WIND SPIRIT

By Aimée and David Thurlo

ELLA CLAH NOVELS

Blackening Song
Death Walker
Bad Medicine
Enemy Way
Shooting Chant
Red Mesa
Changing Woman
Tracking Bear

Plant Them Deep

LEE NEZ NOVELS

Second Sunrise

SISTER AGATHA NOVELS

Bad Faith

WIND SPIRIT

✖ ✖ ✖ ✖ ✖

AN ELLA CLAH NOVEL

AIMÉE & DAVID THURLO

A Tom Doherty Associates Book
New York

WIND SPIRIT

Copyright © 2004 by Aimée and David Thurlo

This book is printed on acid-free paper.

A Forge Book
Published by Tom Doherty Associates, LLC
175 Fifth Avenue
New York, NY 10010

www.tor.com

Library of Congress Cataloging-in-Publication Data

Thurlo, Aimée.
    Wind spirit / Aimée & David Thurlo.—1st. ed.
        p.   cm.
    "A Tom Doherty Associates book."
    ISBN 0-765-30477-5 (acid-free paper)
    EAN 978-0765-30477-3
    1. Clah, Ella (Fictitious character)—Fiction.   2. Near-death experiences—Fiction.   3. Police—New Mexico—Fiction.   4. Navajo Indians—Fiction.   5. Navajo women—Fiction.   6. Policewomen—Fiction.   7. New Mexico—Fiction.   8. Arson—Fiction.   I. Thurlo, David.   II. Title.

PS3570.H82W56 2004
813'.54—dc22
                                                                    2003062626

First Edition: April 2004

Printed in the United States of America

0   9   8   7   6   5   4   3   2   1

To M. S.,
who's always there to point us in the right direction.
Ella thanks you and so do we.

ACKNOWLEDGMENTS

With special thanks to those Cold War heroes who risked their lives within the uranium mines on the Navajo Nation.

AUTHORS' NOTE

The American Association of State Highway and Transportation has changed the number of U.S. 666, what was known as the Devil's Highway, to U.S. 491.

ONE

It was a cloudless spring morning, and even though a cool breeze was still flowing down from the nearby mountains, a crowd of nearly three hundred had assembled in the remote canyon south of Shiprock. This was a historic milestone for the *Dineh*, the Navajo People. Today, some of the uranium mines that lay like open wounds in the side of Mother Earth would finally be filled in.

Ella Clah, special investigator for the Navajo Tribal Police, proudly watched her mother, Rose, who was standing among the dignitaries behind the speaker's microphone. Rose had been integral to this effort, generating support for the work through her activism and leadership on tribal committees, and Ella had come to the ceremony today to support the tribe and honor what her mother had worked so hard to accomplish.

There was a saying among the Navajo that seemed to epitomize everything about Rose—"in-old-age-walking-the-trail-of-beauty." Today her mother was looking her best in a long blue velvet skirt and deep purple velveteen blouse fastened at her waist with a big silver concha belt. Around her neck, Rose wore the handcrafted silver and turquoise squash blossom that had been in their family for generations. Her long silver hair was tied neatly into a traditional bun fastened at the base of her neck.

Ella listened as the Christian minister, an Anglo named Campbell, said a brief prayer. Next, her brother Clifford, a respected *hataalii*, or medicine man, began singing *hatals*. These songs of blessing compelled the Navajo gods to bring good luck to the land the yellow dust had corrupted and give it new life.

Navajo prayers were not petitions. If recited just right, it was believed that the gods couldn't fail to comply. All Navajo knowledge was now being brought to bear on this problem that faced the *Dineh*. The People had even named the yellow dirt *Leetso* because using the name of their enemy would rob it of power and bring about its downfall.

Today was a special day for traditionalists and modernists alike. Everyone willing and hardy enough to make the long cross-country trip over the poorest of dirt roads was here to witness the historic occasion. The local television stations had sent crews to film the event, and some of the morning classes at the community college had been postponed so that the teaching staff could attend. She saw several of the Shiprock college professors, including Wilson Joe and Preston Garnenez—who taught organic chemistry in the classroom that adjoined Wilson's. Both men were standing at the end of the row, beside the preacher.

This place was personal to Ella for completely different reasons. Near this spot she'd cornered and captured a cop killer just last year. And she recalled, with a chill running down her spine, she'd also discovered that skinwalkers— Navajo witches known for their evil practices and rituals associated with the dead—were using these old mines for their own purposes. Fortunately, skinwalkers had apparently stopped using this site after authorities had destroyed a few of the larger shafts.

Clifford had cleansed the area last year, and had done so

again today before the crowd had gathered, but Ella still couldn't help but wonder where the skinwalkers had relocated to and when she'd cross paths with them again.

Hearing the enthusiastic countdown, she looked over to where the men in hard hats were standing. Then, as the first blast of explosives shook the earth, the crowd cheered.

So it began. As a demolition crew started the long process of sealing up the old, abandoned mines that had brought so much sickness and sorrow, Ella wondered if the new mining methods and safety procedures NEED was sanctioning would live up to expectations.

NEED, which stood for Navajo Electrical Energy Development, represented the Navajo Nation's first step toward a more prosperous future. Casinos on the large, isolated Navajo Nation would never be able to attract large numbers of patrons like the ones run by other tribes closer to population centers. The Navajo tribe's one small casino, being test-marketed at To'hajiilee, west of Albuquerque, had been doing well so far, but it hadn't gone into the black yet. Even if it was a big success, the facility wouldn't be able to make a substantial impact on the poverty that shadowed the Rez. Lack of funds still took a heavy toll on the tribe's ability to provide and maintain emergency services. Police equipment was badly outdated and salaries hadn't been improved in years. Even the hospital was understaffed these days and it was becoming nearly impossible to persuade many of the health professionals to remain there for long.

Ella was standing at the back of the gathering far from the speaker, but she could hear her brother's voice clearly as it rose in a Song of blessing. When his voice softened slightly toward the middle of the Song, she became aware of the faint sound of children's laughter somewhere behind her. Recognizing the dangers inherent in that area because of all the uncovered and undocumented mine shafts, she wondered why anyone would bring kids here, even if it was Saturday.

Ella turned her head and caught a glimpse of one of the boys peeking around a washing machine–sized boulder. Julian, her brother's eight-year-old son, had recently told his father that he wanted to become a *hataalii* when he grew up. Like any proud papa, Clifford now allowed his son to accompany him as often as possible. But Ella was sure he'd counted on Loretta, his wife, to keep a better eye on him, particularly since they'd allowed Julian to bring his friend, Tim Manuelito.

Ella glanced around, trying to locate her sister-in-law, and finally saw Loretta helping a late-arriving Navajo woman to one of the few folding chairs provided for senior citizens. Ella recognized Susana Deerman. Her husband and son had died of Red Lung many years ago and Susana's granddaughter had not lived to see her first birthday. The child had been born with severe birth defects due to the contamination of the soil and drinking water around their home. The legacy of uranium mining had cast a long dark shadow over many families here in the Four Corners.

The words of her brother's chant, particularly poignant under the circumstances, touched her. "Beauty before me, beauty behind me, beauty above me, beauty below me. Beauty all around me," he intoned.

Feeling the heavy weight of sadness, Ella looked down at the barren soil. She wondered what possible good he could do here after all that had happened to this land.

Once again, Ella was distracted by the scuffling noises created by the two boys who were playing somewhere behind a cluster of boulders several yards away. Annoyed, she decided to haul them back to Loretta. It was dangerous to allow them to run around unsupervised, and Ella was certain Clifford didn't want his son to come across any skinwalker ritual items that might have remained in the area despite numerous searches.

Ella slipped quietly around the rock wall and managed to grab Tim Manuelito by the arm before he realized she was there. "This is an important ceremony, not recess," she said to the startled boy. "Go back to my sister-in-law and stay put."

"Yes, ma'am." Without looking back Tim hurried toward the group gathered around Clifford.

Julian stood up from atop his hiding place on a nearby boulder, climbed down, then came over to her. "I'll go back too, Aunt," he said, looking crestfallen.

"If you really want to become a *hataalii* someday you'll have to do a better job of listening and learning from your father."

"But the ceremony is *so* long."

"This is only a short blessing made up of prayers from the longer Sings. A full ceremony can take more than a week."

"Yeah, yeah, I know," he muttered softly. "But my friend lives way over by Hogback. He and I never get a chance to play together." He kept his gaze fastened on the ground, avoiding direct eye contact with her out of respect.

"I understand," she said, remembering how hard it had been for her to stay still at his age. "You just have to learn to be patient. Now come on. Let's go back. The land around here is sick, so you shouldn't be running around. You could fall into a hole or something."

As another underground blast shook the earth, Ella felt the earth shifting beneath her feet, like quicksand. She took a quick step to maintain her balance, but the ground between her and Julian suddenly collapsed. Julian yelled, then fell back, sinking into an ever-widening hole.

Ella dove forward onto the boards that had obviously been used to cover a mine shaft, grabbing the boy by the hand as he slid down. Sand was slipping out of sight like water down a drain. Ella held on to him, but she didn't have enough leverage to pull him back up. The rotten planks she was lying on were creaking and sagging as the support beneath them fell away.

Julian dangled helplessly over the edge, staring at her with terrified eyes. "I'm going to fall!"

"No. I won't let go."

Ella yelled for help, but as the ground rocked from another blast of explosives, her words were lost in the cheerful shouts of the crowd. Afraid the ground would shift again, she tightened her hold to a death grip, then inched closer to the edge of the shaft. Using every bit of strength she possessed, she slowly raised Julian up. "Grab my other hand and hang on tightly as I pull."

Seconds felt like eternities, but finally she managed to lift him to the edge of the boards and onto the surface where she was lying facedown. Julian was crying and Ella pulled him into her arms.

"I thought . . . I thought . . ." he managed, never quite finishing.

Ella hugged him tightly. "I know. But you're safe now. Crawl off these boards and get back over to solid ground. Then call your father to come and get you."

Ella watched Julian scramble clumsily out of the sandy depression they were in. Worried about the stability of the ground beneath her, she remained still until he'd cleared the area, then started to gently ease off the old wooden cover. The splintering boards were the only thing between her and an open pit that might continue down a hundred feet or more.

As she reached the edge and moved onto what she hoped was solid ground, the bottom suddenly fell out from beneath her. A wall of sand came sliding down and before she could cry out, Ella felt herself plummeting down a narrow tunnel.

Ella clawed wildly for a handhold, but nothing was there except cool sand and the darkness that engulfed her. Then she hit solid ground, the impact knocking the wind out of her. For several seconds she simply struggled to take a breath. She couldn't even scream for help until her lungs recovered.

Although Ella had no way of gauging how far she'd

fallen, she was alive and that was all that really mattered to her at the moment. The soft sand beneath her had cushioned her fall and kept her from breaking any bones, as far as she could tell. She blinked several times, trying to get her eyes to adjust to the darkness, but opened or closed, all she could see was an inky blackness.

Gathering her courage, Ella stood up slowly. She was either at the bottom of the shaft or on a wide ledge. It was cold here, wherever that was. Ella reached out gingerly and felt the sandstone sides of the shaft. The walls were vertical and cut too smoothly to offer any handholds, though she searched by touch as high as she could reach.

Then she reached down, feeling along the ground, hoping to find a boulder or piece of wood she could use to dig with. Her hand touched something soft, and she flinched, thinking it might be a spider. Reaching down again, she realized it was a big feather. Picking it up, she noticed how heavy it felt. Attached to the bottom of the feather were two pieces of string, and at the end of each string was a round, rough-feeling bead.

That's when she remembered the skinwalker den she'd discovered last year. This belonged to one of them. Holding the feather away from her she tossed it aside, wanting to put as much distance as possible between her and the witch item.

Hoping that her nephew had seen her fall, Ella began to yell for help and continued for a long time, but no one came. Soon her throat stung and her voice began giving out. It was difficult to breathe down here and she couldn't help but wonder if she was actually drawing toxic air into her lungs every time she took a breath.

Panic knifed at her gut. Even if Julian hadn't seen her fall, she was certain that he'd soon notice her absence. Clinging to that, she took her pistol out of the holster, where it had somehow remained during all her tumbling and began to tap on the sides of the shaft, hoping the noise would carry to the surface. Then she tried to scrape out handholds. But every time she created a small shelf by digging out the sand, it would crumble away the minute she put any weight on it.

Ella yelled for help again, tapping the butt of her pistol against the sides of the tunnel at the same time. She'd always assumed she'd make it to old age, providing she managed to avoid getting killed on duty. Never once did she think she'd die alone, like this, with her death serving no purpose. It wouldn't even merit a heroic tale her daughter could take comfort and pride in.

Anger filled her. She wasn't ready to go. There was too much she'd left undone. She'd wanted to see her daughter grow up into adulthood. She'd wanted to be there for Dawn's *Kinaaldá*, her womanhood ceremony, and take part as their family sang the first prayer.

She wouldn't die here. Not like this, not now. Determination gave her strength. Ella began to yell again, tapping the sides of the shaft and ignoring the raw pain at the back of her throat. Long after her voice had faded from the exertion, she kept tapping on the wall with her pistol.

Then, surprisingly, she heard an answering sound. Someone was tapping above her. Just to make sure, she tapped twice, then waited. Two taps from up above sounded in reply. Ella cheered, though her voice was scarcely more than a whisper now. But her victory was short-lived. In the time it took to go from one breath to the next, there was a resounding crash and a wall of sand came tumbling down on her. Ella hugged the side of the shaft, covered her head, and tried to make an air pocket as tons of sand closed in around her.

It was a fight she couldn't win. Sand reached her nose, then her mouth. She couldn't scream, she couldn't move. Then something hard slammed against her head and there was nothing.

TWO

Ella woke up to hear her name being called. She opened her eyes slowly, expecting pain, but was surprised to discover that she actually felt warm and comfortable.

"Come on now, Bright Eyes. You're all right," the familiar voice urged.

Ella blinked, clearing her vision, and then stared in shock at the man crouched beside her. It was her husband, Eugene. They'd run off and gotten married when she was barely out of high school, but after his death . . . She gasped. "I'm dreaming—or dead."

"Neither, really—or both—depending on how you look at it, sleepyhead."

Ella sat up, trying to figure out where she was or, more to the point, *what* she was now. "Would it kill you not to speak in riddles?"

"No. Actually, nothing can kill me now," he answered with a wide smile.

She looked at him and laughed, recalling their brief time together with a sweet nostalgia now that the nightmares of his sudden death had long since faded. He was the same man she remembered, with strong, chiseled features, wide shoulders, a gentle touch, and a smile that was contagious. But there was one major difference. His body glowed as if it were lit from the inside. "You're a ghost."

"You know me, Ella. I don't believe in ghosts," he answered. When he touched her face in a light caress, she felt it clearly.

"What are we then?" she asked, aware that her own body glowed too, though less so.

"We are. Let that be enough."

"Okay. I'll let that pass for now if you tell me this—where the hell are we, or can't I use that word here?" She glanced around. They appeared to be in a low valley bordered by tall rock formations, some fifty or more feet high. The spires were colored in layers of yellow, red, and orange. The ground was sandy but it glittered, like wet river sand.

"It looks like Angel Peak, Bryce Canyon, or someplace like that, but much more colorful," she added. Looking back down at the ground, she noticed something odd.

"But there are no shadows . . . and light seems to be coming from all over the sky." She paused, listening. "And there's something else . . . it sounds like water along the shore." She stood up and looked into the distance. "I see a blue line out there, and the air smells moist and fresh. It's a lake, right?" She looked at him again and repeated, "Where are we, Eugene?"

"This place has no name. Like us, it just is."

"And the water?"

"Not just a lake. It's the ocean."

"In New Mexico?"

"You always walked two contrary paths, Daughter," another familiar voice said from behind her. "This place is what your mind creates for you—an in-between place that reflects who you are."

Ella turned and stared at her father. Tall and dark-haired and in a faded corduroy sports jacket, he appeared much younger than she remembered. He looked like the man she'd known as a child. Love for her father softened the pain of bittersweet memories. But he'd been dead for years now. She'd returned to the Rez to investigate his murder almost a decade ago. "I *am* hallucinating. Very kind of you to point it out."

"No, you're not hallucinating, Daughter. This place really exists. As a Christian preacher I believed that there was a veil separating the spirit world from that of mortals. But that's not quite right. You're simply *there* and we're *here*. There's no real division, it only appears that way because the spirit eyes of those in the mortal realm are closed. They can't see us, but we can see them and that allows us to keep watch over our loved ones."

"Then I hope you know that I've finally come to terms with the anger that drove me away from home—and from you, Dad. I really regret not getting to know you better when . . ."

"I was still alive?" He chuckled. "Don't give it another thought. I always knew you loved me in spite of my shortcomings."

"I didn't know you had any," she said softly, then grinned, letting him know she was teasing.

Ella walked around, looking at the plants. They were so beautiful they seemed straight out of a fairy tale garden. Reaching down, she touched a beautiful red rose that was growing between two black rocks that gleamed like obsidian. The colors here were more vibrant than anything she'd ever seen before. She felt the velvety coolness of the petals as a warm breeze drifted past her. It was all too real to be only a product of her imagination.

"Why am I here?" she asked. "What happened to me— besides the obvious, I guess."

Eugene spoke again. "You're to be given a choice, Ella. You can stay and progress with your life here—or return to the other level of awareness."

In this landscape of conflicting features, Ella felt at peace, comfortable and at ease, more so than she'd ever been before. She wanted to stay. She was ready to leave the dangers of her job behind her and never again have to worry if the witness standing in the doorway was about to pull a gun, or if another human being would die at her hand.

She was tired of suspicious looks from strangers who believed in legends of evil associated with her clan, of talk behind her back, and the anxiety of citizens when they found out who she was. Her job was often thankless, no matter what she accomplished. Being a cop often wore her down, and coming home late, day after day, after her daughter was already asleep had become increasingly frustrating. Here there was only peace.

Yet the peace would come at an unspeakingly high price. To possess it she'd have to leave her daughter who needed her. As her love for Dawn tugged at her, she thought of her mother and all the other people in her life who mattered to her. Her life, with all its ups and downs, was still worth fighting for. The scent of Mom's fry bread, the taste of pecan pie, the adrenaline rushing through her system as she collared a criminal, the warmth at her feet when Two curled up at night at the foot of the bed. All these would be gone, too, if she stayed.

She looked around, taking in the beauty and breathing in the sweet smell of peace and serenity one more time. Finally Ella turned and smiled at Eugene and her father, wiping away an errant tear that had run down her cheek. "It's wonderful here, and I'd really like to stay, but . . ."

"Your daughter needs you," her father said with a nod, "and you aren't ready to leave your responsibilities behind. It shows in your eyes."

Ella nodded. "Despite the crazy contradictions I see here, like an ocean beside the desert, this place is very comforting to me. But I'm not ready to stay."

"You'll return to us someday. It's inevitable. But, for now, I think you've made the right choice, Daughter. You've really only just started to discover who you are and who you can be."

"We'll see each other again," Eugene added, reaching out to touch her hand one more time.

Suddenly everything before her faded to black. The next instant she was back in her physical body. She ached, and her throat hurt so much it felt as if it were on fire. She couldn't see; she couldn't breathe.

"I've done the *Ee-nah'jih Hatal'*, the Come-to-Life ceremony, but her wind spirit has drifted," Ella heard Clifford say.

"We can't give up," Justine urged, desperation in her tone. "Let's try CPR again."

Except for muted sobs coming from somewhere close by, there were no sounds for a while, then something soft was placed over her face, probably a blanket. Gathering her strength, Ella pushed it aside and sat up. Justine gasped and jumped back.

"No need for CPR, Cousin. It worked," Ella mumbled, then coughed. Her throat was raw and she couldn't manage anything above a whisper. The sudden bright light made her squint.

Two paramedics she didn't recognize were at her side instantly. Jeremiah Crow, the medical center's helicopter pilot, was standing right behind them, looking very relieved. Ella knew the helicopter was grounded for lack of funding, so he must have been driving a rescue vehicle now. Like her, he went where he was needed.

Clifford's eagle-sharp gaze was focused on her, probably reassuring himself it was really her and not her *chindi*. Rose had paled considerably and her face was moist from tears, but she took a step forward and stood beside her son while the paramedics checked her vital signs.

"Your brother's chant worked," Rose managed. Then in a marginally stronger voice added, "Don't ever scare me like that again, Daughter."

"I'll do my best, Mom."

It was nearly two in the afternoon when, after a series of tests and doctor examinations that failed to indicate any real problems, Ella found herself alone in the small hospital room. Before she had much of a chance to think, she heard a knock at the door and saw Carolyn Roanhorse Lavery, the tribe's ME and her old friend, standing there.

"I came as soon as I heard about the accident. How are you feeling? What happened?" Carolyn asked.

Ella motioned for her to come inside. "I'm not sure—to both questions," Ella said with a weak smile. "I remember falling, then screaming my head off and tapping on the rocks with my pistol to get somebody's attention. Just when I made contact and thought I was about to be rescued, the roof collapsed burying me in sand. I must have passed out. After that, I'm not sure . . ."

Ella reached for the water pitcher but Carolyn got there first and poured her a glass of water. Ella took a long sip, stalling. She just wasn't ready to discuss her experience with anyone yet, which was why she'd deliberately been vague with her family earlier. Instinct told her that it was better to withhold a secret of this kind than expose it to others who would pass judgment on it. She needed time to sort things out in her own mind before she could confide in someone else. But one thing was clear even now—she'd never tell her family that she'd found a skinwalker feather with beads where she'd been trapped. The beads were usually made from human bones taken from a grave. All that would be too much information for a traditionalist to accept.

Carolyn didn't press her for details, fortunately. "I'm nothing short of amazed that you're still here and in such good condition. Those bruises and a strained voice are nothing in comparison to what might have been. From what I heard, the paramedics had already given up on you. Contrary woman that you are, that's when you suddenly sat up and gave half the tribe a heart attack."

"You suppose I was really dead?" Ella asked.

"Apparently not. I spoke to your brother down in the lobby before I came in and he told me that your wind spirit was knocked out of your body for a while. But because of his Come-to-Life ceremony it managed to find its way back."

Ella nodded, taking another swallow of water.

"You find out who got to you first?"

"Yeah. A lot of people were digging, but it was Justine who found me, I guess. Then the paramedics uncovered me completely and carried me over to solid ground. They tried CPR while my brother did his thing. Mom said that Julian helped him out, too, by keeping everyone else back so my wind spirit wouldn't be driven away. I've heard of those Come-to-Life rituals but I never attended one—until now."

Carolyn nodded slowly. "The doctor wants to keep you under observation, so it might be a good time to work out how you're going to be dealing with this event once you leave the hospital. Your life is about to become very complicated, old friend."

Ella looked at Carolyn, understanding what she meant and weighing the implications. "Have you picked up any talk yet about the accident and what happened to me out there?"

"Justine is telling everyone your survival was a miracle. My guess is that Reverend Campbell and some of the other Christians will pick up on that as well, once they know the details."

"I can live with that. What do you think the *Dineh* will believe?"

"Hard to say. But I know something about the history of those old mines. Some Navajo miners died in a cave-in near there fifty years ago. Their bodies were never recovered."

"I know how that works. Some may think I've been contaminated by the *chindi* of the dead miners." Ella shrugged. Her people believed that the good in a person merged with universal goodness, but the bad side remained earthbound to create trouble for the living. Ella didn't want to mention it, but she knew that there would also be others who would remember that the skinwalkers had used the area in the recent past as well. That, to some, would be even more frightening.

"Many will probably not worry about any association with the dead, choosing just to think of you as lucky. But either way, you're going to need to have a Sing if you want to be able to do your job. If you don't have one done, you're going to scare Navajos every place you go."

"Mom acted bravely around me. But were you around her long enough to tell how she really feels about this whole thing?" Rose was a staunch traditionalist and Ella couldn't help but worry about her now.

"When I saw her, she was talking to your brother about finding a Singer who can do the branch of the Holy Way Chant you need. Clifford doesn't know that one, apparently."

Ella nodded slowly, taking another sip of water. Unlike some other tribes who depended on trances or spells, the Navajo equated knowledge with power. A medicine man had to *perfectly* memorize the prayers of a week-long Sing before he was qualified to conduct it. That was why no one *hataalii* knew all the Sings.

"Very few individuals go through an experience like yours and come out of it unchanged," Carolyn said, interrupting Ella's thoughts. "I'll let you rest now, but if you need someone to talk to, just let me know and I'll come by. I'm here for you, Ella."

"Thanks, pal," Ella said as Carolyn waved and left the room.

Alone again, Ella closed her eyes. When she woke up again, Clifford was sitting where Carolyn had been. Ella smiled at her brother.

"You should have woken me up," she said.

"You needed some rest. I just came by to thank you again for saving my son's life. He's already told everyone how you kept him from falling, then pulled him out with just one hand."

He paused and in a voice filled with emotion continued. "You risked your own life to save my son. I don't know how to thank you, Sister."

"I saved your son, and later he saved me. We're even."

"I just want you to know one more time how grateful I am for what you did."

"You would have done the same thing for my daughter had the positions been reversed," Ella said. "Don't give it another thought."

Clifford paused for a long moment, then continued, measuring his words carefully. "I didn't want to mention this in front of our mother earlier, but there's something else you should know." Clifford took a deep breath and regarded her thoughtfully. "The first thing Justine saw was your hand. Your fingers were sticking up out of the sand. Do you understand the significance of that?"

Ella shook her head.

"We, as Navajos, are taught that life begins when wind enters the body at birth and that death happens when it leaves through the fingertips. Some who were there now believe that your wind spirit left your body and that it was the *chindi* who helped your body remain in perfect condition until it returned. I've tried to convince them that once the wind spirit leaves to report to Dawn Woman, it never returns to the person it left behind. It waits for another to be born. So you couldn't have been dead. But there will be some, especially the locals who remember that the evil ones carried out rituals in those mines, who'll now believe you have evil allies."

Ella nodded. "My doctor friend and I discussed the contamination issue earlier when she came by. Once word gets out that I have no serious injuries, that belief is bound to spread," she said. "If I have a Sing done for me, do you think they'll stop being afraid?"

"Yes, but only one *hataalii* knows the Sing you need— *hastiin sání*," he said.

The words simply meant "old man" but everyone knew that they referred to John Tso, who was believed to be in his nineties.

"You see, the ceremony that would be best for you is a branch of the Holy Way Chant that has fallen into disuse so it's nearly extinct. *Hastiin sání* has been trying to teach the ceremony to his grandson, but the younger man hasn't learned it all yet."

"How can I find the *hataalii*? I'll need to have this Sing conducted as quickly as possible. If you remember, when I first returned to the Rez, there were very few Navajos who'd talk to me freely. Conducting an investigation under those conditions was nearly impossible. I don't want to go through that again."

"The Singer you need has gone on a spiritual journey. He's visiting the shrines of his clan and could be nearly anywhere. I spoke to his grandson and he says that his grandfather does this from time to time and may be gone for weeks."

"How long ago did he leave?"

"About two days ago."

"We have to find him quickly. Can you help me, Brother?" she asked.

"I've already sent messages to some of his relatives and clan members."

"Thanks. I really appreciate that. By the way, how's Mom handling this?"

Clifford hesitated. "She's a traditionalist and her beliefs tell her to beware of the *chindi*, but she's also your mother and she's really happy you're alive and well."

There was no doubt that she'd been given a second chance. But Ella still wasn't sure what had happened. Had she imagined her encounter with her father and husband? Logic continued to battle against what her heart was telling her. The simple truth was that, deep down, she didn't believe it had all been a dream.

"What are you thinking about?" Clifford asked.

"I want to see my daughter," she said, changing the subject deftly.

"I'll bring her tomorrow if they don't release you in the morning."

When Clifford stood up she saw the cowhide medicine pouch hanging from his belt. It was a larger version of the deerskin one he normally wore. "Carrying flint?" She knew that was a Navajo's primary defense against the *chindi*.

"Yes. And I've got a bag for you, too. It has flint points, ashes, soot, and ghost medicine."

"Are *you* afraid of me?" she asked, surprised. Even in the darkest times, Clifford had never backed away from danger.

"No, not *of* you—*for* you. A lot of people are going to be scared of you now and that emotion never fails to bring out the worst in people." He exhaled softly. "People from outside our tribe say the *Dineh* are superstitious. Yet when their own religions tell them that someone walked on water or parted the sea, they accept it without question. Everyone chooses what to believe and which path to follow. But since you now live among us, regardless of what your personal beliefs are, you have to take into account the fear of those around you. Carrying the medicine pouch will show your willingness to honor our ways."

Ella took the beaded velveteen medicine pouch he handed her and set it on the stand by her bed.

"No," he said. "Clip it to your hospital gown. You need to start sending out the right message."

She did as he asked and Clifford nodded in approval. "I'll tell Mom that you have the medicine pouch with you now."

"Find the *hataalii* for me," she asked again.

"I will."

Ella watched Clifford leave. Most of the Navajos she'd met seldom said good-bye, they just turned and left. Smiling, she remembered having to adjust to that again when she'd returned to the Rez after years of living on the outside.

Ella glanced down skeptically at the pouch she'd pinned to her hospital gown. She didn't personally find it useful, but it was a necessary compromise. It was a different world here in *Diné bikéyah*—Navajo country—and danger could come from sources one never encountered on the outside.

THREE

The morning sun filtered through the pale green curtains in Ella's hospital room, nudging her awake. Her body ached today, more so than yesterday, but it was time for her to leave. She'd been given a new lease on life, and she wasn't going to waste it lying around here counting ceiling tiles.

Tossing the sheet and thin blanket aside, Ella climbed out of the tall, narrow bed and walked over to the small closet. Her mother had taken her dirty clothes earlier and Justine had left some clean ones for her during visiting hours last night.

Ella closed the bathroom door, then washed up and dressed quickly. When she came out several minutes later, she saw Big Ed Atcitty, the chief of police, in her room. "Whoa, Shorty," he said, using the nickname he'd given her though she was a head taller than he was. "Where do you think you're going?"

"Morning, Chief. I'm getting out of here. I've wasted enough time."

He gave her a long, speculative look. "Well, that cinches it. You're still the same Ella," he muttered. He glanced down at the pouch she now wore on her belt and nodded in approval. "That's a good idea."

"My brother prepared it for me," she answered. "He felt it was appropriate and I agreed." Ella stepped out into the hall and cocked her head toward the nurses station. "Come on. I'm checking myself out."

Big Ed was barrel-chested, short, and sturdy like a tree stump, with graying temples and coal black eyes grown wise with time and experience. He exhaled softly, then followed her. "I guess I should argue with you, but experience tells me it won't do much good."

She smiled and kept walking. "I'm going to need a day off, Chief."

"Take more if you want. You deserve a rest."

"A day will probably do. I'm going to be tracking down a Singer—John Tso. I think I can find him fairly quickly with my brother's and mother's help. They've already put the word out to his relatives. Someone must have seen him by now."

"I've met the man. Well respected, but older than dirt and damned independent, if I remember correctly. If there's anything I can do to help you, let me know." Big Ed paused, then added, "By the way, I think you're right to put him at the top of your list of priorities. You're not currently working a major case, so this is your opportunity to get a proper Sing done. You'll never regain the respect or the trust of the *Dineh* until you undo what's hanging over you now."

Ella stopped by the nurses station so they would know where she was going, and checked herself out. Her physician, who'd been making his rounds, expressed some concern that the lack of oxygen might have left some neurological damage, but was forced to concede that all the tests they'd run so far had come back within normal parameters.

"I need to see my daughter and get back to my life," Ella explained, hoping to make him understand, but determined not to let anyone talk her out of leaving.

After agreeing to watch for headaches and some other

symptoms, Ella signed the discharge papers and walked outside, allowing Big Ed to hold the door open for her. Stopping at the curb, it suddenly hit her that she didn't have her unit here.

"Can I hitch a ride with you, Chief?"

"Of course. Why do you think I hung around?"

They were under way five minutes later. Big Ed kept his eyes on the road, but it was quickly clear to Ella that he had other matters on his mind. "By the way, the place where you . . . had your accident," he said, finding the right words at last, "is expected to attract skinwalkers once again, for obvious reasons. Your brother and a handful of other *hataaliis* are planning to go out there and do another Sing so our people will know it's safe to return and continue sealing off those mines. But even after the Sing is done I doubt we'll ever see another large crowd gathered there again."

"That's just as well. Between the contamination and the undocumented mines, that area is an accident waiting to happen." Ella sat back enjoying the warmth of the morning sun as it played on her face. It was good to be alive.

"A lot of people who go through what you did yesterday never look at their lives in the same way again. Take plenty of time to get your bearings, Shorty. You owe it to yourself."

Ella took a deep breath, then let it out slowly. "I'm okay, Chief, really, though I expect I'll be smothering my daughter with love for the next few days. Of course, knowing her, she'll only take it for a short time, then throw her teddy bear at me and tell me to leave her alone. She's an independent little thing."

When Big Ed laughed, his entire body shook and laughed with him. Yet, despite his wide girth, the man had the stamina of an athlete. Every spring Big Ed insisted on qualifying with the officers on the obstacle course and track. He'd never failed yet, proving that, as it was with most things on the Rez, appearances could be deceiving.

As Big Ed parked behind her patrol unit in the driveway
of her mother's house, Ella saw her nearly six-year-old daughter Dawn playing with Two, the family mutt. When the little
girl smiled and waved, a burst of unmitigated joy filled Ella.
She'd never been happier to be home.

As soon as Big Ed pulled to a stop, Ella got out. Dawn
ran up and launched herself into Ella's arms, an increasingly
rare show of affection that Ella had truly missed.

"*Shimasání* said you were sick," Dawn said as they were
sharing a big hug. "But I knew you'd come home today."

Ella hugged Dawn tightly one more time before letting
her go. "Wild horses couldn't keep me away, sweetie." The
connection between them was strong. Dawn, like Rose, always seemed to know when she was in trouble.

A second later Rose came out the front door. Standing on
the porch, she gazed at Ella with tear-filled eyes. "You're
home!" Rose opened her arms wide and Ella knew then that
no taboo would ever break the bond between them. Yet, as
she drew near, Ella couldn't help but notice the medicine
pouch pinned to the side of her mother's long skirt.

Ella stopped short of hugging her. "Are you sure it's okay
with you, Mom?"

Rose answered by taking Ella into her arms. "The pouch
is there to honor who we are as a people."

Big Ed, who'd remained in his car, called out to Ella, "If
you need more than one day off, Shorty, be sure to take it.
Unless the case load suddenly picks up, we'll manage without
you."

As her boss drove off, Rose looked at her daughter. "Did
you ask for time off?"

"Yeah," Ella said with a tiny smile. "There's a first time
for everything! But, Mom, under the circumstances, I figured
I needed to go find the Singer as soon as possible."

"Yes, I agree," Rose said, then led the way back inside.

"I've been trying to get some word on his whereabouts and I imagine we'll hear soon. Come inside. Your friend the doctor stopped by your hospital room, discovered you'd already left, and called me," she said, referring to Carolyn, "so I kept breakfast warming for you in the oven."

Rose went to the kitchen, the heart of their household, and for the first time since she'd left for work yesterday, Ella relaxed. Her mother brought her a platter of scrambled eggs with green chile, flour tortillas, and sausage links while she sipped freshly brewed coffee.

Breakfast was great and she ate greedily. Once her stomach was full, her spirit felt renewed and she was filled with energy. She looked around the kitchen appreciating the earth tones that covered the walls and the richness of the brick floors. She was home and things were going to be all right.

Hearing a car drive up, Rose started to leave the stove where she was fixing mutton stew for tonight's dinner but Ella, having finished her meal, stood up. "Don't worry, Mom. I'll take care of it."

Out on the porch, Ella saw Jennifer Clani, Dawn's babysitter, getting out of her car. Jennifer usually arrived at seven A.M., except on Mondays and Thursdays. She'd chosen those days off because they coincided with classes she took at the college. "It's Boots," she called back to Rose. "I guess she was running late today." Ella looked at her watch, which had a badly scratched crystal now, but still worked.

Rose came out of the kitchen, drying her hands. "I'm surprised she's here," Rose said softly. "Her grandmother, my dearest friend, is a staunch traditionalist. When she heard the stories about what happened yesterday, she didn't want Boots to come until you had your Sing done, so I really wasn't expecting her to show up. But maybe your brother has finally managed to convince people that you were never truly dead."

They both greeted Jennifer Clani warmly and went inside

the house with her. Dawn was in her room now, watching a children's nature program on the small television set her father had bought for her.

"I didn't expect you," Rose said, "but I'm glad you're here."

"Your son came by to visit us," Jennifer said, looking at Rose. "He spoke to our family, said prayers, and gave us some special things for our medicine pouches. He also told Grandmother that he'd already done a blessing over you, your granddaughter, and your grandson, and that you all have medicine pouches of your own now. Since we're all protected, I saw no need for me to stay away."

Ella looked at Rose, surprised to hear that her brother had done a special blessing over her mom and the children.

Rose looked back at Ella and nodded. "It was the right thing to do," she said. "My daughter-in-law insisted, and for once, I agreed with her."

Ella said nothing, though she was starting to feel like Typhoid Mary.

Jennifer Clani looked at Ella speculatively and warned, "But not everyone will feel like my family does—particularly if they watched the morning news on TV. Do you remember the camera crew that was there yesterday?"

Ella nodded. "Don't tell me they got everything on tape and decided to actually put it on the air."

Jennifer nodded. "It was pretty impressive," she said, and shuddered. "One minute you were beneath the sheet, and the next you were sitting up. It made my grandmother jump right out of her chair."

Ella stared at Boots in surprise. "You saw it too?" Seeing Boots nod, she added, "I'm amazed you still came."

Boots smiled. "Our tribe's medical examiner was interviewed, too, and she said that if you'd really been dead and deprived of oxygen for as long as it took them to dig you out, you'd have permanent brain damage and probably wouldn't be able to even move. Between that, and your brother's assurances that you weren't really dead in the first place . . ." she said with a shrug. "For me, it was enough."

Jennifer paused before continuing. "But others have different opinions and explanations for what happened." Jennifer looked at Ella hesitantly. "You *will* have a Sing done like your brother said, won't you?"

Ella suddenly realized that Jennifer had come despite the fears and doubts she still harbored, and that act of loyalty touched her deeply. "Yes, I will, just as soon as I can find the *hataalii* and make the request. In fact, I'm planning to start searching for him myself today."

"They say he often goes to the area where the Mancos River flows into the San Juan. That's said to be a holy place, and that's where he likes to get the white sand he uses for his sand paintings."

"Then I'll drive up there this morning," Ella answered. Jennifer had done her part by showing up, she'd do hers.

As Jennifer walked up the hall to Dawn's room and Rose went back into the kitchen, Ella picked up Dawn's toys from the living-room carpet, grateful to do this very ordinary chore.

Once finished, her thoughts turned naturally to John Tso and the search she'd begin shortly. She was actually looking forward to the road trip. It would give her time to sort out her thoughts.

Although she'd never be able to prove what she'd experienced hadn't been brought on by her own terror, one thing was clear. If death signaled the end of life, then the path that led to death wasn't an unpleasant one. Death didn't need to be feared. And if there was a life beyond death—and everything in her was telling her there was—then that gave everything a whole new perspective, one she'd never considered before.

Hearing the phone ring and her mother answering, Ella focused on the present. It was time to concentrate on her life here and the work she had to do.

Rose returned to the living room a moment later. "The manager of the trading post at Beclabito said he saw *hastiin sání* just yesterday."

"Then I'll start there since it's closer, then go where Boots suggested," Ella said, standing.

"I'll fix you a thermos of cocoa and a snack to take with you," Rose said. "I wish you could stay home today, but I know it's important that you get this Sing done quickly." She sighed. "The basic problem—what's going to compound people's fears—is our family legacy, you know."

"No one will ever forget the stories about that particular ancestor of ours, will they?" Ella observed.

"When I was younger, Mist Eagle seemed like the epitome of foolishness and evil, but now that I'm older and have seen more of life, I don't judge her quite as harshly," Rose said. "She was just a woman in love."

Hearing soft footsteps, Ella turned her head and saw Jennifer Clani at the end of the hall. "I don't know the details behind your family legacy, but I do know that's the reason some of the traditionalists are afraid of your family. Does the legacy have something to do with the gift of intuition that runs through the women in your clan?"

Ella wasn't surprised that Lena Clani, Rose's old friend, had never given Boots the details. Her mother's friends were fiercely loyal to her. That was a quality Rose often inspired in others.

"Come sit with us," Rose said. "You have a right to hear the story." As Jennifer sat down, Rose continued softly. "It started generations ago, before the *Dineh* had a reservation, even before the war with the white man. Mist Eagle, a woman of our clan, fell in love with Fire Hawk, a man who was also from our clan. Respecting the taboo, Fire Hawk married another, but Mist Eagle's love for him continued to grow. One night when Fire Hawk's wife went out, Mist Eagle went into his hogan and seduced him. Before long, it was clear that she was pregnant."

"Did he leave his wife?" Jennifer asked, a touch of horror in her voice.

Ella heard it and understood. The People considered a physical relationship with someone of their own clan to be incest. "Fire Hawk committed suicide rather than face the shame," Ella said.

"What happened to Mist Eagle?" Boots asked.

"She gave birth to a girl, but she and her daughter were shunned," Rose said. "Alone, Mist Eagle learned about herbs and about healing. Skinwalkers sought her out and were the only ones who would speak to her, so Mist Eagle learned what they could teach her, though she never became like them.

"Then, one day, she helped an old man who had gone out alone into the desert to die. When he returned to his village healed, word about her abilities spread. People started going to her secretly for help, but they were still afraid of her. It was said that Mist Eagle could kill as easily as heal. But the truth was that she never turned to evil."

"That's not a bad legacy," Jennifer said, puzzled.

"It's not the end of the story," Rose said in a heavy voice. "Mist Eagle taught her daughter everything she knew. At first the girl used her knowledge and power only for good, but eventually the darkness that surrounded her birth overwhelmed her and she turned to evil."

"But for the legacy to have continued, Mist Eagle's daughter must have had a daughter of her own, right?" Jennifer asked.

"Yes, a girl, by her father's brother, a man who was much older than she. As the generations passed, each child was encouraged to develop whatever special ability he or she possessed, and make their gift as individual as they were. Yet the roots of evil remained and a few of our ancestors did end up using their gift to harm others. But most of Mist Eagle's direct descendants have chosen to help the tribe."

"It's all mostly legend, you realize that, don't you?" Ella asked softly, looking at Boots. "I mean, so much time has passed that it's really impossible for anyone to verify any of this. Stories can grow all by themselves if the speaker has a strong imagination."

"There's probably a lot of truth to it, too," Boots answered. "Our people have relied on word-of-mouth teachings for generations. It's our way."

"Certainly there's *some* truth to the story, but my intuition at least is not so much a gift as it is training. I've been taught to be especially observant and that's given me an edge, like a person who's gifted in music and studies to become proficient with a certain instrument."

Boots nodded, but didn't say anything for a long time.

Ella didn't interrupt the silence, allowing it to stretch.

"People believe the legacy, so the most important thing now, I think, is for them to see you're a good person and that you respect the ways of our tribe," Boots said at last.

Ella nodded. "That's why I'm going to go find the Singer."

Rose handed her a paper sack filled with two egg and sausage burritos and a thermos filled with hot chocolate. "Go do what's necessary, Daughter."

Ella took the tribal unit and headed north. Once she reached the town of Shiprock, she'd turn east, then follow the road that would lead her past Beclabito and on to Four Corners. As she mapped out the route in her mind, she realized she'd be passing right by Tom Joe's house. He'd filed a complaint the day before yesterday, reporting that someone had poked holes in his water barrels.

There'd been an outbreak of vandalism in that area lately,

but so far she'd turned up no common denominator to tie them together.

Since it was on the way, stopping by the Joes' house seemed like a good idea. From what she remembered from the early-morning briefing, the Joes were modernists, so a visit from her wouldn't be likely to upset them.

Although she was used to traveling across the Rez quickly, particularly whenever she was on her way to interview someone, today she went along at fifty-five miles per hour—at least ten to fifteen miles slower than she would have ever done. She'd spent her entire life living in the future—hurrying from one thing to the next, always focusing on distant goals, but in so doing she'd robbed herself of the present. Maybe it was time to change that along with some other things.

Ella thought about her work in law enforcement. She'd sacrificed everything for it, and somewhere along the way, she'd lost any semblance of balance in her life. She'd spent so much time trying to be better at what she did that she'd forgotten how to be good to herself.

When Ella arrived at the Joes' wood-frame house north of Rattlesnake and beside the river, she was surprised to see a ceremonial hogan behind the main house. Modernists generally didn't have them. If the information she had about the Joes was wrong, it was quite possible her presence would make things difficult for everyone.

Uncertain, she remained where she was and waited. The next move would have to be theirs.

FOUR
—— ✘ ✘ ✘ ——

Time passed, and Ella remained by the tribal unit patiently. Although she saw someone peer out the front window, no invitation to approach was given.

Finally a young, modern-looking Navajo woman with a hard look in her eyes came out. She was wearing a T-shirt, khaki pants with big pockets, and boots. Her hair hung down to her waist. She looked like a blend of old and new, leading Ella to conclude that they were a family of new traditionalists.

"I'm Janet Joe. Now that grandmother is living with us, my mom and dad have become new traditionalists so you're not welcome here. They all heard what happened to you the other day and saw it on TV, too."

"They filed a report of vandalism a few days ago and I'm here to follow it up," Ella said. "I won't stay long, but it's my job to take a look around and get a few questions answered."

"I figured that, which is why I insisted on coming out. They don't like me talking to you," she said, "but I'm not afraid."

Ella sensed the kind of toughness in Janet that came from facing adversity and coming out on top. Janet Joe had survivor written all over her.

"Show me what was vandalized," Ella said.

Janet led her to two large covered barrels kept by the corral. Ella could see that someone had poked holes into the thick plastic sides. Crouching down, she studied the punctures. "My guess is that they used a sharp screwdriver or an ice pick."

Janet nodded. "The holes aren't big, but the barrels can't hold water now."

Ella studied the ground around the barrels carefully. There were tire prints and one of the tires appeared to have a shallow slash across the treads. "Does your family park their truck here sometimes?"

"No. Dad always parks next to the house, where the pickup is now. These tracks are from some other truck."

As Ella took some photos with a camera she kept in her gear, Janet spoke. "Thanks to the jerk who did this we're going to have to scrape up the money to buy new barrels. Big ones like these aren't cheap. Mom's trying to trade one of the trading post owners a rug for barrels, but these days people would rather have cash."

"Is this the only way you've got to store water?"

"For the animals, yes. We have another barrel beside the back of the house for us. I have a patch kit for inner tubes and plan to put a new seal on the inside before lunch. We'll get by."

Ella knew Janet was still trying to make up her mind about her, so she let the silence stretch out.

Uncomfortable with the silence, Janet began to talk at last. "This whole thing is my fault, in a way."

"How so?" Ella asked.

"I used to be with the Many Devils. You know them, right?"

"The gang on this side of the river," Ella answered, careful to have her tone remain neutral and nonjudgmental.

"Yeah," Janet said. "I used to get into a lot of trouble when I hung around with them. Then one day I took a Colt forty-five that belonged to my friend's dad. I was going to take it to school and blow Coach's head off. I was tired of him ragging me in PE every single day. But that morning before I left for school Mom found the gun when she moved my purse. She and Dad refused to let me go anywhere—even school—for a month. They told everyone I'd run away. Instead, they took me to Ben Tso, a *hataalii*. He's not as famous as his granddad, but he worked with kids, to put them on the right track, you know?"

Seeing Ella nod, she continued. "He did a Sing, then kept me at his hogan for almost a month. I had to chop and haul firewood, take care of his animals, haul water, everything. At first, I hated him, but he always treated me with respect. Eventually, we began talking and a lot of what he said made sense to me."

"Did you get over your anger with the coach?"

She nodded. "I realized that anger twists you all up inside and gets you nowhere. These days I help other kids quit the gangs. My old friends don't talk to me now, but I guess it's a price I'll have to pay."

"You think maybe somebody in the gang did this to get back at you?"

"No, but that's what started it all."

"I'm not following you," Ella said.

"Catching me with a handgun really scared my parents. Recently when they heard that Lewis Hunt, the tribal councilman, came out in favor of handgun registration, they immediately jumped on that bandwagon. They believe that most people need rifles out here to go hunting and all, but that handguns are only good for shooting people."

Ella exhaled softly. "Gun registration is a tough sell anywhere in the Southwest, but it's even more so on the Rez. People here, by and large, figure we have more than enough Anglo laws to contend with."

"Exactly, so when my parents went to a Chapter House

meeting and spoke in favor of it, a lot of people got real angry with them."

"Like who?"

"I have no idea. I wasn't there. All I know is that the barrels got punctured later that same night after we all went to bed and Mom's sure the two incidents were connected."

Ella realized that she'd just uncovered a possible link between the incidents of vandalism that had been reported recently. "Need some help with the patches?"

"Thanks, but no," Janet said. "My mom might feel funny using the water, you understand?"

Ella nodded. Then, sensing someone looking at her, she turned her head. As she did, she caught a glimpse of someone ducking back behind the curtain at the front window of the house. "I wish your family wasn't afraid to talk to me," she said.

"They can't help it," Janet said. "Although they heard that your brother the *hataalii* said that you were never really dead, that your wind spirit was just lost, the fact remains that you fell into the place where the yellow monster *Leetso* lives. That's why a lot of new traditionalists believe that you're dangerous. Until you get a Sing done, of course."

In a way, she could understand this explanation a lot more than any of the others. Even people outside the Rez might have second thoughts about being with someone who'd been around radioactive dust until they learned that contamination couldn't be passed on like a disease.

"You're so cool about all this," Janet said. "If I were a cop, I'd get really pissed off at people who act the way my parents are."

"Being angry won't change their beliefs." Ella climbed back into the SUV. "If you learn who got angry at your parents in that Chapter House meeting, send word to me, okay?"

"Sure."

As Ella drove up the dirt road toward the main highway,

she speculated on why or how her intuition had become so sharply attuned. She'd always been able to sense people's feelings, but today she'd known that Janet's parents had been peering at her even before she'd turned around. Before she could think about it any longer, however, her cell phone rang.

"Hey, Ella, how are you doing?" a familiar voice said.

Hearing Harry Ute's voice made her smile. "It's good to hear from you."

"I just heard the news about what happened. Are you really okay?"

"Well, the whole thing shook me up a lot," she said honestly. When Harry didn't comment, Ella wondered if he'd simply wanted reassurance. "But I'm alive and healthy and that's a win," she said in a more cheerful tone.

"You bet it is," he said. "I should have known this wouldn't get to you for very long."

Ella felt a twinge of regret as she realized that all he wanted was a casual conversation. But she wasn't really surprised. Things between them had been cooling down considerably for several months. Every time they'd spoken, she'd sensed him distancing himself emotionally, just as he was now.

"I haven't heard from you in a while. How have you been doing?" she asked.

"You know how it is. Work never ends."

"Are you going to be traveling our way soon?" She regretted the words as soon as she spoke them. One of the main obstacles between them was that Harry's life was now on the outside. Hers was here.

"I won't be going anywhere for a while, not with the caseload I'm juggling. You know how it is, twenty-four/seven." He paused for several moments as if struggling with what to say next.

Ella knew what was on his mind. Neither of them wanted

to bring up the subject, but the fact was they'd reached the end of the road and it was time for them to start seeing other people.

"Listen, Ella," he started, but then someone else approached him and spoke hurriedly to him. A moment later he turned his attention back to her. "I've got to go. My partner's ready to roll. I'll be in touch."

"Later."

Ella placed the phone back on the seat beside her. She was sure that she and Harry would remain friends. It wasn't in either of their natures to hold grudges or mourn for what might have been. They'd actually had a lot in common— maybe too much to make a long-term relationship work.

As Ella continued toward Beclabito and the trading post, she caught a glimpse of a light blue pickup behind her. The late-model Ford seemed to be keeping pace. Spotting a dirt road leading up to somebody's home, Ella slowed and turned off the highway, watching to see if the driver would follow or stop. When the pickup continued down the highway, she laughed softly at herself. She *had* to learn to relax.

A short time later Ella pulled up by the trading post, a long, low cinder-block structure right off the highway among junipers and a few scattered piñon pines. The old building, which also had a garage and gas pumps, attracted many tourists driving through the Rez on their way to visit the only place in the USA where the borders of four states met.

Jim Benally, the manager, was sitting down behind the counter reading the paper. Ella knew that Jim was a devout Catholic and wouldn't be overly concerned about her brush with death. He looked up and smiled at her. "Hey, Ella, what brings you out of the big city?"

Ella smiled at his comment about Shiprock, one of the largest Navajo settlements. "I'm trying to find John Tso. I heard he might be in the area."

"He's around somewhere. He stopped by here yesterday morning for supplies."

"Did he say where he was going?"

He thought about it. "I'm not sure, but I do know he likes to go camping along the San Juan River."

Ella remembered what Jennifer had said about the Singer often visiting the spot where the Mancos River joined the San Juan River. "I'm going to try and find him, but just in case I miss out, would you mention I'm looking for him if he comes by? It's personal, not professional."

"Right, I heard. No problem."

It took nearly an hour to drive through Four Corners, then south on a dirt road toward the river. Before long, Ella found the spot where the old *hataalii* had probably camped the night before. There were traces of a fresh campfire and tracks left by a pickup, but no sign of anyone. She followed the vehicle tracks to the east, heading away from the river, until the ground hardened and the trail fizzled out.

From what she could tell, he was either heading cross-country toward Highway 666 to the east, hoping to catch one of the dirt tracks that followed the San Juan River downstream, or looking for something in particular that only he knew about. Without more information she could search for years and still not find him. For all she knew, he was back in Shiprock at the Totah Café having a big piece of gooey pecan pie.

As Ella turned back north toward the highway and drove down a dirt track that was barely a road, something compelled her to look in the rearview mirror. A vehicle in the distance to the east was raising a cloud of sand and dust into the air.

Remembering the light blue truck that had passed her a few hours ago, she slowed down and tried to get a clearer look, but it was all but impossible because of the layer of sand

and dust kicked up by her own SUV as well as the dust that surrounded the other vehicle.

Her senses alert, Ella touched the stone badger fetish she wore around her neck on a thin leather strap. For whatever the reason, she'd discovered that it always felt hot whenever she was in danger. She'd never been sure if that was a product of her own body temperature, chance, or something more, but right now the fetish felt neither overly hot nor cool against her skin.

As she traveled down one side of a shallow arroyo, then back up the other side, she caught a flash of color in the mirror again. The truck was definitely light blue and was closing the distance between them.

What she needed to do was use the land itself to her advantage. Instead of cutting across the next small wash she encountered, Ella engaged the four-wheel drive and left the dirt track she was following, driving northeast up the arroyo itself. The pickup behind her reached the arroyo, then turned to follow.

Ella accelerated up the deepening arroyo, then as soon as she was around the first curve she encountered, she quickly reversed directions. Rolling down the window to listen, she waited for the other driver to catch up.

First she heard the low rumble of an engine, then she saw a cloud of dust as the driver maneuvered along the sandy bottom of the wash. Without four-wheel drive, the pickup was struggling.

When she finally saw the truck come around the curve, Ella stepped on the accelerator and drove forward, pulling right across its path, lights flashing.

The driver's eyes widened the instant he saw her, and Ella stared back at him in surprise, wondering if she'd made a mistake. It was Professor Garnenez, whose classroom adjoined Wilson's at the college.

Curious, she tried to remember everything she knew about him. He was said to be a new traditionalist who adhered to his new lifestyle with the zeal of a convert, annoying some modernists like Wilson Joe in the process. But there was nothing about that to send up a flag, and he hadn't been doing anything illegal—yet.

As she got out of her vehicle and walked toward his pickup, Garnenez opened the door and stepped out. She could see what looked like a video camera on his seat. Had he been filming her, for some strange reason? "What's going on, Investigator Clah?" he asked, taking only a step away from his vehicle, leaving the door open and the engine running.

He had on a short-sleeved shirt, jeans, and western-cut boots. A large deerskin or suede medicine pouch hung from his belt. The only thing in his hands at the moment was a small rock.

Relaxing a bit, she got right to the point. "It appears that you've been following me, Professor."

He hesitated for a moment, then finally nodded. "It's true. I heard that you were looking for *hastiin sání* to do a Sing for you and I wanted to help."

"Wouldn't that work better if you weren't searching the exact same places I am?" She moved closer, narrowing the gap between them, and he held the rock out so she could see it better. It was shiny and black, probably obsidian.

"By the way, you're supposed to be using flint, not obsidian, if you're trying to ward off the evil ones," she said, biting back a smile. She reached into her medicine pouch and brought out a flint arrowhead, holding it up. "Like this."

Flint was used to defend against skinwalkers—Navajo witches. Maybe he'd been following her, thinking she'd turned evil, and had brought the video camera to catch her doing something that would prove the point. But he hadn't really done his homework about traditional beliefs concerning rocks and minerals, obviously.

Looking uncomfortable, he stepped back, reaching down and placing the obsidian into his own medicine pouch. He then leaned against the side of his pickup. "My mistake," he grumbled.

He stood there awkwardly for a moment, and Ella wondered if he was trying to come up with a believable excuse. A bit annoyed, she decided to press the issue.

"You didn't answer my question. But let me guess. You were trying to find out if I'd turned evil and was about to join forces with the you-know-whos? Did somebody tell you that skinwalkers hang out around here?"

He cringed visibly at the word "skinwalkers" and she thought for a second he was going to jump into the truck and take off right then. But he managed to recover his composure almost immediately.

"Don't be ridiculous, Investigator Clah. I was just trying to catch up to you so I could help out. Maybe take one direction and you take the other. I'd seen you pass by a while ago, recognized who you were, and decided to join your effort. I guess I should have honked the horn or waved."

At best it was a thin explanation, considering she'd also pulled off the road before reaching Beclabito. She said nothing, and waited him out.

"I figured you'd welcome the help," he added. The professor was either a con man, a very good actor, or he sincerely believed she was dangerous.

Ella held his gaze. "Following a police officer is a risky step to take. An action like that can be easily misinterpreted so I'd appreciate it if you'd stop. If you happen to find out where the Singer is, and you really want to help, just give me a call and I'll follow it through."

"I'm sorry if I set off any law enforcement alarm signals."

His eyes shifted away from hers as the cell phone she'd left inside her unit started to ring. Slowly a look of stunned surprise spread over his face and he took a quick step onto the running board of his truck.

Puzzled, Ella glanced at the side of her SUV as she stepped toward the door. "Is something wrong?" she asked.

"It's just—"

"Hold that thought. I have to get this first," Ella interrupted. As she swung the door open and reached for the cell phone on the seat, she heard a low hiss. The SUV suddenly sagged toward her and almost instantaneously she heard a loud pop just to her left. Ella jumped back and saw that her left front tire was rapidly going flat.

Ignoring the cell phone now, she stared at the tire. There was a big hole in the side just above the tread where air was hissing out. Ella crouched down and inspected the tire, then she looked around where she'd just driven her vehicle. There was nothing jagged around that could have poked such a hole.

"How did that happen?" she muttered.

Garnenez pointed toward something on the ground and she saw a large pointed screw probably four inches long halfway buried in the sand.

"When the phone rang I looked over at your vehicle and noticed that lag bolt sticking out of the side of your tire. Then, when you went to answer the phone, it suddenly popped out and landed way over there," he answered, then slowly added, "You're extremely lucky, you know. I can't figure out how that stayed in the sidewall of your tire without giving you a flat long before now—especially driving out here in this terrain. You have a spare and a jack, don't you?"

"Yes, but the jack is one of those generic ones that doesn't really work well on soft ground. Could you give me a ride back to the trading post? I'll hire their mechanic to come back here in the wrecker and change it for me using safer equipment."

"You want to ride in *my* truck?" His mouth dropped open. "Why don't you let me stop by the trading post on my way back to town and send the wrecker for you?"

Ella nodded. He was obviously worried about her, and pushing things wouldn't help. "Never mind. I'll use my cell phone."

Before she could say anything else, he climbed into his pickup and drove off. As he sped away, Ella tried to figure him out. He hadn't really been trying to help her, not judging from the way he'd behaved. Garnenez had been trying to catch her consorting with skinwalkers so he could . . . what? Maybe he wanted to get her off the police force, or shunned, or worse. She shouldn't have been surprised. Janet had told her how the new traditionalists would react to her, and his behavior meshed perfectly with what she'd said.

Deciding not to wait for a wrecker since it would undoubtedly take more time than she wanted to spend out here, Ella searched until she found a large flat rock, then placed it beneath the narrow jack base to give it more stability. Then she carefully jacked up the SUV and put on the spare. As she got under way, her cell phone rang again. Rose barely gave her a chance to identify herself. "Some TV reporters are here," she said in a rush. "Apparently, they weren't allowed in the hospital yesterday so when they learned you'd checked yourself out this morning they came straight to our home. They want to interview you. They already tried to talk to your daughter, but I pulled her inside."

"Tell them to leave," Ella said. She had no love for reporters.

"If you don't talk to them here, they'll hunt you down at your office."

"Better there than at home. I don't want them around my

child." Ella knew successful reporters were persistent. They probably wouldn't give up until they spoke to her, but her family deserved a home where beauty and harmony prevailed, and all this attention would bring neither. "Tell them I'll meet them out in the police station parking lot in two hours."

Ella hung up, then called Big Ed. Although she thought he'd approve of her decision, it was easier to ask forgiveness than permission.

FIVE

When Ella arrived camera crews were gathered beside the building, along with two officers obviously stationed there to keep an eye on everyone. In all her years as an officer she'd yet to see either the press or media make her life easier. This time, depending on how things went, they had the power to make things spectacularly worse.

Despite having time to prepare herself mentally, Ella still had butterflies in her stomach as she pulled up into a parking space. People with cameras immediately began moving in her direction, and as she stepped out of the car, they began firing questions. She closed the door, standing with the vehicle at her back.

"Do you think God brought you back from the grave because you saved the life of a child?" a fast-talking blond Anglo reporter asked, cutting off a tall, skinny man while shoving a microphone toward her.

Ella saw the call letters of one of the Albuquerque television stations on the mike and recognized the woman from recent broadcasts. "Obviously I was never dead. That condition, I believe, is extremely permanent. I got banged up and covered with sand after falling into a mine shaft. Then I passed out, but they obviously dug me up in time. That's it."

She hoped to dispel any other potential troublemakers like Professor Garnenez who'd think of her as the undead, or worse.

"You saved the life of a *hataalii*'s son, your nephew, is that right?" another reporter asked before the first reporter could follow up.

"Yes. I got lucky and was able to reach him before he fell through some old boards into the mine shaft. But then I got unlucky and fell in myself."

"The EMTs had stopped trying to revive you—and had even covered up your body—when you suddenly sat up again," the first reporter asked quickly, refusing to be deterred. "How do you explain the fact that you're here now with not even a bruise on you?"

"Being a police officer means having a thick hide," Ella quipped. She had bruises and sores, just none that she would show in public. "My rescuers did a magnificent job, though. They should be getting the attention, not me."

The reporter wasn't dissuaded. "According to other Navajos I've spoken with, you'll now need to have a special ceremony done before anyone will feel safe around you since you came so close to death. What do you say to that?"

"I'm not going to stand here and explain my Navajo beliefs in front of the cameras, and I'm certainly not going to speak for other Navajos. It's not our way."

"Have you learned anything from this experience that you'd like to share with us?" A third reporter, a stocky black man she recognized from the cable channel, managed to get his question in above the confusion.

"Yes, this taught me something very important." She paused, and a half-dozen microphones came forward, jockeying for position. Ella smiled at the reporters' anticipation. "Be more careful where you step."

Several reporters laughed.

"You weren't breathing, and your heart had stopped

when they finally pulled you out. Did you have an NDE, a Near Death Experience?" a dark-haired woman reporter standing atop a concrete barrier shouted out.

"I did think I was going to die at one point and that was quite an experience, but somehow I don't think that's what you meant." She held up one hand, ignoring other questions shouted at her, and began moving toward the front entrance to the station. "That's all I've got to say on the subject, so if you'll excuse me, it's time for me to go earn my living."

She brushed past those who followed and slipped inside the station lobby. The two officers who'd been outside with her blocked the remaining reporters, turning them away from the door.

Ella thanked the officers, then headed toward the hall and her office.

Big Ed met Ella as she passed the lunchroom. "It seems you've become a celebrity," he said, then smiled. "Keep this up and we'll need a press room."

Aware that some of the officers were staring at her, Ella slid her medicine pouch to the front of her belt, keeping it in plain view. Since not many cops were traditionalists, it would simply be seen as a sign of respect. "Chief, can I speak to you in private?"

"Of course."

Ella walked with him to his office, then shut the door behind them. "I ducked some of the reporters' questions. I had to, and I'm hoping they'll go away for good now, but sometimes that just makes them more determined to get answers. In that respect, I may have just blown it."

"For now, you're news. People are curious to know exactly what you went through. If you say nothing, everyone will speculate and that'll end up making you even more interesting to them."

"I can't win." Ella explained about Garnenez following her, what had happened, and his obvious concern that she was about to ally herself with skinwalkers. When she mentioned him using the obsidian instead of flint for protection, he chuckled.

"Garnenez is said to be a new traditionalist zealot and gossip passes quickly across the college campus. Yet I'm still surprised how fast this kind of reaction has surfaced. It looks like you're going to be facing this kind of problem until people's minds are changed," he said and shook his head slowly. "But if anyone interferes with you in any way, bring them in. You don't have to put up with any harassment."

"I appreciate your support. Hopefully having that Sing will make the difference."

When the chief's phone rang, Ella stood up and started to leave, but as she reached the door, he called out to her. "Wait."

Ella returned to her chair and sat down. Something important was brewing.

"The fire department is there now?" Big Ed asked, then paused and listened. "What makes them think it's arson?" he added after a beat.

Ella leaned forward, curious, but she couldn't make out the voice at the other end. By the time the chief hung up she was eager to hear the entire story.

"I just spoke to Louise Sorrelhorse," he said. "She's the caregiver for Councilman Hunt's wife. When she arrived for work at the Hunt residence in Waterflow it was engulfed in flames. Neighbors had already called the fire department and the Kirtland trucks arrived within fifteen minutes, but Louise believes that Arlene Hunt was inside. There's no sign of the woman now. Mrs. Hunt requires a wheelchair so that might be part of the reason she wasn't able to get out."

"Has the fire crew confirmed that there's someone trapped in the house?"

"No. They haven't been able to get inside the house yet. And, from the looks of it, it's shaping up to be arson. Louise overheard Kenneth Curley, the new fire chief, saying that they'd found a hot spot beneath a broken window and some of the firemen detected the smell of gasoline. It looks like your time off just came to an end. Sorry. Get over there and find out what's going on."

"I'm on my way," Ella said, standing up.

"Mr. Hunt is a councilman, so he's going to want answers quickly. He's also an unpleasant man at the best of times, a real manipulator and wheeler-dealer. So even if we all get lucky and Mrs. Hunt turns up someplace else unharmed, we can count on Hunt second-guessing us every step of this investigation. Start by thinking up possible motives for arson and work from there. And see if you can find anyone hanging around, rubbernecking. You know what they say, sometimes firebugs show up to watch their handiwork."

Ella remembered her conversation with Janet. "I already know of one potential motive, Chief. Councilman Hunt's stand on gun registration is not very popular."

"That's an understatement. I heard about his proposals," Big Ed replied. "Now go. And save time by taking your crime-scene team with you."

"Are Justine and the others here at the station now?" she asked.

"Justine is in the lab. Ralph Tache was in the lunchroom last time I saw him. I'm not sure where Joseph Neskahi is."

"I'll find him."

Sergeant Joseph Neskahi was usually harder to find than the others because he routinely did double duty. If the crime-scene team wasn't currently working on an active case, he would shift back to his job as a patrol officer. The shortage of manpower these days meant that many of them wore several hats.

Today, it took her less than five minutes to assemble her team. Unlike it was for the public, weekends for the crime-scene unit usually meant time to catch up on paperwork.

On the way to the site, Ella drove her own unit while Justine followed in the crime-scene van with Tache. Neskahi was out on patrol south of Sheep Springs and would meet them there as soon as possible.

Ella drove quickly, but not at top speed. There was no urgency since the scene couldn't be processed until the fire was completely out. The structure, what was left of it, would also need a chance to cool. The one thing they'd be able to do right away was interview potential witnesses and firemen. That was usually a very effective way to get quick answers, providing the questions were worded right. Over the years she'd learned that people often saw more than they realized.

As they drove up the long dirt road that led to the Hunts' house, Ella could see emergency vehicles ahead. A thin column of dark gray smoke was streaming from the center of the ruined building into the clear blue sky. As she got closer, Ella could see the modern, wood-framed single-story house had been gutted, though the outline was still essentially intact. Firemen in dirty tan turn-outs and helmets worked inside the shell of what had once been an upper middle-class home.

Ella parked about fifteen feet from the smaller of two fire trucks. She'd just stepped out of her unit when Louise Sorrelhorse, a middle-aged woman wearing loose dark slacks and a light blue, long-sleeved blouse, rushed over to her.

Louise's face was spotted with soot and she smelled like smoke, which was understandable. "They haven't found her yet! And no one knows where the councilman is. Make them work faster."

Ella saw the desperate fear in her eyes. "I'm sure the fire crew is going through the building as fast as they can," Ella said. "If the owner is in there, it won't take them long to find the—" Ella stopped short before adding the word "body." She didn't know for certain the woman had been at home, and there was no sense in upsetting Louise even more than she already was. But the truth was that no one could have survived a fire of that magnitude.

"Look at that place," Louise whispered.

The flames had been extinguished and now the air was filled with the damp, acrid smell of charred wood. Steam rose over residual hot spots that had been covered with water. It reminded Ella of an artist's image of Hell. As it was at any crime scene, imbalance and disharmony now permeated everything here.

"They should have tried harder to get inside," Louise said, crying softly as she stared at the destruction. "She didn't deserve to die like that."

"Are you positive she was in there?"

"If she'd planned on going out today she would have told me. We had a schedule. She was very organized. The reason her car's not there is probably because her brother has it. He borrows it often."

"How long have you worked for the councilman's wife?"

"For about two years now. She doesn't like strangers so I'm paid very well to come every day. On weekends I usually arrive in the late afternoon to help her bathe, and so on."

"Were you two close?"

"Not really. She was my employer but we had a good working relationship. I could read her really well. I could always tell when she needed cheering up or was upset about something."

"Had she been disturbed about anything lately?"

"No, not at all. She talked a lot about working in her garden and, yesterday, she bought dozens of seed packets." Louise wiped her tears away with a rumpled handkerchief. "Now . . . it's over."

The words struck close to Ella's heart. For those faced with death was there always a feeling of being cheated by time? She pushed that thought back and focused on the situation.

As she looked around, Ella saw that Justine had arrived and was already talking to Chief Curley. Tache was with another fireman, and Neskahi, who'd also pulled up while she'd been talking with Louise, was studying the ground for tracks and other evidence.

"Tell me more about her," Ella encouraged, bringing her attention back to Louise.

"She and her husband have been married for nearly forty years, yet they were still very much in love. There was harmony in this house."

"Children?"

She shook her head. "Don't you remember she was shot during a robbery in Gallup just two years ago? That's why she was in the wheelchair."

Ella nodded. She recalled that the robber, an underage Navajo boy, had recently been released from jail. Hunt had fought hard to have the fifteen-year-old tried as an adult, but failed. That was enough by itself to explain why Councilman Hunt wanted handguns registered. "Did she help her husband promote his proposed legislation?"

"Yes, she was behind him all the way on that. She thought that handgun registration might at least reduce the chances of anyone else having to go through what she did, both during the robbery and afterward. They've also promoted an overhaul of the youth offenders program, making young people who commit violent crimes face trial as adults. But nobody has paid any attention to that, though it's a popular issue here in the Southwest. Everyone seems to focus solely on gun registration."

Ella nodded, but didn't comment, her gaze resting on several firemen who were all working the same spot inside the ruined house.

After a few minutes of silence, Louise continued. "The councilman made a lot of enemies by taking a stand for gun registration."

"Has the family received any threatening phone calls, letters, or things of that sort?"

"Not that I know of," Louise said, then after a long pause, added, "Councilman Hunt's only enemy, if you can call him that, is Councilman Tolino. Councilman Hunt got into several heated arguments over the phone with him, mostly on the youth crimes issue, I gather, though they have their differences on gun registration. Get two lawyers together . . ."

She couldn't see Kevin in the role of arsonist, and to Ella's own surprise, the fact that Louise had thought to mention him at all bothered her. Kevin was a politician through and through. He'd argue politically, but that would be it. However, this kind of talk could harm him. Uncertain why she cared at all, she shoved the thought out of her mind.

Maybe she was getting soft now that she was pushing forty and starting to feel a little older every morning. Kevin didn't need her protection. She'd treat him like any other suspect and would follow up this lead. "Do you know what they were arguing about?"

"I think Councilman Tolino thought that my employer was pushing the gun bill too hard. The words 'dead in the water' were the ones Councilman Hunt mentioned to his wife. Apparently Tolino wanted him to change his strategy so he could at least get the violent youth offender program passed. But since I only overheard one side of the conversation, then pieces of the discussion between the Hunts, I obviously don't know all the details."

Ella made a mental note to ask Kevin about it. Her gaze drifting back to the scene, she saw the firemen had moved on and scattered. Obviously the search for Mrs. Hunt wasn't over. "Thank you for your help. I appreciate it."

Louise followed Ella's line of sight. "I guess they're still looking," she said and sighed. "If you don't need me, I'm going to wait over by the fire truck until . . ."

"Go ahead."

Ella studied the charred remains of the house. Arlene had probably had breakfast that morning and gone about her business in the normal way never realizing that, hours later, she'd be lying dead beneath a pile of rubble. Life was incredibly uncertain, but that knowledge was so hard to take most people avoided thinking about it at all.

She took a deep breath. It was time to get to work. Order had to be restored.

While the firemen continued searching for any sign of Mrs. Hunt, Ella's team looked for evidence related to arson. Chief Curley had been right about the hot spot. Justine, Tache, and Neskahi worked to collect evidence, taking photos and collecting samples of charred wood that might contain traces of the accelerant. While they processed the scene, Ella walked around the perimeter of the ruined house trying to reconstruct the sequence the arsonist had followed as he committed the crime.

Ella turned around in a slow circle studying the area. As she did, she suddenly noticed a large, round-faced Navajo man wearing jeans and a cowboy hat walking toward the ruined house. He came to within fifteen feet, then stopped, his gaze on the smoldering rubble.

"Can I help you?" Ella asked, walking toward him.

He continued to stare at the house as if mesmerized. "I just needed to see this for myself," he said, looking at her briefly, then back at the house.

The man was in his early thirties and wore his hair short, a common style almost everywhere. From what she could see, he didn't appear to be wearing a medicine pouch. That, and his willingness to approach this site—a place where a death might have occurred—made her think that she was dealing with a modernist.

"Who are you?" she asked, pushing her jacket back so he could see her badge clearly.

"My name's Hoskie Ben, Officer," he said, finally looking at her closely.

"What brings you here?"

"This," he said, gesturing toward the house. "I wrote copy about the fire for the radio news just an hour ago, but I just couldn't believe it had really happened. I needed to see it for myself."

Ella watched him, suspecting that there was a lot more he hadn't said. "If you write copy for the news you're probably used to hearing about all kinds of unpleasant subjects. Why does this particular event upset you? Do you know the owners?"

He looked at her, then at the ground. "This is different. I feel responsible for this fire."

Ella's antennas went up. "What do you mean?"

"We had an entire program devoted to the topic of gun control yesterday." Hoskie swallowed, then in a taut voice added, "I did the research that provided most of the facts and statistics George Branch used when he went on a tirade against Councilman Hunt's gun registration plan." He paused, then continued. "I stuck to the hard facts, but I knew George would spice them up by adding all the redneck commentary meant to provoke. That's what he does best."

"There was a program that focused on Councilman Hunt?" Ella pressed.

"No, not on Hunt alone. The last show targeted all the current and possible proponents of gun control on the Rez. George said that The People had the right to know that the Tribal Council felt powerful enough to tamper with the Bill of Rights." He looked at her. "You know how he spins things."

Ella exhaled loudly. "Oh, yeah." She was dying to ask Hoskie if he'd also provided background for the comments Branch had made about her last year when she'd become the talk show's target, but decided not to ask. This wasn't the time or place.

"I've studied very hard to become a journalist," Hoskie continued. "I'm working on a Master's right now, but the only job I could get around here was working for Branch at the radio station. I do a great job with news and editorial copy, but George edits anything I give him and uses the information any way he wants. There's nothing I can do about it except find another job. I took a leave of absence once to do just that, but I couldn't find any other openings. I have a family to support, so eventually I went back."

"Give me the highlights of yesterday's program," she asked.

"Branch implied that there was a faction within the tribal government conspiring against the *Dineh*. He told the listeners that the problem with some politicians was that they were insulated from the real world. They received the best police protection, lived in good neighborhoods, and never went anywhere they might actually have to use a gun to protect their family. Of course the listeners knew exactly who he was talking about."

"Naturally."

"I've never owned a gun, but until this came up, I'd always thought that guns had to be licensed."

"No, not in New Mexico. Here it's just automatic weapons, and that's done federally. Other than that, a waiting period and a background check is pretty much all that's required."

Hoskie nodded. "I'd sure like to speak to the issue myself but I have no editorial clout or airtime. I would also like to bring up the Hunt plan to put violent youth offenders away for much longer sentences. My employer conveniently ignores that side of Hunt, though I'm sure he agrees with the concept."

She heard the ambition in his tone and had the strong

feeling that he was the kind who'd never give up trying. "Maybe you'll get your turn someday."

"If there's anything I can do to help you find whoever set this fire just let me know. I can try to write some discussion topic suggestions for George denouncing what happened here and asking people with any information to come forward. If I approach him in the right way, he may go for it."

"Sounds like something that would really help our investigation. Do it."

As he walked away, Ella noted paramedics joining some of the firemen in one of the smaller rooms of the house. They had a stretcher. From the looks of it, they'd found Mrs. Hunt. As she waited for confirmation, Ella joined Tache, who was photographing the hot spot beneath the window. A broken bottle lay in shards around a charred black spot.

Justine came up with a set of forceps and began to collect the glass, placing it in a box.

Ella sighed. "You won't find any fingerprints on that."

"What do you know that we don't know?" Tache asked, looking at her intently.

Ella suddenly realized that she'd spoken aloud. "It's just a hunch." One she knew was right, however. Her intuition, something her mother believed to be something else, was rarely wrong.

A few minutes later, the paramedics came out with a body bag on the stretcher.

Ella stopped them. "The wife?" she asked, not using the name of the recently deceased in accordance with Navajo customs.

"It's hard to tell," one of the Navajo men answered. "The body was so badly burned. But there was a ruined wheelchair beside the remains and that makes me think your guess is right. The ME asked us to transport the body to her lab and she'll be making the final determination."

Before Ella could say anything more she heard running

footsteps. As she turned her head, she saw Lewis Hunt, the councilman. He stopped abruptly inches from the stretcher and stared at the black plastic body bag in horror.

"Is that—" His voice was barely audible. He tried to finish the sentence, but the words wouldn't come.

"We don't know who it is for certain, Councilman. A medical examiner will be making the identification. All we know is that it wasn't your in-home care nurse," one of the emergency medical team members answered.

"Was there a wheelchair nearby?"

The EMT nodded.

"Then it's my wife," he said and began to shake violently. "There's no one else it could be." He took a step back and stumbled, weak at the knees.

Ella steadied him and nodded to the EMTs, who continued on with the body. "We're investigating this now, Councilman," she said, making sure he saw her badge. "It's still too early to be certain, but the fire appears to be the work of an arsonist."

"Arson? Who would do such a thing to my beautiful wife?" he whispered and crossed his arms in front of his chest in an effort to stop shaking.

"We need to find whoever was responsible," Ella answered softly, leading him away from the site.

He stopped by the mailbox that was at the front of the house near the street and looked back. "Who hated me—us, enough to do this?" he asked in an anguished whisper.

"I'd hoped you'd be able to tell us."

Hunt took several deep breaths as he stared at an indeterminate point across the highway. Then his eyes narrowed. "It may be connected to the radio show. Did you hear about that?"

"I've heard a few things. I'll learn more."

"Maybe one of Branch's loony callers decided to come after me." He started to say more, stopped, wavered slightly, then covering his mouth with one hand, ran over to the side of the road and vomited.

Ella waited. His grief and shock were stunningly real. She considered telling him what she'd experienced in her own close call with death, thinking it might ease his pain a little, then decided against it. She had no proof that any of it had been real.

Lewis Hunt returned to where she was standing a few minutes later. Ella's heart went out to him. His eyes were dull and lifeless. His spirit had been broken. "Councilman, I know this is a terrible time, but—"

"Ask me whatever you need," he said wearily.

"Did your wife have any enemies?"

"Not ones who'd do something like this," he said, his voice unsteady. "My wife had a law degree and was active in politics. She didn't run for office because that wasn't what she wanted, but she was actively involved with me campaigning for the gun restrictions I wanted to pass. She spoke to any and every group that would listen to her—from Chapter Houses, to political science classes at the college."

"Do you think she made enemies doing that?"

He shrugged. "Lots of people disagreed with us on gun registration, but that's just because they don't realize how prevalent handguns are on the reservation. Kids carry them around on the streets and in their cars, bring them to dances and social events, even to school. Although, so far, we've averted any major tragedies like the ones that have happened in other places, our luck will run out one of these days. Perhaps Shiprock will be next," he answered, parroting what she suspected was his standard speech.

"Getting back to your wife. Is there anyone in particular who has given her—or you—a hard time recently?"

"I received some nasty hate mail this morning—a backlash from Branch's radio show—but it wasn't unexpected. I put it into a file just in case something comes of it."

"I'll want to examine that mail. Did anyone at the college classes or Chapter House meetings that your wife attended seem openly hostile to her, during or afterward?"

He considered it. "Pam Todacheene and my wife have never gotten along. They're both attorneys and could argue a case nonstop for hours on end—and they did just that several times over the gun proposal. But she wouldn't have hurt my wife or me."

Hunt looked around as if lost, then waved halfheartedly at someone who'd just pulled up. "That's my brother-in-law and chief aide, Cardell Benally. He'll help me with the arrangements I'll have to make. Do you need anything else from me?"

"No, sir. Thank you, Councilman. I'll be sure to keep you appraised on our progress."

"Yes. And I'd like to ask you to do something for me, Investigator Clah?"

"Yes, Councilman?"

"Find the person who did this. And when you do, gather enough evidence so that even the . . . stupidest jury in the world will convict him and put him away for life. My wife has been denied justice once already, I won't have it happen again." Hunt's voice was shaking now, and it wasn't just from grief. He was angry.

Ella didn't know how to answer the man, and he was beyond consoling any more, so she just nodded and walked away. Quickly she joined her team, worked beside them for another hour, then took Justine aside. "I'm going to pay George Branch a visit," she said, recapping what she'd learned about his last broadcast.

"Would you like me to meet you there? I'm going to be finished here shortly, and Ralph can take the evidence back to the station without me."

Ella shook her head. "I need you to do something else. Find out when the last Chapter House meeting around here was held and if the deceased attended. If she did, find out how her views were received and if anyone in particular gave her a hard time."

"Done."

Ella drove to the radio station located in the off-reservation city of Farmington, glad to be working a case again. Arson, murder—these were crimes she understood, and something she was trained to deal with effectively. Trying to figure out intangibles of any kind—particularly what happened after death—was just an exercise in frustration.

As Ella entered the large cinder-block building off Main Street, she found Branch in the hallway getting hot cocoa from a vending machine. He'd easily put on another twenty pounds since the last time she'd seen him. The man had to tip the scales at close to two-seventy or -eighty.

"Hey, Clah," he said, seeing her. "Figured you'd be dropping by. Hoskie told me what happened."

"Then let's cut to the chase and save us both some time. I'd like a list of your callers—the loony ones. Or is that redundant?"

"Charming as ever, I see." The half-Navajo radio personality took the steaming cup from the machine dispenser and sipped it slowly. "But I'm feeling charitable so it's your lucky day. The station won't release phone records, naturally, but you can listen to a tape of the show and take all the notes you want."

Branch led her to a booth down the hall from his office, then brought down a CD containing the audio of his last show and handed her a headset. "I didn't take any callers for the first half hour of the show, but from then on, we had a flood of listeners expressing their opinions."

Ella spent the next two hours forcing herself to listen to Branch's show. Callers usually identified themselves only by their first names and she had no doubt that some of them had used aliases. Most of the callers had been really incensed by the issue and had expressed negative viewpoints, but none of them had mentioned Hunt specifically. There was nothing for her here.

As she walked outside to the hall, George Branch met her and she handed him the CD and headset.

"All done?" he asked.

"For now."

"You and I don't see eye-to-eye on much, Clah, but even you have to admit that *if* this is a reaction to the things said on my show, I'm still not to blame."

"Your radio show is known for stirring up people's emotions and getting them to react. You may have done a better job than you realized. Either way, an innocent woman was killed and I intend to find out who did it."

"I've heard a rumor that Arlene died in the fire. Has this been confirmed?"

Ella nodded. "It's not official yet, but I'm pretty sure the body they found was hers."

"Damn." Branch leaned back against the wall and stared at her, his face drawn. "I met her a few times. The woman had a mouth on her, but I admired her. She had guts and never pulled her punches, and in this day and age when everyone's trying to be politically correct, that's quite a virtue. I always thought *she* should have been the council member, not that spineless idiot she married. She'd have had enough sense to drop that gun issue and carry the ball on the youth offender bill, something most of us can agree on."

"Off the record, and, in your personal opinion, are any of your regular callers capable of something like this?"

Branch shrugged. "My callers, as you've heard, are passionate people. Gun registration is a particularly volatile issue. The People won't take kindly to anyone who's working to restrict their rights."

"Save the speech for your program. Just answer my question."

He scowled at her. "People are people, Clah. They're capable of almost everything."

"Well put. But you might keep that in mind, too. One of these days you're going to piss off the wrong person." Ella walked away from him, glad to finally be able to put some distance between them. Dealing with someone like Branch always left a bad taste in her mouth.

By the time Ella crossed the parking lot and reached her vehicle, she had a plan. Picking up her mike, she called Justine. "I need you to handle something else for me. Go talk to Janet Joe's parents. See if they have any idea who may have wanted to set fire to the Hunt residence. Janet's parents are right there on the front lines with Hunt on this issue. They've been victimized themselves already."

"I'll take care of it," Justine said. "What really bugs me about this case is that even if we catch the perp, chances are all we'll get him for is manslaughter. He'll go to prison and then get out in a few years. Yet the way she died . . . that cries out for tougher justice, you know?"

"We'll make the best case we can against the perp," Ella said. "That's all we can do. Our duty stops there."

A part of her felt just like Justine did, but catching the perp was paramount in her mind now, not the eventual sentence. First, they had to restore order. Harmony wasn't as passive a concept as she'd believed when she'd first returned to the Rez. It required a struggle and watchfulness to make sure that evil was held in check by good—that the balance was maintained.

SIX

✖ ✖ ✖

It was ten-thirty that evening when Ella finally got the chance to open the book on life after death experiences she'd discovered in the Shiprock drugstore's extensive book rack on the way home. Dawn was asleep, and for the first time today, Ella was on her own.

She was still sore, maybe from the accident, or perhaps her many work-related injuries were kicking up again. She had to fidget around on the sofa to get comfortable but finally she put her feet up on the cushions and began to read.

The book was written by an MD who'd interviewed hundreds of people who'd survived what he called "bodily death," and she was amazed at the similarities in the described experiences. She'd finished the first chapter when, out of the corner of her eye, she saw Rose peer into the living room, then leave. About fifteen minutes later, Rose came back in again and quickly left before Ella could say a word.

The third time Rose came by, Ella closed the book and waved at her mother. "Mom, why don't you come in and tell me what's bothering you?"

"Have you found the Singer?" Rose suddenly paused, then continued. "No, let me rephrase that. Are you still trying to find him?"

"I searched for half a day, left word at the trading post

and with some other people I met, but I'm relying on your friends and my brother most of all. I've now started working on a case, so my free time is restricted."

"Finding the Singer is very important, Daughter. I'd hoped that you'd try to get some leads and follow them up, just like you do when you're tracking a suspect."

"I am and will, but I've also got to take care of police business. A leave of absence is out of the question."

"If we were to find him tomorrow would you put your work aside and have the Sing done right away?"

Ella sighed. "Mom, the Holy Ways can last up to a week. I doubt that the department would let me take that much time off all at once right now. I'd have to find some way to work things out."

Rose's expression hardened. "You have to find the Singer, Daughter, and then make the time to be healed. It's been nearly ten years now, but don't you remember how isolated you were when you first returned home? Some of the *Dineh* called you L.A. woman and wouldn't even speak to you."

"Of course I remember," Ella answered. It seemed like a lifetime ago. She'd left her job with the FBI and come to unofficially investigate her father's murder.

"It'll be far worse now unless you honor Navajo ways. You'll be treated like an enemy instead of just an outsider."

"I know that, Mom, believe me. I *will* take care of this."

"It'll help you, even though you're only having the Sing done so that others won't be afraid." Rose gave Ella a long, pensive look. "You still don't really believe in any of our ways, do you?"

"I try to keep an open mind, but honestly, I don't know what to believe anymore."

Rose glanced down at the paperback that Ella had in her lap. "Life after death experiences? It sounds like one of your father's books. Have you decided to become a Christian like him?"

"I don't think picking a religion is something you can decide so quickly or easily. I'm just reading . . . and learning."

"Something happened to you down in that mine," Rose observed thoughtfully. When Ella didn't comment, she added, "Navajos like myself define death as lack of growth—stagnation, if you will. We don't believe in a personal afterlife, just that the good in us merges with universal harmony. The bad, of course, remains earthbound." She held Ella's gaze. "When your wind breath was lost, did you experience something . . . troubling?"

Ella hesitated. Since she still wasn't sure what had happened, it seemed wrong to discuss it with Rose. What she'd seen would conflict with the beliefs her mother had held all her life.

"Mom, lack of oxygen can do all sorts of crazy things to a person," she said, trying to make light of it. When Rose's expression hardened, Ella sighed. "When you come face-to-face with your own mortality like I did, you learn a lot about yourself—what matters and what doesn't," she said, measuring her words. "In a pinch inner strength is far more important than physical. It's the reason I'm here now."

Before Rose could answer, Two suddenly began barking.

"What's gotten into that dog? He was chewing on a bone just a while ago." Rose looked toward the kitchen. Two was on his hind legs, looking out the back window.

Seeing him, Ella felt her skin prickle. As she glanced over at her mother, she saw the same uneasiness mirrored on Rose's face. "Stay inside with Two," Ella said quickly. "I'm going to take a look."

Reaching for both her cell phone and her gun, she hurried to the back door. Even before she stepped outside, she heard the pony running around in the corral, obviously disturbed about something. "Keep Two here. The dog will chase anyone off, and I'd rather catch whoever's out there if I can."

Rose held Two by the collar to keep him from following

as Ella turned off the kitchen lights and slipped outside, edging along in the shadow cast by the house. The moon was out, but the clouds muted its glow. As Ella hurried toward the corral, she caught a brief glimpse of a shadow darting between the hay bin and the shed.

"Stop, or I'll shoot," she called out, hoping he wasn't going to run for it.

The figure crouched low, then raced away.

"Oh, crap, you want to run?" Ella grumbled, breaking into a jog. Picking up speed, she followed him to the large arroyo, a fifty-foot-wide natural ditch, which ran parallel to the fence line. Stopping for a moment to listen, she heard a thump. Figuring he must have jumped down to the bottom, Ella cautiously moved forward and risked a look below. A large impression had been made in the loose sand at the bottom, and other footprints led downhill. Knowing that person would have to climb out again somewhere, and figuring that she could make better speed up here where the ground was harder, Ella opted to run along the top of the arroyo. The soreness she'd felt earlier on the sofa had disappeared, perhaps from the extra adrenaline, and she found an easy rhythm in her stride.

Several minutes later, she stopped and listened for footsteps. It was too quiet. She crept to the edge and studied the area below. There were no footprints visible anywhere. The person had chosen to hide, either by pressing himself tightly against the bank, or maybe crawling inside one of the dark crevices.

The perp was smart, and knew how to blend into the deepest shadows with skill. Backtracking, she found an area of sandstone that intersected the arroyo. Scuff marks showed he'd gone up one of the narrow side channels perpendicular to the main wash.

Going on instinct, she headed toward the road, certain that was his destination as well. As Ella drew near, she began searching for a vehicle. Soon the road became visible, but before she could intensify the search, she heard a car or truck starting in the distance, and then saw a pair of taillights moving toward the highway.

Ella strongly suspected that it was the same person she'd been chasing, but since she had no way of knowing for sure, she remained vigilant as she returned to the house at a fast walk. When Ella reached the back porch, Rose opened the door and let her in. Two was beside her mother, the bone back in his mouth as if nothing out of the ordinary had happened.

"Are you all right?" Rose asked Ella. Seeing her nod, she added, "My special herbal tea will be ready in a minute. It'll help us both relax." Pouring hot water into a teapot, Rose said, "Tell me what happened."

"I'm not sure if it was a burglar, or a vandal, or if someone's watching the house, Mom. If this ever happens when I'm not home—Two going nuts like that and the pony whinnying and running around—keep the mutt with you and call the station. Two will defend you and my daughter. He's very protective."

Rose petted the mutt's head. "Yes, he is."

"I'm also going to request that the department send an officer down this road more often and at random intervals."

As Rose poured them both some of her special tea, the kitchen was filled with a soothing, minty scent.

"Mom, once before, your friend kept a watch on this house. Is it possible that he's doing so again?" Ella asked, remembering how Herman Cloud had tried to protect their family, especially Rose, with whom he had a long-standing friendship.

"Bizaadii?" Rose asked, surprised. Herman Cloud was a very quiet man, so calling him "the gabby one" had been Rose's way of teasing. "If that had been him, he wouldn't have run from you like a criminal. He's a traditionalist and

may not have wanted to be too close to you, but he would
have at least identified himself."

"Yeah, you're right. He's too direct and plainspoken to
do anything less."

"And he's always been very loyal to this family," Rose
said thoughtfully.

"That's because he cares about you, Mom."

"I've been very lucky in my life. I found a mate in your
father, and a very comforting friendship with Bizaadii. But I
worry about *you*, Daughter. The day will come when your
daughter will no longer need you. Your life will be very
empty if she's all you have."

"My daughter's barely in school. I have a long time before
I need to worry," she answered, smiling.

"Time has a way of slipping through our fingers, Daughter. It's the way of life."

Ella got up at daybreak after a restless night. Worries about
the case and, more importantly, the person who'd been lurk-
ing around her home had crowded her mind. She thought of
Professor Garnenez, then recalled how he'd acted around her.
He wouldn't have come around at night, not to a place he
considered contaminated with evil. Traditional Navajos, and
possibly a lot of new traditionalists, avoided doing anything
dangerous at night—the time for evil to roam.

Dressing silently and noting gratefully that she was less
sore this morning than she'd been yesterday, Ella crept
through the house, then went outside. First, she checked her
department vehicle, especially the tires. After changing the
flat yesterday, she'd remembered passing through an old
dump site that had intersected the dirt track she'd been following. The ground had been littered with half-buried junk.
That may have been where she'd picked up the object that
had ended up giving her the flat tire. But a vandal might have
targeted her unit when she'd left it parked at the trading post,

too. There was no way to know for sure, so from now on, she'd be giving her vehicle a frequent once-over.

Assured that her unit was okay she began to search for traces of last night's visitor. Ella quickly found footprints around the area where she'd seen the figure, but they were faint, and an early-morning breeze had softened the features, making the impressions less distinct. Her guess was that he'd worn a size eight or nine shoe, but that didn't tell her much. It was a pretty common size.

Ella took a deep breath. The air was crisp and clear and she felt energized. A long-distance runner since high school, she eased into a comfortable jog and headed to her brother's house, less than three miles away. He would be up now saying his prayers to the dawn.

As Clifford's home and medicine hogan came into view, Ella saw that he'd completed his prayers and was carrying a handful of wood into his medicine hogan. Seeing her jogging up the road, he stopped and waved. "I haven't seen you out running in a long time. You must be feeling well."

"I am," she admitted, slowing to a walk as she got close. She loved jogging, though she didn't do it nearly often enough. "I need to talk to you," she said as he placed the wood down by the entrance to the hogan.

"Sure. Come inside. I'm expecting a patient this morning, but he's not due for some time yet."

"Can we walk and talk instead? I'd like to cool down slowly so I don't stiffen up. I'm still planning on running back home."

"Okay." Clifford walked beside her as they continued past the end of the road and down a trail that led into a nearby canyon.

"I think someone is watching the house," she said, coming right to the point. "Since right now I'm an object of fear to some and curiosity to others, I'd like you to keep an eye out."

"Of course. Do you sense danger?"

Clifford had always honored her intuition. The question didn't surprise her.

"Not particularly, but logic and instinct both tell me to be cautious."

"Logic may fail you, but your instincts never will. Trust them to guide you instead."

"I do. In fact, these days, I seem to be more attuned to everything around me," she said, then regretted having spoken. Clifford wouldn't let it go at that. "I'm not an oracle, don't get me wrong," she added with a chuckle.

"When something frightens you, you always joke. You give yourself away every time, Sister."

One of the many skills Clifford had developed as a *hataalii* was the ability to read between the lines—to sense what people weren't telling him. "I'm not afraid of this. I've just been surprised by how I can predict what people are going to do." She told him about her experience at the Joes'. "I turned around just in time to see them looking at me."

"You faced death. That's bound to make you more attuned to the world around you—to the life you almost lost." He paused, then added, "But keep that new ability of yours under wraps for now. People are likely to misinterpret anything they perceive as a change in you."

"And think that somehow it's a result of my contamination?" she said, finishing the thought for him.

He nodded. "Things are always more complicated on the reservation. You know that."

Ella took a deep breath, thought about mentioning her experience with Professor Garnenez, then decided against it. There was nothing to be gained by mentioning his name, and perhaps within a few weeks, days if she was lucky, she'd no longer be considered a pariah by some. "I better go back. I have to drive over to see my child's father this morning. I'm also going to ask him to keep an eye out whenever he's at the house visiting."

"Good. He should be aware of what's going on."

Ella returned home at a fast pace, showered, then dressed for work. Boots was already in the kitchen fixing Dawn's breakfast when Ella joined the family.

Seeing her come into the kitchen, Dawn gave Ella a hug and a kiss, then immediately began talking about the pony and her latest riding lesson with Boots.

"Boots said that I have good hands," she said proudly.

Boots glanced back from in front of the stove and nodded. "She does, and great balance too. She doesn't depend on the stirrups as much as other kids her age."

As Boots and Dawn began talking about riding Ella felt a twinge of jealousy. For a moment, she wondered what it would have been like if she'd married Kevin, who could have easily provided for them. She would have had the financial freedom to be a full-time, stay-at-home mom, maybe even home-school her child as more and more people were doing across the country.

No sooner than the thought formed, Dawn, who'd been demonstrating how to neck rein while seated at the table, knocked over her glass of milk, which tipped over her cereal bowl. Dawn managed to catch the bowl in time—upside down.

As Two rushed up to express his divine right to spillage, Ella, who'd jumped up to grab a dish towel, tripped over the animal and nearly fell. Two yelped, Dawn began to giggle, and chaos ensued.

Dawn had somehow managed to get oatmeal in her hair. As Boots took her to wash up and change clothes, Ella sighed and helped Rose clean up the floor and table. Who was she kidding? She wasn't cut out to be a stay-at-home mom. Not now, not ever.

Ella reached for her weapon, kept on the top shelf, removed the trigger lock that she'd added recently now that Dawn was getting taller and could stand on a step stool, and clipped the holster onto her belt. "I better get going."

"I hope your day is less eventful than our breakfast," Rose said, smiling.

Ella laughed. "I'll see you tonight, Mom."

Kevin didn't live too far away, having constructed his own home a few years ago on land allotted to his family. The location was perfect for him now because he wanted to be as much a part of Dawn's life as he could. Though his busy schedule meant that his visits weren't as frequent as he would have wanted, Ella knew that he really loved their child.

Today, besides the heads-up on their intruder, she had other serious matters she wanted to discuss with him. She'd never had a will made, for one. It had never seemed like a pressing concern. That was about to change. She also needed to find out more about his arguments with Councilman Hunt.

As she pulled up, Kevin walked out to the porch and waved, obviously having heard her vehicle coming up the road. He looked like he'd been just about ready to leave for work. He was wearing dress slacks, a long-sleeved shirt, and a bolo tie. His boots were crafted of the finest leather.

"Are you back on duty already?" he asked, leading the way inside.

"I'm working a case," she said. "Early bird gets the worm."

"Pity the early worm." Kevin chuckled. "So what brings you by?" he asked, pouring himself some coffee and offering her some as well.

Ella noticed that the *Dineh Times* was on the breakfast table, open to the editorial page. She sat down in the chair he offered opposite his, but Kevin remained standing, leaning against the counter as he sipped from the cup.

Ella told him about the person she'd seen near the house last night. "I'll ask for extra patrols, but I'd like you to keep your eyes open anytime you come to visit, and let me know if you see any strangers in the area who don't seem to belong here."

"You can count on it," he replied. "And thanks for the heads-up." He refilled her coffee cup, then joined her at the table and turned the paper around so it was right side up for her.

"You hadn't commented about it, so I suppose you don't know there's a letter to the editor that concerns you professionally. The writer doesn't think you should be working with the PD until you have your Sing."

Ella groaned, and looked down at the signature. She didn't recognize the name. "I *am* going to have a Sing, but first I have to find the medicine man who can conduct the right one. I'm looking for John Tso, but he's hard to track down."

"So I've heard." He nodded slowly. "What really happened to you at the mine, Ella? I was in Window Rock all that day, but I've heard a lot of variations of the story since then."

"Well, obviously, I didn't die. I'm here and feeling just fine, but the whole thing scared the hell out of me, Kevin."

He nodded. "That's to be expected."

"The accident woke me up and made me think about a lot of things, including writing a will and getting life insurance so Dawn will be provided for even if I'm gone."

"I would always make certain that our daughter never lacked for anything. You know that, don't you, Ella?"

"Sure, but I still want to leave her something . . ." She shrugged.

"Everyone should have a will, of course, but in your profession, life insurance is going to cost you a fortune."

"Probably, but I still need coverage at some level. I'd also like to have you draw up that will for me. Can you do that?"

"Sure," he answered. "The will should designate a guardian for Dawn, but I assume that'll be me, right?" he asked.

Ella gave him a wry smile. "Kev, I know you mean well, but be realistic. You're not suited to being a full-time daddy. You don't realize how complicated that can get. I think Mom's the logical choice with Clifford as backup."

"You're wrong about that, Ella. She's my daughter and I'm the one who should take care of her if something happened to you. But even setting kinship aside, she'd be far better off with me than with the others you mentioned. Rose's life has changed drastically in the past few years. She's taken on a lot of responsibilities. She's the main reason those mines are now being sealed up. I don't think it's fair to ask her to give up the work she's started so she can become a full-time parent to Dawn. She raised you and your brother. That should be enough, especially at her age. Your brother, too, has his own concerns and I'm not convinced Loretta would welcome Dawn into her household."

Ella sat back and considered what he'd said. Kevin was right, her mother was working for the tribe as a consultant and resource on several environmental and cultural concerns, not to mention getting up in years. Her brother Clifford had his hands full with his patients, and she couldn't see choosing Loretta to raise her child.

"Good points," Ella conceded. "But so was the one I made about you."

"I'd bring Boots over here. She would continue her role in Dawn's life, like she does now while you're at work. Of course, this is all assuming that you passed away while Dawn was still a child."

"Of course." Ella weighed what he'd said. "Let me see how Mom feels about all this. She has to be given first choice on whether to keep Dawn with her or not. But if something does happen to me in the future, and Mom is unable to take care of her, Dawn should come to live with you as long as Boots is here to help. As Dawn gets older, of course, I'll amend the will to meet whatever new circumstances arise."

"Fair enough. But make sure you let Boots in on this before I start on the paperwork."

"I will." Ella looked directly at him as she got ready to move on to another subject. "I've been working on the Hunt case and your name came up. I understand you two got into an argument over the phone recently."

"We argued whenever we saw each other, too. Both of us want better laws to address the problem of violent crimes committed by minors, and to be honest, I never thought his idea to push for handgun registration was so bad either. But the way he was going about it all stunk. Hunt has a reputation as a manipulator, getting others to lead the way and then taking the credit later. But in this case he's not even bothering to try a little arm twisting. He's thinking with his heart instead of his head. It all goes back to his wife getting shot, of course."

"Can you think of anyone, maybe another councilman, who might have had a serious grudge against Hunt?"

He shook his head. "It's been said he'd sell out his best friend to get what he wants, and maybe he has a few times. But, no, in general, we're all politicians, Ella. We present, discuss, argue, then deal. It's the way things get done."

Ella drove to the police station in Shiprock thinking about what Kevin had said. Maybe a compromise hadn't gone the way someone else had expected, or he'd twisted somebody's arm just a little too hard. Retaliation could be termed the flip side of compromise.

As Ella stepped inside the lobby, which was pretty quiet today, she saw Justine standing by the candy machine, sorting through her change. "Did you get anything new from the evidence collected at the arson site?" Ella asked.

"Tests reveal an accelerant was used, which was proof of arson. Other than that, we don't have anything that points to a particular individual."

"Then let's go canvas that neighborhood again."

"We worked it all yesterday, Ella. No one knew any-thing—at least nothing they were willing to share."

Something in her tone alerted Ella. "Did you think some-one was holding back?"

Justine took a deep breath, collecting her thoughts. "I don't know anything for sure, and it could be nothing . . ."

"But?"

"One of the people I spoke to was Vernetta George. She and I go back quite a ways and I had a strong feeling that there was something she wasn't telling me."

"Did you press her?"

"You bet, but it didn't work. I was planning to go back today and work on her some more. I had a feeling that Netta was being secretive because her husband Norman was there beside her."

"They must have a lot of money if they can afford to live in that area. What do they do for a living?"

"Norman used to work for the power company, but he got laid off because he missed too much work. Netta is a CPA for the tribe."

"Why do you think she's reluctant to talk around Nor-man?"

"I have no idea. After she got married three years ago we quit hanging around as much as we used to."

Ella motioned toward the parking lot. "Let's go pay her a visit and see what we can get from her." Ella tossed Justine the keys once they stepped outside.

Although they took Ella's unit, Justine usually drove. That left Ella free to think without having to worry about the road. Soon they were heading east toward Waterflow.

"Tell me more about Netta. In your opinion what's the best way to handle her?" Ella asked as they left the commu-nity of Shiprock.

Justine considered it. "She and I were good friends once,

and that means that she's not likely to be intimidated by me, even when I'm visiting her in an official capacity. You'd probably have a better chance of getting answers from her. If we do the hard-soft approach, I'll take good cop. But my gut feeling tells me that the key is making sure Norman is not around."

They arrived in the higher income area south of the river fifteen minutes later. A winding, paved road led into the housing development. The Hunt home was clearly visible from here and Ella could see the yellow crime-scene tape that had been erected there after the firemen had moved their equipment from the area.

Since this was a residential area occupied mainly by modernist Navajos there was no need for them to wait for a customary invitation before approaching the door. Ella and Justine got out of the unit, but even before they reached the front porch, Netta came out to greet them. "I knew you'd be back," she said, looking at Justine with a relieved expression. "Come in. We'll have some privacy today. Norman drove to Farmington for a job interview."

Ella introduced herself, then sat across from Netta at the opposite end of the couch while Justine took a seat on the easy chair.

"This is now officially a murder investigation, Mrs. George, so you should know that before we begin," Ella said, polite but firm.

Vernetta nodded. "I heard that the poor woman's body had been dug out from beneath the wreckage of the house. We've been talking a lot about it."

"Who's 'we'?" Ella asked. "You and . . ."

"Norman. Right before you came, Justine, Norman told me not to volunteer any information even though I thought there were some things you needed to know. Norman figured that the police would find out everything sooner or later so there was no reason for us to muddy the waters or put ourselves in the middle of it."

"If you know something that pertains to this case, you're doing the right thing telling us," Ella said quietly, trying to motivate her without coming on too strong—unless it became necessary.

"I'm not sure how much this is going to help, but here's what I know." She hesitated, gathering her thoughts, then continued. "Lewis Hunt has made lots of enemies, and more recently because of his stand on the gun control issue. But one guy stands heads above the rest. He's a loudmouth who has a tendency to go off half cocked. In fact, two days before the Hunts' home burned down, he took a swing at Lewis right here in my own home after they got into an argument about the issue."

Ella knew that it was a mistake to rush most Navajos. They told their stories at their own speed and attempts to interfere with that process usually backfired. Forcing herself to be patient, she waited.

Vernetta paused and cleared her throat. "I should tell you that Norman thinks I'm overreacting and that the man is completely innocent. But I think that, like me, he's afraid of retaliation. If this man ever found out that I told you about him, he'd come after me for sure. Can you keep my name out of it?"

"I'll do my best, but you do need to tell us the other person's name," Ella said firmly.

"Bruce Smiley," she said.

Ella didn't know him, but when she glanced at Justine her partner nodded.

"You should have a police file on him," Netta said. "He was arrested last year for bringing a gun into a Chapter House meeting."

Ella recalled the incident although she hadn't responded

to the call. "Smiley's a tribal activist, right?" she asked, searching her memory. "Doesn't he travel all over the country fighting for Indian rights, stirring people up?"

"Yeah. Bruce isn't happy unless he's fighting something or someone. Lately, he's been focusing on the gun control issue here at home."

"And you think he might be the one who burned down the Hunts' home?" Ella pressed.

"I have nothing to offer you that might be even remotely considered evidence, but I do think he's capable of doing something like that. Last year Hunt pressured other councilmen to vote for using the revenue from the casino in To'hajiilee to fund an addition to the health clinic, then was absent himself when the vote was taken. It ended up a tie, and Hunt's vote could have made the difference—if he'd have shown up. Bruce took a baseball bat to Lewis's car, he was so mad."

"That was a hot issue," Justine said, remembering. "A lot of people felt that the money could be better spent."

"Bruce was afraid that if the tribe didn't channel those funds to the clinic, the money would end up being spent on salary increases at the tribal administrative level or more government. Later on, Hunt voted in the majority when it went toward a new tribal office, exactly what Smiley predicted would happen. But it's the fight he had here with Lewis that made me think of him when the Hunts' house burned down. It may be coincidence, but there it is."

"Did you see him hanging around the neighborhood the day of the fire?"

"No, but he was here that day. I'd gone shopping and when I came back I noticed several empty cans of beer in the trash. The brand was Coors, but Norman buys Budweiser and he seldom drinks more than one. I asked my husband about it during lunch, and he told me that Bruce had stopped by with some cold ones earlier."

Netta paused thoughtfully, then continued. "But I will say this for him—if Bruce is responsible, I can almost guarantee that he didn't know the councilman's wife was home. His argument was with Lewis, not his wife. Although she campaigned with him on the issue, Bruce would see it as a wife supporting her husband, nothing more. His enemy was the councilman."

"Maybe he thought killing her would be a way to demoralize or destroy Hunt," Ella suggested.

Netta shook her head. "Bruce is not a deep thinker—he just reacts." She looked at Justine and then back at Ella. "Will you be checking this out?"

"Yes, but we won't mention your name or your husband's," Ella assured, addressing her concern.

"Thanks. Oh, and one more thing. If Bruce set that fire, I'm sure he's heard about the death and knows the police will be working extra hard on the case. So be very careful around him. When Bruce feels threatened, he gets even more aggressive."

"Thanks for the warning," Ella said.

They were in the SUV moments later when Ella glanced over at Justine. "Head for the station. Once we're there, get me an address, a rap sheet, anything and everything you can get on Bruce Smiley. Also ask Special Agent Blalock to run him through the NCIC and then check the sheriff's department and Farmington PD. Let's see what we're up against before we pay him a visit. I have a bad feeling about this."

SEVEN

✖ ✖ ✖

It was late morning by the time the two FBI agents who worked the Rez met with Ella and her special investigations team in Big Ed Atcitty's office. Dwayne Blalock, the senior agent, was an Anglo the *Dineh* had nicknamed FB-Eyes because he had one brown eye and one blue.

Lucas Payestewa, a Hopi, was at least twenty years younger. He had been assigned to the area two years ago to concentrate on a long-term investigation on organized crime, but Ella had heard a rumor that he was about to be transferred. Several complaints had been lodged against the Hopi man and he was making too many waves—a situation the Bureau didn't like at all.

Ella began their meeting by briefing everyone on what she'd learned, then continued. "Men with Bruce Smiley's reputation sometimes think of themselves as crusaders. They like headlines and sometimes they will do anything to get attention. So, before we pay him a visit, I wanted us all to be prepared. Smiley lives in a house less than a mile inside the Navajo Nation over by Hogback, so I asked Sheriff Taylor to loan us a deputy who could help us study the house from the off-Rez side while Neskahi kept watch from inside our borders. My caution paid off. Both men found a good surveillance site and Neskahi reported seeing Smiley carrying assault rifles from an outside storage into his house. Then the deputy saw him filling sandbags and bringing them inside. My guess is he suspects we're coming and is getting ready for a siege."

"If those weapons are fully automatic and not registered we can arrest him right now and figure out the rest later," Payestewa said. "I'm sure we can round up an ATF man to do the honors."

"I agree that he's trouble, but maybe he's just paranoid. Let's come up with a more subtle approach than a clear and direct confrontation," Blalock said. "Those sandbags make it sound like he's going to make a stand and is going to try and set himself up as a martyr. A shoot-out might eventually force us to kill him so that'll play right into his hands and, unfortunately, a few of us may also go down with him.

"If he's responsible for Mrs. Hunt's death, he may be trying to confuse the issue hoping he'll be remembered not as a killer, but as a man who was willing to fight for his right to bear arms. Or he may have rationalized Mrs. Hunt's death as collateral damage, and convinced himself that he's a patriot and we're the bad guys. I don't know, but experience tells me that men willing to die for what they believe in all too often take others along with them. I want to cut the chances of that happening—to him and to us."

"From what I've heard so far this guy sounds like a loon," Lucas said. "I recommend we suit up and go out there expecting a war. If it goes down easy, then we'll take it as a win."

"Who wants to make the initial approach and try to get him to come out and talk?" Big Ed asked. "You want to handle this?" he asked the FBI agents.

Blalock looked at Ella, then back at him. "I was going to suggest Clah. Her track record for cheating death is pretty good, and it's her turf," Blalock said with a half grin, then growing serious added, "But Lucas and I will go with your people to provide backup."

"I don't blame you for not wanting to be the first face he sees." Ella took a deep breath. "I vote for an initial low-key approach. I'll drive up alone and the rest of you stand by behind cover and hidden from view. There isn't much ground cover, but there are plenty of low hills and boulders that have tumbled down from the Hogback just east of there. We'll play it by ear after that and see what he does."

"When you first get there, stay in your unit, and see if he'll come out to meet you. You'll be safer outside," Big Ed said.

"And he'll think I'm treating him like a traditionalist," Ella said with a nod. "Good plan. That little courtesy might make things go easier. I like it." Ella looked at the others. "Any objections?" When no one spoke, she added, "Then we're all set. Let's roll."

Bruce Smiley's wood-frame house was north of the highway and just west of the twenty-mile-long ridge known as Hogback. His closest neighbor, Victor Garcia, lived nearly two miles east on the sliver of non-reservation that stood between the Navajo Nation to the west and south, and the Ute Mountain Indian Reservation on the north.

While the other officers were getting into position, Ella decided to pay Victor a visit first. The man's house, in the middle of a rough section of desert dotted by old coal mines and depleted oil wells, gave him an unobstructed view of the road all the way to Smiley's house. There was no telling what he might have seen that could be helpful to them now. All things considered, it was worth a stop.

Ella let the backup team know what she was doing, then proceeded to Garcia's house.

Victor was working in his small vegetable patch as she drove up. Jabbing his shovel into the ground, he came over to her. "Can I help you?"

Victor was in his early eighties, but he looked strong and in good health. Although he didn't live on the Rez, Ella could see he had Navajo in him.

"How's it going?" she greeted.

"It's a good day for loosening up the soil," he answered, then wiped his brow with the sleeve of his shirt. "What brings the Navajo Tribal Police here? I usually see the Utes instead."

"I hope you don't mind. You're not really in my jurisdiction, but I'd like to ask you a question or two."

"About my neighbor?" He gestured to the small pitched roof house in the mouth of a canyon to the west.

"What makes you assume that?"

"That's one very angry young man over there. I always figured that it was only a matter of time before he got into trouble. Mind you, I have very little to do with him, but we run into each other whenever his goats get out and come over to browse in my cornfield. At first I'd try to help him round them up, but he always acted as if I was actually saying he couldn't handle it alone so I quit offering."

"I didn't realize he had any animals," Ella said casually.

"For a long time he did. But in the last few months he sold them all. I thought he was getting ready to move on but then he got involved in reservation politics when the gun issue came up. That's all he talks about whenever he comes by. His truck is filled with bumper stickers and his favorite says that the only way you'll get his gun is by prying it from his cold, dead hands."

Ella had seen the sticker dozens of times. Many law-abiding New Mexicans had that particular one on their vehicles. But violent lawbreakers who had a personal armory gave that particular sticker an entirely new meaning.

"You've got a real clear look at his home from here," she said, looking in that direction. "Have you seen anything unusual going on down there?"

"You mean besides the fact that he's been target shooting

that automatic rifle of his? He's aiming into the side of an arroyo, but it still makes me nervous when I hear a bullet ricochet. I spoke to him about it, but it didn't do any good."

"Is he a pretty good shot, or could you tell?" Ella asked.

"He showed me his targets—which by the way are drawings of people aiming guns straight at you, not the circular bull's-eye type. He groups his shots tightly and aims for the head."

"How far is the arroyo from here?" she asked.

"It runs kind of northeast and southwest just on the other side of the fence down there. That's the reservation boundary, you know."

She saw where he was pointing and nodded. "Does the rifle fire full auto, or does he just squeeze off several quick shots?"

"I think it's an M-16. He fires it full auto in short bursts, three or four rounds at a time. Maybe he doesn't want to overheat his weapon."

"Did you notice if he has any other firearms like that?"

"I can tell you he's got at least one M-1 carbine, a paratrooper model with the folding stock. The others I've seen him toting around are an M-1 Garand and a big Colt forty-five autoloader. I asked him once why he had all those former military weapons and he said he's been collecting them for years."

Once again she remembered Payestewa's suggestion. Before coming here, they'd done a quick check and found that Smiley didn't have the federal firearms permit necessary to own an automatic weapon. Arresting him on that charge would be one way to solve the problem if they couldn't get anything more substantial on him right away.

"Does your neighbor get many visitors?"

"Not really. I saw him shooting one time with a Navajo man I've met at the trading post a few times—I think his name is Norman—but that's about it."

"Do you remember seeing your neighbor at home yester-day afternoon at around three-thirty or so?"

"He drove away at around two as I was putting away my gardening tools. I know it was two because that's when I go inside to watch my favorite TV show, *Doctor Bill*. Then, when I came back outside after dinner, at around six to do a little cultivating, I saw him drive up. Of course he might have come back and left again while I was in the house."

"Thanks for your help," Ella said, walking back to her unit.

"If you're thinking of trying to arrest him for something, you better take some reinforcements. No one forces that guy to do anything he doesn't want to do, and he's liable to put up a fight."

Ella considered it. "Would it be all right if Sheriff Taylor put one of his deputies up here on your land for a few hours?"

"Like a sniper?" He shrugged. "If you really think he's done something bad, then go ahead. But tell me, are you go-ing to question him about that fire at the councilman's house? The one that killed the poor woman in the wheelchair?"

Ella's radar went up. "What makes you ask that?"

"The timing . . . and the fact that I just remembered some-thing. I had to go to the Quick Stop for a few groceries yes-terday morning and I saw him outside by the gas pumps. He was filling up gas cans and loading them into his truck. He never saw me because when he came in to pay he got into an argument with the clerk and I ducked behind the row where the dry goods are. After he stormed outside, I went up to pay for what I bought and I saw him through the window. He walked off the concrete pad and grabbed up a handful of mud where the water had pooled from spray. You know how they wash off the concrete with a spray hose?"

Ella nodded and smiled, wondering when he'd get to the point.

"Well, he smeared the mud all over the license plate, then flipped his hand to splash a little more mud on the bumper. When he turned around, probably to see if anyone was watching him, I stepped to the right and the cash register hid me," he said. "I remember thinking that he was acting like a crook straight out of the Dick Tracy comic strips. Do you remember those in the newspaper?"

"Yes, I do." Actually Ella knew who Dick Tracy was, but the comics were a little before her time. "Thanks for taking the time to talk to me this morning," Ella said, getting back into the vehicle. Victor sure liked to talk. Maybe it was because he lived basically by himself out here and missed the kind of conversation TV just couldn't offer him. But he'd given her valuable information.

As soon as she was under way, she called Blalock and updated him. "Call Sheriff Taylor, and get him moving on this. We need one of his SWAT boys with sniper training up there, just in case. The owner has given his permission."

"I'll do it right now. Drive back to the main highway and take a break. We're still waiting for the county officers to get into position."

It was around two when Ella pulled up in front of Smiley's house. According to plan she stayed in the vehicle, waiting and trying not to remember that a high-velocity rifle bullet wasn't likely to be deflected by the windshield. Time passed slowly. Someone pushed the curtains in the living room back enough to peer at her, but no one showed up at the door.

Blalock hailed her on the radio. "Don't get out of that vehicle unless you place some solid cover between you and the house. Something about this stinks. He should have come out by now."

"He's there—or someone is," Ella said. "I'm going to step out and lean against the side of my unit, but I'll make sure the vehicle is between me and him. Let's see what happens."

Ella got out, then waited. After fifteen minutes passed, she got tired of waiting. Following a spur-of-the-moment idea, she pretended to see someone coming up from behind the house. She held her hand over her eyes, peering into the sun, and called out, "Good morning!"

Ella walked around her vehicle, taking a few steps toward the house when a voice suddenly boomed out from behind the front window. "Don't come any closer. Get off my property."

"Mr. Smiley, is that you?" Ella called out, then pretended to look into the distance again.

"Cut that out. There's no one out there but you."

Ella gave up the pretense. It had already accomplished what she'd hoped for—getting his attention. "I'm with the Tribal Police, and I just need to ask you a few questions. If you don't want me in your home, can you come outside?"

He stuck a rifle barrel out the window and fired a shot. Ella saw it coming, dove to the ground, and rolled behind her unit, coming up in a crouch behind the engine block with her pistol in hand.

"That was a warning," Smiley yelled. "If I'd meant to shoot you, you'd be dead now."

Ella heard a call coming over the radio, then her cell phone started ringing. Opening the car door, she picked up the handheld. "I'm all right. He didn't appear to be aiming at me."

At that precise moment, the cell phone went silent. It had probably been Justine, and she'd heard Ella's radio response.

"We're moving in, Clah. Stay in place and keep your head down," Blalock said first. "Taylor is here. He and his men will cover the north and east in case he rabbits on us."

Justine and Neskahi spoke next. They were coming from the east. With Blalock behind her to the south, Payestewa accompanying him, Smiley had no escape route. Before long more Tribal Police units and county sheriff deputies had come to help.

"You're surrounded, Mr. Smiley," Ella called out to him. "Set your weapon down and come out now."

There was no response. As one of the county sheriff deputies made a dash toward a large boulder fifty feet from the house, Smiley fired from one of the windows to the east. Ella saw the deputy fall to the ground hard, clutching his leg.

"I don't want to kill anyone," Smiley yelled out from inside. "Leave me alone. I'm on my own property and I haven't broken any laws."

"You have now. You've wounded a deputy," Ella countered. "But we don't have to do this the hard way. Lay down your weapon and come out."

Blalock pulled up in his unit, then hurried toward her. "There's no cover anywhere close to the house, so coming up undetected is out. He's got a clear line of fire all around for a hundred feet."

"I'll shoot to kill if anyone tries to enter my home," Smiley called out. "You've been warned."

"I want his phone service disconnected," Ella said. "I don't want him calling out or anyone calling in. We also need to cut off power to the house."

"He's already done that himself and started up the generator. It'll run for hours probably," Blalock pointed out.

"Can we disable it with something? Like a well-placed bullet?"

"It's over there beside the propane tank. If we hit that gasoline-powered generator we could start a fire—right next to the propane. The last thing any of us will ever hear is a loud boom."

"He's been getting ready for us, that's obvious." Ella raised Justine on her handheld radio. "Turn off his phone service."

"We can shut off his regular phone, but if he has a cell, it's going to take a while to find out what carrier he uses."

Before Ella could reply, Sheriff Taylor called Ella on the cell. "I have bad news. A camera crew from the cable station in Farmington bypassed our roadblock by going cross-country. They're being detained by my deputies about a quarter of a mile from your position."

"Can you keep them there?"

"Yes, but I thought you should know that they're claiming Mr. Smiley invited them."

"Our Mr. Smiley?" Ella asked.

"He told them he wants to be interviewed on the air, live," Taylor said.

"No way. He's not getting any publicity until he's in custody."

Taylor spoke to one of his deputies, then added, "Make that two camera crews. A second station is at the roadblock now."

Ella considered her options, then called Justine. "Have you found out yet if he has a cell phone? I need to talk to him."

Less than two minutes later, while Justine was still looking into it, dispatch at the Shiprock station called Ella on her cell phone. "We have a call from Bruce Smiley. He's demanding to speak to you."

"He just saved me some time. Give him my number," Ella said, then updated Justine.

About two minutes later, her cell phone rang again. "This is Detective Clah," Ella said.

"You're the woman who came up first. Are you really in charge, or should I talk to someone else?"

"You're talking to the right person."

"You sure? I've seen FBI jackets and county cops."

"This is Rez land—our turf. The FBI is here because you're known to be in possession of at least one unlicensed automatic weapon and that's a federal violation. Since you live right beside the boundary between our jurisdiction and the county, sheriff's department deputies are also here. I'm here on behalf of the tribe because we need to question you regarding the death of Mrs. Hunt and the arson attack on the Hunt residence."

"I'll consider coming out *after* I talk to the television reporters. Send them in when they get here."

"They won't be allowed to come into the perimeter at all until you're disarmed and in our custody. Lay down your weapons and come out peacefully. Then you can have a few minutes to make a statement to the press or whoever you want."

"How stupid do you think I am? The minute I step out this door, you'll blow my head off."

"With all those TV cameras aimed at your door from behind our lines? We're not stupid either. We'd like this to end peacefully as much as you do."

"Don't lie to me. By now you know exactly what happened at the Hunts' or you wouldn't be here. It wasn't my fault the woman couldn't get out of her house. There was no car there so how could I have known anyone was inside? All I was doing was standing up for the rights of the *Dineh* before those fools on the council leave us defenseless. Cops and crooks will always have guns."

"You'll have your day in court," Ella replied, weary already of his twisted logic. "That's *your* right. We don't want to shoot you nor do we want you to shoot at us. If what you really want is to die in a spectacular firefight that'll be broadcast across the entire country, it's not going to happen. We're prepared to wait you out for as long as it takes. Eventually you'll fall asleep or the generator will run out of gas."

There was a long pause, but Ella didn't interrupt the silence. Finally, Smiley spoke again. "You've had firsthand experience on what it's like to die, Clah. Tell me about it."

This was definitely not something she wanted to discuss with anyone, but at least when he was talking he wasn't firing his weapon. "First, I didn't die. Without immediate medical intervention the dead tend to stay dead. All that experience did for me was bring home the fact that life is too precious to waste."

Ella waited, then realized he'd hung up. She tried calling back but all she got was a message saying the call couldn't go through. It hadn't been Justine's doing, so Smiley must have turned off the phone himself. She was trying to think of something to yell over to him when a redheaded woman reporter suddenly ran up in a crouch and shoved a tape recorder in Ella's face.

"Did you really come here to confiscate his guns? Have your actions forced this standoff?"

"How in the hell did you get over here? Get down behind the engine block! He's already shot one deputy."

A moment later another police unit drove up right next to hers and stopped. With her vehicle protecting him from direct fire, Neskahi slipped out the door, staying low, and came up.

He grasped the reporter's arm firmly, then looked at Ella. "Sorry! She got out of her vehicle at the roadblock and managed to get a head start before I saw her."

He pulled the reporter toward his car. "Get going. If you refuse to cooperate, I'll arrest you and you'll be sitting in jail when this story breaks."

As soon as Neskahi got the reporter into his car, Blalock and Justine took advantage of the extra cover and joined Ella behind her unit.

"This is getting us nowhere," Blalock said. "He's hunkering down and going to remain uncommunicative."

"I've got an idea." Ella explained quickly and Justine left to get what was needed.

A half hour later when Justine finally returned, no progress had been made.

"I've got what you wanted, Ella," she said, opening a case and bringing out a tranquilizer rifle borrowed from the local vet.

Blalock shook his head. "You're going to have to get close to your target for this to hit the mark and too many things can go wrong. We're not after a feral dog who's attacking sheep. What if you miss or the dart's deflected?"

"I'm going to try and place a shot through one of the open windows," Ella replied. "This is the only way to avoid killing him. I don't think he has any intention of surrendering."

"Agreed. But he may end up killing *you*."

Ella shook her head. "I won't make myself a target, and I'll have my regular pistol with me too."

"I know that the possibility he'll go out as a martyr rankles you, but is it worth this?"

Ella didn't reply. A week ago that would have probably been her motivation, but things had changed. Life meant a lot more to her now. Although she had no desire to risk her own for his, she had to at least try to give him a chance to live. She'd received a second chance of her own, and she just couldn't bring herself to deny someone else that same opportunity. But she'd be extremely careful.

"I'm a good tracker because I move silently. My brother taught me that skill years ago. I can do this. Several windows are partially open for circulation and, hopefully, I'll be able to take advantage of that."

Ella watched as Justine loaded the rifle with a tranquilizer dart. "Tell me what the vet said, Justine."

"Dr. Goldman uses this to help the animal control people capture animals that can't be approached, like vicious dogs or a cornered bull. He said the dose will drop a two-hundred-pound man within fifteen seconds, at least theoretically. But you have to hit him in a fleshy area, not the skull or backbone or kneecap. You know what I mean."

"What if he just plucks it out?" Blalock interjected.

"Too late. The impact injects the knockout drug," Justine answered, handing Ella the rifle.

"It'll be up to you guys to keep him distracted," Ella said. "Use the bullhorn to try and strike up a conversation."

"We'll do everything we can," Blalock said. "Just remember that once you go around this car you'll be out of cover. And keep your eyes on the ground because he could have easily booby-trapped the area and that armored vest you have on only protects your upper body. If he reloads his own ammunition, and most of these guys do, he probably has plenty of gunpowder to make pipe bombs. And they may not be easy to spot, particularly if he buried them just below the surface."

"I'll watch my step. We've got plenty of daylight left. As long as his attention is on you, I'll be fine. And even if I don't get a chance to dart him, it's going to help us a lot if I can take a look inside the house and see what kind of ammo, weapons, and gas masks he has." Ella took the small pair of auto-focusing binoculars from the ground beside her and stuck them in her vest pouch.

"Just don't try and go into the house," Blalock said, then shook his head. "I wish you'd reconsider this, Ella. Too many things can go wrong with this plan. At least two of those rifles he's supposed to have will easily penetrate that vest."

"I'll be careful, and if I see an opening I'll take the shot."

Blalock walked over to the rear of the vehicle and announced who he was. Then he began trying to convince Smiley to turn on his phone and talk.

As he spoke, Ella crouched down and made a dash for the corner of the house where there was a blind spot, and then waited to see if Smiley reacted. When nothing happened, she inched around the side, checking the ground below her as she moved. Aware that a rifle bullet could go right through plaster and wood, she was careful not to even rub up against the wall and make a noise.

Halfway down was a small bathroom window. The glass was frosted, but the casement glass was open about three inches. Once she made it there, she'd peer inside and try to figure out where he was. If that didn't work, there was a bedroom window farther down at the other end.

As she crept slowly, she heard another vehicle pulling up somewhere behind the police line by the front of the house. Blalock was using every technique he knew—including building a wall of cars up close that would help them tactically—to keep Smiley focused on them.

Ella sidestepped to the bathroom window. It was up high and she had to stretch to peer in. No one was visible. All she could see was the wall in the hallway through the open door. Inching toward the bedroom window, she suddenly spotted a strand of transparent fishing line stretched across the ground, connected to something buried beneath a thin layer of earth.

She stepped over it carefully, now doubly alert. There was no telling how many of these were hidden here or around the other side of the house. Before she could take a look through the bedroom window, the crack of a single gunshot blasted through the air.

Ella froze, then ducked and reached for her cell phone. "What's happening?" she asked in a whisper.

"You tell me," Blalock said, matching her soft tone. "I thought he took a shot at you. We can't see you from here. Let me see if I can raise Smiley on the phone." A moment later Blalock spoke again. "No luck. He has it switched off."

"Let me take a look in there before anyone moves in. And alert everyone to watch where they step around the house.

There are trip wires beneath some of the windows. Maybe elsewhere too."

"Then he's probably rigged the windows and doors." Blalock paused, deep in thought. "That one shot we heard means that he either committed suicide, or wants us to think he did. If he did off himself, then you can bet he's left some surprises for us."

"There's smoke coming out of the side window. Maybe he's hoping to create a smoke screen to use as cover when he makes his next move," Ella said.

"Fall back, Ella," Blalock said.

Before Ella could reply, flames shot out the back window. "The place is on fire. I think he rigged it up so that it would catch after he was dead. No one would try to fry themselves alive. But I need to go in now because he might still be alive. A lot of suicide attempts miss."

"No, hang back and wait it out. This was his call."

"If he's still alive I have to try to get him out." Self-preservation told her to stay where she was, but she had to finish what she'd started. When she'd fallen into that mine, her rescuers hadn't assumed she was dead, and that's why she was here now. Everything was interconnected. To find harmony, one's life had to be in balance. She'd survived against the odds. She owed the man inside the same chance, even if he was a criminal.

Ella stood and peered in the bedroom window. No one was inside and the door leading to the rest of the house was closed. Leaving the air rifle propped up against the outside wall, she slid the casement window open and was about to crawl through when she heard footsteps behind her.

Ella reached for her service pistol instantly and whirled around.

"Whoa, Ella." It was Neskahi and he was stepping over the trip wires.

"I've got some explosives training," he said. "I took the classes the FBI offered last winter. Let me go in first."

Ella lowered her weapon. "If you're expecting me to turn you down, you're going to be disappointed," she said with a tiny smile. "Lead on."

She followed him in, staying low to the floor, trying to remain below the thin cloud of smoke coming in from beneath the door. Ella closed the window to cut down on oxygen feeding the fire while he looked around. Neskahi soon spotted a wooden clothespin and wires attached to the door.

"It's a old trick. When you open the door you pull out a piece of wood keeping the jaws of the clothespin apart. They snap shut and the wires around them touch, connecting a circuit to a battery and blasting cap. The explosives on the other side of the door then go off," Neskahi quickly explained.

The sergeant took a pair of wire cutters from his pocket and cut the wire leading from the top jaw, then bent it out of the way. After cutting the wire to the other jaw, he pulled out the clothespin. "It's safe."

Ella touched the door. "It's warm, but not hot. I think we can open it and this time I'll go first. Fair's fair. Ready?"

Ella pulled the door open, then went through low and fast. The fire seemed to be concentrated in the kitchen, but it was spreading fast. The smoke was as thick as a wall, but it gave them some cover.

Through the ever-thickening haze in the short and narrow hallway, Ella saw a figure lying back in a recliner with what appeared to be a forty-five auto on the floor by his feet. She didn't have to move any closer to see the gaping hole where his temple had been. "He's gone," Ella said. "Let's get out of here."

Neskahi pointed to wires leading away from the front door. Following his gaze, Ella saw a stack of ammunition, gunpowder, and a can of kerosene on the floor in the doorway between the kitchen and living room. A blasting cap and lantern battery were wired into the center of the makeshift bomb. A second nonelectrical blasting cap was beside the first, connected to detonating cord that extended into the kitchen.

The wooden table had been turned on its side and pushed against the kitchen window. Smiley's second-to-last act had apparently been to throw a kerosene lantern against the table and set the fuel on fire.

Flames had already ignited the detonating cord. They only had seconds and the front and back doors were blocked. Ella grabbed a folding chair from beside the computer desk and threw it out the front window. Then reaching for a sofa cushion and keeping it in front of her, Ella dove through the shattered window. She hit the ground a heartbeat later and scrambled to her feet, Neskahi right beside her.

"Bomb!" Ella shouted to the others behind the police line. As everyone dove for cover, Neskahi and she raced away from the house.

When Ella heard the sudden pop of a blasting cap behind her she instinctively stretched out in a desperate dive to reach cover. A wave of hot air and heat caught her like a leaf and flipped her over in midair. Deafened by the roar, she landed on the ground faceup, then rolled over and covered her head as a storm of debris came raining down on her.

EIGHT

Moments later Ella felt someone helping her off the ground. Her ears rang and she couldn't quite focus as someone carried her back behind the police line, then eased her down onto the sand behind one of the vehicles. Trying to get her bearings, she looked up, blinking, and saw Dwayne Blalock and Justine looking down at her.

"Damn, Ella," Blalock said in a breathy voice, "you gaining weight?"

There was a moment's confusion, then Payestewa and a big county deputy she didn't recognize eased Sergeant Neskahi to the ground beside her. Joseph was covered with dust and pieces of wood and gravel, had a cut on his cheek, but still insisted on sitting up. Everyone around them crouched low as rounds of ammunition continued to go off at a rapid rate. For a brief moment she was reminded of the Fourth of July celebrations at the old drive-in movie theater in Farmington.

Sitting up, Ella looked at Justine, who handed her a bottle of water, then at Blalock. "I think you darned near pulled my arm out of its socket when you drew it over your shoulders, Dwayne."

"Beats being dragged over the ground by the arms," Neskahi grumbled, then smiled at the Hopi agent who'd hauled him from danger to let him know he was grateful.

"Next time, FB-Eyes, I carry the girl, you carry the guy," Payestewa announced. Blalock scowled at him and Payestewa laughed. Justine joined in, and finally Blalock smiled as well.

"This makes the second time this week you've tried to get yourself killed, Ella," Blalock sighed.

"Maybe I'm going for the record," she joked, reaching down to ensure that her medicine pouch was still intact. Her luck was still holding.

A loud but less spectacular explosion suddenly shook the ground and everyone ducked. "Maybe I should just keep quiet," Ella said, glancing around for her car. "Where's my unit?"

"I moved it before the big blast," Justine said.

"What happened in there?" Blalock looked back and forth between Ella and Neskahi, who was now drinking from the water bottle.

Ella shook her head, trying to clear her thoughts. "Smiley took himself out with his forty-five, but he had the entire house rigged."

"Was all this just about his gun collection?" the same redheaded reporter rushed up, holding a small tape recorder.

Although Ella's thoughts were still in the process of clearing, her response was automatic. "What the hell are *you* doing here?"

"I came back. Were you there when Bruce Smiley killed himself? Do you blame yourself for his death?" The woman crouched low, inching closer but watching the burning house with anxious eyes.

"Get out of the crime scene," Blalock growled at the woman, then looked at Payestewa and added, "You can carry *her* all the way to Farmington—if she won't leave under her own power. *Now!*"

The reporter glared at Blalock, took a step back from Lucas, who was reaching for her halfheartedly, then stomped back toward the van where the press had been detained. A county deputy followed her, making sure she didn't circle back.

"I don't know what Smiley told those reporters over the phone before we moved in, but I've got a feeling we're going to be under attack on this one," Blalock said. "No comments until we debrief," he told them.

"Good idea," Ella said, wondering if her hearing would ever be the same again. The fire department was coming up the road, and their sirens made her head hurt.

An hour later, after receiving first aid for small cuts and bruises, Ella left Justine and her crime-scene unit on-site with Lucas Payestewa to gather evidence. She, Blalock, and Big Ed met back at the police station.

"Give me your Cliffs Notes version of what went down," Big Ed said once they were all seated.

"I think Smiley wanted to go out like a hero. He hoped that once he was dead and his home destroyed, we'd never be able to find enough evidence to link him conclusively to the fire and Mrs. Hunt's death. That would have left the element of doubt in people's minds as to whether he was really guilty. He could be remembered as a martyr and patriot who'd stood up for a cause he believed in."

"Do we have proof that he was the arsonist?" Big Ed asked.

"We have witnesses that'll attest to suspicious behavior, but that's all circumstantial. The glass bottles that held gasoline used to torch the place shattered, and according to Justine's report there were no prints on the fragments and shards. Without finding evidence in his home that linked him to the crime, we would have had a tough time making a case against him. He admitted to me over the phone that he'd set the fire, but that's not a signed confession—all we have there is my word," Ella explained.

"We'll also never be able to prove to the press that our actions didn't precipitate the incident that led to the man's death and the explosion," Blalock said. "No matter how you slice it, we're going to be screwed on this one."

"It goes that way sometimes," Ella said, standing up. "If we're done for now, I'd like to go jot down some notes for my report."

Blalock remained seated. "I've got a few other things to discuss with your chief. I'll catch you later."

Ella returned to her office. At the end of a good day she was always filled with an incredible feeling of accomplishment, but today all she felt was a sense of futility and the weariness that came from swimming against the current. She'd lost a battle today and the cost had been a human life.

Ella went directly to her desk but as she passed the fax machine she saw that someone had sent her a copy of the statement Smiley had sent the media and press before she'd arrived at his home. From the telephone number printed at the top that identified the sender, she realized that this copy of the original had come from Jaime Beyale, the editor of the *Dineh Times*.

As she retrieved the fax, her phone rang and she reached for it with her free hand.

"Did you get the fax I just sent you?" Jaime asked.

"Yeah, I have it now."

"I thought you might want to see it. According to Peter Finch of the Albuquerque paper, Smiley sent this letter to a targeted few. All I have is a fax of his fax, but basically it's Smiley's rant on the rights of gun owners and his unqualified support of George Branch. But what's most interesting is the last paragraph. He calls Lewis Hunt an enemy to anyone who believes in the Bill of Rights.

"He wanted to be remembered as a martyr in the fight to preserve The People's rights to bear arms."

Minutes later, Ella took the letter into Big Ed's office. Blalock was still there. "Just to make a bad day worse," she said, handing the papers to the chief, who read them over quickly, then passed them to Blalock.

"We're going to have a tough time with Councilman Hunt unless the crime-scene team finds something that ties Smiley to the arson," Chief Atcitty said. "The man lost his wife and will want definitive closure."

"We'll do our best," Ella said.

An hour later, after her team came in, Ella learned that they'd found evidence in the outbuilding near the propane tank and gas generator. One metal can that had fallen behind some old trash cans held traces of gasoline and several blades of bluegrass were stuck to the bottom where a store label had been peeled off. The Hunts had such a lawn around their home but Smiley didn't.

"It's the best we're going to get, Ella," Justine said.

Ella nodded. "Finish making out your report and leave one copy on my desk and another for the chief. It's almost eight now. I'm going home."

As she drove home Ella felt the same peculiar sense of restlessness that always followed her after a bad day. Glancing at her watch, she wondered if Rose had waited to make dinner for both of them tonight. She did that every so often.

Ella called home. "Mom, have you eaten yet?"

"No, not yet. Your daughter just went to bed, and I was going to give you some time to get home."

"Great. Don't cook dinner."

"You're picking up something?"

"No, Ma, I'm cooking tonight. I'll come up with a decent meal using whatever we have on hand. And don't worry. I can follow cookbook instructions."

"I don't have a cookbook."

"Then I'll make up my own recipe."

"Daughter, I don't think we're ready for that."

"Don't worry. I'll make something easy. Maybe Texas chili. It's hard to kill beans."

Even with a pressure cooker, the beans had refused to soften for some reason. It was ten o'clock and neither of them had eaten anything yet.

"How long can it take beans to cook?" Ella said, exasperated after tasting one.

"I usually soak them overnight," Rose said, then took one bean from the pot. Sampling it, she added, "I think we've got a shot at refritos."

By eleven, they finally had a meal on the table. The burritos, stuffed with chili, refritos, and sausages, were wonderful.

"It's not bad at all, Daughter."

"I'm a Renaissance woman, Mom. I just have to apply myself."

Rose gave her a long, thoughtful look. "You were on the news tonight—the national news. Did you know that?"

"Really? Must have been a slow news day for them to focus on a Navajo. What was the story about?" Ella hoped it wasn't about the incident with Bruce Smiley. She reached up and touched one of the scratches on her forehead, then noticed Rose watching her closely.

"They talked about you saving your nephew, then being buried alive. The reporter called it a miracle. They showed film from some old mine, not the right one, of course, then you in front of the police station being interviewed by that local reporter. But you didn't have that scratch on your forehead this morning, Daughter. Is there something I don't know about yet that may be in tomorrow's news?" Rose asked nonchalantly as she took a bite of burrito. "You also have some new bruises."

"You don't miss much, do you, Mom?" Ella recounted the events and the explosion. "Everyone believes it's all over now, and the evidence seems to support that, but I have a real bad feeling about this."

Rose began clearing the table. "I don't know how you stand your work. From what I see, it's a never-ending job with few real victories."

"This is what I was meant to do. It suits me," Ella replied honestly. "But I haven't been paying enough attention to the details of my personal life. I should have seen to it that I had life insurance, and a will. Nearly getting blown up today brought the urgency of it home to me again."

"That reminds me, you got a letter from a life insurance company." She reached up to a wooden shelf above the counter and handed Ella the thick packet.

Ella immediately recognized the name of the company. As she glanced at the forms, she realized that she'd need to do more than fill out the questionnaire. She'd have to go see Carolyn and get a physical. But that wouldn't be a problem.

"I can understand why you'd want to leave your daughter a cash settlement," Rose said in a heavy voice. "These days everything revolves around cash, check, or credit cards. There was a time when having lots of sheep in the corral was the same as being rich. You could always trade for whatever you needed." Rose stood up wearily and rubbed her eyes. "You can leave the dishes to soak in the sink tonight if you want. Good night, Daughter."

As Rose left, Ella thought about how different her mother's generation was from her own. She couldn't help but wonder what the world would be like when her daughter grew up.

Ella cleared the table and washed the dishes and pans, placing everything in the drain rack to dry overnight. After wiping the table and counter, she hung the dishcloths up to dry and walked wearily out of the kitchen, turning off the light.

Stopping by Dawn's room, she slipped inside and brushed a light kiss on her daughter's forehead. Dawn had grown a lot this past year and become very independent. Her baby was gone forever and now in her stead was this little person. The realization was bittersweet. She wished that Dawn could stay just as she was forever.

Ella slipped out of the room as quietly as she'd come in. Her job now was to safeguard her daughter's future and make sure Dawn was protected until she was strong enough to face life on her own terms.

The following morning Dawn dressed for school while Ella made the oatmeal. After one taste, Dawn put the spoon down and made a face. "Yuck. This tastes like glue with sugar, *Shimá.*"

Ella tasted the oatmeal herself, then grimaced. "You're right."

"See? You don't want to eat it either." Dawn shook her head, then looked through the entryway toward the front door as someone walked inside. "Boots, help!"

Ella smiled at Dawn's sitter. "You heard my daughter's cry," she said as Boots stopped to pet Two, who'd greeted her at the door. "Breakfast is in your hands."

Boots was still laughing when the phone rang and Ella went to answer it. Whenever they got a call this early in the morning it was invariably work-related and it was no different today. Even before he identified himself, she recognized Sheriff Taylor's voice. From the sound of the connection and background noise, he was speaking from a cell phone.

"I thought I'd better give you a heads-up, Ella," he said. "Someone drove a car right into George Branch's living room via the picture window. That started a huge fire. The fire department is out here now."

"The car—did it belong to someone from the Rez? Or was it stolen?"

"Can't say yet."

"Where's the big guy?" she asked.

"Branch is sitting inside his Mercedes in his pajamas. He's fine. He got out okay."

"Pajamas, huh? Be thankful he doesn't sleep in the buff."

"Now there's an image I could do without," he said with a chuckle.

"I'll be there shortly," she said.

Ella gave Dawn a quick hug and a kiss, then smiled at Boots. "You take good care of her. Thank you." Ella glanced over at Rose, who'd just come inside after putting a soaker hose in her garden. "I may be late again tonight, Mom."

"Take care of yourself, Daughter. Remember, you're famous now. I'll keep checking the news to see if any other stations are doing your story. Want me to record it for you if they do?"

Ella scowled, then noticed her mother was trying to avoid cracking a smile. "Yes, Mother, definitely. Check *every* station to make sure."

Ella drove directly to Branch's house, located outside the reservation boundaries and northeast of where the Hunts had lived. If the car's owner lived on the Rez, then this incident would be a jurisdictional nightmare.

The smoke from Branch's house could be seen for miles, a bit reminiscent of the plume from the coal power plant, which had polluted the area for years before filters had been added. But this smoke was black and oily-looking, not the white, feathery plume she remembered. As she got closer she could see the frame of a sedan protruding from the front of the old farmhouse, which faced the road. Bright orange and yellow flames enveloped the pitched roof and shot out the window openings. The glass had already been blown out.

Several vehicles were beside the road, the drivers watching the action. Another vehicle, a Mercedes, was on the property but well back from the house beside an old apple orchard that had seen better days.

As Ella pulled up beside two county sheriffs' cars, she saw Sheriff Taylor standing behind the fire truck with several firemen. It was the same station that had responded to the fire at the Hunts' and she recognized some of the men immediately.

Ella climbed out of her vehicle and walked toward them, curious to find out why they were standing there instead of fighting the fire. Taylor saw her and motioned for her to stay low.

She'd only gone another step when she realized what Taylor was signaling to her. A series of loud pops and whistling sounds like bottle rockets sent her crouching low to the ground. Then she remembered Branch's gun collection. He'd had several wooden gun cabinets in his living room, she recalled from a previous visit, and even more in what Branch called his gun room. He'd never let her really see them, mostly because she'd never had a warrant to check. Now ammo stored in the house was going off, but fortunately it didn't seem like Branch had any explosives on hand. Ella ran back and ducked behind her SUV.

A few minutes later, after the noise had died down again somewhat, Sheriff Taylor ran over to join her. "It's not as bad as what you all encountered at Smiley's place. There haven't been any big explosions, but no one can get close because of the arsenal he kept in his house."

"Who decided to play torpedo with the Dodge Stratus?" Ella asked.

"The fire has obscured some of the tag, so all we have is a partial. Once it's safe, we can go take a closer look. Whoever was driving either bailed or is extremely dead."

"Where's Branch?"

Taylor pointed. "Behind the house in the orchard, still in the Mercedes. Special Agent Payestewa came down from Farmington as soon as he heard the call. He questioned Branch immediately when he got here, but the only substantial thing we got was that Branch saw a truck speeding away from here when he ran outside. That was just after the Dodge went through the front wall."

"Interesting. So we're talking two suspects doing a smash and grab on a residence. Vehicle number two was for the getaway. Were any guns stolen? Did Branch take a look before he had to leave the structure?"

"I don't know. We need to continue to interview him, but we thought we'd give him a few minutes to get himself together before we try again." Taylor shook his head sadly. "I understand the man had a lot of historic weapons in there. Hate to see them go like this."

"I saw a few one time. Quality firearms, all right. If you're willing, I'll continue the interview with Branch. I may be able to get something else from him we can use."

"Give it a shot then."

As Ella approached the luxury sedan parked beside a gnarled old apple tree gray with age, she saw Branch's face. He was still in shock. He was staring at the fire, his hands clenched tightly around the steering wheel.

She came over and tapped on the passenger-side window with her knuckle.

Branch jumped. Seeing it was her, he relaxed and nodded. "Get in."

Ella opened the door and sat down on the plush leather seat. A Mercedes even smelled classy. As she looked over at Branch she noticed that his face was the color of ashes and his breathing unsteady. Wondering if he was all right, she watched him carefully. Branch was a large, heavy man and years of carrying that much bulk around couldn't have done his heart any good. For the first time in her life she felt a little sorry for him.

"Do you want me to call the paramedics to check you out? This must have scared you witless."

"It did, but I'm okay. Don't call anyone."

"Were you in bed when it happened?"

"No, flannel pajamas and slippers are this year's sportswear," he snapped. "What else do you think I'd be doing at six-thirty in the morning, for Pete's sake! I was sound asleep, then I heard what I thought was a crack of thunder so loud it made the house shake. When I came out of the bedroom I saw the car right there in my living room. Dust was everywhere and the damn engine was still running. I was so pissed off I went over to drag the driver out of the car. He was already gone. I ran outside to look for him and that's when I saw a truck speeding off."

"So you went back inside, right?"

Branch nodded. "But the living room was on fire by then. I grabbed my cell phone from the kitchen counter and ran back outside to call the police and fire department. After that, I walked around the house to see if there was some way I could go back in and save something. But the smoke was too thick."

"People don't usually ram somebody's house with their vehicles on purpose, but then again, you have a knack for pissing people off. Any thoughts on that?"

"Well, there's no way this could have been an accident. My house is a hundred yards from the road, and anyone losing control on the highway would have crashed through the fence at the angle they left the road. Besides, the driver had somebody waiting for him so he could make a getaway."

"I agree. So do you have any idea who might have done this?"

"No, not really." As he shook his head a rivulet of perspiration ran down his forehead. He wiped it away impatiently with the back of his hand. "Don't just sit there," he said, shifting restlessly. "Go and find the lunatic who demolished my life. Everything I've worked for was inside that house. My gun collection alone represents twenty years' worth of acquisitions."

"Did you notice if anything was taken from your home after the car hit?"

"None of the gun cabinets had been opened, though flying debris had broken some of the glass fronts. The TV and sound systems were still there, that's where the sparks were coming from. Everything happened so fast." Branch gave a long sigh and wiped the perspiration from his forehead again.

It was cool in the car, so the heat wasn't a factor here. "Just relax and take deep breaths," she said, concerned. "I'll call a rescue unit and let the EMTs take a look at you. It can't hurt."

"Clah, I'm fine. Give it a rest. What I need now is a little justice for the crime that's been committed against me."

Ella focused on his breathing and realized it was more uneven now. "You're a heavy man. All this stress . . ."

"What are you trying to do, harass me into having a heart attack? If I were out of the way it would make things a lot easier for touchy-feely cops like you."

The biting comment, though typical of Branch, irritated her enough to drive away any compassion she'd felt. "Have it your way."

As she climbed out of the car and walked back toward the fire truck, Sheriff Taylor came up to meet her. "No more ammo has gone off for a while and the fire crew is making some progress. We should be able to go in and take a look around within fifteen minutes or so."

"Great."

"What did you get from Branch?" he asked, his gaze on the firemen manning hoses and attacking the fire.

Ella told him what she'd learned and the likelihood that robbery wasn't a motive. "What about the plates on the Dodge? Have you got anything on that yet?"

"Yeah. The vehicle's registered to Arlene Hunt. She's the dead woman from Waterflow, right?"

"Yeah. We can safely say she wasn't driving," Ella noted acerbically. "Arlene was in a wheelchair so I don't know if she could drive at all. My guess is that this is the second vehicle that the nurse's aide, Louise Sorrelhorse, drove. But I do remember Louise saying that Arlene's brother, Cardell Benally, borrowed it from time to time."

"How fast can you check on both their whereabouts?" Taylor asked.

"I'll do it right now," Ella said, then called Justine and told her what she needed.

"I'll get on it," Justine answered, then disconnected.

As Ella put the phone away she glanced around. There was another house close to the highway beside the road leading to Branch's home. That's where she wanted to go next, but she was out of her jurisdiction. "I'd like to talk to the residents of that house," she said to the sheriff and pointed.

"Okay, but take one of my deputies just to keep it legal," he said.

"How about her?" Ella asked, pointing to a woman deputy who was studying the ground searching for evidence.

"Sergeant Emily Marquez is a top-notch cop. She patrols this sector now and our new policy has field officers actively involved in investigating crimes committed in their areas."

As she walked toward Sergeant Marquez, Ella heard one of the firemen mumble something about "Detective Lazarus." Ella exhaled softly. So the stories had followed her out here, too. Hopefully, she'd be old news soon and comments like that would stop once and for all.

"Hi, I'm Investigator Ella Clah from the Tribal Police," Ella said, offering Emily her hand.

Emily shook it and smiled. "I've heard a lot about you lately."

Ella decided not to comment. "I'd like you to accompany me for a few minutes. I want to question the neighbors and find out if they saw anything. Will what you're doing wait?"

"Yeah. I'm just searching for footprints, and others can do that just as well. We know that the driver climbed out of the car once he crashed through the wall. Since there was no gap between the car and the wall for him to slip out, he escaped through the front door."

"This won't take long," Ella said.

"Did Sheriff Taylor okay this?"

"I wouldn't have asked if he hadn't," Ella said. "You ready to roll?"

"That's my cruiser," Marquez said, pointing to a county squad car less than twenty feet away.

"Let's go."

"Okay. Hey, since we're riding together, do you think some of your incredibly good luck will rub off on me? I heard all about you and that accident at the mine."

Ella looked at her in surprise, noting the difference between Anglo and Navajo ways, then laughed. "If I'd been really lucky, I wouldn't have fallen into that mine in the first place."

"Good point," Emily said, chuckling as they climbed into the county car.

As they drove up the bumpy gravel road Ella glanced over at Emily Marquez. Her blond hair was wrapped up in a tight bun at the base of her neck. It was a severe hairstyle, but Ella had a feeling she was trying to downplay the fact that she was pretty. Good looks weren't always a plus when working in a department filled with men. As a sergeant, she undoubtedly was far more concerned about commanding respect.

"You must have worked pretty hard to earn those," Ella said, gesturing to her stripes.

Emily gave Ella a guarded look, then realizing the compliment was sincere, relaxed. "I've chosen law enforcement. When you love what you do, you give it everything."

Ella nodded. "I know exactly what you mean. I feel the same way about my work."

Emily glanced at Ella's hands. "Which is probably why neither of us is great marriage material."

Ella smiled. "I have a little girl. That and my job is all I can handle. No more kids for me, even if I do get married again."

Emily nodded, her eyes on the dirt track ahead. "I had a daughter, but she passed away before she turned one. A blood disorder," she added, her voice taut.

When they exchanged a glance, Ella saw the depth of her loss mirrored in her eyes and her heart went out to her.

"That was a long time ago. Now I have my work," Emily said.

"There have been times in my life when working was all that kept me sane," Ella said, remembering the death of her father. But what Emily had gone through was in many ways far worse. The loss of a child upset the natural order of things. No preparation could ever be sufficient. No matter how well Emily seemed to cope, as a mother, Ella knew that Emily lived with a hole in the place where her heart had been.

As if reading her mind, Emily added, "At first you think you'll never get over it. You can't understand how time continues to tick or why the sun continues to rise. But, eventually, you go on."

But you're never the same, Ella added silently.

"I'm active with kids in a different way now," Emily said, her voice stronger now. "I coach a girls soccer team and they're a terrific bunch. You should see my girls play." They pulled up in the driveway of the house by the main road and Officer Marquez parked, turning off the engine.

"It's too bad I didn't know you before my kid got interested in horses. Believe me, I would have much rather bought her a soccer uniform and ball than a pony."

Emily laughed. "We should get together sometime. You can teach me about horses and I'll teach you about coaching soccer."

"You're on."

As Emily and Ella stepped out of the car, a middle-aged Anglo woman came out her front door and stood on the porch.

"I saw the fire and heard the commotion, Officers. What's going on? Is George all right?"

"Mr. Branch wasn't injured," Ella replied. "The fire began after someone rammed a car into the front of his house. The driver got away in a second truck. Were you up at the time, and did you happen to see a pickup go by your home right after the first disturbance?"

"I was and did. My husband leaves for work at seven so we're up early. A truck came past here from the direction of his house, cut the corner, then went up onto the highway, tires squealing. I know he cut the corner because he broke off the corner fence post of my garden." The woman pointed to the square post, which was hanging from the wire now.

"I ran outside and managed to catch a glimpse of the license plate," she continued, pulling a piece of paper from her pocket. "Here. I wrote it down." She handed the paper to Ella. "I have no idea if these are the same people who are responsible for what happened at George's place, but I saw them hit my fence, and they can't weasel out of that."

"How many people were in the pickup?"

"Two, but I can't tell you if they were men or women, or one of each. I didn't get a close enough look. It happened too fast."

"What color was the pickup and did it have any distinguishing marks?" Ella asked.

"It was old and dark brown. There might be some paint scraped off onto my fence post," she said and pointed. "But I got you the license plate. Isn't that enough to catch them?"

"Usually, but sometimes people steal license plates and put them on different vehicles—particularly if they're about to commit a crime."

"Oh, I didn't think of that," she said.

Ella glanced around for Emily and saw her taking a photo of tire prints near the garden. "That's where the truck fishtailed, right?"

The woman nodded and followed Ella to where Emily was working. "Take all the photos you want and let me know if there's anything more I can do to help. Someone that crazy needs to be caught. You can take the fence post too if the paint on it will help."

"We'll do that. If you see that truck around here again, give us a call, okay?" Emily said, handing her a card. "The department will send out a deputy right away."

"Okay," the woman answered.

"Thank you for your help," Ella said, then glanced at Emily, who was placing a chip of paint taken from the post into a paper envelope. "Ready?"

"Just a second." Sergeant Marquez labeled the envelope, writing down the address of the house as well.

After they were in the car, Ella handed her the license plate number. "Run a make on that, will you?"

Once they returned to Branch's house, they had their answer over Sergeant Marquez's handheld.

Ella was standing close enough to hear the report from the county sheriff's dispatcher. Hearing Cardell Benally's name come up once again, she quickly jotted down his address.

"That address is on your turf," Emily said. "Do you know it?"

"I know the general area." Thanking Emily for her help, Ella started to walk off.

"Wait a second." Emily reached into her shirt pocket and pulled out one of her cards. "Give me a call and we can get together sometime."

"Thanks. I'll do that," Ella said, giving Emily one of her own cards in return, then went to join Sheriff Taylor.

"We're starting to work the scene," he said. "But it's going to take forever to process what the fire left of that car. From what we've been able to tell, there was a gasoline can tossed onto the engine to help the fire along after the crash. What did you turn up with the neighbor?"

Ella filled him in. "Cardell Benally is Arlene Hunt's brother so he certainly would have had motive to pull something like this."

"If we can place *him* at the scene, not just his truck, then we've got him and maybe whoever it was that provided the getaway vehicle."

"While your people process the scene here, I'm going to head back to the Rez and see what I can get from that end."

NINE

✖ ✖ ✖

Ella called her team together and, after meeting in Big Ed's office, filled everyone in on the early-morning events.

"You're going to have a big problem with this one, Shorty," Big Ed said.

"You mean because there are going to be people sympathizing with Cardell even if he did ram Branch's home and set it on fire?"

"That, the influence of his brother-in-law, Lewis Hunt, and the fact that about twenty years ago Cardell was a Tribal Police officer," Big Ed answered.

"Did you know him?" Ella asked.

Big Ed nodded. "He served for about five or six years. He worked from the Window Rock station and I was his lieutenant."

Ella looked at the chief speculatively. "So, do you think he did this?"

Big Ed considered it for a while. "He might have, but if he did, he also probably found a way to cover his back or create some reasonable doubt for a jury, probably with the help of Councilman Hunt, who's in a position to know how to cover his trail. We may have his truck linked to the scene, but we're still going to have to place him in the vehicle at the time."

Ella glanced at Justine. "What about Louise Sorrelhorse, Mrs. Hunt's nurse. Did you check her out?"

"I spoke to her on the phone and she said that Arlene kept the car there for their use. That way they'd both have reasonably comfortable transportation if Arlene had a doctor's appointment or needed to go shopping." Justine paused and checked her notes. "Louise also has a very good alibi. Early this morning she was at mass. Father O'Riley served her communion and vouched for it. Then she served breakfast to her church group."

"Any ideas who was driving the getaway vehicle?" Big Ed asked.

"Logic says it was Lewis Hunt," Ella said. "But he's an attorney as well as a councilman, so approaching him without some evidence already in hand is going to be tricky."

"Be careful. Besides being very powerful politically, he's also very smart. If you make one misstep, he'll turn on you and the department," Big Ed said. "The man has done some fancy maneuvering as an attorney, putting a spin on things so that the bad guys look squeaky clean when compared to the police."

"He's right," Justine said. "I remember some talk about two years ago when Hunt filed civil charges against an officer at the Window Rock station. Hunt's nephew had been hauled in for vandalism but Hunt got all the evidence thrown out of court on a technicality and then sued the officer and the department for harassment. Eventually, the suit was dropped, but if we go after him, we better make sure we do it by the book."

"I'm on patrol today," Neskahi said. "I'll keep my ears open and if anyone I come in contact with has seen Hunt or Benally, I'll pass the word along."

Tache looked at the other officers with his normal, glum

expression. "I've got photos of the Branch crime scene coming in, including those of the post that was knocked over and plenty of vehicle tracks. There will be footprints as well. I'll study those and make a report based on what the county crime-scene team has found."

"One more thing," Chief Atcitty said. "The Benallys are traditionalists, for the most part. I know because my wife is a friend of that family. The entire clan was up in arms when Arlene married a modernist. They disapproved of the match, and of Lewis in particular. Then when Cardell went to work for Lewis, they nearly disowned him. I believe that the extended family—with the exception of Arlene—live next to one another over by Cudei."

Ella considered what he said. "So if we can't track down Cardell directly and we end up having to go to his family, they probably won't talk to me—not until the Sing is done."

"Exactly. But there's more. Since Smiley decided to blow his own brains out yesterday, some new and very disturbing stories about you have been added to the ones already circulating out there. The way I heard it, you came out of the place where death lives and now it follows you like a friend. People who oppose you will die just as Smiley did."

Ella's stomach sank. She'd been alienated before when she'd first come back to the Rez but this promised to be far worse. Her very existence would become a source of contention for the tribe. The modernists would make a great show of not caring, as would the Christians. But to the traditionalists, she'd become a sign of everything that was wrong on the Rez—and of how Anglo influences that had supplanted the Navajo ways could end up endangering everyone. Religious beliefs, no matter the culture, seldom depended on logic and rationality and often brought out the worst in people. Hopefully, not all of the traditionalists would be against her. Clifford had a fine reputation and he'd said she was untainted. His opinion might carry among some of the *Dineh*.

"Do you plan to have the Sing done?" Big Ed asked, interrupting her thoughts.

Ella took a deep breath and let it out again. "I have no other choice, not if I want to continue working as a cop on this Rez."

He nodded. "Until then, I'm sure you'll find ways to get things done. In the meantime, I'm going to see if we can get you a search warrant for Cardell Benally's house. Under the circumstances, I think we can persuade a judge."

"Justine and I will drop by his home while that goes through and maybe we'll find what we need without a warrant. If he's there, he can answer some questions for us."

As they all left the chief's office, Justine glanced at Ella. "Let me check my computer real fast and get some more information on Cardell. Then we'll go."

"Too bad we don't have computers in the cars like some of the bigger departments," Ella said.

Justine laughed. "Computers? I'd settle for new tires."

Ella went with her, then waited while Justine checked the databases. A moment later Justine hit the print command. "All I've got as an address is Cottonwood Canyon, which is northeast of the Cudei Chapter House. But it'll be enough."

Ella was quiet as they got under way moments later. Finally Justine glanced over at her. "What's eating you, partner?"

"This whole business with the Sing bothers me. I'm having it done just to appease people and that seems wrong to me."

"When you live and work on the Rez you have to follow certain rules and customs. You can't change what is."

Ella nodded thoughtfully. "I'm aware of that, and I'll do it out of respect for others here. But it still bugs me."

"My advice is accept it and don't give it another thought."

Ella nodded, but didn't reply.

They drove through Shiprock and headed northwest on

a road that paralleled the San Juan River. There were lots of small farms and fields in this area along the river valley.

After about fifteen minutes, they came upon several small homes along a curve in the river. Cardell Benally's residence was a simple wood frame home with a cleared field to the right of the house. The small irrigation ditches that ran along one side toward the river were overgrown with weeds. No crops were being cultivated on the land and there were no animals or corrals anywhere, though a metal post in the ground with a long, light chain attached suggested that he'd owned a dog in the recent past.

"There are no trucks or other vehicles around. I don't think he's home," Justine said.

As they got out, Ella noticed that two rosebushes by the front door were in need of water, though a garden hose was coiled nearby, still attached to a faucet. Ella knocked on the front door, but no sounds came from inside. After a moment, Ella walked around the side of the house and peered through an uncurtained window. The bed was made, and there was no sign that anyone had been there recently.

Justine came up beside her. "We still don't have a search warrant so we can't go in. But we can try the tribal offices where Benally works. If that doesn't pan out, we can try his parents' house." Justine pointed toward two hogans farther down the road. "I think it's one of those."

"First, call Hunt's office and see if Benally's there."

Justine did, then a moment later shook her head. "The secretary said that Cardell never came in this morning."

"Then we go to the Benallys'."

It took just a few seconds by vehicle to reach the two buildings. The smaller octagonal hogan in the back was probably used for ceremonial purposes. To the right side of the large hogan, which had a conventional door rather than a blanket across the entrance, was a corral made of interlocking branches. About thirty sheep were gathered there and an elderly man was in the process of feeding them.

"We stay in the unit until we're invited," Ella said.

Time passed slowly, but the elderly man made a show of ignoring them.

"Follow my lead," Ella said, getting out. She and Justine stepped out and leaned against the SUV, watching the sheep and talking back and forth in whispers but never looking at old Benally directly.

Before long the elderly man approached, but stopped about fifty feet from where Ella stood. "What do you want from me?"

"We need to find your son. Is he here?" Ella asked.

"No." The man's eyes were wary as he regarded them. "He doesn't come by very often. Try his house." He pursed his lips, indicating the direction to Cardell's house.

"We just came from there." Ella pointed out the obvious.

"And you didn't find him, did you? You might go to where he works."

"We called. They haven't seen him today."

The old man shrugged and wiped some perspiration from his brow with a red bandanna. "I don't know what else to suggest. My son is a grown man. He does as he pleases."

"We think he may be in a lot of trouble," Ella said, then told him about George Branch's home being destroyed.

The old man looked sorrowful. "My son had great respect for his sister. But he is *not* a criminal."

"If your son is innocent, he can save embarrassing his family by coming forward quickly. By avoiding us, he's just making things worse for himself and his clan. The police will keep after him, and I have no idea what will happen if he resists arrest . . ." She let the sentence hang.

It had seemed like a good tactic, but as she saw his expression change, she suddenly realized that she'd made a huge mistake.

"Death follows you and that's what you'll bring to my son," he said coldly. "Get off my land."

"If you truly believe that death follows me, then your son would be better off if he turns himself in quickly to another officer before *I* find him," Ella said.

He gazed at her for several moments, then spoke in a clear, steady voice. "I don't think you even realize the danger you pose. You're like the *bilagáanas*, the whites, who judge everything and understand nothing."

Ella wanted to counter his accusations by naming all the things she'd done to protect the *Dineh* and to keep everyone on the Navajo Nation safe, but it was obvious Mr. Benally had already made up his mind about her. "I *will* get a Sing done as soon as someone finds the *hataalii*," she said, then got angry with herself for explaining that to him. She was a Tribal Police officer. She deserved his respect on that basis alone. Yet, even as the thought formed, she realized that respect went both ways. The man was just scared.

As he walked away and went inside the hogan, Ella remained where she was. "Go talk to him, Justine. See if he'll tell you where his son is. I have a feeling he knows, but if I go after him I'll just make things worse."

Justine returned to the unit about ten minutes later. "You were right not to get any closer to him. The only reason he invited me inside was because you weren't there, and because I'm wearing a *jish*, a medicine bundle out of respect for traditionalist beliefs. I guess the one you still have on your belt isn't enough for him."

"Did he tell you where Cardell is?"

Justine shook her head. "All he told me is that if his son wanted to avoid us, he'd go someplace away from town where he could think. He grew up hunting and fishing and can take care of himself for as long as necessary."

"We could get the word out to trading post owners all

across the Rez, but there's a good chance not all of them will cooperate," Ella said. "Cardell's going to have a lot of support, particularly in the more remote areas where traditionalists live. They think of the department as a *bilagáana* invention already. It's no secret that they liked things a lot better when the tribe handled their own problems through small councils and local chiefs. And if he's getting help from his brother-in-law, Lewis Hunt, he's probably been well funded and supplied."

"So what do you propose?" Justine asked.

"Besides notifying the officers on patrol, we should get in touch with the tribal forestry department and those who work for the tribal sawmill. They're more likely to come across a camper anyway, and as modernists by and large, they'll be more inclined to help us."

"Okay, I'll get the ball rolling," she said, picking up the mike. "Where to now?"

"Head for the tribal offices back in Shiprock. We're going to track down Lewis Hunt and pay him a visit."

As they got under way Justine put in a call to dispatch, and had their request relayed to the appropriate agencies. By the time they arrived at the tribal offices, what promised to be a long process had already been put into motion.

Ella led the way inside, and before long they found Lewis Hunt's office. Ella knocked on the open door as she walked in, and a harried Navajo woman in her early twenties glanced up. "May I help you?" she asked.

"We're here to see Mr. Hunt," Ella said and flashed her badge.

"He's in a meeting right now, but I expect he'll be out shortly. Would you like to wait?"

Ella nodded. "Sure. In the meantime, will you check to see if Councilman Hunt had anything on his calendar for early this morning, say between six-thirty and seven-thirty?"

She hesitated. "I'm not sure I should answer questions like that without specific permission . . ."

"You can answer her," a man's voice came from the doorway.

Ella turned her head and saw Lewis Hunt enter the room. "I understand that the police have been looking for my brother-in-law because they think he's guilty of setting the fire that burned down George Branch's home. But, for the record, that's nothing short of preposterous. His pickup and my wife's car were both parked in the driveway of the house I'm now using and were stolen sometime during the night a few days ago. We never reported it because we've been too busy, and frankly, we knew that the police's track record for finding stolen vehicles is dismal."

Ella was about to defend the police department, but then realized he was trying to put her on the defensive so he could slip a really lame alibi past her. "Come on, you expect me to believe you had *two* vehicles stolen and didn't report it?" she demanded, staying on track.

He didn't even change his expression. Here in his office Lewis Hunt projected complete confidence. She had a feeling that nothing she could do would ever put a dent in that armor.

"What I can't understand is why you asked about my schedule and activities? Am I under suspicion as well?" Hunt folded his arms across his chest.

"There *were* two men involved in the incident," Ella said, fully aware that she had no way of proving that the two perps had been men.

"Your wording suggests that you don't know *which* two men, so you're obviously still fishing for information. Well, you can scratch me off your short list, if you have one already. This morning at seven my administrative assistant and I were working together, getting my notes ready before I met with an aide to the Secretary of the Interior. I've been lobbying for matching funds so we can update some of the equipment at our Navajo sawmill."

Ella glanced at his assistant, who nodded eagerly but failed to make direct eye contact with her. Instead, her gaze quickly shifted to Hunt, who smiled at her. The exchange made Ella suspect that Hunt's assistant would have verified that they'd just returned from Jupiter on a moonbeam had he asked.

"Can you tell me where we can find your brother-in-law?" Ella asked.

"Cardell? I haven't got the remotest idea, but you better have solid evidence and a very credible witness if you plan on arresting him. I won't have a member of my family rail-roaded simply because you need to close at least one of the cases you're working on."

"We close almost every case that crosses our desks," Ella said, then bit her tongue. She was letting him bait her and that just wasn't going to cut it. "Your brother-in-law needs to answer a few questions. If you see him, advise him to come to the station for an interview. Going into hiding isn't going to erase his name from the list of possible suspects."

"*Into hiding*? He's probably just gone off somewhere where he can be by himself to mourn his sister's passing in private. And he's certainly entitled. Using innuendo and loaded terms to pressure me just won't work. And, to be honest, I doubt you'll find much support for those tactics anywhere else on our Navajo Nation either. I'm going to be watching you very carefully, Investigator Clah, and I won't rest until everyone behind the death of my wife is brought to justice."

Ella nodded once, then looked at Justine and gestured to the door. "I hate politicians," she muttered as they walked out of the building. "And I hate lawyers who become politicians."

"I wouldn't say that around Dawn, if I were you," Justine teased, reminding her that the father of her child was both.

Ella smiled. "Kevin's different. He's in a league all his own. I'm not exactly his number one fan, mind you, especially when it comes to politics, but Hunt makes my skin crawl. The way he handled my questions back there tells me that he's very used to distorting the facts and even the law for his own purposes. I find that offensive on principle. And how he's calling for justice, as if the death of Smiley, the man who set the fire, wasn't enough. Come to think of it, he's probably not terribly unhappy about what happened to Branch."

"He had a hand in what happened to Branch's house, I'd bet on it," Justine said.

As their call number came over the radio, Ella picked up the mike and identified herself.

"We have a 20 on Cardell Benally," the dispatcher said, using the shortened term for a 10-20, which meant location. "One of our officers who was off-duty and at Navajo Lake yesterday afternoon says that he saw Benally there in a campsite area just above the dam. Once the officer began his shift today, he heard you were looking for Benally and told his duty officer to pass the word along."

After getting a good description of the actual location where Benally had been, Ella racked the mike. "I think we better bring in Lucas Payestewa. His office is closest to Navajo Lake, and if we have to go onto state park land, county, or any of the local communities he'll still have jurisdiction." Ella dialed up the FBI resident agent's number in Farmington and got him on the second ring.

She explained what she needed quickly. "Can you meet us at the Pine River Recreation area just north of the dam? Officer Goodluck and I need to question campers in that area. We're trying to find a suspect in an arson case, but Pine River is out of our jurisdiction."

"You've got it."

Ella and Justine met with the FBI agent about an hour later at the camping area where Benally had last been seen. "If we can split up, it'll save us some time," she said, explaining that they were trying to track down Benally, and why. "If anyone spoke to him, or saw him, maybe they'll have an idea of where he'll be headed next."

"We can give it our best shot, but my guess is that Benally won't be in any one place long. He's probably moved on to another location, and I doubt he chatted with anyone and told them where he was going," Lucas answered.

"Yeah, probably, but for now, this is all I've got."

They searched the campsite first, which was not occupied at the moment, but found nothing to suggest where he'd been heading to next. The campers questioned didn't remember seeing anyone who fit Cardell's description.

"Cardell was a cop. If he doesn't want to be found, he's going to be careful," Justine said.

Studying the ground, Ella discovered the direction the last two vehicles parked at that particular site had taken when they'd driven away. "If either of these tire tracks belong to Cardell's truck, he's heading toward Bloomfield. That means we've lost him, unless he stopped at one of the businesses along the way and left us a clue we can follow next."

"That's doubtful," Lucas said, coming over to check the tracks and walking with Ella at his side.

As they searched, Lucas glanced over at her. "By the way, I've been relocated to another Bureau office," Lucas said.

"I'll be sorry to see you go."

"Thanks. I expect you're in for a whole new experience with my replacement. I hear he's still wet behind the ears."

"Rookie, huh? Well, we all have to start somewhere," Ella said with a shrug, "but thanks for the heads-up."

"It'll be interesting to see how Blalock handles him. Blalock's been thinking about retirement, so the last thing he needs is trouble. But if this guy screws up, it'll come right back at FB-Eyes."

Ella nodded, then focusing back on the business at hand, added, "We better split up again and visit some of the other campsites around the lake and talk to a few more campers, just in case Benally circled around south and drove up the eastern side."

Ella and Justine worked together and eventually found a fisherman who'd seen an Indian man matching Cardell Benally's description. He pointed toward another camping area farther down the small ridge that extended out into the lake about a half mile like a peninsula. "Hmm. He's gone now."

"How long ago was that?" Ella and Justine asked at the same time.

"I can't rightly say, Officers. I was out in my boat earlier when I saw him packing up his gear. Then another Indian family came up. Last time I looked over they were standing around talking, but I never saw when he left. That was around two hours ago, maybe less. The family set up their own camp, it looks like." He pointed in that direction and they could see a small ribbon of smoke rising a short distance away.

"We're going to have to work a little faster if we want to catch up to him," Ella said, glancing skyward at the cumulonimbus clouds starting to build over the mountains. "It might start to rain, and if that happens, it'll drive everybody into shelter and we'll have to start knocking on tent flaps and camper doors."

"Never thought a native New Mexican would want it *not* to rain," Justine teased as they walked back to the vehicle.

Ten minutes later they arrived at the location the fisherman had pointed out to them. Ella and Justine saw an old wall tent, like the kind sheepherders often used, pitched down by the lake. A green pickup was parked beside it and on the bumper were several stickers for the Shiprock Lady Chieftains basketball team. The license plate was for San Juan County.

Justine pulled to a stop, seeing a Navajo woman beside a campfire cooking something that smelled like fry bread in a large Dutch oven. She was wearing a traditional-looking long skirt and cotton blouse. "We should wait in the vehicle even if this is only a campsite," Ella said.

The woman, in her fifties, turned around and looked in their direction, but didn't acknowledge them. Instead, she went into the tent and brought out a blanket to air out, draping it over a rope tied between two trees. Then, without looking at either of them, went back to cooking the fry bread.

Minutes ticked by and Justine began to grow restless. "If she waits any longer and I have to keep smelling that fry bread, I'll die of hunger."

Ella was about to risk barging in on the woman when she finally turned and waved at them. Ella and Justine left the unit and walked toward her. As they drew near, Ella saw recognition flash on the woman's face.

"Stop there," she said as Ella came within ten feet of her. "I live in Shiprock too, down by the river behind where the old trading post used to be. I know who you both are."

"We're looking for a Navajo man who may have been camping here a few hours ago," Ella said.

"Just my husband and me here now. Look around."

The answer, as curt as it was fast, let Ella know that the woman knew exactly who they were looking for. Not only that—she had no intention of helping them catch Cardell Benally.

Ella took a deep breath. "The man we're searching for is wanted for questioning only," she began. "He may have been leaving this site when you arrived."

"I know who you want," she admitted, "but you'll have trouble finding any *Dineh* willing to help the police catch him.

You people should have taken care of the real problem—that half-Navajo radio talk man. He stirs up all kinds of trouble and then stands back and pretends it's not his fault. Well, this time he paid for the trouble he created. If the police had muzzled that man years ago, none of this would have happened and the councilman's wife would not have died."

"We can't restrict what a person says on the radio. He has the right—"

She held up a hand. "And we have the right to do as we please."

"If you believe that you have the right to withhold information, you're mistaken. The man I'm after is wanted in connection to a serious crime. To shield a criminal is to become an accessory. You could go to jail."

"You should direct that anger onto the radio man who started all this though he doesn't even live on Navajo land."

The woman continued on a tirade directed toward George Branch, and when she started to repeat herself, Ella decided that the woman was deliberately trying to keep them there. Perhaps Benally had parted within the past hour and was still in the area.

"Let's go, Justine," Ella finally said, starting to walk away while the woman continued to rant.

Justine took one last look at the woman, apparently decided not to speak, then glanced up at the sky. "Going to rain anyway."

Back in the SUV, Ella fastened her seat belt immediately. "Let's get moving. She was trying to keep us here, so Cardell probably hasn't been gone long." She paused, then added, "What bugs me is that now he's seen as a hero and the Tribal Police as the bad guys."

"In a lot of ways, Cardell's type of justice is something people can get behind. That eye-for-an-eye stuff is a lot more direct than the courts," Justine said, climbing in and fastening her seat belt.

Ella glanced over at Justine. "Vigilante justice never fixes the problem. The only thing it does is start a new one."

"Do we keep working our way around the lake?" Justine asked, starting the engine.

Although Ella thought it would probably be a waste of time, she knew they had to try. "Let's keep at it."

They met with a tired Payestewa an hour later. Lucas's sour expression said it all. "Benally's probably left the area, and for what it's worth, I think you're going to have one heckuva time finding him."

"He'll head back to the Rez soon," Justine said. "He'll be more protected there than anywhere else."

"Not everyone will shield him," Ella said. "We'll find him."

"I love your optimism, but it can be tough to make progress when the tribe closes ranks," Lucas said. "If you don't need me anymore, I'll be heading back."

"Okay, we'll take one last pass by the area where he was seen last," Ella responded, catching Justine's eye, who nodded.

Before long the sky began to darken even more, a breeze began to build, then raindrops appeared on the windshield. Justine slowed, turned on the wipers, and was forced to watch the road closely.

"We're never going to find him in this weather in the forest." Ella shook her head, trying to peer out the side window at a forest road that led to a campsite farther downhill. There was a silver-gray pickup just visible beneath a pine, and she couldn't tell from the angle if someone was in the cab.

The SUV fishtailed slightly as the rain started to beat down hard now. "The road is getting a little slippery too. I doubt we'll get stuck anywhere, but visibility is getting low . . ."

Justine reached over and turned on the lights. "Getting to be an actual downpour."

Ella checked back into the side mirror and noticed the gray pickup had come out of the side road and was now following them. The driver had on his lights too, and they glared in her eyes.

"We've got company. Where did he come from?" Justine asked, speeding up a little as the pickup drew closer.

"One of the campsites. Maybe it's a fisherman who decided to call it quits." Ella saw the outline of the driver, but the rain on the window and the driver's windshield distorted everything.

"He's in a hurry, but I'm not going to go any faster. The mountain is a long ways down, and I'm not familiar with these roads," Justine said, staying focused on her driving. "Too bad we can't give the guy a ticket for tailgating."

They continued on for another half mile, but the pickup remained right on their tail. Between the downpour and the cooler air around the lake, a cloud layer descended, and wisps of fog began to appear in the low spots. "Ella, next wide spot in the road, I'm pulling over and letting this idiot by. See if you can catch his plate number. Maybe we can ask a local officer to pull him over and give him a hard time."

"Whoa!" Justine exclaimed suddenly, maneuvering their vehicle around a large boulder that had washed off the hillside and into the one-lane road. It had been barely visible, even with the windshield wipers at high speed.

"To hell with this, I'm pulling over now until the downpour subsides. I'm not used to rain this heavy," Justine grumbled, slowing and watching over to her left. "Help me look, will you?"

"Right," Ella added, hearing the beat of water on the hood and roof of the vehicle. "Better safe than sorry."

"Hang on." Justine touched the brake lights and pulled

over as far as possible but suddenly there was an increase in the glare from behind. "Go ahead, you bas—"

Justine's curse was cut off by a loud thump on the hood of their car. Ella saw something red hit the hood, bounce off the windshield right in front of her, then pass over the car, landing somewhere behind them in the road.

Their unit slid to a stop. "Call it in," Ella yelled, jumping out into the rain to see what had struck them.

The rain was freezing and Ella began shivering, but it was the scent of gasoline that got her heart beating overtime. "Turn off the engine," she shouted back at Justine.

Looking over at the windshield, she saw a thin stream of clear, pungent liquid that was obviously not water flowing down the glass. Turning, Ella spotted the outline of a plastic gasoline container lying by the side of the road.

"I smell gasoline," Justine yelled across the hood of the car. "Did we break a fuel line?"

"No, that idiot hit us with an open gas can when he passed by. Talk about road rage!" Ella yelled back.

"At least the rain will wash it off." Justine looked back toward where the red container was resting, now in the stream of muddy water flowing beside the inside slope of the road.

"You don't suppose that was Benally?" Ella yelled, ignoring the downpour and checking the car, looking for damage or any place the gasoline might have seeped inside.

"If so, he's getting away. Do I risk starting the car again? One spark and we're an instant bonfire," Justine said.

"Use the radio, I'll grab the container in case he left some prints. In a minute, we should be safe enough to roll." Ella looked up into the rain, her face soaked along with her clothes. It was easy to wish she were out on the front porch at home, watching this downpour from a dry spot, a cup of coffee in her hand, like a normal New Mexican.

––––––

Neither of them had been able to read the vehicle plates, and they had no luck finding the silver pickup. Neither did the county sheriff's deputies. But the water had washed away the gasoline, along with most of the vehicle's wax job, and the smell was gone by the time Ella and Justine reached the reservation.

The rain was just a memory now, and the ground here, out of the mountains and over forty miles away, was dry. Though tired and uncomfortable in her still damp clothes, Ella's thoughts remained on the case.

"I have a real bad feeling about this manhunt," Ella said. "Despite what I told Lucas earlier, I think we're facing a big problem. People need heroes, and stories about someone like Cardell can grow into legends in a hurry. If the pickup that doused us with gas turns out to be his, he's also on to us in a big way, and is not above trying to stop us permanently. If we don't get results fast, we'll never be able to build a case against him or Lewis Hunt. Any evidence can disappear, and alibis can be bought and paid for if we give them enough time. Call Sheriff Taylor and Farmington PD and ask them to bring in Benally if they locate him. And when we get to the station, check that gas can carefully for prints. If we can lift any that belong to Cardell, Hunt can squawk all he wants and it won't help his brother-in-law get out of this one."

"Right. I'll take care of it."

"And turn up the heat, will you? I'm freezing."

Sometime later they finally arrived at the station, their clothes dry at last. It had been a miserable, frustrating, nerve-wracking day and the next two hours didn't improve the matter. Unable to put it off any longer, Ella had been forced to work on some overdue reports.

When she finally finished and reached for her car keys, she'd had it. It was time to go home. She'd take off early tonight and spend some time with her daughter. She wouldn't be any good on the job if she didn't wind down.

Ella said good-bye to Justine, who was still in her lab trying to lift some fingerprints from the textured plastic gas container. As Ella walked out to the parking lot and approached her SUV, a cold chill enveloped her. Written in the dried-up water spots of the hood was the word *"chindi."*

TEN

Ella stared at the one-word
message, anger building inside her. Every day she put on a
badge she worked to restore order. To even imply that she
was in league with the *chindis* was beneath contempt. This
kind of attack on her—and on her integrity—infuriated her.

Justine walked up to her, followed her line of vision, then
glanced back at Ella. "I couldn't get squat from the gas container, too uneven a surface. But maybe there will be some
prints here. Want me to give it a try?"

"Go ahead. I can't press charges—this isn't even a mis-
demeanor—but I'd like to know who did it. The implications
go way beyond a joke or harassment—at least to me."

As Justine went to get her kit, Ella spotted the top half of
a bird feather on the ground and picked it up. There was
nothing remarkable about it except for the fact that it was
dusty and scuffed up. Checking the finish of the car, she saw
traces of the feather on the hood. Unless she missed her guess,
the perp hadn't used his finger at all.

Fifteen minutes later they'd checked all the prints they'd
lifted, but unfortunately there were no surprises. Most of the
ones that had enough points to get a match belonged to either
Ella or Larry Jim, the police mechanic.

"The creep used the feather," Ella said, deep in thought,

as she paced inside Justine's lab. "We both saw traces of it on the hood. I was just hoping . . ."

"Will the type of feather tell us anything?" Justine asked. "For example, if it's from an owl . . ."

Ella shook her head. "It's just a pigeon feather, probably selected because it was convenient. Whoever wrote this was particularly careful not to leave prints. I'm thinking that it may have been a cop."

Justine sat back in her chair. "It could be. Some of the new traditionalists here in the department resent the fact that you came back to work before the Sing was done. To them you're now like a magnet for bad luck. I've seen many of them carrying medicine bundles. Some others have them in their pockets, out of sight, not wanting to look foolish, but not taking any chances either. To them, working around you is like being around an unexploded bomb—it's possible nothing will happen, but if it does, there'll be hell to pay."

"Spoken like a Christian," Ella said with a tiny smile. Yet the knowledge weighed heavily on her. "I sure hope I don't get into a jam where I need backup."

"It won't keep any of them from giving you their support, Ella. They *are* police officers. But don't expect them to shake your hand or invite you out for a drink in Farmington."

Ella rolled her eyes. "You have such a way with words, partner."

"I calls 'em like I sees 'em."

Ella reached for the doorknob. "Before I leave, do you know if there's been any more reports of vandalism against the families who are for gun control?"

"Nothing's come in so far, but since Arlene Hunt died, it's been very quiet. By the way, Arlene was buried yesterday after a private ceremony. Her husband insisted on a funeral claiming that his wife was a modernist and would have wanted it that way."

"I bet Arlene's clan wasn't too happy about that," she said, then added, "I'm going home. And to think I was hoping to quit early!"

Ella drove south slowly down Highway 666. It was dark, but the route was so familiar she knew she could probably drive it in her sleep. Her mind wandered as she gazed at the moonlit expanse of dry desert that descended to the river valley to her left, and rose gently toward the mountains to her right, the west.

The possibility that a fellow officer had left that message on her vehicle bothered her and she couldn't quite put it out of her mind. She had to find John Tso and make time to have that Sing done. That was all there was to it.

As she reached the top of a long, gently sloping hill, Ella passed a billboard advertising a guided tour of Navajo cultural sites to visitors on the Rez. Suddenly there was a flash of light near the ground at the base of the sign and she heard a loud pop. The left front of the car trembled and the steering wheel pulled hard to the left, taking her over the center line. Ella gripped the wheel tightly, her heart in her throat as she looked ahead for oncoming traffic.

She knew instantly that the tire had blown out, and reacted automatically, her senses now at their peak. Resisting the urge to hit the brakes, Ella lifted her foot off the gas pedal and allowed the vehicle to slow, compensating for the pull by steering more to the right, bringing the car back over the center line into her own lane. As the car slowed quickly from the drag, she checked the rearview mirror, applied the brakes, and pulled off to the shoulder of the road.

No vehicle lights were visible in either direction, but if this had happened in traffic, she would have had real trouble avoiding a collision. Experience and her own intuition told her this hadn't been an accident or a faulty tire. The flash of light she'd seen almost at the same time she'd heard the tire blow led her to another conclusion—someone had shot out her tire. The absence of a really loud boom also suggested the shooter had used a small-caliber weapon.

Realizing she could come under fire again, Ella scooped up her flashlight and dove quickly out of the passenger side. Crouched low, she peered back down the road from around the rear bumper. The badger fetish she wore around her neck felt hot against her skin—a sure sign of danger.

Ella brought out her pistol, then called for backup, staying low and letting her eyes adjust to the darkness. When dealing with a sniper, patience was crucial. She'd expected more shots, but when none came after five minutes, she worked her way around the vehicle, this time peering out from the left front fender.

In the distance, perhaps several hundred yards away, she could hear the sound of a vehicle. It seemed to be fading, which meant the driver was moving away from her. No vehicles had passed by, so this engine noise was coming from off the main road. Ella holstered her pistol, reached for the cell phone clipped to her belt, and called Justine.

"Are you under fire now?" Justine asked quickly.

"No, and I can't see any sign of the sniper either. I just heard what may have been a vehicle driving away, so I'm going to wait another few minutes in case it's a trick, then move to the site where the shot was fired and take a look around."

"Wait until I get there. There could be more than one perp. If they're setting you up, you'll need backup."

The badger felt cool against Ella's skin now and she saw a cottontail sitting up watching her from across the highway not far from the sign. "I think the danger's past."

"All right. My ETA is less than ten minutes."

Ella came out from behind cover slowly. The darkness emphasized the silence, which she used to her advantage. Anyone approaching *would* be heard, because she intended on being as quiet as a jackrabbit. Using a penlight instead of her large flashlight to avoid spotlighting herself, she checked the front tire and confirmed her suspicions. There was a small puncture in the sidewall, but the bullet hadn't been very large, so the air hadn't escaped all at once. An almost instantaneous blowout from a heavy-caliber round or a shotgun could have flipped her car or caused her to lose control completely.

Ella crossed the highway quickly, then, after waiting and listening for a moment, walked over to the billboard and used the flashlight to examine the immediate area. Without more light, she could inadvertently end up obscuring evidence if she got any closer to the spot, so she stayed where she was and scanned the area with her flashlight. There was a flattened place in the dirt where someone had obviously been, and she could also see a pair of tracks leading away from the road and over a small rise. The trail led toward the spot where she'd heard the vehicle earlier, confirming her belief that the shooter was long gone.

As Ella returned to her SUV ready to change the tire, she canceled her request for backup. All she needed now was her crime-scene team.

Several minutes later, Ella pulled the damaged tire free, examined the outside, and located the small entry hole. Turning the tire over, she looked at the back of the sidewall and, unable to find an exit hole, rotated the tire. Something made a tiny thunk inside the tire casing. The bullet was still in there. That would give them something to work with.

Ella got busy replacing the tire with the spare and was just hand-tightening the lug nuts when Justine pulled up. "Tache and Neskahi are right behind me. What's the situation?"

Ella filled her in as she lowered the jack. "He was over there on the ground just below the billboard. The bullet trajectory supports that." Ella stood up and glanced around.

"And there's a round still inside the tire. My guess is that it came from a twenty-two," she said, nodding to Neskahi and Tache, who'd just driven up.

"Only one shot was fired?" Justine asked.

"Yeah. He had to time it just perfectly and lead the target—which isn't easy even at close range," Ella said. "I wonder if this attack is connected to the one-word message written on my unit."

"The two incidents happened within a few hours of each other, that's true."

"Most officers wouldn't ordinarily pick a twenty-two caliber, but to make a difficult shot like this one—where the target is a moving car—it's not out of the question. If I'd been attempting the same shot, I would have chosen it—or a shotgun."

"We should also consider Cardell Benally as a possibility," Justine said thoughtfully. "You pass by here on your way to and from home every day. Maybe he decided to find you before you could find him."

Ella nodded slowly, speaking loud enough so the two approaching officers could hear, "I'm not high on Lewis Hunt's favorite people list either. Maybe he sent someone after me—to throw me off the search for Cardell. If I'd had a wreck or been forced into the path of an oncoming car and put out of action, I'd be out of their hair, possibly permanently."

"Quite a fan club you have there, boss," Neskahi said.

As they began working the scene, they found several eight-and-a-half-size shoe prints behind the base of the billboard, and signs that a vehicle had been parked just over the next rise. There were also impressions leading to the vehicle, where the shooter had probably run right after taking the shot.

"It's still not much to go on," Ella said. "There wasn't even a shell casing left behind, which means he either picked it up or was using a revolver—which would have been a really tough shot. We need more."

She considered their options silently, then looked at Justine. "This is a bit of a long shot, but go to the closest business south of here that sells twenty-two shells. Then try to find out who has purchased a box, say within the past few days," Ella said. "I'll take the businesses leading into Shiprock in the opposite direction. Tache, I need you to go develop the photos you took here and see if they'll give us any more info about the shooter—height, weight, make of shoe—like that. Neskahi, take all the light you need from the van and follow the trail the shooter took after reaching the vehicle. Any house within sight of that route will need to be visited. Interview the residents and see if they saw or heard anything we can use. Also, when you reach the highway, see if the dirt tracks on the asphalt tell you which direction he went. If you can tell for sure, go in that direction and check every house you pass for a reasonable distance.

"You've got it."

"Talk to as many area residents as you can and find out if they've seen anyone walking around studying the terrain, or shooting a rifle or pistol. The sniper planned this very carefully and may have done a trial run with some dry firing, studying the angles and so forth."

As Ella went back to her SUV, she realized that, by now, Dawn would be getting ready for bed. Once she finished questioning the clerk at the convenience store and she finally got home, Dawn would be asleep.

She took a deep breath and pushed her personal concerns aside. She had a job to do, and it was time to get to work again. At least the shooter hadn't been gunning for her directly. If he could hit a moving tire, he could have also easily taken a shot at her head. The shooter had either wanted to put her out of action or else scare her silly. But obviously didn't know much about her. All he'd succeeded in doing was pissing her off.

Although Ella spoke to everyone, even the regulars who stopped by to get their oversized soft drinks or snow cones on the way home, no one had seen anyone rabbit hunting or just hiking around the hillsides that bordered the highway.

By the time she got back into her unit, Ella was tired, frustrated, and angry. It was nearly nine o'clock and she still hadn't had any dinner.

Going home in her current mood didn't seem like such a good idea, so she reached for the card Emily—Sergeant Marquez—had given her and dialed her cell.

Emily answered on the first ring.

"It's Ella Clah. I'm just getting off work but I'm not ready to go home. Do you want to meet me for a late dinner in Farmington?"

There was no hesitation. "You know what? I'd love to. I'm just getting off work myself. I've been filling out reports and I'm ready to go nuts."

Ella had no doubt now that they were kindred spirits. "Do you have a favorite spot?" Ella asked, suddenly looking forward to this.

"Most of the family places are closed, but there are a few all-night places. Have you ever gone to the Terminal Café?"

"The wha-at?" She'd had enough of death to last a lifetime.

"Not 'terminal' as in fatal," Emily said, laughing. "It caters to truckers and the food there is fabulous. The clientele is a bit rough around the edges, but they're okay. The café has a large-screen TV and most of the guys are so engrossed in sports they don't pay much attention to anything else."

"Great," she answered, laughing. All in all, it sounded just perfect.

Ella called home, told Rose that she was meeting a friend, then drove directly to the Terminal Café on Farmington's east side. When she arrived forty minutes later Emily was already seated and waiting at one of the corner tables. She waved as

Ella came in the door, though in her tan uniform she'd have been easy enough to spot.

Ella noted that Emily had chosen a table that would give them both a clear view of the entire room, including the entrance. That particular vantage point had been a cop's logical choice. "Hey, I'm really glad you could come, Emily."

She nodded. "Me, too. I don't get to do things like this very often."

Soon they were eating, and at ease with each other, their conversation flowed smoothly. "You know, hearing about what happened to you at those mines was a real eye-opener for me. Deep down we count on having lots of tomorrows to catch up on all the things we've sacrificed for our careers. But we may never get them before it's our time to check out. Death doesn't play fair."

Ella nodded somberly. "Putting off something you really want to do just means that you may never get to do it at all."

"Sobering thought."

Ella nodded. "I'm not superwoman, but I really believed that I could always get myself out of a jam. Yet down there I was helpless. Now I want to stay in control. If I die, I want to be calling the shots all the way."

"That's one way to deal with it," Emily said. Silence stretched out between them for some time before Emily spoke. "I was told by some of the other officers that Navajo beliefs about the dead are making your life a little rough at the moment."

"Yeah, but in all honesty, the hardest thing I've had to deal with is that I just don't know for sure what happened to me down there," she admitted, needing to confide in someone. "If I really did die, then what I saw must have been part of what some people call a 'near death experience.' If I didn't, then it must have been a hallucination from lack of oxygen."

"What *did* you see?" Emily asked, leaning forward.

Ella told her, surprised by how good it felt to talk openly about this with someone. Carolyn, the tribe's ME, was a dear friend of hers, but ever since Carolyn had gotten married, they seldom got together, especially after hours.

Emily sat there, listening closely but not saying a word.

"I just wish I knew if it was real," Ella said, concluding.

"Why not just let go and accept it as an NDE?" Emily asked. "It obviously gave you comfort when you needed it most and you said it felt real, so why fight it?"

Ella shook her head. "It's not in my nature to accept things that I can't prove or quantify."

"Sometimes logic has to take a backseat to other things, like love, intuition, and . . . well, faith."

"Are you a religious person?" Ella asked.

"I am, I guess. I mean, you won't find me pounding a Bible and yelling, 'Repent!' but I believe in God and I try to live by the Ten Commandments."

"With your religious background and experiences, how would you explain what happened to me?"

Emily paused. "I'd say you were given a blessing. What you experienced calmed your fears and gave you comfort. That's what a blessing is. All that's left is for you to decide how—or if—it's going to change your life."

"The one thing I know for sure is that I'm meant to be a detective for the tribe. I live and breathe my work. It's part of me, and I can't stop being who I am," Ella said. "But I intend to take more time from now on to actually have fun and relax. What my life lacks most is balance."

"I work a lot, too, but I also have hobbies that help me unwind. Besides coaching the girls, I grow orchids in a greenhouse."

"I thought those were expensive, fragile, and only grew in the tropics."

"The plants I have grow in a small greenhouse that's equipped with a humidifier. But some varieties don't require much more than strong indirect light and some attention. What do you do when you're not working?"

"Up to now? Sleep—and eat occasionally," Ella added, laughing. "But it was great to do something impromptu like this. Let's do it again," she said, picking up the bill.

"You bet. I really enjoyed this, but next time it'll be on me."

As Ella drove home, she felt more relaxed than she had in days. Until now, she hadn't realized how badly she'd needed time to decompress.

When Ella arrived home, she went directly to Dawn's room and kissed her sleeping daughter lightly on the forehead, then tiptoed out. Rose was waiting for her in the hallway.

"Who's this new friend of yours?"

Ella laughed. "Mom, did you stay up just to ask me that? If you did, you're going to be disappointed. It was a woman deputy from Farmington. She patrols the area over by Waterflow and Fruitland."

Rose smiled. "It looks like getting together with her did you a world of good. I've always said that women need women friends most of all. Our sitter's grandmother," she said, referring to Lena Clani, "has given me strength many times when I had none of my own. She's helped keep me balanced. For a long time now I've wished you would find a friend like that."

As Rose ambled off to bed, Ella thought about what her mother had said. It was true, of course, that she didn't socialize much, but few people outside work could understand the demands of her career. Carolyn and she would remain close friends, but it was good to have met Emily. In a lot of ways they had even more in common.

The next morning, shortly after her alarm went off, the chief called on her cell and asked her to meet him in his office at seven-thirty. Ella ate a quick breakfast at Rose's insistence, then walked through the station doors at seven-fifteen.

Big Ed was in the hall talking to a uniformed officer and, seeing her, waved. "Shorty, my office."

Moments later, Big Ed closed his office door, then sat down behind his desk across from Ella. "Fill me in on what happened yesterday after the gas can incident. Any idea who took a shot at you?"

Ella gave him a list of suspects, then added, "Of course to that list we can also add a gazillion others who'd rather see me dead than alive." She paused thoughtfully. "But whoever was responsible wanted to make it look accidental . . . and coupled with the timing . . ."

Big Ed nodded. "I heard about the message left on the hood of your department vehicle."

"I suspect that we're dealing with someone who thinks I pose a danger because of what happened to me at the mine."

"Shorty, this department needs you. If you were unable to carry out your duties, that's one thing. But there's no way I'll condone having a perfectly healthy officer on leave until he or she gets a Sing done."

"I understand what you're saying and agree with you. That's why I'm here. But there are plenty of people around who don't agree. Remember what I told you about Professor Garnenez, tailing me on the back roads way up by Four Corners, trying to keep an eye on me."

"You haven't encountered him again?"

"Not that I could verify. But I know he's eccentric. And I'm nearly certain that seeing that big screw sticking out of my tire spooked him into thinking I have some kind of special power or magic."

"Then maybe he's the one who took a shot at you. The flat tire concept—one doesn't harm you, but the next one does—might have been his attempt to restore balance. You see all kinds of interpretations of the Way, especially among new traditionalists. Don't be too quick to discount him just because he's a professor. I've seen the strangest takes on religion and culture from so-called highly educated people, and the fact that he mistook obsidian for flint doesn't mean he's any less sincere. Go find out where he was last night and follow it up."

"I intend to. But first I was going to track down Wilson Joe and see what he has to say about Professor Garnenez."

"Good idea. And, Shorty, don't rule out Benally and Lewis Hunt. If they had anything at all to do with the fire at Branch's home, Hunt, in particular, will be out to derail the investigation. Lewis certainly knows it's your case. If he could put you up in a hospital for a few months . . ."

"I haven't ruled them out either, Big Ed. Thanks for the reminder."

Ella left the chief's office, then checked in with her partner, who was busy in the lab. "Justine? Anything on that bullet that was trapped inside the tire?"

"I've recovered it and verified that we were right about the caliber, but it suffered a lot of damage striking that steel-belted radial, then bouncing around inside. I don't know if we'll be able to connect it to a particular weapon or not."

"If you learn anything more, call me. I'm going to the college."

Justine nodded and Ella knew she'd understood that she'd be paying Wilson a visit. Justine and he had broken up months ago but Ella still avoided bringing up his name around her. Her partner wasn't quite over him yet.

Ella set out moments later. This time, she kept her eyes open, searching the rises and the desert around the highway for any movement or unusual activity. She really didn't expect another attack during broad daylight, but she wasn't going to be caught off guard again. She'd just made the turnoff to the local community college when her cell phone rang.

Ella recognized her mother's voice right away. "Is something wrong?"

"Daughter, I have some exciting news for you. A man from Hollywood called. He wants to buy the rights to your life story."

"What?"

"That's what he said. He left a number," Rose read it off to Ella.

"Mom, I can't deal with that right now. What if it's just some con man who saw it on the news? I'll tell you what. I'll look into it when I get home."

"It could just as easily be for real, Daughter. I only spoke to him for a short time, but he was very interested in talking to you about your experience in the mine, saving your nephew and all that. I remember reading in a magazine at the dentist's office that those rescued miners back East sold their life stories for a hundred thousand dollars. Think of what they might pay you!"

"Mom, trust me. It's not the same thing. The whole nation was waiting to see what happened to those men and if the rescue attempts would be successful. What happened to me made the *Navajo Times* and the *Daily Times*, then was TV for what, thirty seconds?" she teased.

"That was the network news, seen all over the country. You *have* to call him back, Daughter."

Ella laughed. "Mom, those guys are slicker than lard on a doorknob. You agree to one thing, then later find out that it's not what you thought at all. There's a million stories about them."

"So keep your eyes wide open. But it's raining soup, Daughter. You have to get your bowl and run outside."

Ella chuckled. "Okay, Mom. I'll call the man back later. I promise."

As Ella put the phone back on the seat she wondered how

much her life story would be worth. The fact was, she could use some extra money. Who couldn't, here on the Rez? She'd call when she returned to her office. Even if they offered a third of what they'd given the miners, or a fifth, it would be more money than she'd ever seen at once in her life. Maybe she'd finally be able to get a new roof for their home and buy that shed they'd wanted. Anything left after that could go into an account for Dawn. In theory, it sure sounded like a great opportunity, but experience had taught her that things were never as simple as they appeared to be at first glance.

ELEVEN

—— ✖ ✖ ✖ ——

As Ella pulled into the parking lot beside the college's Science building, she worked to focus her thoughts back to the case. First, she'd talk to Wilson, then she'd go see Professor Garnenez.

Ella's thoughts shifted to Wilson as she made her way to his office. They'd remained close friends throughout the years, but though Rose had once had hopes they'd get together, their relationship had never gone past friendship.

She was about to turn the corner when she heard someone calling out her name. Glancing back, she saw Wilson coming in the side door. In his hands were two pastries on a paper towel and a cup of coffee.

"Hey, you're just in time to share these crispies. They're fried sweet rolls just loaded with piñon nuts. It's Mrs. Yazzie's special recipe. She makes them to raise money for her kids' college expenses and they're sensational. You've got to try one."

"No, thanks. I'm really not into sweets—unless they have chocolate," Ella said, then followed him into his office.

As Wilson sat behind his desk Ella pulled up a chair. "I came hoping you could tell me something about Professor Garnenez," she said.

"Then you've heard what he's been saying about you?"

Ella reached over and tore off a piece of his crispie. "Just a bite," she muttered, then answering his question, added, "I didn't know the professor was talking about me at all, though it figures. Fill me in?"

Wilson motioned toward the coffeepot, silently offering her a cup. She shook her head, and he began. "Garny, that's what some of his students call him behind his back, was actually reprimanded by the president of the college because he started discussing you in his classes. He said that until the *hataalii* did the proper Sing, you were a danger to the entire community. He claimed that the death of Bruce Smiley was a perfect example of what's going to continue to happen. Smiley, according to him, wasn't suicidal until *you* got near him."

"But that's not the way it went down," she said, absently taking another piece of the crispie. "There were plenty of cops at the scene who can verify that."

Wilson nodded. "And it's not uncommon for criminals trapped by police to take their own lives. Anyone who reads the newspaper knows that. Either way, what amounts to gossip and character assassination of a Tribal Police officer isn't an appropriate subject for an organic chemistry professor. Academic freedom isn't even close to an issue there either. That's why he was reprimanded, but personally I don't think it'll shut him up. He'll just be more careful of who he says it to. I heard that he's asked all his students to help you locate John Tso, unofficially, of course."

As Ella took another piece of the crispie, Wilson slid it over to her. "Take it," he said.

"No, thanks. I'm just not hungry."

Wilson stared at her skeptically, but Ella continued, ignoring his reaction. "I *can* use help in tracking down John Tso, so maybe this is a blessing in disguise." She took another small piece of the crispie.

Wilson looked down at what was left of the remaining sweet roll. "There's just a tiny piece left. Why don't you take it?"

Ella looked down at it. "Okay, I give in. A little bit won't hurt." She finished what was left of the crispie in one bite, then stood. "Listen, you really should cut back on these homemade sweets. I bet they're loaded with cholesterol."

Wilson scowled at her. "Recently I've been eating fewer of them."

"I have to find Professor Garnenez. His office is in this building, right?"

"Yes, but first try the faculty lounge down the hall. He likes to grade papers there. He says that if he stays in his office he's constantly interrupted by students with questions, even if it's not during posted office hours."

"Why doesn't he just lock the door?"

"I gather it breaks his concentration when people knock," he answered, then shrugged. "Just between the two of us, the guy is a little strange."

With a nod and a wave good-bye, Ella left his office and walked down the hall. The wonderful taste of the crispies still lingered in her mouth. She'd have to try to get some to take to the station one of these days.

Ella found the faculty room moments later and since the door was unlocked she walked inside. Professor Garnenez never glanced up until she pulled a chair out and sat across the table from him. The second he saw her, his expression changed from mild annoyance to horror and he scooted his chair back quickly.

"I'm sure you'd like me to leave as soon as possible, and I'll be happy to oblige—after you answer a few questions for me."

He moved his chair back another foot, then stood, reaching down to put his hand on the medicine pouch attached to his belt. "You're not supposed to be in here. This room is for faculty *only*."

"And here I was thinking you'd be thanking me for not knocking."

"What do you want?" he asked through clenched teeth.

"Where were you last night at around eight?"

"At home."

"Can anyone verify that?"

He stared at her. "Why? Am I some kind of suspect?"

"Just answer the question."

"I was alone," he said, then shook his head. "No, wait, I did go to the Quick Stop for a while, I think."

"Will the clerk remember seeing you there?"

"You'll have to ask him," he said coldly. "One Navajo doesn't speak for another."

Ella held his gaze, saying nothing but thinking to herself what a hypocrite he was, using Navajo customs just when they suited him. He'd been spreading gossip about her all over the place, including, probably, the insinuation that she was a skinwalker candidate.

"Look, I don't know what this is about," Garnenez said at long last. "All I can tell you is that I stayed here working late, then went by the store on my way home. It must have been about eight or so."

Ella made a note to check it out later, then stood. "Thank you for your cooperation." She started toward the door, then turned with a sly smile. "Find any actual flint for that pouch of yours?"

His return gaze was laser-sharp. "With someone like you around? Of course." Garnenez reached down to his medicine pouch again to make the point.

Ella headed out to the Quick Stop. She'd go there first, then after she finished, on to her brother's. Maybe he'd finally turned up something on John Tso's whereabouts.

As she drove down the highway, Ella's thoughts drifted and she thought about Emily's coaching and her orchids. Her own life just wasn't structured for a hobby because her free time was best spent with her daughter. Considering Dawn's interest in horses, Ella wondered if she could make time to take up riding again. That would allow her to share in her daughter's favorite activity and to spend quality time with her.

Lost in thought, Ella stared across the mesas and canyons of the region known as the Colorado Plateau. The morning light was warm and bright. It was a cloudless day, and only a faint breeze stirred the branches of the hardy sagebrush and thin clumps of grass that dotted the ground all too sparsely. Yet as peaceful as it was now, by this afternoon the wind would invariably rise and gust at thirty miles an hour or more. Dust and sand would fly, tempers would get thin, and calls to the station would increase. There was always a correlation between the crime rate and the movement of the thermometer and other weather factors.

Ella arrived at the Quick Stop less than fifteen minutes later. As she stepped through the doors, she discovered an old high school friend of hers behind the counter. Juanita Franklin had played on the Shiprock High Lady Chieftains basketball team. They'd made state their senior year and memories like that were hard to forget.

Juanita had put on a good fifty pounds since high school, but her face held a youthful quality that was accentuated by her dimples. "Hey, Ella! It's good to see you. It's been a while, girl. What brings you here? You playing hooky from work?"

"Don't I wish!" Ella said, laughing as Juanita and she exchanged high-fives. "I'm here working a case. I need to talk to whoever was behind the cash register last night. Did you work that shift?"

"No, on Tuesdays it's usually my brother, Clyde. What's he done now?" she asked, instantly worried.

"Not a thing that I know of. I just need to verify something with him. Any idea where I might find him?"

"He's in the back," she said, gesturing Navajo style by pursing her lips toward the rear of the store. "He's putting away some crates. Do you want me to call him out?"

"Nah, I can go back there if it's okay and talk to him while he works," she said.

"That's fine."

Ella found Clyde transferring cases of canned goods from a wheeled cart to a pallet against the wall. Clyde had been two years ahead of Ella in school and she'd had a crush on him for months. He'd been the quarterback of the Chieftains football team.

Seeing her, he smiled. "Hey, Ella. I haven't seen you in ages!" He gave her a friendly hug, something traditionalists would never have done.

"It's been a long, long time," she agreed.

"What brings you here today? Are you looking for a job?"

Ella laughed. "No, I've already got one," she said, pushing back her jacket and revealing her badge and handgun.

"Hey, I know all about that," he answered with a grin. "I'm just having fun with you. Don't shoot!"

Ella laughed.

"What can I do for you?" he asked, still smiling.

"I needed to ask you a few questions. Do you have a minute?"

"Sure." He waved her to a stack of crates about three feet off the ground. "Have a seat."

As he leaned back against the wall, Ella studied him. She'd heard that Clyde and his wife had six kids now and another on the way. She wasn't sure how he made ends meet just working here at the Quick Stop, or how he managed to stay so cheerful. Raising six kids was expensive, even on the Rez where people had learned to get by with just the basics. Raising one child was hard enough.

"Do you remember seeing Professor Garnenez in here lately?"

Clyde nodded. "Yeah, a real night owl, if you'll pardon the expression. He comes by almost every night on the way home. Sometimes, when there are no customers waiting, he and I will play a quick game of chess. He teaches at the college, but I don't think he's got that many friends."

Ella caught his reference to owls, which, due to their tendency to hunt at night, had a bad reputation among traditionalists. "Do you remember if he was in here last night, and if so, about what time?"

"Let me think about it. The days all seem to flow together sometimes, you know? Don't get much rest nowadays."

Ella nodded, realling that three of Clyde's kids were still too young for school.

"I think he was here last night. Yeah, it must have been at right around eight. I remember because I was planning on catching the new TV series about the cop who hears people's thoughts. It was part two, so I really wanted to see it." He exhaled loudly. "But I felt sorry for him, so I turned the volume down and we had a game of chess instead."

"How long was he here?"

"About an hour and a half. The show lasts an hour, and he didn't leave until the next show had started and was about halfway through. I wouldn't have missed my show at all if I'd tried to lose the match, but you know me, I've always been too competitive."

She smiled and nodded. "What do you know about Professor Garnenez?" Ella asked.

"Just what I get from him, which is not a lot. He lives alone way over past Bloomfield, and has that romantic notion about following in the path of the *Dineh*."

"I'm not sure I get what you mean," Ella said.

"He's like the majority of new traditionalists. They want the old ways back—with plenty of modern ideas thrown in.

But Garnenez seems a little more dedicated to the goal than most," he added with a shrug.

"Okay, thanks for your help."

"Take care, Ella."

Ella drove away from the Quick Stop disappointed that Garnenez actually seemed to have a good alibi. The truth was that she'd wanted it to be Garnenez. The man gave her the serious creeps and to haul him in for assault on a police officer would have been very satisfying. But her cases never seemed to be that straightforward and easy. Maybe Benally or Lewis Hunt would turn out to be the ones behind the attack.

Ella glanced at her watch, wishing she'd stopped to buy some of those crispies *before* she'd left campus. It was nearly lunchtime now and she just realized she was hungry. Thinking about returning to the Quick Stop, she quickly rejected the idea of a snow cone or gooey nachos and a soft drink.

Instead, Ella stopped at a fast food place just past the old bridge on the west side and picked up a hamburger and cola. She'd intended to eat it as she drove to her brother's place, but after taking one bite she tossed it back inside the paper sack. It was completely tasteless and she'd forgotten to have them add green chile. Maybe Two would enjoy it. He wasn't quite as picky about his food. At least she had the cola.

As Ella headed south in the general direction of her brother's home she thought about how different Clifford and she were from each other. Clifford was a respected *hataalii* and the old ways came as naturally to him as breathing. He'd spent years learning the proper Sings. Those had to be perfectly memorized, not an easy task considering Sings often lasted eight to ten days. Any mistake, however slight, meant incurring the disfavor or wrath of the gods.

Ella parked outside Clifford's medicine hogan and waited. There was a gray mare tethered outside the blanketed entrance so she knew Clifford was with a patient. About ten minutes later a young woman about Boots's age came out, jumped up onto the horse's back in one leisurely motion, then rode off.

Seeing Ella, Clifford waved, inviting her to approach. Ella joined him just as he was picking up the bags of herbs and the jars that were on the ground near the sheepskins. "What's on your mind, Sister?"

"I was hoping you'd received some news about the Singer I need," she said. Here, no proper names would be used out of respect for her brother's traditionalist views.

"A few people have sent word to me that they'd seen him driving by their home, or campsite, but that's about it. He's clearly on the move. I've now left word everywhere I can think of asking people to tell him that I'm looking for him. I'm sure he'll be in touch."

"He's a hard man to catch. I've discovered that there are a lot of people trying to help me find him," Ella said with a rueful smile, then told him what Professor Garnenez had apparently asked his students.

"His students may get somewhere with the search, but I wouldn't count on the professor himself being able to help you. A man like the Singer you're searching for would probably go out of his way to give the professor a wide berth. The professor is like many of our generation—caught between the old and the new. They aren't comfortable in either world, so they try to walk a path between both. But, in my opinion, that's an even harder road to travel. You understand that quite well, I'm sure."

"All any of us can do is follow where our hearts lead us. What other choice do we have?" Ella asked rhetorically.

Clifford considered it for a moment. "You're right, but it reminds me of something our Christian father used to say about 'a house divided.' Remember that?"

Ella nodded. She'd loved her father deeply but she'd never understood him. Then after his murder all she'd felt was guilt—for not having taken the time to get to know him, and for never having understood that he had the right to follow his own path, even if it created division in their household. "I still miss him, you know?"

"I do, too." Clifford sat across from her on the sheepskin rug. "I loved him though he and I never agreed on anything from the time I hit my teens. I think deep down he always knew that I'd never worship the Christian God, no more than Mom would. But he never gave up trying to convert us— which bugged me to no end. Mom was far more gracious about it than I ever was," he said.

Ella nodded slowly, remembering. "I have a question I'd like to ask you, but this is something that must remain between you and me."

"Go on."

"I know from my biology classes that a practical definition of dead is when all the body processes stop and cannot be restarted. That obviously didn't happen to me, but there's more than one definition of death. What do you think happened to me that day in the mine? Is it possible that I died— on one level or another—then came back?"

"As a *hataalii* I have to believe that your wind spirit was just lost for a while. Our ways don't include a belief in a heavenly afterlife, like Dad's did. To us death is stagnation—a failure to grow and thrive—not an inviting place."

Ella nodded slowly. She knew that she'd made a conscious decision to return and that was why she was here now, talking to her brother. But she just wasn't sure whether that pointed to a greater power, or if it was evidence that her own stubbornness and force of will had reversed a biological process.

"You saw or experienced something when you were down in that mine shaft that you haven't been able to understand, didn't you?" he asked softly, his gaze on her.

Clifford's beliefs were set and rooted in the Navajo ways.

She'd been wrong to try to discuss something like this with him. It would only add confusion to his life. "I have no idea what happened to me in that mine. I'll probably never know for sure. But I'm here now and that's the important thing."

TWELVE

✖ ✖ ✖

Ella was walking to the blanket-covered doorway when her stomach growled loudly.

Clifford laughed. "When's the last time you ate?"

"I had bits of a crispie a while ago . . ."

"The ones they sell at the college?" Clifford asked.

"You've heard of them?"

"Oh, yeah. If you ever see her with some of those crispies for sale, pick some up for me."

"Okay, Brother. I'll bring them over and you and I can pig out like we did with fry bread when we were kids."

"Suits me," he said, chuckling. "But in the meantime, why don't you come into the house and I'll fix us both something to eat."

"Are you sure?" she asked, worried about how Loretta would react since she hadn't had a Sing done yet.

"My wife and son aren't here today. So come on, I made some of my Texas chili last night and there's still some left. We'll add some potatoes to it and use it as stuffing for burritos."

"Sounds great."

Ella followed him in. Clifford's house was simply furnished and the wooden furniture well worn. There were no luxuries here, unless one could count a thirteen-inch TV set as a luxury.

The kitchen was slightly more modern, but there was no microwave oven. Loretta felt the same way Rose did—it would be a waste of money to buy what their stove could already do. At least the refrigerator was large, and although purchased from an appliance renewal place, it hummed along nicely.

"Sit down. I'll cook," he said.

"Don't you want me to fix the potatoes while you get the other ingredients ready?"

"No, I still remember the time you made hash browns for Mom. They tasted like wood shavings by the time you finished with them."

She remembered the incident well. It was Thanksgiving and she was helping Rose with breakfast. She'd started to cook, gotten stuck on the phone, then remembered the potatoes only when the smoke alarm went off. It had happened over three years ago, but it had become the family's favorite joke. Every time Ella offered to help in the kitchen someone brought up the story.

Ella sat down and watched Clifford work. "How's my nephew doing?"

"He realizes he could have been seriously hurt, if not worse, and that really frightened him—for about a day. He was really quiet when we came home and didn't even want to go outside to play. But now he seems to have forgotten all about the incident and is completely back to normal. Kids are amazing little beings. They live in the present so their recovery time is zero flat." He switched on the radio to the Navajo station, realized George Branch's program was on now, and switched it back off. "I know that man must have some redeeming qualities, but I've never been able to discover what they are."

"He's a pain, but even so he sure didn't deserve what happened to him. His house is nothing more than rubble now."

"Don't waste time feeling sorry for the radio man. I listen to the news on that station and apparently he's managed to turn his tragedy into a publicity bonanza. Supposedly his ratings have tripled, if you believe the hype. I'm told that he's asked his listening audience to cooperate with the Tribal Police and help them find the man suspected of setting the fire at his home. He told his listeners that anyone who hides and protects the suspect is mistaking vigilante justice for the real thing."

"I think the people shielding the man I'm trying to locate believe in our tribe's traditional methods of justice, not the law as we know it," Ella said. "It'll take more than words, particularly those coming from a reactionary like the radio man, to change thinking like that."

"Word has spread that the one who ended up killing the councilman's wife, then himself, was at the radio host's home several times."

"What? I hadn't heard that."

"My sources are good," Clifford said and shrugged.

Ella didn't doubt that for a minute. Her brother traveled everywhere on the reservation and spoke to a multitude of people. "I'll have to look into that."

Ella accepted the finished burrito her brother handed her. It was excellent—filled with cheese, spicy ground beef, pinto beans, and salsa. "Good job. Do you have a paper plate?"

"Why? You won't have to do the dishes," he said, frowning.

She laughed. "I wasn't worried, but I can't stay and I'd like to take the food with me. I've got a radio personality I'd like to speak to as soon as possible."

He looked in the cupboard and found a paper plate with

a cartoon Great Dane on it. "Here. It's leftover from my son's birthday party. Are you sure you can't eat like a normal person—at the table?"

"I really want to follow this up. But, listen, this burrito is quite a treat. I'm used to generic fast food for lunch. You should experience the hamburger I bought before I arrived. I took one bite and threw it back into the paper sack."

"Did you get it from that new place near the bridge?"

"Yeah."

He made a face. "You don't want to know what I've heard about the way they cook their food. Just don't go there again."

"I was going to save the burger for Two, but I just changed my mind."

Ella drove back through Shiprock, eating her lunch on the way, then directly to Branch's radio station in Farmington. The first person she met when she walked into the lobby was Hoskie Ben.

"What brings you here?" he greeted with a warm smile. "Are you looking for George?"

"Yes, I am. Will you tell him I'm here?"

"Can you wait a few minutes? Right now he's with a nervous sponsor. Despite the jump in ratings there's a lot of negative publicity going around. This businessman is afraid it'll hurt his company's image if he continues to run his ads on George's show."

"I bet the station isn't too happy about that."

He shrugged. "One sponsor might pull his ads, but another two will come along soon to bid for those open slots. Controversy is good for the show."

"And how are things for you? Busy?" Ella asked.

"Yeah," he said, adding, "I just keep reminding people that it's my program notes and research that helps Branch get those ratings."

She chuckled. "No one can fault you for wanting to get ahead."

"Unfortunately some people do," he replied somberly. "Councilman Hunt's assistant called, wanting us to do a story about Navajo justice. When I asked if the councilman was trying to capitalize on the sentiment surrounding the death of his wife to justify the burning of George Branch's home, she cussed me out real good."

Hearing a commotion, Ella glanced down the hall. A door opened about then and an angry Anglo man in an expensive suit stormed out. George Branch came to the door and tried to call him back.

"Jack, wait a minute—"

The man brushed by Ella and Huskie, then continued out the front door without comment.

Branch's scowl intensified when he saw Ella. "My day isn't bad enough?" he muttered, then added, "What brings you here?"

"I need to ask you a question."

"First, did you catch Cardell Benally? That lunatic might set fire to somebody else's place if he doesn't happen to like what they say. Lewis Hunt is stirring him and a lot of others up by calling for 'Navajo justice' when the court system fails."

"My investigation is still ongoing. But I need to know something concerning the first arson. I've been told that Bruce Smiley, the man who set the fire that killed the councilman's wife, was an avid listener of yours and, in fact, visited you at your home more than once. That might explain why Benally and Hunt have you in their sights. You and Hunt have a way of inciting people."

"That's such a distortion of the facts, Ella. And I don't invite listeners into my home. Smiley was a nut job who somehow managed to get my address. He came by to talk to me a couple of times and really pushed to be invited inside. But each time I told him that I really valued my privacy and if he wanted to talk, he should call while I'm on the air." Branch paused suddenly. "Wait. Come to think of it, things did get a little weird the last time he stopped by. Smiley wanted to talk about my gun collection, and was so interested in the details I was afraid he was planning to break in later and try to steal something."

"Did you ever discuss the councilman with him?"

"No. I'm telling you, our conversations lasted only long enough for me to get him off my porch so he'd go home."

By the time Ella left the radio station she was convinced that Branch had told the truth about Smiley—especially because she'd confirmed the story with Hoskie before leaving. Apparently Branch had grilled everyone at the station trying to determine who'd given out his address, but he'd never managed to get an answer.

Glancing at her watch after she pulled out into traffic, Ella decided to stop by her home once she reached Shiprock. She needed to ask her mother for a favor. As a traditionalist, Rose knew every single rumor that concerned that group. With a little luck, and using her own connections, Rose might be able to get a lead on the sniper for her.

As she pulled up at the house forty-five minutes later, she saw her mother hanging up some laundry outside.

Ella went to join her. "Mom, why are you doing that? I thought part of Boots's job is to help you with the house-keeping."

"She asked for some time off today, and I gave it to her. To be honest, I like having the house to myself sometimes."

Ella smiled ruefully. "And so today of all days, I decide to come home."

Rose chuckled softly. "I'm glad you're here. A friend of yours dropped off a small gift for you."

"Who dropped what by, Mom?" Ella asked, instantly on her guard.

"She said she was a sergeant in the sheriff's department and her uniform and badge looked real." Rose led the way inside, then reached for the small flowering potted plant. One long shoot had a half-dozen purple, white, and yellow orchids.

"Here's the gift she left for you," Rose said, handing it to her. "I've never tried to grow an orchid in this desert, but I've heard that they can thrive in a bright window." She touched one of the petals. "Your daughter will love it so make sure she doesn't water it to death."

Ella looked at the beautiful plant and sighed. "I wouldn't worry about that if I were you. I'll kill it long before she does." She glanced at Rose. "You know it's inevitable."

Rose sighed. "You're probably right. I still remember when you were going to the Plant Watcher meetings with me. I gave you a cactus I knew needed almost no attention at all. Although it had the exact same sun exposure in my room, it died three weeks after you took it to your room." She shook her head, still perplexed. "This type of ornamental plant doesn't have a prayer. It's downright delicate in our environment."

Ella read the note attached to the pot. "She says to put the pot in a tray of gravel and keep that moist, then stick it in a bright window and water it every five days." Ella looked at Rose. "She's trying to be helpful, but this is her hobby, not mine. I barely have time to do the things I have to do now, let alone nursemaid a plant."

Rose remained thoughtful for a moment. "The closest to a hobby you have is that thing," she said, pointing to the computer. "At least your friend's hobby cultivates beauty."

"And I cultivate . . . pixels?"

"Pixies?"

"Never mind," Ella said with a chuckle. "Mom, I don't have leisure time so I can't have a hobby."

"It's not good to work to exhaustion and nearly pass out every night, Daughter."

"It's not always like that, just when I'm working on a pressing case."

"As your daughter grows older, she'll be spending a lot more time with her friends and maybe even travel with her father. You'll need to find something to do with yourself when you're not working and she's not there. This isn't the big city, so you have fewer choices, but I can't see you as a couch potato, watching mindless TV."

Ella grimaced. Her mother had just pointed out a fact of life she just didn't want to face—Dawn growing up. "I'll think about it, Mom," she said at last.

"Oh, and here's the telephone number the Hollywood producer left for you," she said, reaching for the pad of paper beneath the phone.

"Thanks, Mom."

"Call him now. I'm dying of curiosity."

Ella spent about fifteen minutes on the phone, and had just hung up when she saw Rose standing at the door.

"Well?" Rose asked.

"The man I spoke to is the producer, and he owns his own production company. He gave me a list of credits— which meant absolutely nothing to me—then offered me sixty-five thousand dollars for exclusive rights to my story."

Rose's eyes grew wide. "That's a fortune. Did you say yes?"

Ella shook her head. "There was more to it, Mom. I wouldn't get that money unless a TV station or network actually decided to film the project. Then he threw at least half a dozen terms at me that I've never heard of. It would have been crazy for me to agree to anything without an attorney at this point."

"Will you talk to your child's father?"

"Yes, absolutely." She remained silent for a few more moments, then at long last added, "It's not going to be easy, Mom. The bottom line is that I hate letting outsiders into my private life and that's exactly what will happen as soon as I say yes. The only reason I'm considering it at all is in hopes of giving my daughter a nest egg she can rely on someday. That's it."

"Then talk to your child's father before you sign anything, and get as much money as you can," Rose said flatly.

"My thoughts exactly. Now I need a favor from you."

"Name it."

Ella led her mom to the couch in the living room and sat down beside her. "Someone took a shot at my car, Mom," she said and explained about the bullet and the flat tire. "I want you to ask around and find out if there's anyone out there who believes that the only way I won't pose a danger to the tribe is if I'm dead."

Rose weighed her daughter's request. "What you're asking won't be easy. People won't speak freely to me about something like that." Rose considered it, then smiled as a new thought occurred to her. "But they might talk about it to another friend of mine, Boots's grandmother. Despite the fact that she's a traditionalist, she knows you're doing your best to find the *hataalii* and is on your side."

Ella knew who she was referring to. Lena Clani and Rose were very close friends. Lena wouldn't refuse Rose. "Great, Mom. If you hear anything, let me know right away, okay?"

Rose nodded. "Do you think this sniper is also the person who was watching our home?"

"I don't know," Ella replied honestly.

"Then I'll ask my friend to work fast."

Ella went back to her office at the police station, then spent the next hour filling out reports, her least favorite duty. When the intercom buzzed, she reached for it with the eagerness of a drowning man grasping for a log.

"Shorty, come to my office." It was Big Ed.

Ella stood, glad for a chance to stretch her cramped muscles, and walked to his office. When she knocked lightly on his opened door, he glanced up from his paperwork and waved at her to come in. "I've had something on my mind I need to discuss with you."

"Shoot," she said, sitting down.

He rocked slowly back and forth in his chair, indicating that he hadn't made up his mind about something yet. "You went through quite an ordeal in that mine," he said after several long moments. "I know I encouraged you to return to work, but I want to make sure I haven't been pushing you too hard. I've seen officers who've had a close call seem perfectly fine for several days, then all of a sudden lose it. Everything gets all scrambled in their minds."

"I'm doing okay," Ella assured him quickly. "Really. I won't tell you that the accident didn't affect me at all. It has. For example, I'm going to be getting life insurance, even though it costs an arm and a leg, and I've tied up some loose ends I should have never ignored. But I'm back on the job and dealing with the usual pressures pretty well."

"Okay, you've always been honest with me so I'll accept your answer. But if you change your mind and feel like you want to talk to a doctor," he said, pointing to his head, "just let me know."

"No shrinks or counselors," Ella said with a groan, "but thanks anyway."

Ella returned to her office and found Justine waiting there for her.

"Hi, Ella, is there anything you need from me today? I'd like to head out," her second cousin said.

"Hot date?"

"No, nothing even remotely exciting, unfortunately. My sister Jayne is repainting her house and asked all of us to come help. Since she asked us in front of Mom, it's not exactly an option anymore. Mom expects us all to be there tonight."

"A command performance."

"Exactly."

Ella picked up her keys from the top of the file cabinet. "Well, I'm going to head out now too while it's still daylight. I'd like to spend some time with Dawn this evening."

Ella arrived home at six and found that Dawn had already eaten dinner and had gone outside to ride her pony in the arena. Boots was standing in the middle, holding the pony's tether line.

"Sit up straight and don't hold the reins so tight. And remember to cue him with your legs," Boots said.

Ella watched for a while, remembering her own riding instructor telling her the same thing. But Dawn moved with the animal fluidly and seemed more attuned to her mount than she'd ever been. Although Ella loved being around horses, she'd hated riding them.

"She's a natural," Rose said, coming up behind Ella. "But if memory serves, you weren't so bad at it yourself."

"You've got me confused with my brother, Mom. I was dreadful. He was the one who could ride. I just sat on the horse and let it carry me."

"That's not true, Daughter. The real problem was that you were always competing with your brother. If he wanted to learn how to rope, you wanted to learn, too. But you weren't satisfied unless you could be even better than he was."

"True," she answered, laughing. "But whenever my brother rode, you could see his oneness with the horse. I never achieved that." Ella looked at Dawn as she leaned forward to pet the pony's neck. "My daughter, on the other hand, has the same gift for riding my brother did."

Rose nodded. "She does have a way with animals." Rose paused and glanced at her daughter. "I have a great idea. Why don't you take up riding again? It would be something you two could do together."

"You know, I'd been thinking the same thing. But it's been ages since I've been on a horse. And finding the right animal . . . well, it takes time. You need to locate one that suits your personality and abilities. In my case, one with the energy of a slug."

Rose laughed. "You'd hate a horse that didn't challenge you every once in a while. But, for now, why don't you just go see what's available? Or, better yet, have your brother do the ground work for you. He's got a good eye and he knows a lot of people who own horses."

"I'll think about it."

"Daughter, have you noticed how much of *that* you're doing lately?"

"How much of what?"

"Thinking. You keep postponing nearly every decision you have to make. One example is the Hollywood producer. It's as if you're afraid of making a mistake. That's not a good thing."

"I *am* afraid of making mistakes that'll come back to haunt me, Mom." Ella watched her daughter and thought of all the time they could share if she did take up riding.

"Moments pass and then they're lost forever, Daughter," Rose said softly.

"I'll take care of things, Mom. But I'm not familiar enough with Hollywood to make a snap decision. If we were talking about something I know, it would be different. I wouldn't have to take things at a snail's pace."

"I'm so glad to hear that! You certainly know horses, so buying one will be easy! I'll call your brother and ask him to help you find one."

Ella burst out laughing. "Mom, you set me up!"

"Yes, I did."

"Okay, Mom. I'll consider buying a horse. But I'll make the arrangements myself, understand?"

Rose nodded, smiling.

The moment Dawn's riding lesson was over, she ran over to Ella and threw her arms around her. "Did you see me, *Shimá*?"

"I sure did! You were great!"

"Your *shimá* is going to get a horse so she can go riding with you," Rose said. "Won't that be exciting?"

"Really?" Dawn squealed.

Ella's eyes grew wide and she turned to look at her mother. By then Dawn was jumping up and down.

"Now you can't change your mind—just in case you were considering it," Rose said with a smile.

"Mom, shouldn't you be looking for a horse too? We wouldn't want to leave you behind when we go riding." Ella smiled wickedly at her mother.

"Wow! Three horses?" Dawn looked back and forth from Rose to Ella expectantly.

"Absolutely not! *Someone* has to stay home and have supper ready when you young people return home from a *long* trail ride," Rose announced, then turned and walked toward the house.

Dawn snickered. "Never argue with your mother, Mom."

"You've got that right, Pumpkin."

Ella was up early after a restless night. Around two in the morning, she'd woken up from a sound sleep for no apparent reason. As she'd lain there staring at the ceiling, she'd come up with an idea for finding Cardell Benally. It wasn't something that Big Ed would approve of wholeheartedly, so she'd have to sell him on it. Still, it would be one way to get the job done.

Ella had just walked into the kitchen when Rose came through the back door, anger etched on her face. She held the contents of a paper sack away from her in disgust.

"What's that?" Ella asked.

"I was looking out the window while adding water to the teakettle and caught a glimpse of something odd in the backyard. I went out to see what it was and found this." She opened the sack and showed it to her.

To Ella, it looked like ground beef at first, but then she spotted tiny slivers of shiny glass hidden in the meat.

"It was meant for Two, obviously," Rose continued. "Good thing I found it before he did."

Ella glanced out the kitchen window. "Where did you say you found it?"

"There." Rose pointed to a sunny spot against the side of the shed where Two often lay.

"Keep it in the sack," Ella said. "I'm going to take it to the station for analysis. In the meantime, I'm going to see if there's anything else out there."

"Good. I'll keep Two inside with me until you're finished."

Ella was hoping to find footprints, but the area around the shed appeared devoid of any fresh prints except those of her mother and Two.

Walking a loose spiral search pattern out from the location of the meat, Ella quickly discovered recent footprints leading away in the opposite direction of the road in a trail that led to the big arroyo. They were boots in a size and pattern nobody from her household wore.

Hurrying along, she noted the footprints seemed to be farther apart just ahead, though the person hadn't been running. She stopped short of the first footprint to think about it.

The space between the two footprints was about six inches more than the ones on either side, as if the person had decided to take one giant step among the regular ones.

There was nothing in the trail to step over, just a small bush that looked tilted to one side. Inching forward, Ella disturbed the loose ground slightly with her foot. Suddenly a large piece of metal flew up from the ground and snapped with a horrible crunch.

Ella jumped back, her heart pounding. It was an old bear or wolf trap, and she'd just set it off with a touch of her shoe.

The jagged jaws of the cruel device gleamed, having recently been sharpened.

Ella froze, trying to calm down as she searched the ground all around her for a second trap. She didn't dare take a step now. The meat for the dog had served two purposes. First, to possibly take out Two, and secondly, to take out anyone who tried to follow up on the bait.

Then her fear was replaced by a cold, dark anger, more intense than any she'd ever known. What if Dawn, her mother, or even one of the animals had ventured down this path instead of her?

Turning around completely, Ella noted that she was still quite alone. Stepping in her old prints, she walked back to the barn and grabbed a long bamboo pole from beside the shed.

"What did you find, Daughter?" Rose poked her head out the door.

"Keep everyone inside, Mother. Whoever set the poison out also set at least one big animal trap along the trail to the arroyo. I managed to avoid being caught, but barely."

"Are you sure you're okay?" Rose looked Ella up and down carefully. "Want me to call the station?" Rose's face had turned pale.

"I'll check it out first. If I find any more, we'll call the station," Ella said, weighing her options and trying to decide on the best course of action. "Wait, doesn't Bizaadii have a metal detector?" Ella was referring to Herman Cloud.

Rose nodded. "It's a good one, too. We've used it to help some of the Plant Watchers figure out where they could dig in their yards without hitting utility lines. I'll give him a call. You be careful, Daughter."

Ella nodded, then walked back toward where she'd set off the trap, probing the ground in front of her. She checked the area from where the tracks started all the way to the arroyo. From that point on, after the trail led down into the wash itself, the tracks disappeared across hard sandstone exposed by the elements. There would be no traps here.

Knowing there could be no traps where nobody had walked, she checked the ground carefully around the house, barn, and yard, searching for anything, from footprints to a cigarette or wad of gum, but she found nothing. Taking the trap, she handled it with gloves and placed it safely in the back of her unit. It would go to the station for examination.

By the time she came back inside, Boots had arrived and Ella learned that Herman Cloud was on his way. He'd check everywhere with the metal detector.

After cautioning everyone, including Dawn, to remain watchful of strangers, Ella took her mother aside. "It would be a really good idea for you to invite Bizaadii to visit on evenings when I work late. He's still got a very sharp eye."

"I'll definitely do that. After the search for any more traps is completed, I'll tether the pony closer to the house, too. If anyone harms that little animal your daughter would be heartbroken."

Ella nodded. "Tether Wind near her window. She'll love it. Plus, that little horse works as a good watch animal. Last time, between his whinnying and running around, he was the one who first let me know someone was outside."

"That furry little gelding doesn't like strangers. That's true," Rose agreed.

Ella left home in a black mood. She was more than willing to put herself on the line out in the field, but when her family was attacked her perspective went out the window. Knowing that anger would only hamper her ability to think clearly, she struggled to calm down.

As she reached the end of the gravel road that led to the highway, Ella decided on impulse to make one quick stop before going in to work. Turning, she headed toward Kevin's home.

As she drove up several minutes later, Kevin came out

onto the porch, then waved at her, inviting her to come inside. "Two days in a row! Am I part of your rounds now, and should I be honored or worried?"

Ella didn't crack a smile. "Kev, I need your help." She told him about the animal trap and contaminated meat they'd found. "I'm afraid that the reason someone's trying to get rid of our dog is so they can sneak up on us at night. And that wolf trap could have killed our daughter or my mother. I've ordered extra patrols, but with our manpower shortages, I know it won't be enough. What I'd like to do is hire some off-duty or retired cops to watch the place while we're sleeping."

Kevin's face had turned red with anger when he heard about the steel trap, and his voice was shaking with barely suppressed rage. "If you need the funds to do that, you've got them." He pulled out his checkbook. "Tell me how much to make it for, and you'll be all set. You might also consider the men I've hired as my bodyguards in the past."

"I don't want a bodyguard. What I need is a sentry, someone to watch for intruders."

"Fine. How much?" he asked again.

"I'll find out later today," she said, placing her hand over his. "And thanks. You know I wouldn't ask you if I didn't need it for Dawn's sake."

"You can ask me for anything—anytime."

"Oh, I'm so glad you said that," she said, a twinkle in her eye.

"I've got a feeling I'm going to regret having said that," he countered with a smile, sensing her change of mood.

Ella told him about the Hollywood producer. "I really don't know any of the terms he was throwing at me, so I'd like you to handle this. First, I need to make sure that it's legal for me as a tribal cop to accept this type of offer, even though I wasn't working at the time. If it is, find out if what he's offering me is a fair deal and what he'll expect from me in return. Get him to spell it out clearly. I don't want any surprises."

Kevin gazed at her speculatively for several moments. "You don't really want to sign, do you?"

"No, but I will because I'd love to be able to set that money aside for Dawn in a trust fund, or something like that. Of course to get the big bucks, they actually have to film the thing."

"One thing that occurs to me is that if one producer is interested, chances are others will be too. Shall I try to check that out? You might be able to get more money that way."

"Go for it."

"Give me some time to get up to speed on this. I need to talk to people who have dealt with Hollywood before and get some pointers from entertainment lawyers. I prefer to come at them informed and knowing exactly what's common practice and what's not."

"Sounds like a good plan."

"In the meantime, if they call you again tell them you're interested and are looking for an attorney to negotiate any offers," Kevin said. "By the way, if I can't get them to increase their offer, do you still want me to accept it?"

"Yes, but look at everything they want me to agree to with a magnifying glass if you have to."

"Of course."

She was about to leave when she saw that Kevin had two of Mrs. Yazzie's crispies.

"Forget it. Those are *mine*," he said flatly. "I know how you like to pick at other people's food. It may make you feel like you're not eating as much, but the poor slob who lets you nibble away at their plate gets shortchanged. So mitts off, flatfoot."

"Geez! What a temper!" Ella smiled. "But okay. Just to show you what a good person I am, I forgive you," she said, inching subtly toward them.

Kevin moved to block her. "Out," he said and pointed to the door.

Ella drove to the station, pushing back her craving for a crispie by concentrating on the current situation. She had to move fast and find out who was stalking her house. Anyone who endangered her family became number one on her most wanted list.

THIRTEEN

✖ ✖ ✖

Ella left the tainted meat in Justine's lab refrigerator, asking for an analysis in case a poison had been added in addition to the glass. The trap, a common design that was probably fifty years old, was checked for fingerprints. None were found, and the tool marks were made with some kind of file. Without the tool used to sharpen it, there was nothing more to go on.

After making out a report about the incident, Ella began going through the list of perps she'd put away in the recent past. Maybe someone with a grudge, who also had knowledge and access to animal traps, had just been released or made parole.

That didn't pan out, and out of leads for the moment, Ella switched gears and concentrated on the hunt for Cardell Benally. As she went over the little they had on him, the idea she'd come up with late last night looked even better to her.

Ella walked to Chief Atcitty's office and stopped in the doorway. Big Ed was behind the desk, engrossed in something on his computer terminal.

"Chief, I need to talk to you for a bit."

"Come on in, Shorty. I'm reading the report you sent me E-mail about the animal trap and the attempted poisoning of your family's dog."

"Nobody's going to harm my family or my animals, Chief. I'd like to hire some off-duty cops or maybe some retired officers to keep an eye out at night when my family and I are sleeping."

"This goes way beyond animal cruelty, I agree. I don't know any retired officers still living in the area, but you can hire any of our off-duty personnel. We won't need them unless there's a crisis. I wish I could assign people to do this for you but that's impossible right now."

"I know. And that brings me to another request I'd like to make. I want to put a tail on Councilman Hunt."

"I've heard he's been making some public statements about a return to old-fashioned 'Navajo justice.' But do you have anything to justify monitoring Hunt other than the fact that he and his brother-in-law Cardell have the best motive?"

"Well, we do know that there were two people involved in what happened at Branch's home, and Hunt *is* the logical second suspect. Except for the vehicles involved we have nothing hard on Hunt, who's been very active lately, apparently trying to justify what happened to Branch. But we believe Benally is hiding out somewhere on the Navajo Nation. If I'm right and Hunt helped his brother-in-law, then I'd bet anything that Hunt knows where Benally is, and is still helping him. If we tail Hunt, and he gets careless, I think he'll lead us to Cardell."

"All right, but be careful. You know Councilman Hunt is aware that you suspect him, so he'll be keeping watch. If he finds out what you're doing, the fur'll fly, mark my words. Is this the only way you have of getting a lead on Cardell?"

"Unless we either get an informant or somebody stumbles across him and calls us."

"All right. Run the operation for twenty-four hours and see what happens. But make *sure* that the councilman doesn't spot the tail. Lewis Hunt is used to manipulating people, and has the ear of those who control the department's budget. I really don't need that kind of trouble right now. You hear me?"

"Absolutely."

"Who are you going to get for the stakeout?" he asked.

"Justine is pretty good. I can also take a turn. I'll probably bring Neskahi in for the night shift. We want to keep this a team effort."

He considered it and nodded. "Okay. But keep me updated."

As Ella stepped inside her office the phone rang. She answered it and recognized her brother's voice instantly.

"I have some information you may find useful. Gossip has it that the radio talk show man is worried that he'll continue to be a target as long as the councilman's brother-in-law is still at large. He's let the word out that he'll pay one thousand dollars for information on the man's whereabouts."

"That's a fortune around here," Ella said, worried. "That idiot is going to stir up a hornet's nest. Do you have any idea what he plans to do with the information *if* he gets it? Will he turn it over to us?"

"I doubt it. Look at the way he made the offer in the first place. It's all word-of-mouth, so if push came to shove he could always deny it."

"Branch is no hit man," Ella said, thinking out loud. "He likes—maybe *liked* is a more appropriate term—owning an arsenal because it's the macho thing to do. But I don't see him as the type to go gunning—literally—for anyone. He lets his mouth do that."

"He could hire someone," Clifford suggested.

"To do what?" Ella asked. "Is there something you're not telling me?"

"No. You now know what I do."

"Okay. Thanks for the tip. I appreciate it," Ella said, hung up, then called in her team. Within twenty minutes they were all gathered in a conference room and she detailed her plan.

Tache looked at her in surprise. "They've got a job now, but what's my part in this?"

"I have another task for you. I want you to go over to the county sheriff's office and ask Sheriff Taylor if you can examine all the evidence they gathered during the fire at Branch's home. Check to see if anything's missing, or if there's something that needs to be followed up on. We're looking for anything to back up what we have on Cardell Benally or Lewis Hunt."

"The county has a pretty competent team, Ella," Tache said.

"Yes, I agree, but sometimes things get missed—particularly details that might have meaning to a Navajo but not to someone who's not from our tribe. Just be careful not to step on any toes by letting them think we're second-guessing them."

"Got it."

"I also want you to go back to Branch's home yourself and take a look around. See if there's anything there along the same vein that might have been overlooked. Get Branch's permission if you run into him, but don't be too specific about what you're searching for, okay?"

"That'll be easy, considering I don't know exactly what it is I'm hoping to find," Tache muttered.

Glancing back at Neskahi and Justine, Ella worked out their schedules. "You take the first shift following the councilman, Justine. Stay in touch with me at all times, and if you think something's going down, call me immediately," she said, then laid out the rest of the watch.

After Justine and the others left, Ella returned to her small office and mulled over what her brother had told her about Branch. She needed to keep closer tabs on the radio commentator now that he was taking matters into his own hands.

This latest move of his shouldn't have surprised her. Like most bullies, Branch was used to dishing it out, but taking it was another matter. Of course they'd hit him where he was most vulnerable. She had no doubt that he'd stewed about it and become increasingly worried when it became clear that neither the tribal nor the county police would be able to find Benally easily. Fear always brought out the worst in a person.

As Ella considered her options, she remembered Hoskie Ben. He probably knew more about Branch than anyone else. She'd start with him.

Ella called the station and after identifying herself only as a friend was put through to Hoskie Ben.

"It's Ella Clah," she explained. "Sorry for the subterfuge, but I need to talk to you off the record."

"Then it's a good thing you didn't say who you were. With Lewis Hunt trying to stir up some of his own vigilante type justice, George is nothing short of paranoid. People like him recognize their own. If the receptionist mentioned that you'd called me, he'd make my life miserable."

"Can we meet somewhere after you get off work?"

"Sure. What did you have in mind?"

"I need to ask you a few questions. Off the record is better, but I can make this official."

"Can you be more specific?" he asked, his voice guarded. "I have a responsibility to this station. Proprietary business stays confidential."

"Let's meet. If you don't like a particular question, don't answer it, and I'll go to the next one," she said, keeping her tone as casual as possible. She wanted him relaxed, not on his guard.

"Fair enough. I live just southwest of where the La Plata River joins the San Juan. It's as close as you can get to Farmington and still be on the Rez. I rent land from an allottee, and since my wife works and my kids are at school, we'll have the place to ourselves. I can get off for lunch at eleven. How about if we meet a half hour after that?"

Ella checked her watch. It was nine-thirty now. "That sounds fine. I'll see you then."

As soon as Ella hung up, the telephone rang. It was Jim Begay, the trading post owner at Beclabito and one of the few traditionalist-leaning Navajos who wasn't afraid to contact her. "Are you still looking for John Tso?"

"Yes, is he around?"

There was a brief pause. "He was. He came in to buy supplies and mentioned that he was going into the Chuska Mountains to find one of his family's lost shrines. I told him you were looking for him, and he said that he'd look you up when he came back to Shiprock. I suggested that you needed his services right away, but he just shrugged and said you'd have to wait. He had to do this other thing first while he was still strong enough to do it. It's part of the legacy he wanted to leave behind for his family. After he left, I thought about it and wondered if he'd really understood how much you needed him. He's been out of touch with all the news around here."

"Any idea when he'll be coming out of the mountains?"

"He bought enough supplies for two or three days at least, but may have had more food in his truck. I really can't say, Ella. Sorry," Jim answered.

"Well, thanks for letting me know." Ella hung up and called Rose. "Do you know anyone out there who might be willing to try to find the *hataalii* and convince him to do a Sing for me right away? I can't take off and go searching for him now. It might take days."

"Let me see if I can get some of the Plant Watchers who live in the area to go check for him."

Ella hung up, satisfied. If it could be done, her mother's friends would find John Tso.

After another quick meeting with the chief to tell him the news about the Singer, Ella got on the road. She had over an hour before she had to meet with Hoskie, so she decided to stop by and see Carolyn Roanhorse Lavery. Ella still needed a physical done and she'd been carrying the insurance papers they'd mailed her in her glove compartment for some time now.

Ella was halfway to the hospital when her cell phone rang. "Hunt made me, Ella. I'm sure of it," Justine said.

"Where are you now?" Ella asked.

"Just off the road west of Hogback. He stopped by the grocery store in Shiprock and came out with a cart full of groceries. Then he got on Highway Sixty-four heading east. He turned off on a gravel road before Hogback, so I went farther south and drove on a parallel course along the ditch levee. The only problem is that the trail here is dry and dusty and the cloud of dust that my unit left behind was impossible for even a blind man to miss. He's slowed down considerably now so I'm sure he made me."

"You say he's still heading east?"

"Yeah, and, Ella, his home isn't out this way and neither is the place he's been staying at. I checked. He's been living with a friend of his just outside Shiprock where most of the power company's tribal employees live."

"Hang back and watch him through binoculars. I'll take over as soon as I can. I'm on my way now."

It took Ella another ten minutes to reach the area Justine had mentioned. "I'm coming alone above you on the main highway. Where's he?" Ella asked.

"About a mile up, close to Waterflow now."

"Okay, I'll take over from here. I'll stay on the highway north of him. Go back to the station for now."

"I'm sorry, partner."

"Get Neskahi and tell him I'll need him earlier than we thought. I can only stay with the councilman for another half an hour or so."

"I'll take care of it."

"He might be watching the road behind him, so double back rather than go all the way to the Morgan Lake turnoff. If you can let him see you pulling back on the highway," Ella said, "that would be even better."

Ella kept her eyes on the large, white pickup slowly heading east. It was one of those trucks that had every amenity in the world and was the size of a white elephant. It must have cost him more than what three average Navajo families grossed in a year.

Ella watched Hunt as her partner got back on the road. Without a pair of binoculars the truck would have been nothing more than a white dot, but with them she could easily see that the bed of the truck was loaded with grocery sacks. She had a feeling he was delivering supplies to someone. His caution and the direction he was heading in, which would eventually take him into a very isolated area, made her suspect that he'd been on his way to see Benally.

Ella had to drive slowly in order not to get ahead of him. Soon, he came to a stop. She parked by the side of the highway and waited. She had a feeling that he was searching for another telltale trail of dust. Then, without warning, he turned the truck around and headed right back to Shiprock, crossing the river at the only bridge between Waterflow and Shiprock.

Ella couldn't figure out if he'd seen her or just suspected he was being followed. But a short time later he entered a housing area at Shiprock's northeast end, pulled into one of the driveways, and began carrying his groceries inside.

Disgusted that this operation had been a bust, Ella contacted Neskahi and turned things over to him. "Hunt's got a sixth sense when it comes to spotting a tail, so hang back and good luck."

Ella drove down the highway, lost in thought, when the back of her neck suddenly began to prickle. She glanced in her rearview mirror and saw nothing, yet her uneasiness continued. The badger fetish at her neck felt uncomfortably warm, almost hot. Acting on instinct alone, she slowed abruptly, pulling off to the shoulder of the highway beside a low mesa. Just then something shattered the windshield and she felt a slight tug on her left cheek, followed by a burning sensation that made her eyes tear automatically. As blood began dripping down her cheek, then flowing onto her neck, she realized that a bullet had creased her face.

Hitting the brakes, she grabbed the mike, keeping the vehicle under control with her other hand. "Officer needs assistance. Shots fired," she yelled. By the time the vehicle stopped she was below the dashboard, out of view.

Her cheek burned like fire, and with her head down, blood dripped freely onto the floor of the SUV. Ella waited a full five minutes, but when no other shots followed, she finally raised her head to look around. It was quiet, there weren't even any cars coming.

Ella studied the hole and the spiderweb pattern around the cracked safety glass of the windshield, then turned around and looked for an exit hole or impact site. She found another small hole in the plastic covering the rear window pillar on the driver's side. Judging from the direction she'd been traveling, and the place where the round had impacted, the sniper had been above and just ahead of her. Had she not turned, he might have scored a direct hit.

That's when Ella started to shake. If she had nine lives, as many in the department claimed, she'd used up at least half of them in the past week.

Hearing the wail of the police sirens, and aware that others were on the way, bolstered her courage. Her team would arrive shortly and they'd scour the entire area together until they found something, even if they had to stay out here all day.

———

Ella's cheek continued to bleed, and despite the annoyance of having to leave the crime scene she decided it was best to go have it checked at the hospital. After reaching into her SUV's glove compartment and grabbing the life insurance forms she'd wanted Carolyn to fill out, she met with Justine. Her partner had insisted on driving her.

"I'll drop you off, then come right back here to look around the mesa," Justine said. "I'll find the spot where the sniper was hiding. Count on it. At least we can rule out Lewis Hunt on this one."

When Ella arrived at the emergency room, a young Hispanic doctor began to work on her. "I'm hoping that you won't need stitches, but let's see how it goes."

"You're calling it, Doc," Ella said. Experience told her that Dr. Martinez was one of the many young physicians who served at the tribal hospital as a way to pay back their student loans, then would disappear as soon as their time was up.

"You got off lucky. Another few millimeters and you'd be in surgery now, a centimeter and you could have been in the morgue," Dr. Martinez said.

"You're nice and upbeat today, aren't you, Doc?" Ella smiled ruefully.

She gave Ella a sheepish grin. "A good bedside manner is hard to come by when you get four hours or less of sleep at night. But I'll work on it."

Ella was about to answer when Carolyn Roanhorse, the tribe's ME, knocked and poked her head inside. "Justine called and said you were on your way in, Investigator Clah. This is getting to be a bad habit."

"Doctor, can I help you?" Dr. Martinez asked.

"We're old friends, Doc," Ella explained.

"In that case, come in," Dr. Martinez said.

Carolyn checked the doctor's work as she treated the wound, then bandaged it. "Very nicely done," she said at last.

"Make sure it stays clean and airtight, and keep a little petroleum jelly on the bandage," Dr. Martinez told Ella. "That'll minimize scarring."

As the doctor left to take care of another patient, Carolyn looked at Ella. "She really did do a great job. She's not so good with her communication skills, but she's a very competent physician. You shouldn't have much of a scar there after it's all said and done."

"I'm glad to hear that." Ella looked at her watch and groaned. "I need to meet an informant, but I'm already late. Justine insisted on driving me here after my unit became Exhibit A, so I'm without wheels. And I absolutely refuse to call one of them away from the scene just so I can have quick transportation."

Carolyn tossed her a set of keys. "Take my car."

"This isn't what you charmingly call the 'meat wagon,' is it?" she asked, knowing that Carolyn had a warped sense of humor.

She laughed. "I considered that one, but I figured you aren't in the right mood for black humor."

"You've got that right. At the moment, what I'd really like to do is find the jackass that's using me for target practice and throw him in a cell until he rots."

"The keys I gave you are to my new Suburban," Carolyn added. "Well, it's not new, but it's new to me. Treat it gently."

"Thanks. I should be back in about an hour or so, okay? When I return can we talk? I need to ask you another favor."

"You know where to find me."

Ella called Hoskie to see if he was still at home. Apologizing for being late, she drove there quickly. He came out to meet her as soon as she pulled up.

"What took you so long? I thought maybe you'd changed your mind," he said.

"No way." She pointed to the bandage on her cheek. "I had a small accident."

He waited for her to elaborate, but when she didn't, he didn't press. "What do you need from me?" he asked, leading her inside.

They sat around a small kitchen table, and he offered her a sandwich, which she declined, and some coffee, which she accepted.

"I need to ask you about George. I know he doesn't socialize with his listeners, by and large, but who are George's closest friends at the station?"

"He's strictly business and doesn't socialize with anyone there that I know of. My wife and I invited him for dinner once but he declined, saying that he preferred to keep his business and personal life separate."

"What about when off the job? Do friends ever come visit him at the station or has he mentioned anyone specifically?"

"I don't have the remotest idea who he associates with outside the station. When we leave work, he goes his way and I go mine."

"One more important question," Ella said. "This is completely off the record, okay?"

Hoskie nodded. "You want to know about Branch's thousand-dollar offer, don't you?"

"So he did make it?"

"Hell, he even offered me a finder's fee if I could recommend someone. 'A tracker,' he said, 'bloodhounds optional.'" Hoskie smiled grimly. "He was dead serious, and was even flashing some cash. I saw it myself. But you didn't hear this from me."

"Of course not. Do you know if he found someone?" Ella watched his eyes.

Hoskie looked right back at her. "I think he did. One of the station's salesmen who goes bow hunting every season asked for the job but was turned down. George told him it was too late." Hoskie put up his hand. "And before you ask, no, I don't have any idea who it is, except they don't work at the station. Nobody's taken any time off since then. I'd know."

"Thanks for your help, Hoskie."

"I couldn't have helped you because this meeting never happened, okay?"

"Meeting? What meeting?" Ella answered. She tried to smile, but it stung her cheek and she winced.

Moments later she was on her way back to the hospital to return Carolyn's car. As she drove down the highway, she telephoned Justine and asked her for an update.

"We recovered a twenty-two shell from the foam at the bottom of the rear window pillar of your unit," she said. "It'll probably match the other round we have from the other incident. They're the same type. The bullet had to have been fired from above at really close range to even penetrate the glass. Any angle except dead on and it would have most likely bounced off. We also have vehicle tracks and shoe prints. Whoever is after you was wearing jogging shoes, not boots."

"Hey, that's something, considering boots are the order of the day on the Rez, but it still doesn't really narrow it down."

"I know. From the depth of the footprints and his stride, we figure he's five feet six or seven, and weighs about one-forty. Also his vehicle was a pickup based upon the tire size. That's all we have right now. We were hoping to find a wad of gum or cigarette butt so we can have DNA to compare to a suspect eventually, but no luck so far."

"No shell casing?"

"No. He must have picked it up or the shell wasn't ejected if it was a bolt-action rifle. We searched a fifty-foot radius."

"There are some residential areas around there and someone might have heard or seen something. Talk to everyone you can, and then go to the gasoline station on the highway about a quarter of a mile from the scene and talk to the clerk there."

"We'll take care of it. By the way, your vehicle was towed to the police garage. Larry said he'd have to get you another vehicle because requisitioning funds for a new windshield would take forever."

"I'll hitch a ride over there with Carolyn later."

"Good luck. By the way, expect Larry to talk your ear off. He's very upset that he hasn't been able to get the funds to service the units that need it, and he's already griped to me about the way you go through tires. I gather from talking to him that the department's replacement vehicles are not in great shape, so the bottom line is that I don't think you'll have much of a selection."

"I'll take whatever I can get."

"If it turns out to be inadequate, I'll trade you my unit until they get the windshield replaced on yours."

"I'll keep that in mind. And thanks."

Ella drove back to the community medical center. Parking near the side door, she took the elevator downstairs and found Carolyn in her office adjacent to the morgue going over paperwork.

"Thanks for the car," Ella said, flipping the keys back to her. "Do you have time to talk?"

"Of course."

Ella told her about the life insurance policy she was planning on taking out. "It'll cost an arm and a leg, but I need to do this for Dawn and for my own peace of mine."

"Do you have the health form they require for the physical?"

Ella reached into her shirt pocket and handed it to Carolyn.

"It's fairly straightforward. Let me give you a physical and get some basics, and then you'll be all set."

After twenty-five minutes Carolyn handed Ella the signed form. "Thanks, old friend," Ella said. "Now how about I buy you a late lunch in return for this and the ride you'll be giving me to the police department's garage afterward."

Carolyn smiled. "Pushy aren't you? But I can be bribed with food. All I've had since breakfast are candy bars and Cokes."

Ella looked at her friend. Carolyn was a large woman but she was comfortable with her size. She made no pretensions about dieting nor did she worry about her weight. She was who she was and others could either accept it or not. Her attitude and self-acceptance alone commanded the respect she deserved.

"Any particular place you want to eat?" Carolyn added.

"You pick," Ella said.

"Hey, that's dangerous. You buying, me eating."

"Not a problem." Ella grinned.

"It'll have to be off the Rez. You know how people who know what I do for a living feel about me around here." She paused, then added, "And come to think of it, it won't do you much good to be seen with me under the circumstances."

"You've heard about the news of my death being greatly exaggerated?"

Carolyn nodded. "Oh, yeah."

"Maybe Mom will be able to track down John Tso for me and hurry him up a bit. At least he knows I'm looking for him now. I'm not expecting a miracle, but I'm hoping that once people find out I've scheduled the Sing, things will get just a little easier for me."

"Wishful thinking," Carolyn said, shaking her head. "The dust won't even begin to settle until long after that Sing is done."

"It's going to be tough to schedule an entire week off for something like that. But I haven't got a choice. A lot of people won't talk to me at all now, and I think it's starting to get to me a little."

"Welcome to *my* world," Carolyn said as they got under way.

Ella felt her gut tighten as she thought about what her friend went through on a daily basis. Although her job was crucial, it had made her a pariah with the tribe. No Sing would ever gain her The People's acceptance. Many of the modernists, who by all accounts shouldn't have minded, were creeped out by what she did, and the traditionalists and new traditionalists avoided her like the plague.

Before long, Ella realized that Carolyn was driving to her own home. "Hey, I told you *I'd* treat."

"I thought of picking out a restaurant, but I have something even better in mind. I baked a chocolate torte last night that's to die for and we had a huge roast that's going to make terrific sandwiches. It'll be the best lunch around for miles. I guarantee it."

"Well, in that case, by all means, the Chez Roanhorse-Lavery it is," Ella teased.

As they pulled up to Carolyn's modest home in Fruitland, an old farming community in the river valley east of Shiprock and north of the Rez, Ella saw a large sedan parked in the driveway.

"I didn't realize Michael would be home," Carolyn said in a guarded tone.

Curious as to the reason for her friend's abrupt change of mood, Ella glanced at her friend, but her expression revealed nothing.

A moment later they went inside and Carolyn led the way into the living room. Oversized leather furniture, a kiva fireplace, and Navajo rugs gave the place a homey, comfortable feel.

Michael Lavery, Carolyn's husband, came out into the

hall and, seeing them, stopped in midstride. "Oh—I'm sorry. Did I interrupt?"

"Not at all," Carolyn said. "I was going to treat Ella to lunch. Why don't you join us?"

He shook his head. "I'm just leaving. There are some brochures I want to pick up at the travel agent's."

Carolyn's features tightened, and she pursed her lips. "Fine," she said coldly.

Ella felt the tension between them clearly as Michael nodded to Ella, then went out the front door without looking at Carolyn directly.

Avoiding Ella's gaze now, Carolyn went into the kitchen and began fixing sandwiches on French bread. "I made the French bread in the new bread maker. It's really good," she said, bringing plates with thick sandwiches to the table.

"I'm impressed," Ella said, taking a bite of the sandwich Carolyn placed in front of her. It was wonderful, the homemade bread giving it that special touch. But Ella knew that Carolyn seldom went on cooking binges unless something was bothering her.

"So what's new?" Ella asked softly.

"I'll tell you after the chocolate torte."

"Chocolate, the closest science has come to a happy pill," Ella teased.

"You bet. And there's medical data to support your conclusion," she added with a twinkle in her eye.

After they finished their sandwiches Carolyn brought out the torte. "This is to die for. Or is that phrase in bad taste right now."

They both laughed at the same time.

Ella tasted the gooey chocolate center and rich cake. "You outdid yourself with this one. I wish I could cook like this, but everything I make ends up crying out for a biohazard sticker."

Carolyn laughed. "I've tasted your cooking. The only reason you have problems is because you're never totally focused on the process. You get sidetracked too easily."

She shrugged. "Mom's a great cook and I hate competitions I can't win," Ella answered with a wry smile. "Her cooking really has spoiled my brother and me. Clifford got lucky when he married Loretta, who, in spite of her crabby attitude, is a very good cook. Like it is with Mom, there's very little she can't fix well . . . though lately, I have to say, she's seldom at home."

"I imagine now that she's working it's hard for her to be in both places at once."

"Working? I haven't heard about this. Loretta's got a job somewhere?"

"Sure. She's an executive assistant over at the college. I was there giving a lecture on forensics and I ran into her. I assumed you all knew about that. Have I let the cat out of the bag?"

"I have no idea," Ella said, considering what Carolyn had said. "But I just can't imagine Clifford approving of this. I wonder if he even knows where she is half the time these days, now that Julian is in school. My brother gets so busy with his patients sometimes he loses track of everything else."

"Marriages are tricky things, Ella. People either learn to adapt or they split up. Those are really the only two alternatives," Carolyn said somberly.

Ella looked at Carolyn. "That sounds ominous. Are *you* okay?"

Carolyn didn't reply for several moments. "Michael has been offered a grant to teach an introductory course in forensics at a university in Hawaii. He grew up in Honolulu but he hasn't been home, except for a few days at a time, in twenty-five years. He really wants to accept the offer and is pressuring me to go with him. But that'll mean being away for five months—maybe more. I can't do that, I'm needed here. The most I can see is going back and forth as often as I can, maybe a weekend a month."

Ella nodded. "Is there any way you might be able to take a leave of absence?"

"Now *you* sound like him," she said sharply, then exhaled and forced a smile. "I suppose I could, but you and I both know that would leave the tribe in a lurch. Face it, I'm working a job no one else wants. The tribe has a hard enough time finding general practitioners as it is. Unless they've got a loan to pay off, most don't want to work on the Rez."

She understood Carolyn's sense of duty because that was a trait they both shared. "If there's anything I can do to make things easier for you, anything at all, just let me know."

"Thanks. I may need someone to talk to . . ."

"I'm here now, and I'll be here whenever you need me."

Carolyn smiled and nodded. "You're a good friend."

"Does that mean I can have an extra slice of that torte to go?" Ella countered with a smile.

"You bet." She cut another slice and placed it in a small plastic container. "Now let's go get your wheels."

"Which I hope will be attached to something more than a horse-drawn wagon. With our budget these days, one never knows."

FOURTEEN
——— ✖ ✖ ✖ ———

Carolyn dropped Ella off at the department's garage twenty-five minutes later. As she strode into the cluttered office of the large metal building, Ella found no one about except an old mutt who lifted his head to look at her as she came in.

"Hi Rip. Don't get up for me," Ella said. Larry had named the dog Rip, after Rip Van Winkle, because all he ever seemed to do was sleep.

"Hello? Anyone here?" Ella called out, noticing that the dog had already closed his eyes again.

A moment later, Larry Jim, the department's chief and currently only mechanic, came through the door leading in from one of the garage bays, wiping his hands on a rag. "Oh, it's Evel Knievel Clah. Your unit is here, but replacing that windshield isn't going to be easy. It's not that the part is hard to get. The problem will be getting the funding. I've put in a requisition form, but it usually takes a month or more these days."

"I'm still going to need another set of wheels right away. What have you got for me?"

"Not much." Larry waved for her to follow and he led her around the building to a fenced-in compound.

When Ella got into the replacement SUV, she nearly

choked. Driving with the windows rolled down would be a must until she could locate some air freshener. The interior reeked of engine oil and another pungent odor she recognized a breath later. "Was this sprayed by a skunk?"

"Yeah, but it was weeks ago. We wiped it down with tomato juice or you wouldn't be able to get within a mile of it. The problem is that these days tomato juice doesn't have the acid kick that it used to." He shrugged. "You'll get used to it. And one more thing. The driver's side door won't lock. Don't leave anything inside it at night."

Ella's first stop was at the closest convenience store, where she bought a can of odor killer along with one of those little pine tree–shaped air fresheners. After spraying down the interior, she hung the little air freshener from the rearview mirror. It helped some.

Ella went to the station after that and immediately headed to Justine's lab. Her assistant was working hard. "Anything new?" Ella asked.

"The ground beef that was meant for your dog wasn't poisoned, but it was loaded with crushed glass. As for the animal trap, it's pretty old. Though it's obvious someone sharpened the blades and made an effort to get it working, we have no way of tracing it. I haven't been able to find anyone who still uses animal traps like these. Coyote traps, still in use in some places, are completely different than these oldies."

"Okay. Thanks for letting me know."

"Also, Neskahi is watching Hunt as we speak. He's confident the councilman won't spot him."

"Anything from Tache?"

"Branch wasn't around the property, so Ralph took a look around what was left of his house. All he found were a few owl feathers scattered near the back of the residence. It wasn't noted in the police report, so either they missed them, didn't write it down, or they simply weren't there at the time. Owls live in this area, so it may mean nothing, but since that bird is considered a harbinger of death, he wanted to pass it along."

"That either points to someone who's Navajo—or a cat who got lucky—but make sure Tache tells Sheriff Taylor. Anything else?" Ella asked.

"Just one more thing. A little while ago I heard a rumor that Branch's show is being canceled or shelved, but I haven't been able to confirm that yet."

"If it's true, try to find out why. You can report to me and the team tomorrow. First thing in the morning, we'll need to meet in my office."

It was shortly after nine A.M. the next day when Tache, Justine, and Ella gathered for a briefing session. Neskahi had worked all night and was off this morning.

Ella shared the information about Branch's tracker and asked everyone to try to find out who he might have hired. Then she asked the others to report their progress.

"I've got nothing new to add, except a verification of what you already know," Officer Tache said.

Ella looked at Justine. "Have you been able to confirm if George Branch's program is being taken off the air?"

"Yeah. It seems that the show will stay on but without Branch. I spoke to the station manager this morning. Despite higher ratings, they've had a problem with several of their biggest sponsors. One, a car dealer, was worried about the ambiguity surrounding Branch's role in the death of the councilman's wife. He thought it might damage his company's image if he continued to run radio spots in that time slot.

"Another of the more conservative companies who make up the bulk of his sponsorship also pulled out because of all the controversy. But when they threatened to stop advertising on that radio station completely, Branch was told to go on vacation until the smoke clears. One of Branch's assistants is taking over for now, a Navajo named Hoskie Ben. He's been told not to discuss either Branch or the controversy on the air."

Ella nodded. Hoskie was finally going to get his shot at afternoon drive time radio. It didn't surprise her. She'd had a feeling all along that he'd succeed. "This will hopefully buy us some peace and quiet for a little while anyway."

After their meeting ended, Ella checked her phone messages. Clifford had called and so had her mother. Ella called Rose first, hoping that one of her friends had tracked down John Tso.

Her mother was waiting for her call and picked up the phone on the first ring. "I wanted to tell you that even though some of my friends have gone out to search for the Singer, no one's had any luck yet. But don't worry. Your brother and I will continue looking."

Ella called Clifford next, wondering if that was why he'd called. Loretta answered the phone.

"Hey, I hear you've got a new job," Ella said, keeping her voice casual.

Loretta didn't say a word for several seconds, then finally answered. "Have you told anyone else about this?" she asked, biting off the words.

"No, why? Doesn't my brother know?"

"It's only been a few mornings so far and I haven't had a chance to discuss it with him. He's been very busy," Loretta said in a tone totally devoid of emotion.

"It's not really my business, but perhaps you should bring up the subject pretty soon," Ella replied. "Someone's bound to mention it, you know. The Rez isn't a great place for secrets."

"I'm aware of that. I intend to speak to him about it later today," she answered coldly. "Shall I go get your brother for you? He's in the medicine hogan right now, waiting for his next patient."

"Yes, please."

Ella heard Loretta walk away. A minute later she heard footsteps, then Clifford picked up the phone.

"I tried to get hold of you earlier, so I could warn you. You may find yourself encountering an additional problem when you deal with our traditionalists."

"What now?"

He took a deep breath before answering and that alone told her that he loathed what he was about to tell her. "After you rescued my son, my wife began to get worried about his contact with you during and after the accident. She asked that I do a blessing prayer for him and I did. Your daughter and our mother were included in that. We were careful to keep it quiet and only told your baby-sitter's family because we felt they'd need the reassurance before they'd allow Boots to come to work at the house. But we asked them not to discuss it with anyone else since we felt that it would only complicate things for you."

"All that happened while I was still in the hospital, right? Why are you telling me now?"

"Late yesterday, one of my patients asked me why I'd protected my son with a blessing if I didn't really believe that my sister was a danger to all around her."

"How did he know you'd done the ritual?"

"It seems my wife didn't realize that we needed to continue to keep things a secret for a while longer."

"I'd like to speak to her."

"Of course."

Loretta got back on the phone. "I'm sorry. I really didn't think I was supposed to keep it a secret forever."

"Not forever, just until we could locate the proper Singer. You seem to be better at keeping your own secrets than mine or your husband's."

Ella could almost hear Loretta's blood starting to boil.

Finally Loretta spoke, her voice low and cutting. "You

want a scapegoat, Sister-in-law, but I won't be one for you. Many people consider you a danger, not just myself. You have to live with that fact, and fix it as soon as you can. If you think it's just a few of the conservatives among us that are creating a problem for you, you're wrong. Even some of the new traditionalists at the college have concerns about you now."

"Who?" Ella knew already, but wanted to see how far it had traveled.

"Professor Garnenez and many of his students have been trying to find the Singer you need because they know that people around you these days tend to end up dead. Death doesn't touch you, but it sure does seem to reach whoever you have a problem with." Loretta paused to catch her breath. "And even if you discount all of that, you can't dismiss what it's costing all of us who are related to you. We're paying a price too. You should talk to your mother and see what it's costing her."

"I'll talk to my mother," Ella said, pausing for effect, "and you can talk to your husband." Then she slammed the phone down.

A heartbeat later Ella suddenly realized what her burst of anger had just cost her. By letting Loretta get to her, she'd lost the opportunity to ask her sister-in-law just how well she knew Professor Garnenez. Loretta might have been in a perfect position to help her. Although the man had an alibi, Ella still had the feeling that she should keep an eye on Garnenez. He had certainly been keeping an eye on her.

Remembering what Loretta had intimated about trouble at home, Ella started to call Rose but then decided against it. Clifford's wife had a way of overstating matters so it was probably not a big deal. She'd talk to Rose later. No matter what her sister-in-law had said, Ella was convinced Rose could handle whatever was thrown at her.

Focusing on the present, Ella realized that now more than

ever it was imperative she find someone to watch her house at night. Leaving her office she walked down the hall and asked several officers she met around the station, but most of them were already pulling long shifts. The department was stretched to the limit. She did get a few names of retired officers, though according to Big Ed, none lived in the immediate area anymore.

Remembering Emily Marquez, Ella returned to her office, looked up her number, and called her next. Maybe she could suggest someone.

The sheriff's department operator said Emily was off-duty, so Ella called her at home. Emily didn't pick up right away, something that surprised Ella. Emily had struck her as a workaholic who lived with the cell phone within arm's reach.

Emily greeted her warmly a minute later. "Sorry it took me so long to answer," she said, as if reading Ella's mind. "I was in the greenhouse with my hands full of moist potting soil. I'm off today. What's up?"

"I wanted to ask you if you knew anyone who would be willing to moonlight, literally, for the next week. I need someone to watch my house at night," she said, and explained.

"Hey, I'm working days and could use the extra money. I have a PI friend who can lend me his nightscope, and should be able to spot anyone who tries to set another of those traps. I'll take from eight to midnight, and should be able to find another off-duty deputy to cover the midnight to dawn hours. When do you want us to start? Tonight?"

"Yes, thanks. Come right after sundown so you can get a good look at the layout before it gets completely dark and be introduced to the dog and pony. If I'm not there, Mom should be. And if there's ever any problem while you or the other officer are on watch, call me immediately. I'll be your backup."

"Sounds good. Shall I have my relief officer stay until

sunrise? That way if anyone plans something while you're still half asleep, he'll be around."

"Sounds terrific. But I want you and him to keep a low profile. Word travels fast around here and I'd rather not tip off whoever's been staking out my place."

"Not a problem. We'll work it like a stakeout, but use our personal vehicles, of course."

As Ella hung up, she felt much better knowing that her home would be covered. During the day the house was filled with activity. Others working with her mother on the plant survey and environmental issues would drop by, and Boots, more often than not, was there, too. Nights were a different story. Rose had meetings two or three times a week. As for herself, Ella knew that now that she was working a case, she could count on being late almost daily. That meant that Boots would be alone with Dawn a lot. With Emily or another deputy there to watch over them, she'd breathe easier.

Ella picked up her keys and headed outside to her replacement vehicle. She'd pay Wilson Joe a visit next. She needed to learn more about Professor Garnenez's activities and find someone who could keep tabs on what he was saying and doing around campus.

Ella reached her car, opened the door, and froze. On the driver's seat was a knife. The blade was crude and white, fashioned out of bone—a skinwalker weapon.

Ella reached for her latex gloves, then picked it up and studied it more closely. Just then, Big Ed, who'd come out of the building, walked by. Seeing what was in her hand, he stopped for a look.

"Shorty, what the heck are you doing with that?"

Ella glanced up, realizing how it looked, and called his attention to her latex gloves. "I'm hoping we can get some prints so I can properly thank whoever left me this little gift."

An hour later Justine and Ella were with the chief in his office. Justine looked worried, the chief angry, and Ella was trying not to let either guess how unsettling this had been for her.

"I found no prints at all. Everything was so clean it all but sparkled," Justine said. "I even checked the door handle and the hood right above the door, since people often rest their hands there when they're putting something inside. But I struck out."

"If anyone had seen that thing in my unit they would have assumed it belonged to me," Ella said through clenched teeth.

"Did you leave the vehicle unlocked?" Big Ed asked.

"It doesn't lock properly. Larry warned me about that," Ella answered.

"And by now everyone knows that the green SUV is your replacement vehicle, so that won't tell us anything," Justine said.

"We're stuck, Shorty. No crime was committed. They didn't take anything *out*, they just left something behind. And that knife isn't contraband, though here on the Rez it should be."

"Tache asked around, but no one saw anything unusual," Justine said. "I wish we could afford a surveillance system for the parking lot."

"It took a lot of guts to do this in the middle of the day," the chief growled.

"Agreed," Ella answered, "though with the door unlocked it wouldn't take long."

"Shorty, I hate to say this, but you better start watching your back even here at the station, at least until we know what's going on."

"I just had an interesting thought," Ella said. "Maybe this wasn't left by someone trying to frame me. Maybe it's a recruitment invitation. If they think I'm mostly evil now . . ."

"The fact that it happened here on our lot makes that even worse news," Big Ed answered.

FIFTEEN
✖ ✖ ✖

Ella drove home slowly, needing to get her thoughts in order. She'd been working long hours lately so taking an hour or so off during the day wasn't a problem.

Today was an in-service day for teachers, so she knew that Boots and Dawn would both be at the house now. As she walked in, Rose was talking to someone on the phone, but her mother pointed to Herman Cloud's metal detector, which was standing in the corner, and gave her a thumbs-up. Apparently no more traps had been found. Ella waved at her, then went outside to join her daughter who was riding under Boots's supervision.

At Dawn's insistence Ella took over for Boots. Taking the reins, she led the pony out of the arena while Dawn continued to ride him. This was a special treat that Dawn was not allowed to attempt on her own under any circumstances. No matter how gentle a horse or pony seemed to be, they were basically unpredictable animals, especially outside the corral where the animal was bound to encounter more distractions. Where Dawn was concerned, she'd always err on the side of caution, and today, despite having had the area searched for traps, she kept a close eye out for anything unusual and avoided the regular paths.

Her daughter chattered nonstop, but Ella enjoyed hearing Dawn talk about her friends and her riding lessons. By the time they returned to the arena and Dawn helped her unsaddle the pony, Ella had finally managed to unwind.

Ella put away the saddle and tack, then stopped to speak to Boots while Dawn stood on her mounting block and brushed the pony's mane.

"Would you keep her out here for a bit, Boots? I need to talk to Mom."

"No problem. Getting your daughter to leave the pony and go back inside—that's the hard part," Boots said with a smile.

Ella found her mother in the living room at the table with a large map and notes and drawings she'd made as part of her plant survey work.

Ella sat on the sofa facing her. "Mom, I hate to interrupt you but I spoke to my sister-in-law earlier and there's something I need to ask you."

Rose looked up and nodded. "I know. Your brother warned me."

"What's been going on? Is there something I should know about?"

"Things have grown a little complicated lately, but as you say all the time about yourself, I'm handling it."

"I'd still like to know what's going on."

"All right." Rose pushed the papers aside and looked at Ella. "What my daughter-in-law was referring to is that I'm not really welcome at the Plant Watchers meetings anymore. I can attend, but everyone except my close friend keeps their distance from me."

"Because of me?"

"Partly. But mostly it's a protest. They strongly believe that I should have made you drop everything to find the Singer. In their defense I have to say that they're truly worried. The stories . . ."

"I'm sorry about that. But I do have a full-time—actually more than full-time—job, Mom."

"I know. As I said I can handle this problem with the Plant Watchers. I'm far more worried about your daughter. Today she told me that no one except her best friend will play with her anymore."

Ella felt her chest tighten as she took in the news. She'd hoped her daughter and her friends would be too young to be affected by this. But at least Dawn's best friend, Cecelia Light, came from a family of modernist Christians who wouldn't be bothered by any of this. Her daughter would have an ally.

"Her friend's parents have made it clear that they won't condone superstition. Their church views what happened to you as a blessing," Rose said. "But that isn't true for every denomination, or even from family to family. It seems they're as divided as we are."

"I hate the idea of *anyone* giving my daughter a hard time." Ella stood and paced around the room. "Mom, do you think I should move out for a while? Would it make life easier for you and my daughter?"

"It would make things easier here, yes, but it may create a new problem all its own. Some might think that I have finally come to believe the stories about you and have asked you to leave. There's no telling what new trouble that'll create."

"Let me give this some thought. My daughter and you are my priorities now."

Ella drove back to her office and sat down to go over the cases she was working on. Cardell Benally was still missing and, so far, nobody in the law enforcement community had turned up a thing. In the meantime, Lewis Hunt was stirring up whatever trouble he could, trying to build support for Cardell by convincing as many people as possible that Branch had deserved what he'd gotten. Somehow she'd have to track Cardell down and bring him in, though there was a good chance the courts would let him off with a slap on the wrist and he would end up being a local hero. It was frustrating, and with all the trouble her own family was facing, Ella felt particularly wrung out.

As she sat there, she thought about Cardell and Hunt, then remembered how Hunt's assistant had verified his statements without question earlier.

Hunt's attempt to supply Cardell had failed, but she knew Hunt would try again, or find someone else to do it for him now that he knew he was being monitored. The woman assistant was a perfect candidate, especially if she was as loyal to Lewis as she had appeared to be earlier.

Ella stood, put away her paperwork, and headed for Hunt's office. She'd keep an eye on Hunt's assistant for a few hours after the woman got off work and see if her instincts were correct.

Five minutes later Ella parked down the street from Hunt's office, close enough to watch the parking lot but far enough away to avoid being recognized. Pulling out her pair of binoculars, she waited, checking her watch from time to time. Hunt, who hadn't been followed today after he was tracked to work, was at work, apparently. His own vehicle was still in the parking lot.

Not knowing exactly when the woman would leave, but figuring it would be between four-thirty and five, Ella was surprised when the woman came out at four-fifteen, in an apparent hurry, and left in a blue Chevy van.

Ella had no trouble at all following her down into the valley to the grocery store. Less than fifteen minutes had passed when the woman came out to her van, opened the side door, and transferred food items to a big black plastic trash bag she'd also purchased. Then she got inside the van and drove east out of Shiprock down Highway 64.

Ella picked up her cell phone, dialed Justine, and filled her in.

"Do you want me to cover Lewis Hunt when he gets off work today?"

"Yes. You just made me realize that this woman might be creating a diversion to lure us away from Hunt. Get to his office as quickly as you can. Let's see what he does. Stay in touch."

Ella ended the call, then slowed as she saw the Chevy van pull off the highway and head down a dirt road leading toward the river. By now they were off the Rez, at least on this side of the river. But this was too good of an opportunity to pass up, and because Cardell Benally was being sought by more than one agency, there wouldn't be any major jurisdictional problems. If she caught up with Cardell off Rez land, she'd hold him there and send for the county sheriff.

Ella pulled over to the side of the highway, then waited, watching the Chevy van through her binoculars as it crept down the road between two cornfields. The vehicle crossed over a high spot where a small irrigation ditch passed underneath in a culvert, then nearly disappeared from view as it turned to the left and proceeded down an apparent road beyond the built-up levee surrounding the ditch. Farther south was the river bosque. All Ella could see was the upper half of the van, but Ella knew the general layout of the area and was comfortable continuing slowly down the highway, driving parallel and to the rear of the woman's vehicle.

Fields of alfalfa, corn, and melons, with the occasional apple orchard, lined this side of the river for a distance ranging from a quarter to a half mile until they reached the highway. Usually, access roads between fields made it possible to reach the bosque, the forested area of mostly cottonwoods, salt cedars, and willows lining the riverbanks.

The van stopped at one of the intersections between the

river road and a perpendicular track leading to the highway, so Ella stopped as well, reaching over for her binoculars.

Hunt's assistant climbed out of the van, looked around, then quickly opened the van's side door. Ella could see the black trash bag containing the food supplies in her hand as she walked around to the passenger side, disappearing for a moment on the bosque side of the road. Then the woman jogged back to the driver's side, jumped inside, and drove off toward the highway.

Ella kept her binoculars on the spot where Hunt's assistant had climbed out of the van. She couldn't see anyone at all, but the top of the black bag was visible beside a gnarled old cottonwood tree. Across the road from the tree a red survey flag, nothing more than a strip of bright plastic, was tied to a bush.

"X marks the spot," Ella muttered to herself. "All I have to do now is wait for Cardell to show up."

Ella ducked down as the Chevy van reached the highway less than a quarter mile ahead, then waited until the van passed by on the opposite side of the four-lane road, heading back to Shiprock.

Once the woman was gone, Ella checked to make sure the black bag hadn't been disturbed, then quickly drove farther east, maneuvering around so she could stake out the black bag from a better vantage point. As she drove, Ella called Justine and updated her, telling her to leave Hunt and come to provide backup for her.

Parking on the side of the ditch road opposite the bosque, Ella climbed out of her vehicle and walked quietly down the field side of the narrow irrigation ditch, which was dry at the moment. Chances were Cardell would approach from the bosque side where concealment was possible. Beyond that was the river, and on the far bank, Navajo land.

Knowing Justine was probably fifteen or more minutes away, Ella hoped that Cardell would take his time making the pickup. Crouching low, she moved up the embankment to take a look.

Cardell was already there! He had to have crawled up on his belly, or else darted out from behind cover while she'd been moving forward. Wearing a desert-style camouflage shirt and jeans, he was nearly invisible in the shade of the cottonwood tree. As a squirrel scampered into some brush, Cardell's gaze swept over the area and came to rest on her.

"What the hell," Ella grumbled, and stood up so he could see her clearly now though he was a hundred feet away. The former officer was barrel-chested and nearly six feet tall, but didn't appear to be armed. "Police officer, Mr. Benally. I need to ask you a few questions. Don't move." She placed her hand on the butt of her pistol and held out her badge as she started walking toward him.

Benally grabbed the bag and ran into the bosque.

"Crap!" Ella sprinted across the narrow road after Cardell. Maybe having the food would slow him down.

Cardell ran parallel to the river, moving west, zigzagging around trees and brush, occasionally hurdling a low log or branch and cradling the plastic bag against his chest.

The ground was quite sandy in places, with stubborn clumps of grass that made the surface uneven and hard to run in. But her hands were free and she could make better speed than Cardell, who was protecting his food source.

Ella thought about yelling out at the man, but she needed the air if she was going to close the gap between them. Benally was several years older than she was but obviously in good shape. She could have used a horse right now. She wasn't getting any younger.

Suddenly Cardell swerved to the left, heading for a narrow gap in the willows that lined the river's banks. He didn't have a chance making good time along the shore, she knew that. The river bottom was quite rocky along this section, and the steep banks dropped down almost twenty feet to the river level.

The river itself was split into two channels here, divided by a half-mile-long sandy island nearly in the middle. It also made a long curve and the inside channel was narrow and deep. He'd have a hard time swimming across with the bag.

Ella slowed down as she bounded up the ten-foot-high ridge of sandy earth held in place by the purple-gray willows and some kind of long-bladed grass. Now she could smell the river, the damp earth, and the vegetation that was blessed by abundant water most of the time. Cardell Benally was down below there somewhere, hiding.

The bosque was thick in this section and several old cottonwoods had long branches dangling out over the rocky riverbed. When she didn't see Cardell, she looked for tracks, and spotted them immediately.

Moving along the high ground above the river, she stopped to listen and heard the trickle of water to the right, and some kind of creaking noise. Looking up through the foliage she saw two ropes had been tied to a stout cottonwood branch, one about four feet above the other. From the direction they led, she knew instantly that Cardell had prepared a rope bridge so he could cross the river and avoid pursuit by a vehicle.

Ella ran up to the branch, climbed up the rough bark two feet, then grabbed the top rope, inching her feet out onto the bottom strand carefully like a tightrope walker. On an afterthought, she took her cell phone from her waist and placed it into her breast pocket.

Cardell had his side to her, and was thirty feet farther out along the drooping ropes, sliding his hands and feet along, crossing over the narrow rushing water just two feet below him. He was almost across already and approaching the anchoring tree growing out of the island.

If she tried to swim the gap instead of crossing over the rope bridge, she'd be swept fifty yards or more downstream and probably be exhausted by the time she made it across. This was the only way. Hanging on tightly, she began to slide her feet along the bottom rope, holding on to the top rope for balance as she inched out over the water.

"Go back!" Cardell yelled, his voice just audible above the sound of the river. He'd obviously felt her body motion once she stepped onto the rope.

"You come back here, Cardell. I've got to take you in for questioning," Ella shouted, but she didn't bother looking in his direction. She was concentrating too hard on keeping her balance as she slid her feet along the rope.

"Don't you believe in justice, Clah?" Cardell yelled back.

"That's not my call, Benally. We only investigate and arrest. You were a cop, you know that." Ella glanced up and saw that he'd already reached the far side and was scrambling onto the other tree.

Cardell wedged the food bag between a junction of two lower branches, then turned around to look at her. "Go back, Clah. I don't want you to get hurt."

"Innocent people don't hurt others," Ella yelled back, now reaching the halfway point. She was confident enough now to keep her eyes on Cardell as she inched along the rope by feel alone.

"Get ready to grab onto the bottom rope, please," he yelled, and Ella saw that he had a shiny hunting knife in his hand.

"No!" Ella watched helplessly as he chopped the upper rope with the blade. It quickly went slack in her hands and she found herself swaying back and forth. Knowing she'd never be able to walk the bottom rope without something to hold on to for balance, she bent down as carefully as she could. Grabbing the bottom rope firmly, she allowed her feet to slip off the rope into the rushing river.

The water was freezing and she gasped, but she managed to hold on tightly to the still-attached bottom line so she could keep the current from sweeping her downstream. Holding her upper body above the water, her legs not touching the bottom, she kicked to help out her straining arms.

"Just pull yourself along arm over arm, Officer. You'll be okay," Cardell said reassuringly, then disappeared into the brush along with his black food sack.

"Thanks for nothing," Ella yelled, then realized she needed to save her strength for the ten feet she still had to go.

Less than three minutes later, sore muscles protesting, Ella hauled herself up onto level ground and looked for tracks in the sand. She found them right away. As she moved in that direction, she brought out her cell phone, which, after shaking it a bit, still worked.

The sound of a car engine distracted her for a second, and she turned in time to see a pickup heading south away from the river. Cardell would be long gone before Justine could reach the spot and she wasn't about to catch him on foot.

"Justine?" Ella sat down on a dry rock, noting that she still had to wade across a slow-moving, shallow lagoon before she'd be across the river completely. "Take the bridge just west of Hogback and go down the dirt road on the south side of the river. I'll be waiting for you, on foot."

"What about Cardell Benally?" Justine asked.

"He got away. I got wet."

The following morning as Rose, Ella, Boots, and Dawn were at the breakfast table, the Hollywood producer called. Ella spoke to the man for several minutes asking, as Kevin had suggested, for time to get an attorney who could handle the negotiations. When she hung up and looked back toward the table, Ella saw Rose's gaze riveted on her.

"I'm surprised he called you on a Saturday. He must really want you to sign." Seeing Ella shrug, she added, "You sounded prepared. Were you?" Rose asked.

"I'd spoken to my daughter's father about this already. But to be honest, if nothing comes of it, I won't exactly go into mourning. I have some serious misgivings."

Hearing footsteps behind her, Ella turned her head and saw Justine come in through the kitchen door. Hoping she'd brought some good news, Ella offered her a cup of coffee, then went into the next room with her. "I thought I detected a gleam in your eyes, Justine. Do you have something for me?"

"The bad news first. Nobody has managed to find any sign of Cardell Benally south or north of the river. But on the good news side, after dropping you off at your vehicle yesterday, I called my gunsmith in Farmington and asked him about a tracker. He called me back this morning and gave me a name. The best one in the area is supposed to be a guy named Daniel Smart.

"Paul, the same gunsmith who helps me with the special pistol grips I need, asked one of his fishing buddies about Daniel, and get this—Daniel isn't available right now, according to his family, because he's hired out."

"I know that name. Do we have an address on the Smarts?"

"Such as it is. They live in a small, protected valley in the foothills near Toadlena, south of Shiprock. They have no phone and no running water unless you count the spring outside."

Ella had heard about the Smarts, a family of hard-core traditionalists who grew their own food and stayed away from modernists as much as possible. There were three boys in the family but the middle son had moved away. The oldest, Daniel, had enlisted in the military but returned after his hitch was up. The youngest, Raymus, had been home-schooled and must have been in his twenties by now.

"I think Big Ed might be able to tell us more about this family. He has relatives down that way. I'll go talk to him. In the meantime, see what you can find out about Daniel Smart. I'll meet you back at the office later."

"Try to stay out of the water today, Cuz," Justine suggested solemnly, taking a sip of coffee.

After Justine left, Ella went back to her room. Justine's joking about water had reminded her of something. The orchid that Emily had given her was in the window, but it looked terrible. The leaves were turning brown, and the flowers had all fallen off.

"*Shimá*," Dawn said as she came into the room. She always used the Navajo word for "mother" that Rose had taught her. "Will you take Wind and me for a walk today, too?"

"I can't promise. I'm not sure what time I'll be back, Pumpkin. But I'll try."

Dawn walked to where Ella kept the plant and looked at it. "It doesn't like it in your room. It's sad here," she said in a pouty voice. Then brightening up as an idea came to her, she added, "Can I have it?"

Ella looked at her daughter and got the distinct impression that this was important to her. "What would you do with it?"

"Water it and make sure it's happy."

"How would you do that?"

"I can learn from *Shimasání*," she said, referring to her grandmother. "Maybe I can make it pretty again."

Ella brought down the small pot. It wasn't going to survive where it was now anyway. "All right. We'll take it to your room."

Rose, who was bringing laundry down the hall, saw them. "What are you doing with that?"

Ella explained.

Rose looked at her granddaughter. "This kind of plant is difficult to keep. It may die no matter what you do. Are you sure you want to try and save it?"

Dawn nodded.

"All right then," Rose said.

Ella placed the small pot in Dawn's windowsill, then kissed her daughter good-bye.

As Ella headed for the door, Rose came to meet her. "Your daughter is growing up quickly. She wants to be given more responsibility. Yesterday she told Boots that she wanted to feed the pony herself. She barely managed to carry the flake of hay but, somehow, she did it." Rose paused. "She reminds me a lot of you at that age. You were just as independent as she is and hated it when anyone thought of you as a baby."

"But she's still a child," Ella said softly.

"Yes, but the personality of the woman she will be some-day is starting to take shape right before our eyes."

"I wish I could stay home with her more," Ella said, then looked down at her wristwatch.

"Go," Rose said, reading her mind. "Your work is impor-tant also."

Giving her mother a quick hug, Ella rushed out the door. Someday she'd figure out how to be all things at once.

SIXTEEN

✖ ✖ ✖

When Ella arrived at the police station Justine met her in the hall outside her office. "Big Ed wants to see us right now. I think he's still worried about the little present someone left in your car. He hasn't said so—and neither have you, for that matter—but I know you're both aware that we could have a skinwalker cop."

Ella exhaled softly. "It's happened before," she said. "But I think it's way too soon to assume that."

Ella walked with Justine to Big Ed's office, then knocked. Big Ed waved for them to enter.

"No more news on Cardell Benally since yesterday's adventure?"

Ella rolled her eyes and noticed Justine was trying to keep a straight face. "Nothing to report," Ella finally said, afraid that Justine would make some comment about that being "water under the bridge."

"Then bring me up to speed on where other things stand right now," he asked, rocking back and forth in his chair.

"Our progress on all fronts has been slow, but maybe talking to the Smarts will fix that," she said, explaining. "We're planning to go out there today."

"They might not have much to say," Big Ed warned. "They barely talk to my family who lives down there. They're really a lot more traditional than anyone else I've met. But what about Cardell? He's obviously going to be playing this game with us now. What else are you doing to find him?"

"Yesterday evening I put out another bulletin on him with state agencies, but he's going to be staying low. We know for certain now that Hunt and some of the locals are helping him," Ella said.

"His assistant claims she was leaving food for a hobo she'd seen living down by the river," Justine said. "Hunt backs her up, and told us to prove otherwise."

"Arresting the woman would only make things worse," Ella added. "Cardell is a hero to many who believe he's provided a measure of justice—Anglo law notwithstanding."

"Four Corners Robin Hood notwithstanding, we need to do something to flush him out into the open," Big Ed said.

"Maybe we can set a fire under Hunt—something that'll make him run to Cardell. But it'll have to be well planned or Hunt will see right through it. He's a sharp cookie and a good game player."

"Any ideas?" Justine asked.

"One—providing Kevin Tolino will help me," Ella said. "I want him to pass the word to Hunt that Branch hired someone really dangerous to hunt down Benally. I think that'll get Hunt to act and if we can maintain surveillance, he should lead us right to him."

"The councilman is tough to trail. He's careful and observant," Justine said. "And he's obviously been busy manipulating public opinion, trying to promote the notion of Navajo vigilante justice."

"Following him is still our best bet. I could bring in Ralph Tache and all of us can do split shifts," Ella said.

Big Ed nodded. "Try it, Shorty, but be sure to give some time to finding out who's been taking potshots at you. A very disturbing thought occurred to me this morning as I recalled the item left in your unit." He met her gaze and held it.

"Someone could be out to ruin your reputation, Shorty, so when they actually whack you, it won't seem like such a loss to the tribe."

Ella nodded slowly. There were too many possibilities, but not enough facts. "Lucky for me that I found that knife and got it out of sight before the shift change," Ella said. "But even so, some people may have seen it was there before I did."

"Any ideas about the identity of the sniper with the twenty-two?" Big Ed asked.

"Cardell Benally should be ruled out. He had the chance yesterday to do me harm, but warned me instead. I did have a possible suspect in Professor Garnenez, but his alibi was pretty solid, I thought."

"What about one of his students?"

"I intend to check that out later today, but first I wanted to pay the Smarts a visit."

"Stay sharp out there, Shorty. One of the boys, I don't remember which one, got into a brawl after a Chapter House meeting one night and dropped three good-sized men."

"I'll let you know what we find out."

They set out in Justine's vehicle and soon left Shiprock behind on their way south. Ella watched the desert stretch out before them. Occasionally the terrain would be broken up by a barren mesa to the left or right or a deep arroyo winding downslope from the mountains to the west. Most of the land here had been carved by wind and water, but it was difficult to imagine where the water had come from. Ella couldn't even remember the last time they'd had a really big rainstorm over here.

They turned west from the main highway, and after passing a solitary trading post with a few vehicles parked out front, the desert rose gently toward the foothills of the gray-brown Chuska Mountains.

"It's just plain lonely out here, isn't it?" Ella observed.

"I don't know why anyone chooses to live out here. Maybe I'm too much of a modernist, but to me hardship is no phone and no Internet," Justine said with a tiny smile. "Without those, my social life—what there is of it—would finally wither and die."

"I think mine already has," Ella said with a quiet sigh.

"You're not seeing Harry anymore? I suppose that explains why he didn't come to the hospital or back to the Rez after your accident," she added.

"Things haven't been working out for some time," Ella admitted. "His life isn't here on the Rez anymore, but mine is. I thought we'd be able to keep things going anyway, but that's not the way it went."

"You sound more resigned than sorry."

"I am," Ella admitted. "I liked Harry but now we just have to say what needs to be said and go on."

"But neither of you has made that move?"

Ella shook her head. "No, but next time I talk to him, I'll end it."

"Then what?"

"I don't know. When I was trapped in that mine, I got a whole new perspective on myself and my life. My work will always be a part of me, but I want more than that. I know the dating pool is getting pretty small for me now, but I'd like to remarry if I can find the right man for me. Down in that hole I realized that I go from day to day, doing my duty and trying to fit everything in, but to really *live* life, you have to reach beyond that. In short, as my mom would say, I don't have balance, so I don't walk in beauty."

Justine nodded. "I think it's the same way for most of us in law enforcement. It's a hard job to leave at the office, so to speak. And since we see the worst of human nature, we become more jaded and cautious about our relationships. We tend to see the bad in a person a lot faster than we see the good."

"My mother was right. I should have married a Rez doctor, so I could stay home and have babies," Ella said, then burst out laughing.

"Oh, yeah, that's you, all right."

It took them another hour, the last fifteen driving down two ruts that pretended to be a road, to get to the Smarts' hogan. It was a large one by most standards, constructed of pine logs that must have been hauled down the mountain. There were horses munching on hay in wooden troughs and a big wagon with rubber tires that looked as if it was used frequently. "I think they all live in there in one big room," Justine said.

"I couldn't do it," Ella said truthfully. "No walls, just one big family with no privacy? No way. Could you pull it off?"

"Not in a million years."

Ella watched the entrance to the hogan, which was covered by a heavy wool blanket, and saw someone peer out. "They know we're here," she said.

Just then a tall, lean Navajo man in his twenties came out and walked toward the unit. He was wearing jeans and a loose flannel shirt. "This must be Raymus," Ella said, getting out.

The moment he saw her he stopped in his tracks, his gaze direct and challenging. "You're not welcome here."

Ella pushed her jacket back, making sure he could see the medicine pouch she wore at her waist, but it didn't seem to calm him.

Ella caught a glimpse of the flint amulet he wore around his neck before he reached up and grasped it in his fist.

"I'd like to speak with your family," Justine said, coming forward.

He looked at her, then shook his head. "You can't enter the hogan. You've been riding with her and until she has the Sing done she contaminates whoever she's near. The cross you wear around your neck can't protect you."

Justine's expression hardened. "I'm here on official police business. If you won't talk to either of us here, we can do it at the station."

Ella was surprised by her cousin's determination. Somewhere along the way Justine had become a force to be reckoned with.

"If we do that, you'll have to ride with us all the way to Shiprock. Choose now," Justine said, moving toward him.

"Here. Ask your questions, then leave."

"Where's your brother, the tracker?" Justine asked.

"He's not here."

Justine glared at him. "*Where* is he? We'd like to talk to him."

"My brother is over twenty-one. He comes and goes as he pleases. If he comes back or we hear from him, I'll send word to you." He looked at Ella again. "I've answered you. Will you leave now? As it is, I'm going to have to go to a Singer before my mother calms down again. You create problems wherever you go. Even your child is a victim."

Ella took a step toward him. "Are you threatening my daughter?"

"I wasn't threatening," he said, taking two quick steps back. "I was just remarking on something I overheard at the trading post. Your kid's class went to a weaver's home this morning to learn about rugs. But when the weaver saw your daughter, she refused to allow her or any of the others inside her home."

Ella's heart twisted, thinking of Dawn and how hurt she must have been. Anger rose inside her. "She poses no danger to anyone. She even carries the special medicine pouch my brother gave her."

"She's your daughter and she shares your fate," he said with a shrug.

Ella took a step toward him, but Justine grabbed her arm gently. "Come on, partner. We got what we came for."

Ella gave Raymus one last hard look, then got inside the vehicle.

"As soon as we get to the station, I want you to do a complete background check on Raymus Smart."

"All right. Are you looking for anything in particular?"

"Priors, that sort of thing, I want some leverage against him in case we need it." Ella picked up her cell phone. "I'm going to call home. I have to know if Raymus was telling us the truth about the field trip."

"He probably was, Ella. I don't think he would have made up something like that."

"That's what worries me," Ella answered, and dialed. Rose picked it up on the first ring, and without even stopping to say hello, Ella asked her mother about the incident. "I just heard some news about my daughter's field trip."

Rose said nothing for a second. "The teacher is an Anglo. It never occurred to her that your daughter wouldn't be welcome along with the other students. She apologized to me personally for the trouble it caused."

"That's not going to help my daughter."

"Your child is fine. She's outside with the pony and Boots. At first she was upset but it's all behind her now. I've explained to her that your job as a detective means that there'll be times when people won't like you. During those times we have to show the same courage you do." Rose paused. "She told me very seriously that she knows that the police don't have many friends. Apparently, she'd heard it on television. Then she told me not to worry, that it would be okay because it always turns out right."

Ella laughed. "Well, I'll never underestimate the power of TV again."

"Speaking of that, the Hollywood man called again. They wanted to know who was going to be negotiating for you. I gave them the telephone number of your child's father."

"I was supposed to stall!"

"You did. I thought it had been long enough."

"You better call my child's father and tell him to expect the producer's call."

Ella hung up and glanced at Justine. "All's well at home for now," she said. "But this whole episode just convinces me that I should move out for a while." With Emily and the other deputy watching the house, she felt more confident about not being there at night.

"You mean move out without Dawn?"

"It would make her life easier," Ella said with a nod.

"Where would you go?"

"I have no idea. Maybe a short-term rental somewhere."

"I have a better idea. Come and be my roommate for a while. I'm renting a place over by where the old farm training teacher lived, just northwest of the high school. The place is pretty large and I'm getting it for practically nothing. But there's one catch."

"What's that?"

"The rent is low as long as I take care of the owner's horse. Legger is a very surly beast. He actually bit me."

"Ouch, that can really take some skin." Ella winced, remembering that having happened to her as a teen. "What breed of horse is he?"

"He's a mustang. Curtisy, the owner, got him at one of the round-ups the Bureau of Land Management sponsors."

"Whatever you do, don't tell my mother that there's a horse on the property. She's after me to buy one as soon as possible so I can go riding with Dawn."

"This particular animal isn't for sale. Curtisy's brother exercises him three times a week and the family loves him for some strange and mystifying reason. But I'll be happy to keep my ears open and if I hear of a good horse . . ."

"A *gentle* horse. It's been a long, long time since I rode."

When they arrived at the station, Justine left to do the

background check. Ella turned to go to her own office, then changing her mind, headed back outside. The college had Saturday afternoon classes and she knew Wilson would still be there. Climbing into her replacement vehicle, Ella drove over there needing to talk to him.

It was nearly three P.M. by the time she reached Wilson's office. Seeing her, he waved her inside. "What brings you here? I'm just about done for the day."

"I'm looking into the possibility that one of Garnenez's students is the sniper who has been taking shots at me," she explained. "Since the professor has been doing his best to get everyone stirred up, I need to check out that possibility. I'd like to talk to someone who regularly attends his classes and might be able to give me a lead—a teaching assistant, for example. Can you recommend someone?"

"Cindie Dodge. She's one of the department aides, so she works for me too. She's a great kid, well, young lady, and works hard. Cindie also seems to be as honest as they come."

"Where can I find her?"

"She'll be taking home some of my students' papers to grade before Monday so I'm waiting for her to stop by and pick them up. She should be here any minute."

No sooner had he finished speaking than a sturdy-looking young Navajo woman wearing jeans and a white and red Chieftains sweatshirt came into the room.

Wilson introduced them. "I missed lunch, so I'm going to go pick up a sandwich and let you two talk privately. Then I'll be back and we'll go over the answer sheets, Cindie."

As he left, Ella sat down in one of the empty chairs. "I need to talk to you confidentially about Professor Garnenez. I understand that he's been saying a lot of things about me."

She looked directly at Ella. "He acts like he's afraid of you, Investigator Clah. I think he really believes that you pose a threat to others and he presents what could be a convincing case—providing you believe in the old ways—which I don't. Right now, he's asked everyone to keep a look out for that medicine man, John Tso."

"One more question. Do you know if he's a member of any of the local gun clubs?"

"I have no idea. I don't know anything about his personal life. But you might ask his new helper—Loretta Destea. She's your sister-in-law, isn't she?"

"What has she got to do with this?"

"She's the new departmental executive assistant and has been working mostly with him. They've been rearranging the storeroom—which is a really hard task because everything in there has been randomly stacked on the shelves for years. Some of the other aides have started to gossip about them because they've been spending so much time alone. You know how people talk." She glanced at her watch. "They were back in the storeroom a few minutes ago and are probably still there, if you want to go ask them something."

Ella had been in the storeroom before so she knew where it was. Although she wasn't sure she wanted to interrupt her sister-in-law, she wanted to see for herself what was going on. If Loretta was having an affair, it would destroy her brother. Brushing her misgivings aside, she went to talk to her.

Ella went through the door at the back of Wilson's classroom that led to the supply area beyond. As she stepped inside and closed the door behind her, she recognized Loretta's voice coming from the other end of the crowded room. The storeroom had rows of shelves containing supplies and equipment that reached up nearly to the ceiling. Several rows stood between Ella and where Loretta was working so neither could see the other, but a man carrying a box was visible for a second as he stepped from a classroom into the storage area. It was Professor Garnenez.

Before she could say anything and let them know she was

there, she heard Loretta talking about her, so Ella remained quiet.

"My husband is a very good *hataalii*, but his perspective is off when it comes to his sister. If it was up to me, I'd have my sister-in-law move off the Navajo Nation completely until the Singer can be found. It would be for her sake as well as everyone else's."

"I tried to keep an eye on her, at least right after the accident, but I have other responsibilities too," Garnenez replied. "Now, she's likely to show up almost anywhere without notice. I can certainly understand your concern for your son."

"I try hard to be a good mother. I want to protect my son, but my husband's making that very difficult right now."

"It's too bad that your husband's loyalties are so divided. You deserve better," he murmured.

There was something in Garnenez's tone that alerted Ella. Instinct told her that the man wasn't just being sympathetic—he had a thing for Loretta.

"He's always so busy with his patients he just loses track of everything else, including his family."

From Loretta's harried and slightly impatient tone, it was clear to her that her sister-in-law had no clue.

"He should put you ahead of his work. Any good husband would do that for his wife," Garnenez added.

Ella got ready to go up to them and surprise Garnenez, who was clearly making his move on her brother's wife, but then Loretta rose to Clifford's defense.

"He does his best," Loretta said firmly. "His job is extremely important. But his allegiance to his sister just makes me crazy. She's like that Typhoid Mary woman we heard about in history class. Worst of all, she just doesn't see it."

"She *is* a danger, and unless she watches her step, someone is going to take matters into their own hands and remove the threat."

Ella didn't pay too much attention to Loretta's comment, but Garnenez's response and his tone of voice got her cop instincts going.

As Loretta switched the conversation to matters pertaining to the workroom, Ella slipped back out the door. Garnenez had just moved way up on her list of suspects, despite his alibi. It was possible that he'd found someone to eliminate her and the threat he believed she posed. From now on, she'd be keeping really close tabs on the professor.

SEVENTEEN
————— ✖ ✖ ✖ —————

As Ella left the campus, she carefully considered her next move. Garnenez made her skin crawl. He was a zealot, and that type either created trouble or was part of it. Of course the fact that he was coming on to her brother's wife in a very sleazy, underhanded way only fueled her hope that she'd be able to throw his sorry butt in jail someday soon.

As she drove away from the campus, Ella considered going to her brother and telling him what was going on, but the possibility that she'd do more harm than good stopped her. Placing it at the back of her mind for now, she decided to go home instead.

By the time Ella arrived, Dawn was sitting on the floor with her back to the sofa, watching TV and petting Two, who had his head in her lap. Ella gave her daughter a hug, and Two a pat on the head, but before she could sit down to talk to Dawn, Rose appeared at the doorway to the kitchen.

Seeing her signal, Ella joined her in the kitchen instead. "What's up, Mom?"

"I got another call from your daughter's Anglo schoolteacher. She wanted to warn me about another situation she just heard about. It seems that some of the mothers have complained about your daughter attending classes with their children. They believe that since it's a tribal run kindergarten, you should comply with the demands of the Navajo Way or be forced to take your child out of school. Even two of the modernist mothers agreed. They feel that honoring our culture is what differentiates this program from a regular public school, and that what you're doing goes against the spirit of the program."

"*Nobody* is forcing my daughter out of school. If they have a problem they can withdraw their own children. But I've been thinking about this already and it may be time to try another solution," Ella said. "I'm going to move in with my cousin until I can have the Sing. That'll take some of the pressure off all of you here."

Rose nodded slowly. "Your daughter will have an easier time at school if you're not living under the same roof with her. But, as I said before, that may create new problems for you. Some will assume that I've asked you to leave."

"I can take care of myself, Mom. I'll be fine. I'll call my cousin and move out tonight," Ella said, her hands clenching into fists.

"You're angry," Rose observed.

"You bet I'm angry. It shouldn't have to be this way."

"It would be no different on the outside, daughter. Even there, anyone who's believed to pose a threat to others is isolated—socially or physically. Our beliefs are not universal, but what you're experiencing is."

Ella glanced toward the living room. "Somehow, I've got to get my child to understand all this. It's a lot to ask of a little girl." Moments later Ella joined her daughter and sat down on the rug beside her. "Will you turn off the TV for a bit? You and I need to talk."

Dawn switched it off, then looked at Ella. "You look sad, *Shimá*."

"I have to move out for a while. I'll try to come back and

see you every day, but I want you to try real hard not to tell your friends or anyone else about that. It'll be our little secret. Can you try to do that?" Ella knew the secret wouldn't last long, even though Dawn was much more responsible and mature than her friends, but hopefully a little caution would make things easier for Dawn for a while.

Dawn furrowed her eyes and thought about it for a while, then nodded. "Okay, I'll try real hard. But why are you leaving?"

"Because it'll make things easier for you at school and for your *shimasání.*"

She nodded, her eyes even larger than usual. "It's okay if some of the mothers don't want their kids to play with me. It doesn't hurt me."

"Thanks, sweetie. You're a brave daughter. But we're going to fix all that so it won't be a problem anymore."

"Okay. Where are you going to stay?"

"I'm going to live with Aunt J for a while," she said, using Dawn's name for Justine.

"When will you come home?"

"Soon. I promise. I'm working really hard to get everything straightened out. But, for now, this is best for everyone."

"People aren't very nice when they're scared," Dawn said somberly.

Ella sighed. Her daughter understood far more than she'd realized. "You're right about that."

"Can I watch TV now?"

Ella smiled. Despite her obvious maturity at times, Dawn still had a short attention span. "Sure you can." Switching on the set, Ella quietly left the living room and walked to her bedroom. While packing, she dialed Justine's number.

"How about if I move in tonight?" Ella asked.

"Sure. That's fine. Joe's here, though. That okay?"

"Joseph Neskahi?"

"Yeah. He comes by to visit pretty often. He brought pizza tonight, so if you haven't eaten . . ."

"Save me a slice."

As she hung up, Ella saw Rose at the door, watching her. "You're very troubled about something . . . more than just about leaving us for a while."

Ella nodded. She couldn't tell Rose about Loretta, her job, and Professor Garnenez. If she told anyone, it would be Clifford, and she'd already decided against that.

Ella closed the suitcase. "I'm only a phone call and twenty minutes away. Remember that," she said, and then told her about Emily. "She's a good cop, Mom. Make sure she's introduced to the animals so they won't get upset."

Rose nodded. "Fix things soon. Your daughter needs you here, not at your second cousin's."

"I think my kid's more independent than either of us give her credit for, Mom. When I told her I was leaving she took it calmly and gave me the impression that she understands exactly what's going on."

"She's growing up fast, but maybe that's a good thing. We can't shelter her from the world."

"I don't want her to grow up too soon." Ella sighed and shook her head. "I'd better get going."

"We'll take care of things here. Just do what you can to settle this matter quickly."

It was tough saying one last good-bye to her daughter. Then as Ella looked at Dawn's tranquil face, she suddenly realized she was far more upset than Dawn was. Ella smiled. "Be a good girl and if you want to talk to me, you can call. Okay?"

"Okay." Dawn looked up at her and smiled. "You're coming back soon, *Shimá*. Don't worry."

Ella sighed and walked out without looking back. If she did, she was certain she'd change her mind. She hated being forced into doing anything, and this was nothing short of surrender. As a fighter, that went against everything she was, but when it came to her child, the rules changed. Nothing was more important to her than Dawn.

When Ella arrived at Justine's, she was welcomed warmly. "I'm really glad you'll be staying here," Justine said. "This house is too empty with just one person. Let me show you around."

Justine took her down a very long hall that had rooms on both sides, some small, some large. Most weren't furnished, but all had curtains or blinds. "How many bedrooms does the house have anyway?" Ella asked.

"Five, and a study. It's also got two and a half bathrooms."

"It really is huge. From the front it looks like any other frame house, but it goes back quite a ways."

"The rent's incredibly low, too. But you'll understand why once you meet the horse," Justine added with a wry smile. "So which room would you like? I have a spare bed in the garage and we can set it up wherever you want."

Before long, with the three of them moving and assembling the bed, Ella was settled into the bedroom next to Justine's office. The window that faced east would give her a beautiful view of the river valley when morning arrived.

As soon as she'd unpacked, Ella followed the voices and headed for the kitchen. Joseph Neskahi was pouring himself a beer as she walked in.

"I nuked your pizza," Justine said, setting the plate before her.

Ella realized that she had six slices. "This is too much. Why don't you each take one?"

"We've eaten like horses," Justine said and shook her head. "Joe brought two pizzas."

Neskahi smiled. "I'll take one off your hands."

"This is a wonderful place, Justine. You were lucky to find it."

"You're right, but it's so quiet! I'm used to living with lots of brothers and sisters. That's why I've been looking around for a roommate. But I'm pretty choosy."

Soon, the conversation turned to the case, not unexpected with three members of the Special Investigation team in the room.

"While I was patrolling, I made it a point to stop by the campus," Justine said. "My niece Julie is taking a few classes and knows a lot of people. But all I turned up was what you already know—Professor Garnenez hates your guts."

"Yeah, so I've been told. Unfortunately, he's got an alibi."

"You want to take him down," Justine noted from her tone. "The man really bugs you, doesn't he?"

"Is it because of your sister-in-law?" Neskahi asked. "I've heard some talk."

Ella glanced at Neskahi in surprise. If he'd heard, then it was only a matter of time before her brother did as well. "The gossip is just that—gossip. I know that for a fact. But I have to admit, if he didn't have an alibi, he'd be a great suspect," she said and explained what she'd overheard him saying to Loretta.

"Maybe we should take a second look at his alibi," Neskahi said.

"It's pretty solid," Ella said. "The professor told me he was at the Quick Stop talking to Clyde Franklin. Clyde remembered talking to him that Tuesday because he'd been trying to watch part two of that TV show with the cop who hears people's thoughts and Garnenez ruined it for him. By the time the professor left, he'd missed it all."

"Wait a minute. I watched that episode. The program doesn't come on Tuesdays. It comes on Monday nights, and they don't rerun it like with some shows."

Ella stared at Neskahi. "If you're right . . ."

Justine stood up. "Want to go verify that alibi again with Clyde?"

"Yeah, as a matter of fact, I do."

"Then let's go. We can take my truck. Joe, you want to tag along?"

"No, I'll pass this time. I've got to go home and feed my livestock."

"I didn't know you had any," Ella said, realizing how little she knew about Sergeant Neskahi.

"Just one horse and two goats. It's all I have time for."

Ella started to ask him if his horse was for sale, but before she could, he continued.

"That old horse has been with me for years. I think he's close to twenty-five now. He's as much a part of my life as my gun and shield. I just wish I had more time to ride him."

"If you hear of a nice gelding, a really gentle horse, let me know, okay? I'm kind of in the market," Ella asked.

Neskahi nodded. "I'll ask around."

"Dawn been pressuring you?" Justine smiled. "It was just a matter of time, wasn't it?"

Ella laughed. "With my mother on her side, I never had a chance."

As they headed out moments later, Ella glanced over at Justine. "Thanks for letting me stay with you, partner. I'm not sure if I said that already or not."

"It's not a problem at all. Really." Justine smiled slowly. "But you owe me one next time I ask for a day off."

Ella burst out laughing. Her cousin never asked for a day off unless it was a full-out emergency—and she'd never been turned down.

When they pulled up at the Quick Stop, Justine looked over at Ella. "How do you want to handle this?"

"I've known Clyde for a long time, so I think I'll just play it by ear. Be ready to back up what I say."

"Got it."

As Ella went inside, she saw Clyde behind the counter watching a small screen color TV set. Seeing them enter, he smiled.

"Hi, ladies. Back again, Ella?" he asked, smiling. "I bet you came in for a snow cone, right? Everyone seems to be dropping by to try out the new raspberry vanilla flavor."

Justine bought a small one, but Ella declined. "I need to ask you about Professor's Garnenez's visit last Tuesday."

Clyde looked serious. "You want to talk about last Tuesday?" He shook his head and shrugged. "The man has come in several times since then, and my memory's not too good, so take that into account, okay?"

"Remember that you told me he interrupted your TV show?"

His face brightened. "Oh, yeah, that I remember. I'd waited all week. It was the second episode of a two-parter."

"Are you sure it was Tuesday? I thought that show was on Mondays?" Ella pressed.

His eyebrows knitted together. "Yeah, I think you're right about that. Maybe I got the day wrong. But he comes by practically every day."

"When does he usually come in?"

"Anytime between five and eight at night, depending on how late he stays on campus."

"Try to think back to Tuesday. Was he here that day?"

Clyde considered it, then finally shook his head. "I can't remember Tuesday from Monday or Wednesday. Days run together for me here at the store."

"If you happen to remember Tuesday . . ." Ella said.

"I do," a voice piped in from the back. A second later a skinny girl barely out of high school came in. "I filled in for you at the last minute, Clyde. Don't you remember that your daughter was in her school play and you went to see her?"

He thumped himself on the head. "Oh, yeah, Maria, I totally forgot. I'm sorry, Ella. My wife and I went to see her, but I fell asleep. After it was over we went straight home. Not exactly a memorable evening," he said. "I sure wish she'd gone out for basketball or track instead—not that I'd ever tell her that, of course."

Ella turned to Maria and introduced herself. "Do *you* remember seeing Professor Garnenez that night?"

The young clerk thought about it for several long moments, then finally shook her head. "No. Sorry, officer. But that doesn't mean he wasn't here. I just don't remember specific customers any particular night. After a few hours they're all talking heads to me."

"Thanks." Ella considered what they'd just learned as she and Justine returned to the SUV. "Garnenez never said who the clerk was that night . . ."

"Then we should go ask him," Justine said.

Ella smiled slowly. "Good idea. Let's go pay him a visit."

"Now? It'll be really late by the time we get there. Since it's not an emergency, let's do it first thing tomorrow."

"All right," Ella said, wishing they could just continue working. Once she stopped, her thoughts would focus solely on Dawn and she'd dwell on what she'd been forced to do. And once she did that, anger would eat her alive. It wasn't just that she'd left her child—it was that she'd allowed public opinion to dictate what she was doing. The only thing that made it even remotely tolerable was that she was doing it for her daughter.

"By the way, do you remember Reverend Campbell from the ceremony at the mines?" Justine asked.

"Vaguely."

"He's the pastor at my church, Fellowship Christian. He'd like to talk to you about your experiences in that mine."

"Does he think he can convert me?" Ella asked with a skeptical smile.

Justine shook her head. "He's not like that, believe me. I've known him for years. He's interested because he sees it as nothing short of a miracle and wants to find out more about what happened." Justine paused, then added, "You can trust him, partner. He'll listen to you, but he'll only give you his opinion if you ask for it."

Ella nodded. "All right. I'll stop by and talk to him when I get a chance." Although she'd never categorize it as a miracle—at least not in the sense he meant—there was a possibility that he'd give her an insight that could help her get a better handle on things. At the very least, it was worth a shot.

The "night squirrels"—what Rose called the random thoughts that often scampered back and forth through one's mind late at night while lying in bed—kept Ella awake for hours.

As soon as the lights were out and her head hit the pillow, Dawn's beautiful face appeared in her mind as clearly as if her eyes had been open. Dawn was safe at home, well cared for and loved by her grandmother. And after her experience at the mine, Ella believed in her heart that her own father watched over all of them as well. She couldn't prove that what had happened to her was real—no more than others who'd had similar experiences, but something inside her compelled her to trust what she'd experienced.

Rolling over onto her side, she pushed back the blanket and sheet, hoping cool air would drive away the nagging thoughts that were keeping her awake. Ella imagined herself walking into Rose's kitchen tomorrow and with the mental picture came the realization that it was her mom's kitchen, not hers. Dawn and she needed a home of their own. Her mother had made a life for herself and it was time for Ella to do the same. They were happy at Rose's house, of course, but after having raised two children, her mother deserved to have more privacy than life with a small child could give her. Ella, too, wanted a home where there was enough space for her to have an office, and where her own likes and dislikes would be reflected. She needed to make a home with Dawn—and she needed a second horse.

As Ella's thoughts continued to drift, she remembered the special men who'd come in and out of her life. There had been so few—only Eugene, Kevin, and now Harry. Gene's death had robbed them of a future together. Kevin had been the wrong man for her, and now Harry . . . it just hadn't been meant to be.

She turned over again, punching her pillow and trying to get comfortable. Justine's pillows were just too soft, or fluffy, or something.

Harry's image popped back into her mind—those damned night squirrels. *If* he had remained on the Rez or *if* either of them had been willing to make some major career changes, they might have been able to stay together. The attraction had certainly been there. But Ella knew that neither a physical attraction nor genuine friendship and respect were enough to sustain a long-term relationship. The fact that she and Harry were both cops hadn't been a good thing after all. The thought that Dawn could end up with two parents in constant danger had placed a very real obstacle between Harry and her.

She lay there for a while, looking at the ceiling, then glancing at her watch. Harry was probably still awake, and they needed to have an uninterrupted talk. Their relationship had gone as far as it could and it was time for them to call it quits.

As Ella reached over for the cell phone, attached to the recharger plugged into the wall outlet, she nearly fell out of bed. Catching herself in time, she sat up. This bed was higher than hers.

Taking a deep breath, she punched out his number. The phone rang four times, then she got his voice mail. "Pick up, Harry, pick up," she urged, not wanting to have to do this twice. Finally, with a sigh, she realized he wasn't going to answer. "Uh, Harry, it's me, Ella. I've been thinking, and I wanted to talk, you know . . . Don't worry about calling back, I'll try again tomorrow or whenever. Bye."

"How lame can you get?" she groaned, ending the call. She was looking around for the cord to the charger unit when the phone rang.

"Hi, Ella, I'm here. I think I know what you wanted to talk to me about."

Harry's voice faded a bit, and Ella wished they could be face-to-face right now. It would be harder, of course, but at least not as cold as over the phone.

A half hour that felt like an eternity later, she hung up, feeling sad but also relieved. They were still friends, and there was something to be said for that. The truth was that she'd miss what might have been more than what they'd actually shared.

Ella turned off the cell phone and plugged it back into the charger. Flopping back down onto the pillow, she kicked the covers off, then curled up into a ball and closed her eyes. The night squirrels were finally gone.

The following morning Ella and Justine set out to Professor Garnenez's home right after seven.

"It's going to be a long haul, Ella. He lives south of Bloomfield over by the Huerfano Chapter House. Why a college professor would live way out there is beyond me. He's a new traditionalist and most of them prefer living closer to town where the houses have more amenities."

"He could still have electricity and gas. A generator and propane would be all he needs."

After driving east along the river valley through Farmington and the small community of Bloomfield, they headed south up and across a high, dry plateau. There were many natural gas wells in the area, and to the west were large circular-sprinkler irrigated fields that were part of the Navajo Irrigation Project. Tall mesas mainly to the east dotted the landscape and relatively flat desert stretched out to the west.

Ella knew this part of the Rez like the palm of her hand. She'd come out here often as a kid. Her father had spent a good portion of his life trying to convert the *Dineh* to Christianity and he'd held many revival meetings south of Bloomfield. She still remembered those clearly. There'd always be plenty of fire and brimstone talk, as well as a free dinner—which was the only reason many attended.

"This section of the Rez would be an ideal place to raise kids," Ella said thoughtfully. "They would have lots of room to play without ever worrying about street gangs or traffic."

Justine glanced at Ella, then back at the road. "You're really bugged about having to move away from your family, aren't you?"

"You bet."

"How's Dawn handling it?"

"A hell of a lot better than I am."

"Then let it go, partner."

"Easier said than done."

"If you don't, Ella, it's going to make you crazy and it still won't change anything."

"Speaking of change, I broke up with Harry last night."

"I thought I heard your cell phone. Do you want to talk?"

"There's not much else to say about it."

Ella remained silent for the rest of the trip. At long last they arrived at a small stucco home nestled in the shadow of a solitary mesa near Huerfano. As Ella had predicted, there was a generator and a huge propane tank.

Ella glanced around. The professor didn't have any livestock and there were no dogs visible. All she could see were five crows pecking at the ground where a garden had been at one time, judging from the rows of dried-out plant stalks. "Looks kind of dead around here, doesn't it?" Justine commented.

Ella nodded. "Maybe 'Garny' has a black thumb."

They'd just stepped out of the SUV when Professor Garnenez came out to meet them.

"Is there something I can help you with?" he asked coldly. The professor was dressed in jeans and a sweatshirt and looked as if he'd been up awhile.

"We came to ask you a few questions," Ella replied, noticing he wasn't wearing his medicine pouch. "Shall we go inside?"

"No, let's not. I wouldn't feel comfortable with you inside my home," he said pointedly.

"I understand you've had quite a bit to say about me in your classes," Ella prodded.

"What I've said there, I'll gladly say to your face. Your blatant disregard for our beliefs is an affront to everyone on this reservation. And your willingness to risk the safety of children—even that of your own child—"

"You *don't* want to bring my kid into this," she warned.

"Easy, partner," Justine said softly.

"As the sister of a *hataalii* you should show more caution, not to mention respect."

"It's strange that you should mention my brother. I understand that you don't approve of him either," Ella shot back.

"When he actually does his job, I hear he's a skilled *hataalii*."

"Meaning?"

"He should be spending more time looking for the Singer who's needed for your ceremony. He knows the circumstances and the urgency involved. As a *hataalii* nothing should be taking precedence over that for him. But then again, he seems to have a problem with priorities."

Ella took a step closer to him. "Listen, you little weasel, I know you're trying to make a move on my brother's wife. She may not realize what you're up to, but I do. So watch your step."

"Or what? You can't touch me. I've broken no laws."

"Your alibi for the time someone shot at me doesn't hold water. You've also made it quite obvious that you consider me a threat, which explains why you've been stirring up trouble. The question that remains is whether you're capable of attempted murder as well."

He backed up a step. "You've lost your mind."

"Who was the clerk at the Quick Stop when you were there on Tuesday?" Justine asked.

He gave her a bewildered look. "I have no idea. I think it was probably Clyde."

"Wrong. He wasn't there that night." Ella held his gaze. "Someone's been taking shots at me. And you have no alibi . . ."

"You think it was *me*?" His voice rose an octave and he looked at her in horror.

Ella weighed his reaction carefully. Garnenez was as much surprised by the news of the sniper as he was by the fact that he was a suspect. She had a strong feeling he was holding back on them.

Deciding on a tactic, Ella turned wordlessly and headed back to the vehicle with Justine. As soon as they were under way, Justine glanced over at Ella. "I don't think he's the sniper. I thought he was going to faint when you mentioned murder."

"He may not be the sniper, but gut instinct tells me he knows something about the incidents. Let's let him sweat for a while. Then we'll try again. His own fears will work against him far more effectively than we could."

EIGHTEEN
——— ✖ ✖ ✖ ———

They stopped by the station next. As she entered her office Ella found Joseph Neskahi placing something on her desk. "Hey, Joe, what brings you here on a Sunday morning?"

"Since I was planning to come in today, Justine asked me to finish the background check you'd asked her to do on Raymus and Daniel Smart. I completed it just a few minutes ago and there's nothing particularly significant about Raymus. He's had a few DWI arrests, but that's about it. Daniel's another story. The guy's been in trouble for years. He got a 'less than honorable discharge.' That's not a 'dishonorable discharge,' but it's the next step up."

"I'm almost sure he's the tracker Branch hired. But I've got to go talk to Branch and squeeze some information out of him," Ella said.

"Branch is currently staying on the Rez at the Lazy Pony Inn," Neskahi said.

"Thanks for the tip. I'll go pay him a visit right now."

Ella made sure Justine would be able to catch a ride with Neskahi, then left the station. It was nearly ten in the morning. The motel Branch had picked was an upscale one on the Rez that catered to tourists. What had surprised her most was that he'd chosen to come to the Rez—that this was where he'd felt safest despite the political muscle of Councilman Lewis Hunt. The pull that the four sacred mountains had on those of her tribe, even those of mixed ancestry, was as real and tangible as the sand that covered the desert.

As Ella pulled into the motel's parking lot, she searched for Branch's luxury sedan and found it parked in front of a door at the end.

Leaving her SUV next to his Mercedes, she went to the motel-room door and knocked. Branch came to the door moments later and peered out. He was wearing a half-open, untucked shirt and slacks that, even with her limited perspective, looked as if he'd slept in them.

Branch's reddened eyes were narrowed into slits. "What do you want, Clah?"

"I'd like to talk to you about Daniel Smart."

Branch rubbed his eyes, then gave her a heavy-lidded look. "What's he done?"

Ella took half a step back. His breath could have qualified as a biological weapon. "The real question is, what have *you* done?" Ella slipped past him and stepped inside his room. Stopping by the window, she opened the blinds.

He groaned and covered his eyes with one hand as light streamed in. "Are you here to torture me?"

Ella leaned against the wall and regarded him thoughtfully. "Why don't you sit down and tell me what's going on?"

"I have no idea what you're talking about," he said, stepping around her to close the blinds.

"Did you hire Daniel Smart to go after Cardell Benally?"

He sat down on the bed, then poured himself some water from a pitcher on the nightstand. "You're wasting my time, Clah, and even more tragically, you've interrupted my sleep. Go away."

"You do understand the term 'accessory to murder'?"

"Do you understand the term 'harassment'?" he countered, now fully awake.

Ella remained quiet for a moment, trying to find yet another way to get through to him. Finally, she opted for the direct approach. "You hired someone to go after Cardell. We have a witness to that," she said, though she knew that what she really had was a lot less substantial. "But Daniel's not as reliable a partner as you might think. Do you know he was kicked out of the military because he was unstable?" she challenged, taking some liberties with the truth. "I wonder what charges he would have faced had he been a civilian?"

George Branch's breathing became heavy and she could see the vein on his forehead pop out. "You checked him out with the military? No wait—more to the point—*why* did you take the time to check Daniel out?"

Despite his bravado, Ella saw the uncertainty in his eyes and knew that she now had his complete attention. "I know Cardell Benally scares you. You're convinced he burned down your house with Hunt's help, and now that Benally has dropped off the radar, you're afraid he's getting ready to make another move."

"Of course I am. Hunt is throwing out that smoke screen of Navajo justice, trying to justify what Benally's done in case Benally's ever caught. He's using Cardell to do what he'd like to do himself, but he's smart too. He won't let Cardell go down because there's no telling what Cardell might say on his own. The crazy thing is that they both hold *me* responsible even though Smiley's the one who burned down that house, not me."

"We haven't proven that Smiley was guilty of arson," Ella pointed out.

"That's only because he killed himself and blew up everything he owned in the process. But everyone still knows he's the one who set fire to the Hunts' home. Unfortunately for me, I'm the focus of Benally and Hunt's revenge because I'm the only target left. They burned down my house, sure, but it won't stop there. Hunt doesn't have the stomach to try and kill me himself—it's not his style. But Benally would. Then, Hunt would produce a dozen people who can give his brother-in-law an alibi—people who swallowed that Navajo justice crap hook, line, and sinker."

"So you hired Daniel Smart to kill Cardell before he could kill you?"

"Kill? I did no such thing," he snapped. "I'm not a murderer, even by proxy."

"Then why did you hire Smart?"

"I never said I did." He held her gaze. "If anything, what I needed was a tracker—someone who could tell *you* where Benally is."

Ella considered what he'd said. "If you hired a tracker and he ends up killing the target, you'll have one hell of a time proving you're *not* an accessory to murder, particularly if Smart turns on you. Remember, you'd be the best witness against him."

"I get your message loud and clear, Clah. But we're speculating here, that's all. I haven't done anything except sit in this motel room—just me and Jack."

"Jack who?" she looked around.

He pointed to the bottle next to the TV set. "Jack Daniel's."

"Take some friendly advice. If you hired Smart, call him off. Chances are he's more than you bargained for." Ella stood up. "By the way, do you have any idea where I can find the guy?"

"Not a clue, and that's the truth," he said, looking directly at her. "Why don't you ask weirdo Professor Garnenez from the community college? The two are cousins."

The news took Ella by complete surprise. "Come again?"

"Second cousins, actually, but Garnenez and Smart grew up together. Garnenez was the nerd; Smart, despite his name, isn't very, but his muscles kept Garnenez from being pounded all through high school."

"Where did you pick up the nickname 'weirdo' for Garnenez?"

"Some used to call him that in high school. He pretty much kept to himself, one of those quiet, intense types who was always looking for something to identify with. Before he became a new traditionalist obsessed with being Navajo, he was hooked on heavy metal, if you can believe it. His notebooks looked like album covers for Black Sabbath and groups like that. Talk about a turnaround."

"Let me guess, Branch. You prefer Grunge." She waved her hand around the room.

"Smart-ass."

Ella chuckled and headed for the door. "Thanks for the information."

"Remember who gave it to you."

Ella nodded once. "And, Branch, do yourself a favor. Go on a diet, stop drinking so much, and consider seeing a medicine man or a doctor. You look like hell."

"Gee, does that mean you won't go country-western dancing with me next Saturday night?"

Ella closed the door between them before she said something she knew she wouldn't regret. As she walked over to the SUV her cell phone rang.

"It's me, Kevin," he said, identifying himself. "I've been trying to find ways to get the producer to up his offer and I think I've found one. I can have you hired as a 'consultant' on the film. That means they can call you with questions, but don't have to take your suggestions. Are you interested?"

She groaned. "Kevin, it's bad enough I can't walk away from this. Now you want me to talk to these characters?"

"It'll give you an extra ten thousand. Think about it, Ella. So you answer their questions if they call. Provide your expertise. What harm is there in that? At least you'll have a chance of influencing what they do—maybe a little."

"I'm going to have to think about this. I want to leave a

nest egg for Dawn, but I'm a Tribal Police officer and there's no telling what they'll do with the script."

"They'll show it to you. I'll make sure of that."

"But I won't be able to force them to change anything?"

"You can suggest, but they don't have to comply. All things considered, I'd still advise you to take the deal. I'll look after your rights. They won't walk over you legally."

"Yeah, but there are a lot of other ways they can leave cleat marks on my face," Ella answered. "Can you stall a bit? Before I agree I want to be sure I'm doing the right thing."

"I spoke to the California guy on Friday, Ella. They're interested in you *now* but they have incredibly short attention spans. I'd take the money and worry about it later."

"I can't do that. It's not my way."

"All right. It's your call. Dawn will never lack for anything anyway."

"I know. I just wanted her to have something extra for when she was ready for college. I'll be getting life insurance, but since I don't plan on dying, this would be a chunk of money she could have when she grows up—money I could never give her otherwise."

"Then I advise you to take the best deal I can get you."

"Give me a chance to mull it over and I'll call you back later," she said.

Ella hung up, deep in thought. What she hadn't told Kevin was that she dreaded answering questions about what had happened to her in that mine. She hadn't been able to explain it to herself in any way that made sense, let alone to someone else. And if she'd noticed anything about television and the movies, it was that exaggeration and sensationalism were common. She was very reluctant to allow what had happened to her to be exploited like that.

Ella glanced at her watch. It was two hours past lunchtime, but she wasn't hungry for food—just for answers. What Justine had said about Reverend Campbell came to her mind.

Her partner had spoken highly of him and she was a shrewd judge of people most of the time.

Ella called Justine on the cell. "Do you think he's around the parsonage now?"

"Services are over by now at Faith Fellowship, and he usually stays in the church office afterward. Give it a try," she said, giving Ella directions to the church.

Ella turned the vehicle in the opposite direction. If the pastor was around, she'd speak to him. If not, she hadn't lost anything except a little bit of time.

There was one vehicle in the parking lot and another in front of the small house that served as the parsonage when she arrived. Ella parked near the open side door to the main building and went in. As she walked down the hall, she discovered small classrooms and the church nursery—judging from the cribs and children's toys. Down the hall she could hear voices. A moment later she saw Campbell, an Anglo man in his mid-fifties with thick eyebrows and a shiny bald head, talking to a Navajo man who was wearing a tool belt and overalls.

The Navajo, apparently the maintenance man, nodded as he passed her, going in the opposite direction. The Anglo man smiled. "I'm Reverend Campbell. Can I help you?"

"Perhaps. My partner, Justine Goodluck, said you were interested in talking to me. She also said you might be able to help me figure out a few things—without trying to convert me," she added pointedly.

He laughed. "I give you my word of honor, Detective. Fair enough?"

"Yeah," she said with a smile.

"Then come in and have a seat."

As she followed him to his office, she couldn't help but remember her father. He'd been a Navajo Christian minister, a real zealot who could never resist the urge to try to convert people. She wondered if Reverend Campbell would really be any different.

"I'm working on a paper for my doctorate," he said. "The topic is Near Death Experiences from a Theological Perspective. I understand that you were pronounced dead for a short time, and I wondered if you had seen, or heard, or felt anything you'd be willing to share with me." He paused, then smiled. "If not, I'll still be happy to help you with whatever you're trying to figure out."

Ella smiled. "Traditional Navajos believe in balance. I'll help you out with what I know or remember, and then you can try to help me. How's that?"

"Okay. Fair enough."

"I would imagine the first question you have is whether I was really dead." Seeing him nod, she continued. "I stopped breathing and my heart stopped beating, so I think it's a pretty good bet—but I'd appreciate it if you didn't tell anyone else that. It's a touchy subject for most Navajos."

"Whatever you tell me will remain in the strictest confidence. The paper, if it's ever published, will never list you by name either. Just so you know, I'd like to compare your experience to the NDEs of people who come from a different belief system."

"I'm not sure how much help I can be to you. The truth is I haven't figured it all out yet. First of all, it's possible I may have been hallucinating. I know I passed out at one point, but after that, it's hard to say when I actually stopped breathing and . . . the rest." She shrugged. "Logically, I have to admit that what I went through could have simply been my brain trying to cope with lack of oxygen."

"Deep down, do you believe you were hallucinating?" he asked, his gaze steady as it met hers.

"No," she admitted after a brief pause. "What I felt . . . what I saw . . . it was as real to me as the conversation we're having now."

"Did you see a bright light?"

"The place where I found myself was bright and filled with colors, but there was no being of light."

"Were you alone?"

"No. My husband and then my father were there."

"I didn't know you'd been married."

"I got married right out of high school but my husband was killed," she answered, not bothering to elaborate on the details.

"Would you say you were in heaven?"

"Probably not in the way you mean. I was told that it was an in-between place and my thoughts determined what I saw. It was desert—and ocean. Contradictions existed there harmoniously."

"Was it the kind of place *you* would categorize as heaven?"

"I never thought of heaven as a specific locale. But based on what I saw ... what I learned ... I'd say that there are many different kinds of 'heavens.' "

"Did you have any kind of life review?"

She shook her head. "But I was asked if I'd finished what I'd wanted to do on this plane. That took some thought on my part. Then I was given a choice—I could stay there, or return. I didn't want to leave, but I knew my daughter needed me so I came back."

"Has your experience changed you in any way?"

She nodded slowly. "I think so. I'm not afraid of dying, but I'm much more aware of the ticking clock, if you understand my meaning."

He nodded. "Is that what troubles you?"

"Not directly, but it's linked to that. You see, I used to think that I was in control of my life, that my choices determined my present and my future. But that's not necessarily so." Ella considered her words carefully before continuing. "I like to plan things. It's the way I am. But all of a sudden I've come face-to-face with the fact that you can plan to a point, but after that you might as well roll the dice."

"There are few guarantees in this world, but faith can make the path you have to walk a little easier. What do you believe in?"

"Just a few weeks ago I would have said 'me' and things I can prove with hard facts. But now . . ."

"Maybe that's why you feel so lost. You have to have a foundation—something that'll give meaning to your life and put things into perspective. Christianity gave me what I needed, but you may find it through Navajo beliefs. I think what you're searching for is a staff of sorts, something to lean on that'll help you make more sense out of the things you experienced. My advice is to read. Find out as much as you can about different religions, philosophies, and belief systems and see what makes sense to you. From what you've told me, I don't think you'll fit in perfectly with any one group, but you may find your own niche somewhere between the cracks."

Ella smiled. "Thanks for your help. And I'm amazed. You never mentioned fire or brimstone!"

"I go out of my way never to alarm anyone carrying a gun," he said and laughed.

"You're okay, Reverend."

"Come back anytime," Campbell said. "I'm always here."

Ella left feeling more at peace. Maybe that was what she'd been doing wrong—trying to find her answers all in one place. But she'd always been *alní*, someone who's split in half, or in her case, with one foot in two different cultures. She couldn't expect her search for answers to be linear—nothing else about her life was that way.

Ella took a deep breath, then let it out slowly. She believed in order and harmony and the need to restore both. She believed in freedom of choice and she now believed that death wasn't the end. She'd hold to those for now.

It was almost three by the time she reached the highway again. As she was waiting at the stop sign her cell phone rang.

"It's Justine," the familiar voice said.

"What's up, partner?" Ella asked.

"Come by the house. There's something you have to see."

Something in her voice made her muscles tense up. "Is everything all right?"

"Yeah, but come over as soon as you can."

Ella resisted turning on the sirens, but she put the pedal to the metal. Something bad had happened. She knew Justine too well not to have picked up on that.

When Ella arrived less than five minutes later, she didn't even have to step out of the vehicle to see what the problem was. Spray-painted on Justine's door in red was a message— "Leave the Rez or die."

NINETEEN

✖ ✖ ✖

As Ella came up to the door, her fists were clenched. "You realize that this message was meant for me, don't you?"

"Yeah." Justine nodded. "But this is *my* home and you're my guest. And, frankly, this really pisses me off. When I pulled up, the perp was racing away in a blue pickup. I went after him and called it in. Joe backed me up and we chased him to the Rez border, but after that we had to turn it over to the county police."

"Did you get a license plate?" Ella asked. "And was it light blue or dark blue?"

"More dark than light, and the plate was smeared with mud—deliberately. But, Ella, I'm almost sure there was a campus parking sticker on the rear window. They're bright orange, and I spotted something that color at the left-hand corner."

"Garnenez," Ella muttered. "But his pickup is light blue. Are you sure about the color?"

"Yeah. Maybe he borrowed a friend's truck," Justine replied.

"As usual, we have nothing we can prove," Ella muttered. "What happened with the sheriff's department? Have you heard anything?"

"They put up a roadblock in Kirtland but I don't think they've turned up anything, or I would have heard," Justine said.

Ella called Sheriff Taylor for an update, her thoughts racing. The last thing she'd wanted to do was to expose Justine to this type of harassment.

Sheriff Taylor came on the line and greeted her. "I have Sergeant Emily Marquez out there working this, Ella. Let me give you her cell number."

"Thanks, I've got it already." She reached into her wallet and pulled out Emily's card and dialed.

"Marquez," came a curt voice.

"It's Ella Clah. Anything on the vandal in the blue pickup?"

"No, and I don't think we'll find him. He never passed through Kirtland. My guess is that he headed back to the reservation, either north or south as soon as your officers called off the chase."

"Yeah. Could be," Ella said. "Hey, how is it going, watching my home? Any problems."

"Not at all. I was going to call you later today about the other officer who covers from midnight on."

"Is it someone you've worked with?"

"Yeah, and he's a good cop. I wouldn't have recommended him otherwise. He's a member of our SWAT team and will be taking the sergeant's exam next time around."

"All right. Remember, if there's any trouble, whoever's watching can call me."

"Understood. I briefed him on that. What's going on at your end?"

Ella told her about the vandalism of Justine's door. "I hate to have brought this to my partner's doorstep."

"If either of you decide to move out for a few days, you can come to my place at the east end of Kirtland. But I should warn you that everything is a mess. I have to move out by the end of the month. They just upped my rent, and I can't afford it."

"I don't want to endanger my partner by staying here, but I'm not sure it would be any better or safer for you."

Justine glared at Ella. "Don't you dare move out! I'm a cop and I can defend myself as well as you can." She paused, then in a soft but determined voice, added, "Don't give this creep a win."

"You've convinced me, partner," Ella said. "Okay, I'm staying here," she told Emily. "But listen, I know my partner is looking for a permanent roommate. You two should meet. I think you'd get along." Ella looked at Justine, who nodded.

A call came over Emily's radio and she signed off quickly, promising to be in touch if anything turned up.

"She's looking for a place to live?" Justine asked.

"I normally wouldn't have butted in on your business, but I think you'd like her. Since she works for the county sheriff's department, she wouldn't have to travel far to get to work. It's almost the same distance for us, only we go in the opposite direction."

"Living on the Rez isn't for everyone," Justine said cautiously.

"She didn't strike me as the type who'd have a problem with it. But this is your place. You decide what's right."

Working together, Ella and Justine searched the ground for any evidence the vandal might have left behind. An hour later they still had nothing except for the tire prints.

Ella pursed her lips and weighed her next step. "My sister-in-law is very chummy with Garnenez. I'm going to have a talk with her," she said at last. "I'd haul her in for questioning, but my mother and brother would have fits."

Justine chuckled softly. "You'll probably get more from her if you go easy."

"Yeah, but she's soooo annoying," Ella answered with a wry smile. "I'll be in touch later."

Ella got back into her unit and called Loretta at home. "We need to talk," Ella said when Loretta answered the phone.

"You can't come here, sister-in-law," she said firmly. "My son is home."

Ella's hand tightened around the steering wheel. "Where then?"

"Here." Clifford's voice boomed from the background. "I've had it. My sister can come to this house whenever she wishes."

"This is *my* house," Loretta said.

Ella scowled. Loretta was right. Navajo Way dictated that the property always belonged to the woman. Ella bit back her anger. "I just need to ask you a few questions. It won't take long."

"Not inside my home," Loretta repeated firmly. "But I'll go outside and talk to you there."

"I don't care if we talk in the henhouse," Ella said impatiently. "You may be able to give me some insights. I understand you and Professor Garnenez have become . . . 'friends.' "

"What have you heard?" Her voice suddenly became tight.

"More than was my business and much more than I cared to," Ella answered truthfully, then added, "I'll see you in twenty-five minutes."

Ella drove to her brother's house, wishing she hadn't put Clifford in the middle. But maybe it was better this way since it had meant that Loretta would meet her outside. Her questions would have undoubtedly upset Clifford even more. Her brother always kept a firm hold on his temper, but he wasn't above anger. Ella wasn't worried that he would show up on the professor's doorstep and punch his lights out, but she was reasonably certain he'd insist Loretta quit her job.

The problem was that Ella knew how badly they needed

the money. People didn't always pay in cash for Clifford's services, but her brother never placed a cash-paying patient ahead of one who could only pay in trade or service.

She arrived at her sister-in-law's house a short time later. As she parked, Loretta came out to meet her. Clifford, seeing her, came out too.

"We can talk out here as long as you like," Loretta said. "But you *cannot* go into my house."

"This is foolish," Clifford said. "We all have our medicine pouches and my sister has had a prayer done over her. That's enough for now."

"I don't agree," Loretta said simply. "She will *not* enter the house."

"Let me talk to your wife here," Ella said, glancing at Clifford. "It won't take long." She motioned toward the house with her head, indicating he should leave.

He looked at her curiously. "You don't want me present," he observed. "Why?"

"It's police business. She knows a suspect, and it's the way we interview people," Ella said firmly and hoped her brother wouldn't press it.

With a shrug, Clifford walked off.

Anger bubbled inside her. She'd hated doing that to her brother, particularly after all he'd done for her. And none of this would have been necessary if his wife hadn't allowed Professor Garnenez to get close to her.

"Thanks for keeping this between you and me," Loretta said softly. "I don't know what you've heard, but it's all just jealousy and gossip. I haven't done anything wrong."

Ella didn't comment. She needed information from her sister-in-law and putting her on the defensive wasn't the way to do it.

Loretta pursed her lips. "Nothing improper is going on. I give you my word of honor."

Ella gave her an impatient nod. "Let's go on. We need to

get down to business. How well . . . no, *do* you know the professor well?"

Loretta hesitated. "I guess so. I mean we talk about things other than business."

"Would you say that he's truly worried about the threat I may pose?"

"Very much. But, Sister-in-law, you know he's just one of many."

"Has he ever become violent or lost his temper around you or his students?"

Loretta shook her head. "Never, and, believe me, he's had plenty of provocation. There was one time a student really mouthed off to him because of the grade he'd been given. You wouldn't believe the things that came out of that kid's mouth! If it had been me, I'd have slapped him, but the professor didn't even blink. He just told him to leave the office."

"So he acts cool and rationally even when he's angry?"

Loretta took a deep breath, then let it out again. "Well, I haven't worked there very long, of course, but he doesn't seem to stew on things. He takes action immediately to correct them. For example, when he failed to get the parking spot he'd asked for, he went to administration and presented his case. Even though he got turned down, he told me he'd keep at it until he got what he wanted."

"What if he felt threatened in some way—would he get violent?"

She considered for several moments. "I don't know him that well, but I think that's like asking me whether I would ever take a life. In most cases, no, but if anyone attacked my family, I would, without hesitation."

"Fair enough. Do you know if the professor does any target shooting for pleasure or in competition?"

"Sorry, it's never come up. We don't talk about repairing cars either, though, but that doesn't mean he's not a mechanic."

Ella nodded. "All right. That's all I have. I would appreciate it if you didn't tell the professor that I asked about him." She paused, then continued. "I'd also like you to keep your eyes and ears open. If you find out that he owns a twenty-two rifle, or that he's a duck hunter, let me know right away."

"What is it that you think he's done?" she asked, her eyes bright with curiosity.

"I can't answer that right now," Ella replied. Meeting her sister-in-law's gaze with a level one of her own, she added, "But be careful that you don't lead him on in any way. You may get more than you bargained for."

Loretta looked at her in confusion, then shook her head. "You're just reacting to rumors that there's something between us. I know you're just trying to protect your brother, but I'm telling you, there's nothing between us."

As Loretta walked back to the house, Clifford came out of his medicine hogan and approached her.

"I'd like to talk to you for a moment," he said, gesturing toward the hogan.

"Okay, but I won't be able to stay long," she warned.

Ella followed him, then sat down on the sheepskin rug across from him on the south side, which, according to custom, was the spot reserved for women. "I've always liked your medicine hogan," she said softly. "There's such a sense of peace here."

"There's not much of that in your world right now, is there?"

"No, there isn't," she answered.

"I heard that you moved out of Mom's house."

"I didn't really have much of a choice. Do you know what happened to my daughter at school?" Seeing Clifford nod, she continued. "And to make matters worse, someone's after me. Just a few hours ago, a spray-painted message was left for me on our second cousin's door."

"Will you be leaving her home now?"

"No. She'd have a coronary if I did," Ella said, laughing. "It's our nature to fight, not to run."

"Do you have any idea who's after you?"

"Yes, but I have to prove it."

"Is that why you came to speak to my wife? Do you think she knows the person you're after?"

Ella hesitated. This was the last topic she wanted to pursue with her brother. He'd always been able to read her much too easily.

She nodded, but didn't say anything.

He exhaled softly. "In case you're wondering, I know about her job at the college," he said. "She just went to full-time, and had to tell me. I didn't like the idea at all, but she's right. We're strapped financially and need the extra income."

"It's a great job, with benefits," Ella said carefully.

"It is. But it makes things complicated. I now have to take care of my son until she gets home. Of course Julian's seven and doesn't need constant supervision, but when I'm with a patient he gets shortchanged."

"You'll find a way to make things work," Ella said, standing up.

"Sister, there's one more thing I need to know. My wife has been working closely with one professor on some kind of inventory project and she talks about him a lot. Could he be the one you suspect has been coming after you?"

Ella hesitated, then nodded. "Yes, but as I said, I have no proof. Right now I'm trying to find out if he owns a twenty-two rifle or if he's a duck hunter. The sniper who's after me is very skilled at hitting a moving target."

"My wife will help you all she can," Clifford said. "She may resist doing something you asked because you two don't get along very well, but in the end she'll come through because you *are* family."

"That's good to know."

Ella started to leave, then remembered something else

that was on her mind. "Brother, this is totally unrelated, but I've decided to buy a horse so I can start riding with my daughter. I'm looking for a well-behaved gelding, probably. If you hear of any possibilities from one of your patients, let me know, okay?"

"You haven't been on a horse in what, fifteen years?" Clifford looked amused.

"It's like riding a bicycle, right? Once you learn, you never forget." Ella scowled at him.

He laughed. "I know this stallion named Lightning that might be available."

"Find one named Molasses, or Rocking Chair, okay? I'll see you again soon." Ella smiled, then left the hogan.

As she drove away, in the rearview mirror she saw her brother standing just outside the entrance to the hogan, and Loretta walking toward him. She wondered if Clifford had heard the rumors about his wife and the professor. It seemed unlikely that he didn't know. But Clifford wouldn't pass judgment on Loretta until he found out for himself how much, if any, of the rumor was true.

Ella decided to stop by her home and see Dawn for a bit, but first she called her mother to make sure she didn't have guests. The sacrifice she'd made by moving out would all be for nothing if anyone saw her at the house.

"Some people will be stopping by later, so come now," Rose said. "Your daughter misses you."

The words tugged at her heart. When Ella pulled up a short time later, she saw Dawn and Boots outside in the arena, brushing the pony. As Ella joined them, Dawn gave her a hug. "Riding is fun, *Shimá*. When will you come riding with me?"

Rose came out and, smiling at her daughter, answered for Ella. "She'll get a horse soon, little one."

Ella glared at her mother, then saw her laughing eyes. Rose was enjoying this.

"Tomorrow?" Dawn said.

"No, Pumpkin. It's going to take time for me to find the right horse. But I've got some people who will help me, including your uncle."

"Make sure you keep reminding her, Granddaughter. Your mother might forget," Rose added, chuckling.

"Okay!" Dawn answered.

"Great, Mom," Ella answered with complete insincerity.

Finished with the pony, Dawn tugged at her mother's hand. "Come see the flowers."

"What flowers?"

"The dying plant she took from your room," Rose explained.

Ella, curious, followed her daughter. The pot was on a window facing east, just like it had been in Ella's room. But, here, the plant had done a dramatic about-face. One tiny bud clung to life on the long, bare flower spike and the leaves looked green and healthy again.

"Good job, Pumpkin!"

"It likes it in my room."

"So I see. You've done a marvelous job. What did you do to it?"

Dawn shrugged. "I gave it water and I talked to it. We are connected. All things are. That's what *Shimasání* says."

"And she's right," Ella said, realizing that she'd also come to accept that belief.

"Daughter, some of the Plant Watchers will be stopping by today. If anyone comes early . . ." Rose warned with a sad smile.

"Right." Ella smiled at Dawn. "I have to go now, but I'll see you again soon. Be a good girl."

"I will." Dawn gave her mother a hug.

Ella walked away quickly, not looking back. Dawn was in the best hands. She'd take comfort in that.

Moments later, Ella was in her unit heading back to Justine's. It was a shame that her brother hadn't known the Sing she needed. It seemed odd for her to have to rely on another *hataalii*. At least Clifford would have understood why she was having it and not expected her to act or feel any differently after the ceremony concluded. As she pulled up by Justine's, she saw her partner cleaning a paintbrush in a bucket of soapy water beside the front porch. From what she could see, there was now a new coat of paint on the front door, which was open.

"Anything new turn up on this vandalism?" Ella asked.

Justine shook her head. "Officer Marquez made an official report. The county police were unable to locate the vehicle the suspect was driving. For them, the matter's closed, at least for now."

"That's that then."

"Why don't you go on in to the kitchen? I bought a bucket of chicken when I went to get the paint. You can nuke a few pieces and some of the mashed potatoes in the microwave." Justine paused, then added, "Just don't touch the door when you go in."

Ella smiled. "Mom's never let me buy her a microwave. Do you like yours?"

"I don't know how I ever got along without one. There's nothing like nuking coffee in the morning, or a bowl of oatmeal. And you can bake a potato or apple in just a few minutes."

As Ella went in, her cell phone rang. It was Emily. "Are you going to be home tonight?"

"I'll be here at Justine's unless something comes up. Why do you ask?" Ella said, placing a drumstick and a chicken breast on a paper plate—the only kind Justine seemed to have.

"I thought I might come over and meet her. The officer who's watching your home offered to take my place on stakeout tonight, so I'm free."

"How much time do you have left before you have to move out?"

"Less than two weeks. Finding a house or duplex within my price range—that also has a large yard—has been nearly impossible. The sticking point is that I need some space for my little greenhouse. It's about the same size as a large shed."

"You'd have room here, but it's Justine's place so you'd have to work it out with her. Why don't you come over now? We're both here."

Emily arrived a half hour later in her personal vehicle, a red pickup truck with a matching camper shell. Justine and Ella went out to meet her.

"As I was driving up I noticed that your horse is going crazy back there," Emily said. "He's bucking and running around everyplace."

"I better go check and see what's upset him," Justine said.

"We'll come with you," Ella said.

A moment later they were in the paddock area behind the house. The wild-eyed horse was running around inside the enclosure, bucking and leaping before spinning around and running in the opposite direction. Seeing them, he settled down, still breathing hard and snorting from all the exertion, and watched them.

Ella laughed. "There's nothing wrong with him. He's just feeling good. The weather's cool, but not cold, and we have a pretty strong breeze right now. He's just having fun."

Justine grumbled. "Tell that to the bucket he kicked half-way across the paddock," she said, pointing to the large, dented-in galvanized tub she'd been using as a feeder. It was sitting on its side now.

"Leggar's the most temperamental creature I've ever come across," Justine added. As she approached him, the horse pinned his ears back, lowered his head to below the withers, and nipped at the air, barely missing her. "Hey!" She jumped back.

Ella laughed. "You don't like him and he knows it."

"I don't like him because he bites."

"He bites because you're forcing things," Ella said. "Don't look at him, just turn away from him and wait. He'll approach you."

Ella went inside the paddock and demonstrated. The horse trotted in a circle around the enclosure, then stopped and watched her. Ella turned sideways, facing away and remained where she was. The horse waited, then finally came up to her. Ella patted him on the neck and the animal remained calm.

"Wow, you're great with horses," Justine said.

"No, not really. I'm good with horses—but only when I'm standing on the ground," Ella said. "Unfortunately, my daughter wants a riding partner. Why couldn't she have been interested in cars or motorcycles?"

Emily burst out laughing. "That's the *first* time I've ever heard any mom say that!"

"Hey, I know what I can expect from a motorcycle," Ella countered. "You want to stop, you put on the brakes. With a horse, you never know."

Once they were back inside, Justine showed Emily around the house. "There's plenty of room and the rent is super low." She quoted Emily the price. "My roommate would pay half of that and half of the utilities. We'd also take turns feeding and grooming the horse."

"That's a great deal."

"Yeah, it is, but you should know that this place is hard to maintain. With no landscaping it can be a lot of work keeping the weeds at bay. Tumbleweeds, in particular, can grow to the size of VWs if you let them."

"I like gardening, so I wouldn't mind taking over that chore permanently. Maybe we can plant some sunflower plants just for color around the house. That's a hardy southwest plant," Emily said, then after a pause, continued. "I have a greenhouse that I maintain, but the temperature control and humidifier run efficiently because it's a small space. I could get it set up on the north or south side of the house where it would be out of the way."

Ella listened to the two of them talk as they all sat in the living room. Their lives, though different, were similar in the ways that counted the most and they soon grew comfortable with each other. Before long, as it always was when cops got together, shop talk took over.

"I really wish we could have caught that vandal for you guys today. We tried, but we just don't have enough people out on patrol."

"That's okay. I have a pretty good idea that it's one of the professors at the college here," Ella said. "He considers me a threat because of my experience at the mine. Anything connected with death gets tricky here on our land."

"I've been giving that a lot of thought, partner, and I think there's another angle we need to consider," Justine said. "We've assumed that he considers you a threat because of what happened at the mine. But there's another possibility. Your sister-in-law works with him, and Loretta's never liked you much, as you know. If they're as involved as rumor has it, Professor Garnenez may think he's doing her a favor by trying to scare you away from the Rez."

Ella wasn't surprised that Justine knew about the rumors, but before she could answer, Emily spoke.

"Garnenez? Wait—doesn't he teach organic chemistry?"

"Yeah, that's him," Ella answered. "How do you know him?"

"He was part of a forensics workshop the college in Farmington sponsored for our department. After the workshop was over we saw each other a few times socially."

"Are you seeing him now?" Ella asked. "Dating?"

"No, I never really felt comfortable with him. He was always watching me out of the corner of his eye, assessing me in some way. And I got the feeling he was putting on an act, pretending to be exactly what I expected of him. I gave up trying to figure out what he was really like."

Ella nodded. "What's your take on him otherwise?"

"Outwardly, at least, he's idealistic and very proud of being a Navajo."

Justine brought her up to speed on the little they knew about the sniper and why they'd linked the incidents to Garnenez. "But it's all circumstantial. We don't even know if he owns a twenty-two rifle."

"I may be able to help you there," Emily said.

"I'm all ears," Ella answered. With luck, Emily would become an ally as well as a friend.

TWENTY

—— ✖ ✖ ✖ ——

It was early Monday morning when Justine and Ella drove up a low hill near Garnenez's home near Huerfano.

"Do you think she'll be able to pull this off?" Justine asked.

"Yeah. Emily's very pretty and that'll give her the edge. When she shows up at his home way out here, he'll think that she's missed him and is trying to get something going between them. His own ego will work against him. I think she's right about that."

"Good thing Garnenez only has a late-afternoon class today," Justine said. "There's Emily pulling up to his house now," she added, passing the binoculars to Ella.

"Now we wait."

"That was a really good idea you two concocted," Justine said. "At first I wasn't sure she'd agree. She'd only volunteered to visit him at his home and look around."

"Everything changed when she happened to mention that he'd asked her to go target shooting several times and duck hunting once," Ella said.

"I think that men who consider themselves marksmen, or at least good shots, love to go target shooting with a cop just to rate their own skills," Justine said. "Or show us up."

"That's why I figured it wouldn't be too big a stretch for her to steer things back in that direction and see if he'd go target shooting with her. The trick will be making him think it was his idea."

"When she didn't agree to your plan right away, I was sure she'd say no."

"She was only mulling it over, like I would have. That's why I pointed out that even if she saw a rifle with a Post-it note attached to it saying 'used to scare Ella Clah off the Rez,' we wouldn't be able to do anything. Legally, she couldn't take it without his permission, and without running a ballistic test, we'd still have no evidence," Ella said.

"This plan of yours is brilliant—providing it works the way we hope. They'll go target shooting in one of the dry arroyos and we'll dig up the bullets after they leave. If the ones fired from his weapon match the ones we retrieved, we've got him."

"Of course that's assuming he uses the twenty-two in question," Ella said.

"It's a good bet. He'll want to be accurate, particularly if Emily's a good shot. If he uses a lower-caliber weapon, he'll have less recoil and that'll make it easier for him to maintain accuracy."

Forty minutes passed slowly as they waited for Emily to emerge from the house. Ella glanced at her watch for the umpteenth time.

"Do you think she's in trouble?" Justine asked.

"No," Ella said, hoping with every breath that she was right. "I think she probably wants to move slow and set things up so it all appears to happen naturally."

They waited another ten minutes, which seemed like several eternities to Ella. Finally, Emily emerged, Preston Garnenez at her side.

"Here we go," Justine said. "They've got targets, two long gun cases, and a box which is probably filled with ammo and shooting equipment."

"If they go to that dry arroyo over there," Ella said, pointing north, "it'll be a piece of cake to dig out the rounds from the earthen sides. And it's off his property, so we won't need any warrants either. See the fence line?"

"She still hasn't given us the sign," Justine said, using a smaller pair of binoculars. "She told us that she'd put a piece of licorice in her mouth if he had a twenty-two with him."

Ella held her breath and watched through the binoculars. Emily placed the box in the back of the truck, then reached into her jacket pocket. Ella saw her pull out a long piece of licorice and stick it into her mouth.

"Bingo. She's got it."

"It's the blond hair. Men love it," Justine said.

Ella laughed softly. "Jealous?"

"Not at all," Justine said. "I have access to the same bottles at the drugstore."

"Meow!" Ella answered, laughing as they walked back to the SUV. "Follow them, but at a distance."

At the site, less than a quarter mile from the house, Ella waited while Emily and Garnenez fired round after round. At first Garnenez brought out skeet-shooting gear and they took turns launching clay targets for each other. Garnenez was particularly skilled with a shotgun, hitting at least seventy-five percent of his targets. Emily barely managed fifty percent.

Then they switched to the twenty-two, firing into the arroyo at small paper bull's-eye targets that Garnenez had stapled to an old real estate sign with a cardboard backing.

"We have what we need now," Ella said after they'd both fired at least twenty rounds. "Go ahead and call her on the cell phone as we agreed. She's done enough work for one day."

Justine called her. "Sergeant Marquez, we need you back at the station," she said seriously just in case Garnenez could overhear.

"Right now?" Emily asked plaintively, then added, "Never mind. I'm south of Bloomfield, so give me an hour."

They saw Emily and Garnenez pack up their shooting supplies, and within five minutes, they were on their way back to his home. Leaving Justine behind to dig out the rounds they'd need for comparison, Ella headed to their rendezvous point farther north near the Angel Peak recreation site.

"Everything go okay?" Ella asked, walking up to Emily's driver's side window as soon as the woman arrived.

"He had no idea." Emily paused thoughtfully, then continued. "I've got to tell you, Ella, I just don't think you're right about Preston. He's a game player, but is just too insecure to take direct action unless driven over the edge. In my opinion, if he were really going to try and kill you himself, he would make sure you didn't survive. He'd be more . . . efficient. He has a .30-06 Winchester in his house that would have been perfect for the job. Just one round through the windshield would have done it. My gut feeling is that you're barking up the wrong tree. Of course, I could be wrong. He's playing a role, even now."

After saying good-bye to Emily, Ella went to pick up Justine, then they drove back toward Shiprock and the station.

"Have you decided if Emily's the type of roommate you want?" Ella asked.

"I like her and I think we could get along. I'm going to call her in a bit and invite her to move in with me. But I sure hope she likes staying up late. That way I won't have to tiptoe around the house at night," she added with a rueful smile.

"Before Dawn was born I used to be a night owl, too. These days, I go to bed at ten-thirty, if I can manage it. Motherhood changes everything—but it's a good change," she added.

"I'm not going to be ready for motherhood for a long, long time," Justine said. "For now, I don't want to be accountable to anyone except myself."

"I was that way, once," Ella answered. "But needs change. There was a time in my life when I would have never considered getting married again, too. Now, I'm not as willing to shut the door on that possibility."

"Navajo Ways say that neither sex is complete without the other."

"Everything exists in two parts and both are needed to balance one another," Ella said softly, remembering her mother's teachings. "When I was younger I'd tell my mother that a woman needed a man like a frog needed roller skates. She'd always counter by reminding me of the story of First Man and First Woman."

"Which one's that?" Justine asked. "I was brought up Christian, so I'm a little fuzzy in that department."

"First Woman told First Man that women could get along without men. The men ended up moving across the river and then destroying the rafts that had transported them. After that, both sides ended up with calamities and great suffering. It was only when they finally came together again that harmony was restored. They needed each other."

Justine smiled. "It makes sense."

"Yeah, it does, doesn't it?" she observed, then lapsed into a long silence.

Later, after Justine went into her lab, Ella met with Big Ed and filled him in. Big Ed, as she'd expected, was far from happy about the way she'd worked things out.

"Shorty, what you did is recruit an officer from a different police department without authorization. There are channels we have to follow for that sort of thing and you know it. If

Sheriff Taylor gets wind of what happened, there'll be hell to pay. He likes things done by the book."

"Normally, so do I, but this opportunity just presented itself and I took it. Had I waited and gotten other people involved, word might have leaked out. This way was fast and neat."

"You did get the job done," he admitted. "But you always do. Next time at least clear it with me first. And let me know what you learn after Justine does a ballistic comparison."

Ella started to head to her office, then changed her mind and went to Justine's lab instead. Justine was busy at the microscope so she sat at Justine's desk and waited.

Although Justine knew Ella was there, she made it a point not to look at her. That was her way of letting Ella know she didn't want to be interrupted.

About ten minutes later Justine finished her tests and paperwork and looked over at Ella with a smile. "It's a match. We can move on this guy."

"I'm ready."

They were at Garnenez's house less than an hour later, but Garnenez wasn't at home and neither was his truck.

Justine took a look around, then peered inside through the curtainless back window. "He's not here and there's a half-eaten sandwich on the table. Do you think he's rabbiting on us?"

"I don't know if he's on the run, but I have a bad feeling about this. Let's head over to the college. He was supposed to have a class there later today anyway. Maybe he just drove over early."

Once they arrived on campus, they went to Garnenez's office first but the door was locked. Ella then led the way to the faculty lounge, but he wasn't there either. "Let's go find Wilson. He may be able to help us find the professor." Ella saw Justine's expression tighten but she nodded.

When Ella and Justine reached Wilson's office they found

him just saying good-bye to a student. "What brings you both here?" he asked, curious.

"It's good to see you, too," Ella said with a tiny smile.

"Hey, when *both* of you show up, I *know* it's pressing business."

"He's got you there," Justine said quietly.

"We're looking for Professor Garnenez," Ella said. "We understood he had an afternoon class to teach."

"It's strange that you should ask. He called Charlie Nez, our department head, not long ago and told him that he has to take off for the rest of the week on personal business. He's entitled to the leave, but Charlie's going to have a heck of a time finding a replacement on virtually no notice."

"What kind of personal business?" Ella asked.

"I have no idea. All he told Charlie was that there was a pressing matter he needed to attend to and he'd be out of touch for a while."

"If you hear anything else, call me," Ella said, then motioning for Justine to follow, left.

"Where to now?" Justine said, keeping up as Ella hurried toward their vehicle.

"I have an idea. Let's go talk to Loretta."

As soon as they were on their way, Ella picked up her cell phone and called her sister-in-law's home.

Loretta answered in a very shaky voice after the fifth ring. Noting it, Ella felt her gut tighten. "Sister-in-law, is everything all right?"

There was a pause, but then as if the flood tides had opened, Loretta began speaking very quickly. "No, I'm not all right. Everything's gone crazy all of a sudden. I thought the professor and I were just friends. I knew he found me attractive, but I never thought it was anything to worry about. I thought you were overreacting."

"And now?" Ella pressed.

"My husband has gone to see a patient and the professor

is coming here *now*. He wouldn't take no for an answer. He said that I'm only staying with my husband out of loyalty and that I belong with him."

"When he gets there, don't open the door."

"Can you come over? Please? Maybe that'll be enough to get rid of him."

"I'll be there as soon as I can."

Ella updated Justine as they hurried toward her brother's home. "I had a feeling all along that this wasn't just going to go away. My guess is that once Emily left, the professor began having second thoughts about the reason behind her surprise visit. He must have put two and two together and decided it was time to get out of Dodge. But he didn't want to leave without Loretta. Remember that he believes she's in danger because I'm part of her family and visit a lot. More importantly, in my opinion, he's in love with her."

"So he wants to take care of Loretta by taking her with him," Justine said with a nod. "It makes sense and also substantiates what I thought—that he took those shots at you as a way of protecting her."

"And now Loretta and her family could be the ones in danger. Step on it."

It took twenty minutes to get to her brother's home. When they entered the driveway, Ella saw a vehicle she recognized.

"That's Garnenez's pickup," Justine said.

Seeing that the front door of the house was open, Ella climbed out as soon as Justine stopped the vehicle. "I *told* her—"

Loretta suddenly pushed Garnenez out onto the front porch. The professor stumbled, then recapturing his balance quickly, reached for her hand. In a flash, Julian stepped in front of his mother and kicked the professor resoundingly on the shins.

Garnenez cursed, but before he could reach for Loretta again, Ella was there, her hand on her weapon. "Step off the porch, slowly, then kneel on the ground, hands behind your head." Ella kept her weapon in her holster. Garnenez didn't appear to be armed, unless he had a knife in his medicine pouch, and she knew she could use physical force effectively if necessary.

"*You're* the problem here, so do your own family a favor and leave," Garnenez said, refusing Ella's order.

"If you don't get down on the ground *right now*, I'll do whatever's necessary to get you there—including kicking your butt or shooting you."

Garnenez reluctantly complied. His eyes still on Loretta, he added, "I only wanted to take you and your son away from here, someplace where he could have a proper Sing done and you two would remain safe from contamination."

"My dad can take care of us!" Julian said angrily. "Go away!"

Justine handcuffed Garnenez and read him his rights as Ella went up on the porch to make sure her sister-in-law was all right.

As she approached, Loretta pushed Julian back inside. "The professor didn't mean any harm," Loretta said. "You didn't have to be so rough or rude to him. He's out of my house now."

Ella glared at Loretta, struggling against the urge to throttle her until her teeth rattled. "You're going to press charges, correct?" she said through clenched teeth.

"Oh, no, I'm not. The professor didn't come here to harm anyone. We're both fine."

Ella pointed to the door. "Then why did you let him in? I specifically told you not to do that."

"He just slipped past my son. I was trying to be polite and it backfired, that's all. I just wanted to explain . . ."

"Explain it to your *husband*. He deserves to know before everyone around Shiprock finds out what happened. Am I clear?"

Loretta nodded once. "But I still won't press charges," she said, looking down at Justine who was escorting a handcuffed Garnenez to the unit.

"He has much bigger problems than a domestic distur-bance to deal with now." Leaving Loretta to ponder that, she joined her partner.

"Where are you taking me? She said she wasn't going to press charges," Garnenez whined.

"You're not only pathetic, you're a suspect for attempted murder. You tried to kill a police officer—me," Ella clipped.

"I did no such thing." His voice rose. "Have you lost your mind?"

"Then perhaps you can explain why bullets fired from your twenty-two rifle match the bullets that we found at the crime scenes."

He started to answer, then clamped his mouth shut. "I'm innocent and I want an attorney," he finally said.

No one spoke on the trip back to the station and Ella made it a point not to turn around and look at Garnenez. His assertion that he was innocent and the sudden silence that followed bothered her. Gut instinct told her that things wouldn't be simple after all.

Ella sat across from Garnenez in the interrogation room. His attorney, a Navajo man by the name of Jim John, now sat to Garnenez's right. Justine stood behind Ella, leaning against the wall.

"My client knows his rights and understands why you've made the assumption you have. But he has an alibi."

"We checked it out and it's no good."

"My client mistook the date. He wants to correct his error now."

Ella looked at Garnenez. The man didn't seem at all wor-ried about his situation. "You lied to me, Professor, and you got caught. How many times is your story going to change before we get the truth?"

"He made a mistake," Jim John said firmly. "Shall we move on?"

"All right. What's his new alibi?"

John nodded to Garnenez.

"No one was supposed to know this," he said slowly, then paused. "I was following Loretta that day."

"Come again?"

He took a deep breath, then let it out slowly. "I was concerned about your contact with death and the danger it presents to others, and so was she. She'd been so worried about the risk to Julian from contact with you and those mines that she hadn't been concentrating on anything else. She told me that she was going to drive to Farmington to go shopping, then drive back to pick up Julian at his friend's house. I was afraid that she wouldn't pay enough attention to traffic and that could lead to an accident. That's why I followed her. I just wanted to make sure she arrived home safely."

Ella shook her head. "I don't buy it." She didn't think even Loretta was *that* worried about contact with her.

"Ask Lea Benjamin, she's one of my students. I was following Loretta while she shopped in the mall when Lea saw me. From the look on her face, I have a feeling she knew exactly what I was doing."

"*Stalking* my sister-in-law."

"No, not at all. I just wanted to make sure she was okay."

"My client has answered all of your questions, and his alibi can be corroborated. Now I want him released," the lawyer asserted.

Ella gave Justine a nod, then as her partner walked out of the room, continued. "If this new alibi of yours turns out to be true, how do you explain the fact that the bullets from your rifle matched those at the crime scene?"

"The rifle was stolen," John answered smoothly.

"It was," Garnenez added with a nod. "Well, not stolen exactly. Just borrowed without my permission. I had no idea what he'd done."

"He—who?"

"My cousin, Daniel Smart. He spent almost a week with me recently. His heart has always been in the right place, but his brain's never fired on all eight cylinders. And, lately, he's been worse than ever."

"Explain what you mean," Ella clipped, thinking that Garnenez was the wrong person to gauge someone else's excessive behavior.

"He and I have always been close. For the past five years we've been going duck hunting and fishing as often as we could. Then last week he showed up at my door and asked to stay with me for a while. He said he needed time to think, and since he had business in Shiprock, he figured my place was perfect. Of course, he was more than welcome."

"What changed?"

"I quickly realized that Daniel wasn't thinking straight. What scared me most was seeing the list he'd made of people he felt were a danger to the tribe—something he compiled by listening to George Branch's radio program, reading the papers, and sitting in the back during Chapter House meetings taking notes. The list had names associated with the gambling issue, or NEED—the Navajo Electrical Energy Development project—and gun control. Hunt and his brother-in-law, Benally, were both on Daniel's list, I know that. You were there too, as was Police Chief Atcitty."

"We're in the process of getting a search warrant, but you could save us some time if you willingly turn over your rifle, ammunition, and supplies. We may be able to lift Daniel's prints from something and that would corroborate your story."

"I'm sure my client cleans his weapon, Investigator Clah. The absence of Smart's prints won't mean much."

"But their presence might," Ella answered.

"Fine. Knock yourself out," Garnenez said with a shrug. "My attorney can loan you the key to my home."

"Now it's your turn to do something for us," John said. "You can release my client."

"Not until we check out his alibi."

"All right. But do so quickly."

Ella went back to her office as Garnenez was escorted to lockup, and began filling out a lengthy report. She'd been working on it for nearly an hour when Justine came in.

"I checked out his alibi," Justine said. "Lea Benjamin remembered seeing him at the mall. She could vouch for the date because she'd gone to the store to pick up a birthday present for her brother. She said that she was almost sure he was following Mrs. Destea. She watched him for a while, and then finally decided to go say hello, but he was really nervous and rushed off. The last time she saw him was in the parking lot. According to her, he pulled out just a few seconds after your sister-in-law left."

"Did she ever tell Loretta?"

"I asked her the same thing. She said that she considered telling Mrs. Destea, but she thought the professor might deny it. Since there was no way she could prove anything, she decided to keep quiet. But it probably fed the rumor mill at the college about Garnenez and Loretta."

"I want that twenty-two gone over with a fine-tooth comb. What I'm looking for is Smart's prints. Check the cartridge boxes, the magazines, and even the cardboard box he used to store some of his shooting gear—everything."

"I'll take care of it. Joe's on his way over to the professor's house with Ralph Tache now. I'll work on the rifle and the rest the second they return."

An hour and a half later, while Justine processed the rifle, Ella signed Garnenez's release papers. Once that was finished, she called her sister-in-law. "I'm releasing Garnenez now so be careful. And under no circumstances should you ever open your door to him. Do you understand?"

"Yes," came a muted reply. "And I thought you'd like to know that your brother is home now and I've told him everything." There was a long pause before she added, "He got really angry when he found out."

"Let me talk to him."

"He's in his medicine hogan now. You know how he gets—when he's upset he doesn't say a word. But if the professor ever comes around here, I'm not sure what will happen," she said softly. "You might tell the professor that for his own good."

There was an emotion laced through Loretta's words that Ella had a difficult time identifying.

"My husband dislikes confrontations, but he won't let anyone threaten his family," Loretta added.

As she heard the pride and satisfaction in Loretta's voice, Ella suddenly understood her sister-in-law. Loretta was relieved and happy to see Clifford jealous.

"My brother loves you," Ella answered, tempted to add "though I can't understand why." "Did you ever really doubt it?"

"He gets really busy with his patients and sometimes it's hard to tell what he feels," Loretta said, her voice heavy with resignation. "He keeps it all inside, and as a wife, I can tell you that's not easy to deal with."

Ella shut her eyes, took a deep breath, then summoning all her self-control, said good-bye. It was hard to deal with a blockhead.

Justine came in just then. "I didn't find any prints except Garnenez's on the rifle. Since there was only a light trace of gunpowder residue on it, my guess is that it had been cleaned recently—prior to this morning, that is. Then I thought of dusting the clip since most people don't clean that very often," she said, and smiled. "I found Daniel Smart's prints there, big and bold."

"Okay. Now we're cooking."

Before Ella could say more, Preston Garnenez appeared at her open door, escorted by the desk sergeant. Garnenez knocked, though it was scarcely necessary since she was looking directly at him.

"May I come in?" he asked.

Ella nodded, and gestured to an empty chair as the desk sergeant walked away. Garnenez came into her office and took the seat she'd offered. He didn't seem the least bit concerned about being close to her now, and he held his medicine pouch nonchalantly in his hand.

"I don't know how dangerous you are to other Navajos, but you do have a reputation of catching those you're hunting, Investigator Clah. So there's something I need to tell you. My cousin Daniel is *not* a bad person. He's had a hard life, but in his own way, he's trying to make things better for everyone—to restore harmony. In that respect and others, you two are alike."

Seeing her start to protest, Garnenez raised one hand, stopping her. "But the way things stand, he's a danger to you now. If you go up against him, you'll each follow your own instincts and nothing good will come of it. Both of you will dig in your heels and blood will be shed."

"I have to bring him in. Whether it goes down easy or not is totally up to him."

"There's no need to turn it into an all-out confrontation. I'm sure I can talk Daniel into giving himself up. Let *me* help you. When you find him, let *me* talk to him first, before you do anything else. No one has to get hurt."

Ella looked at him thoughtfully, thinking that maybe she was seeing the real Garnenez for the first time. He'd never really been afraid of her at all, but it made for good theater and was a way of getting attention. It was also clear to her that he didn't want his cousin to be killed. All things considered she could see no harm in making sure Garnenez talked to him, maybe by phone where he'd be out of the line of fire.

"I'll keep it in mind," she said. "Now there's something I have to say to you." Ella leaned forward, resting her elbows on the table, and looked directly at him. "Stay away from my sister-in-law. Am I making myself clear?"

He nodded. "I had thought she and I . . . But that doesn't matter now. I won't go where I'm not wanted."

"Good," Ella said.

As he left her office, Ella looked at Justine. "Smart is after Cardell Benally, but Cardell's no easy target, as I know from personal experience. If those two meet . . ."

"We can't head this off. We have no idea where either of them is. Unless we get to one of them first . . ."

Ella considered it for several moments. "Let's go pay Branch another visit. Last time we spoke, I rattled him. Let's team up and see if we can get even more from him this time."

Ella rode with Justine to the motel where Branch was staying, but his sedan wasn't parked in the lot and knocking on his door didn't do much good.

"Last time I was here, I made sure Branch understood how unstable Smart is and how, if Smart harmed Benally either of his own accord or while trying to bring him in, Branch might be charged as an accessory. But I may have used the wrong tactic. Branch is probably trying to find Smart himself so he can stop him, most likely by buying him off. Of course if that doesn't work, Branch will have no choice but to lead us to Smart so *we* can take care of the problem."

"So if we can locate Branch, we should follow him for a while?" Justine asked.

"Yeah." Ella then called Hoskie Ben, on the off-chance that the two had been in contact recently. When that proved unsuccessful, she put out an APB with a Code 5, which instructed officers to keep the vehicle under surveillance but not make any attempt to contact the occupant. "Let's go to the nearest gas station that sells diesel fuel," Ella told Justine. "Maybe we can find out if anyone's seen Branch recently."

They arrived a short time later and Justine parked at one of the parking-lot barriers beside the attendant's "island" in the middle of the pumps. As Ella reached for the door handle, her cell phone rang. Remaining where she was, she answered the call.

"Ella, this is Branch," the caller said. "I met with Daniel and tried my level best to get him to come in and square things with you. But you were right about him. He's gone off the deep end on some nut job vigilante crusade. He wants Benally and Hunt first and then he's coming after you. Smart is more dangerous than those two jokers put together."

"And you were the one to light the fuse. Where did you see him and when?" Ella snapped.

"Beside Highway Six-sixty-six where it passes by Table Mesa. While we were talking in the cab of his pickup, I managed to slip a global satellite positioning device under the seat. It's a demo model I'd been carrying around in the trunk of my car that one of my old sponsors had loaned me for evaluation. The system works the same way as one I had installed in my Mercedes, so I know it's reliable. You should be able to track him yourself with a computer from the Web site once you get the system's code number," he said, giving her the information she would need, including the passwords to get onto the Web site.

"I assume you're still tracking him?"

"Of course. He's been circling the area around the south end of the Hogback, east of Table Mesa, for a long time now. Once he headed back to the southwest and stopped by the store at Little Water. But by the time I got there he'd already moved back to the east—in the Burnham area. I spoke to Leroy Joe, the clerk at Little Water. Daniel bought some heavy-duty rope there. From the map on my screen, right now he's at the base of the Hogback near some old mines. My guess is that he's found Cardell Benally, but I'll follow him and verify it."

"No, that's too dangerous. Hang back. We'll take it from here."

"No way. This is a *story*, and I'm seeing it through. Something this big could get me back my show. Besides, I don't want to be responsible for the murder of Cardell Benally— legally or morally. I hired Daniel to find him, not blow him away. I've got to see this through."

Before Ella could argue, Branch hung up. "Damn!" Ella said, tossing the cell phone back on the seat.

"Hogback? You mean the north end near the river, or way down south past the Four Corners Power Plant?" Justine asked, only getting one side of the conversation.

"South, about fifteen miles from where Smiley lived. At least there's no question of jurisdiction. Daniel Smart and Branch are definitely on the Rez," Ella added quickly.

"Come on. We've got to get moving." As they headed south on Highway 666, planning on joining up with reinforcements at Little Water, Ella notified the chief and made sure any patrolmen in that area would be on hand to provide backup.

"I'll get you all the support possible," Big Ed said, "though our closest officers right now are just north of Tohatchi and at the Two Gray Hills Chapter House. Sergeant Neskahi just left Shiprock and is en route."

"Two more things," Ella said slowly. "Have Neskahi pick up Garnenez at the college and bring him to the Little Water trading post. We'll pick up the professor there. There's going to be very iffy cell phone reception from here on out, and if there's really a chance that Garnenez can get Smart to surrender peaceably, I think we owe it to ourselves to try."

"Done. And the other?" Big Ed asked.

"I want someone to find Lewis Hunt and let him know he's being watched. I believe he knows where Cardell is hiding, and I don't want him to show up right in the middle of all this."

"It'll be done. But you watch yourself and your people down there, Shorty."

TWENTY-ONE
——— ✷ ✷ ✷ ———

An hour later Ella and Justine met with Neskahi at the intersection of two dirt roads near the Hogback Ridge.

"What do you want me to do with him?" Neskahi gestured toward his unit, where Garnenez was sitting in the passenger seat, looking around anxiously. "He's scared to death of his cousin and what might happen."

"From everything we've learned so far, he's got reason to be," Justine added. "Daniel Smart sounds like he's really out of touch with reality. Does Garnenez still think he can talk him into surrendering?"

"Yeah. What he's counting on is the fact that Daniel trusts him. Plus the professor has come up with a strategy to convince Daniel to give himself up."

"What's that?" Ella asked.

"He's going to point out that a real soldier's first duty is to live so he can carry on the fight. Dying out here won't accomplish anything."

Ella nodded. "If *that* works, we still have reason to worry about Daniel Smart. But maybe he's not that far gone yet. And one more thing, about Garnenez. His nervousness may be more of an act than reality, so don't turn your back on him. Just call it an instinct of mine."

Justine and Neskahi nodded. They were familiar with how reliable her instincts tended to be.

As Ella stood by her unit with Justine and Neskahi, she unfolded a map of the area on the hood so they all could follow her plan. "Smart's somewhere ahead of us and I want to make sure we trap him with the ridge to his back," she said, pointing. "Neskahi, I want you to go here," she said and pointed to a crossroads leading north and parallel to the Hogback. "Justine and I will cut off his escape to the west and south."

Suddenly her cell phone rang. Suspecting it was Branch, she picked it up even before it finished the first tone. "Ella Clah," she said briskly.

"It's Branch. We're too late. He's moving in on Cardell now and I have no way to cut him off or stop him."

"Where are you?"

"There's a dirt track, actually an old mining road, that turns east just north of the junction at the end of the ridge. This track runs up a small canyon that ends right up against the base of the Hogback where there's an old coal mine. There's a shack there against the cliff side where the miners probably stored their equipment."

Ella looked closely along the base of the Hogback and spotted a small, gray wooden shack in the shadow of the tall sandstone ridge. It was too far away to make out any details, though, and the distortion coming from heat rising off the desert didn't help. "I think I see it from here." She pointed out the spot to Justine and Sergeant Neskahi.

"I don't see any other shacks around, so we must be talking about the same place. Benally's inside that shack, I saw him," Branch continued. "Smart is a hundred yards away, downhill and on foot now after leaving his truck hidden farther back. But the ground seems clear all around that shack and I know Smart's not going to just run up or drive there. My guess is that he'll find a hiding spot behind a rock and ambush Benally the second he steps outside again."

"Can you get out of there without being seen?" Ella asked, noting that Neskahi had a pair of binoculars and was examining the area closely.

"No," Branch answered. "I was watching the tracking display real carefully and didn't come up right behind him, so he doesn't know I'm here, I don't think. But if I start the engine up again, he's going to either hear my sedan or see the dust trail I leave."

"Then stay put in your car. We're less than five minutes away," she said, then hung up. Focusing on her team, she continued. "Okay, listen up." Ella filled in Justine and Neskahi quickly. "We've got to get up there and in position fast. Any suggestions?"

Neskahi nodded, handing her the binoculars.

"There's a ridge on the south side. We can go up the canyon to its right and not be seen, then cross over the ridge and come up behind Smart—if we're careful," Neskahi pointed out.

"But there are a lot of boulders in that canyon that have broken off the ridge over the past million years or so. We may high center on a rock and tear out the oil pan," Justine added.

"You're driving so I know you'll make it," Ella said. "Once there, we'll surround the cabin, but we need to stay behind Smart, putting him between Benally and us so neither of them can make a move without coming out in the open."

"What if Smart manages to reach the cabin and capture Benally?" Neskahi asked.

"Then we rely on his cousin Garnenez to talk him out of the shack. If that doesn't work, and Benally is still alive, we'll have to talk Smart out of a hostage situation. If we need to use force, we'll move fast and decisively. In either case, neither of those two men leave unless they're in our custody."

After a brief discussion, it was decided that Garnenez would ride with Ella and Justine, and Neskahi would proceed on foot the last quarter mile, covering them from behind

Branch's position to the north. Neskahi was a good shot with a rifle and they wanted him free to act if the opportunity came.

Neither Justine nor Ella spoke on the bone-jarring ride up the narrow canyon, at this point not much more than a boulder-littered arroyo. Occasionally, Ella would glance back at Garnenez. He looked terrified and kept trying to moisten his lips with the tip of his tongue, but she had a feeling it was just for show. His face showed one emotion, but his body seemed too relaxed, considering the situation. There was something about Garnenez that didn't add up, and that made her uneasy.

They left the SUV after coming up to a spot they estimated to be a short distance behind where Branch was hidden, then climbed up onto the ridge to look north and hopefully down upon Smart's location. On the top now, lying on their stomachs and peering from behind tufts of brush or rocks to avoid showing their silhouettes, Ella and Justine kept in contact with Branch and finally, thanks to Neskahi's binoculars, they found where the talk show host was hiding.

Branch, who'd ignored Ella's warning and was no longer in his car, poked his head out from behind cover and pointed east of his position.

Ella studied the area between Branch and the shack, but couldn't see any sign of Smart, though there was a dark blue pickup that apparently belonged to him. Then she spotted what was nothing more than a slight movement in a deep shadow. She focused carefully and the extra light-gathering power of the binoculars enabled her to spot Daniel behind a large boulder about a hundred yards from them. He was lying down, studying the wooden shack.

The ramshackle cabin was a rectangular structure about fifteen by twenty with a small window on the two sides Ella could see. The building was about fifty yards uphill from Smart and less than twenty feet from the west side of the steep Hogback ridge. Farther to the south and about fifty feet from the structure was a black hole about ten feet in diameter leading into the cliffside.

"Smart's camouflaged well, wearing desert fatigues," Ella said, handing Justine the binoculars. "Call it in to Neskahi and give him the location."

Justine spoke into the phone, then looked over at Ella. "Joe still can't see Smart from where he is even with the rifle scope. He's moving closer to Branch to get a better angle."

Garnenez, who'd been a few feet farther down the back side of the ridge, crawled up beside them.

"Get down. He'll see you," Justine whispered harshly, pushing Garnenez onto his belly.

"Sorry. If you're ready now, I'll talk to him."

"No, not yet," Justine said, interrupting him. She handed Ella the binoculars. "Look at the west window of the shack."

Ella saw the barrel of a shotgun poised on the sill of the window that faced downhill to the west. "Benally knows he's got company." She shifted back to Smart's last position. "Smart's out of sight now, which means he's on the move. The road drops off to the side, so there must be a drainage ditch over there. I can't see him anymore. I wonder where the door of the shack is? The north side? The east?"

Ella pulled out her weapon but before she could shout a warning to Benally they heard a crash and the sound of splintering wood. Ella knew Smart had kicked down the door, which was apparently on the north side because they couldn't see it. A moment later her suspicions were confirmed.

"I know you're out there, Clah. I saw somebody moving up on the ridge. I've got Benally. If you come closer, he dies, and so will you and the other officers," Smart called out, using his enemies' names, like a traditionalist, to take away their power.

"No one's going anywhere—including you," Ella shouted back. She could see Neskahi now, coming up from below in the same direction Smart had taken. "Release your hostage and we'll talk."

"Back off, Clah. You don't want the councilman's right-hand man dead because of decisions you made. You're going to assure me safe passage to my pickup and then out of the area. Once I'm out of the area, I'll release Benally."

"You're not leaving here with a hostage. This is non-negotiable. Release Benally now!"

Ella saw movement out of the corner of her eye, and turned her head as Garnenez came out of cover. Justine dove for the professor's feet but Garnenez slipped the shoestring tackle and was already sliding down the ridge. He barely managed to stay on his feet, but once he reached the bottom of the slope he was running full speed toward the shack.

"Get back!" Ella yelled at him, but by then Garnenez was in the middle of the clearing.

"Danny, it's me," Garnenez called out to him, slowing to a walk now.

"You led them here! You're a traitor!" Smart's voice came from the cabin.

"No, stay cool. You're all wrong about this," Garnenez said, his voice surprisingly calm. Ella noted that he was hold-ing something in his hand, having taken it from his medicine pouch. She could make out a feather. It was some kind of fetish, no doubt.

Ella could see Neskahi moving up the far side of the road, but he was still too far away to help. Branch had moved too, unnoticed, and was closer.

"Get back, Professor!" Branch shouted, stepping out from behind the last big rock before the clearing. Garnenez turned, surprised, then waved Branch away. But the radio man kept coming.

"Hey, buddy. This is George. We need patriots like you to speak out, but not with violence. It'll only prove they're right in taking away our guns. A wise man knows when to walk away from a fight. This is that time, trust me, I know what I'm talking about."

"Listen to me, Cuz," Garnenez added. "Branch is right. You know me, I've never steered you wrong. I know you're trying to help the tribe, but nobody ever won anything by getting themselves killed. Use your head. Set down your gun and turn yourself in. We'll hire the best attorney around. The tribe is on your side, you'll see. Trust what I'm saying. I'm not just your cousin, I'm your friend."

"You *were* my friend. You sold me out."

A shot rang out and Garnenez yelped, grabbing his leg and crumpling to the ground. "You shot me, you moron!"

Ella saw Branch move forward, trying to reach Garnenez.

A rifle shot came from the far side, striking the shed up high, forcing Smart to duck below the window. It was Neskahi.

"Give him some cover, but shoot high, we don't know about Benally yet!" Ella yelled at Justine and began firing on Smart's position, forcing him to keep his head down. She and Justine then took advantage of the situation, taking turns firing as the other moved, working their way down to a massive boulder at the foot of the ridge.

With all of them providing cover fire, Branch finally managed to drag Garnenez out of the line of fire into a low spot.

That accomplished, Ella and Justine both stopped firing and so did Neskahi, who had moved into position to cover the north side. Smart was trapped now from every direction. While Justine tried to get a connection with the chief via cell phone to apprise him of the new situation, Ella worked to focus Smart's attention on her.

"Daniel Smart," she said, using his belief that names had power to diminish him.

"I've still got Benally," he answered, "and it'll only be a

matter of time before he gets shot, by you or by me. Unless you want more blood on your hands, you'll let me drive away from here."

"I can't make that kind of decision. Let us get some help for the man you wounded, then we'll talk."

"Let my worthless cousin bleed. He's a phony, always talking, trying to con people with that act of his."

"Then why did he risk getting shot trying to talk you into ending this? Think, man!" Ella countered.

"He betrayed me by leading you here."

"How would he know where you were? We brought him, he didn't bring us," Ella replied truthfully. "And if he dies, you'll never forgive yourself for killing a friend," Ella said.

"Then *you* come and get him—alone."

Justine looked over at Ella. "No. You can't trust anything he says. Remember you're on his list. He'll blow you away. Let either me or Joe go."

Neskahi contacted Ella on the handheld radio. "I'll go. I'm closer than either one of you, and I'm strong enough to carry Garnenez out of danger. Smart doesn't even know me, so there's no reason for him to shoot."

"He's right, Ella. You and I can cover him," Justine said.

"All right, but let me tell Smart first." Ella peered out from behind the rock again and called out to him. "I'm not strong enough to carry the professor. One of my men will go in. If you fire, the talking is over and we'll take you down hard. Clear?"

"Go ahead. But after that's done, you and I will cut a deal, or Benally dies. Am *I* clear?"

"If *anyone* dies, all deals are off."

Ella watched Neskahi approach Branch's hiding place, his rifle on the sling over his shoulder. Neskahi crouched down, out of sight for a moment, then a second later, he contacted her on her handheld radio. "Garnenez took a bullet just above the ankle, but I think he'll live. But Branch is gone."

For a moment Ella didn't understand. "What do you

mean gone? He couldn't have left without either Smart or us seeing him."

"I mean dead-gone. Garnenez says he clutched his chest, had trouble breathing, then just died."

The news took Ella by surprise. Branch had finally done a selfless act—probably the first in his entire life—and had died in the process. Life—and death—never made much sense.

"Grab Branch's car keys and get Garnenez into the Mercedes. It's the closest vehicle. Then once you get him in the car, keep going."

"The paramedics should meet him halfway between here and the hospital. They've been dispatched," Justine said.

"I heard," Neskahi said, "And I've got Branch's keys now. I'm going."

Ella and Justine kept their pistols aimed at the windows of the shack. Smart couldn't leave the building now the same way he'd entered when assaulting Benally because of their new positions. But they had a hostage to worry about now. "Smart, listen to me. You can leave here, but not with Benally."

"Do you think I'm that stupid? You'll shoot me the second I step out of this shack. I want guaranteed safe passage *with* my hostage. I'll let him go once I'm sure nobody is following me."

Ella waited a moment before answering. "All right. We have a stalemate here, so I'll see what I can do. But I'm going to need several minutes. There's no radio reception here. I have to move back to a better location so I can talk to Chief Atcitty."

Justine looked at Ella. "You're not really considering letting him go, are you? He's at least partially responsible for Branch's death—and kidnapping too. Not to mention shooting his cousin."

"You know me better than that. But I need some time. Keep him distracted. I'll work my way around and use the same ditch he used before to sneak up on the cabin."

"He's crazy, not stupid. Well, maybe just a little. But he'll suspect something's up if you don't come back soon."

"Then I'll have to work fast."

"There's a better way," Justine said. "I'll go. I'm not a target he wants to blow away so he might think about it a split second. If you show up you're giving him exactly what he wants."

"I've had more training and experience in these kind of situations, Cousin. If anyone is going to pull this off, it'll have to be me."

Justine exhaled softly. "You're the boss. Just come back, okay?"

Ella moved farther west in the same direction Neskahi had gone with Garnenez, passing by Branch's prone body. On the ground beside the dead man was what looked like an owl feather with two white beads attached by strings. It was probably Garnenez's fetish. She stared at it for a moment, trying to figure out where she'd seen something like that before, but Justine's voice interrupted her thoughts.

"We're trying to convince our chief to deal with you, Daniel Smart. What's the condition of your hostage?" Justine yelled.

"He's unharmed, but he won't stay that way for long. Your boss better make up his mind, quick!" Smart yelled back. He sounded more confident now.

"You've already been warned—if anything happens to the hostage, all deals are off," Justine answered.

Ella moved silently, now circling around to the north, hoping to find that ditch that led up close to the shack. Unless Smart was in the doorway, he wouldn't be able to see her coming without her seeing him.

She came up quickly, moving from boulder to boulder, approaching the shack in the shadow of the Hogback itself. But once she got close there'd be no more cover. If he heard or saw her coming, there'd be only one way to get out of his line of sight—coming right up against the building itself.

"We just got a response from the chief," Justine called out. "If we let you walk away, how can we be certain that the hostage will remain unharmed? Also, we need to come up with a way for you to turn him over to us."

Ella smiled. Attaway, Justine! Forcing him to think and come up with answers will keep him distracted. Ella shot toward the rear of the shack, sprinting as fast as she could and making it in five seconds. In the middle of the wooden back wall was a tiny crack between the boards. As Smart answered Justine, she crouched down and peered inside.

Ella saw Benally lying facedown on the floor, his hands and feet bound with a rope.

Ella grabbed a rock and tossed it up into the air above the cabin. Then, before it came down, she slipped around the corner and hurried to the open door. When the rock thumped on the roof, Ella reacted instantly, going through the doorway in a crouch, her pistol up.

Smart was still looking up when she fired. Two rounds hit him in the left side of his chest before he could swing the shotgun around, and he dropped to the floor.

Ella picked up the shotgun and stepped around the dying man. Verifying that Benally was alive, she contacted Justine on the radio. "The hostage is secure. Come on in."

TWENTY-TWO

──── ✖ ✖ ✖ ────

Ella woke up early Saturday morning when Wind, her daughter's pony, began whinnying loudly for his breakfast. Ella hid her head beneath the pillow, but it didn't work. The animal's cry could have been heard for miles. Ella had only been back home for four days, but in that time she'd come to accept the fact that her days of sleeping past daybreak would be gone for years.

She'd just tossed the covers back when Dawn and Rose came through the door. "*Shimá*, there's a present from Auntie!" Dawn said. "Come look!" she yelled, then dashed out of the room.

"Come on, Daughter, get up. Your sister-in-law was kind enough to bring you a gift. The least you can do is go take a look."

Ella looked at her mother through narrowed eyes. "My sister-in-law brought *me* a present? Does it have thorns? Is it ticking?"

Rose started to laugh but then shook her head. "Come on, get up and try to be gracious. She's probably sorry she caused you so much trouble. Apparently she and her brother bought you a gift to make peace. I hope you'll like it."

Ella heard the pony outside still whinnying excitedly.

"Why doesn't someone feed the little guy?" she said with a groan.

"Wind was fed a half hour ago."

"Then why is he still carrying on?" Ella pulled on her jeans and looked at her mother, who seemed inordinately pleased with herself. Suddenly she understood. "There's another horse out there, isn't there? You got them to buy me a *horse*?"

"No, I did not! I'm just as surprised as you. But he's a beautiful animal."

Ella groaned. "Mom, I was looking for one, really. You shouldn't have done it without me."

"I didn't do this, I promise. But don't look a gift horse in the mouth. After the Hollywood people withdrew their offer because the stations no longer wanted original TV movies, your hope of getting extra cash vanished. So count your blessings. Now hurry up and get dressed. I'll wait for you outside."

Ella pulled a sweatshirt over her head, slipped into her jeans and boots, then went out the back door, still brushing her hair away from her face. Seeing her brother holding on to the beautiful, tall, black gelding, Ella smiled. The animal eyed her curiously as she approached, his ears standing up straight.

"Here's Chieftain," her brother said. Hearing his name, the animal tossed his head, but Clifford kept a firm hold on the lead rope. "He's spirited, but has a gentle soul."

"I'll remember that the first time he dumps me on the trail," Ella said, watching the animal prance. Then she turned around and whispered something in Dawn's ear.

Dawn started laughing.

Ella turned to Rose, who was starting to look a little bit confused. "Don't you dare pretend not to know what's going on, Mother. I should make you feed and water him, arranging for all this without telling me."

Rose's mouth fell open. "But I had absolutely nothing to do with this, Daughter. Honestly." Rose looked back and forth from Clifford to Ella, trying to figure out what was going on.

"Mother!" Ella tried to look angry, but finally couldn't help but laugh.

Clifford started to snicker, then looked over at Ella and winked. "You got her, Sister. But this is what, the very first time?"

"What do you mean, *got* me?" Rose frowned at Ella.

"Mom bought Chieftain all by herself, *Shimasání*. She wanted to surprise you," Dawn chimed in. "Don't be mad."

Rose sighed, then smiled grudgingly. "Okay, maybe I deserved that, just a little, for sometimes pushing you too hard to do things my way. But, Daughter, don't ever try to trick me again, or you'll have to start cooking for yourself."

"Ugh. Will you cook for *me*, *Shimasání*?" Dawn asked.

Rose laughed. "It's good to know I'm needed."

Dawn turned back to Ella. "*Shimá*, will you let me ride Chieftain double with you?"

Ella shook her head. "Not until I've ridden him in the arena many times and we've connected with each other. First, he has to learn to trust me and I've got to trust him as well. That'll take time."

Dawn pouted. "*Everything* takes time!"

"Yes, it does," Ella replied, laughing. Ella led the horse around, studying his gait.

"Let's show him to Wind!" Dawn said.

"No, we can't put them together yet. Horses and ponies don't always get along and we don't want them trying to bite or kick each other. For now, one will be in the stall while the other is in the corral. Eventually, we'll build a second stall," Ella said.

"For the next few hours keep Wind tethered near your daughter's window and put Chieftain in the corral. He needs a chance to work off some of his energy," Clifford suggested.

Ella took Chieftain into the corral and unhooked the rope from his halter, letting the big gelding trot free. He stopped at the far end and looked back at her, his ear flicking in her direction.

Ella smiled. "We'll become friends at your speed, Chieftain," she said, then closed the gate.

"You picked out a fine horse—with your brother's help," Loretta said as Ella joined them.

"He really is beautiful," Ella said with a nod. "Thank you both for your help bringing him here," Ella said, then lowering her voice, added, "And for helping me teach Mom a small lesson."

As the others went inside to have breakfast, Clifford hung back with Ella. "If you need any help working with him, just call."

"Count on it," Ella said with a smile, then turned to watch the animal trotting along the corral fence.

"I have a gift for you—in the way of good news, that is."

Ella looked at him curiously.

"I heard from the *hataalii* we've all been searching for. He's finished with his other business and will be here today. The Sing can begin this afternoon."

Ella nodded slowly. "It's a good time."

As Clifford went inside the house, Ella remained standing near the corral watching Chieftain. Order had been restored and the case was now closed. Smart had spray-painted Justine's door. Unfortunately, there was still nothing to tie him to the holes in the water barrels at the Joes'. They'd probably never know for sure, now that he was dead, how many acts of vandalism he was responsible for.

As a cool breeze swept over her, Ella allowed herself a

moment to enjoy the peace. Experience and instinct told her that it wouldn't last long.

She had enemies in the police department—ones who were hoping to convince her fellow officers that she was a skinwalker. Soon, if it hadn't happened already, they'd find allies like Garnenez who'd help them try to destroy her.

It had taken some time for her to get a handle on the professor and see through his act but she now knew him for what he was. The owl fetish he'd carried, similar to the one she'd found in the mine the day she'd nearly died, had given him away. The professor was a skinwalker—only they would have ventured inside a place contaminated by evil.

It was clear that she'd have her work cut out for her during the coming months, but for now she'd restore her own inner balance and harmony by joining her family. It was time to walk in beauty.